Praise for #1 *New York Times* bestselling author

NORA ROBERTS

"You can't bottle wish fulfillment, but Nora Roberts
certainly knows how to put it on the page."
—*New York Times*

"Roberts nails her characters and settings with
awesome precision, drawing readers into a vividly
rendered world of family-centered warmth."
—*Library Journal*

"Roberts has a warm feel for her characters
and an eye for the evocative detail."
—*Chicago Tribune*

"Nora Roberts is among the best."
—*Washington Post Book World*

"Roberts is indeed a word artist, painting her story
and her characters with vitality and verve."
—*Publishers Weekly*

"Roberts' bestselling novels are some of the
best in the romance genre. They are thoughtfully
plotted, well-written stories
featuring fascinating characters."
—*USA TODAY*

Dear Reader,

Love—it is the most sought-after treasure in the world! In these two classic stories by *New York Times* bestselling author Nora Roberts, we see the lengths that people will go to in order to attain it.

In *Treasures Lost, Treasures Found* Kate Hardesty realizes she will never locate a rumored gold-laden sunken ship without Ky Silver's help. Though Kate left Ky four years ago, frightened of the feelings he awoke in her, she needs him now more than ever. Still, Kate knows that working with Ky means more than searching for gold—it means plunging her heart into the depths of love.

The Welcoming finds federal agent Roman DeWinter undercover at a seaside inn with orders to destroy a criminal organization operating out of the premises. It's just another case—until he meets the inn's owner, Charity Ford. Roman hadn't expected to fall for his prime suspect, but soon he finds himself under the beautiful innkeeper's spell...and fighting to prove her innocence.

For some it may take years to discover what their hearts really want, and sometimes we need love to be threatened in order to see its true worth. But in the end, hopefully we are all lucky enough to find this priceless gift at least once in our lives!

The Editors

Silhouette Books

NORA ROBERTS

Golden Shores

Silhouette Books

Published by Silhouette Books

America's Publisher of Contemporary Romance

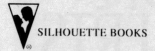

SILHOUETTE BOOKS

Recycling programs for this product may not exist in your area.

GOLDEN SHORES

ISBN-13: 978-0-373-28163-3

Copyright © 2012 by Harlequin Books S.A.

The publisher acknowledges the copyright holder of the individual works as follows:

TREASURES LOST, TREASURES FOUND
Copyright © 1986 by Nora Roberts

THE WELCOMING
Copyright © 1989 by Nora Roberts

This edition published by arrangement with Harlequin Books S.A.

For questions and comments about the quality of this book, please contact us at CustomerService@Harlequin.com.

® and TM are trademarks of Harlequin Books S.A., used under license. Trademarks indicated with ® are registered in the United States Patent and Trademark Office, the Canadian Trade Marks Office and in other countries.

Visit Silhouette Books at www.Harlequin.com

Printed in U.S.A.

CONTENTS

TREASURES LOST,
TREASURES FOUND

To Dixie Browning, the true lady of the island.

Chapter 1

He had believed in it. Edwin J. Hardesty hadn't been the kind of man who had fantasies or followed dreams, but sometime during his quiet, literary life he had looked for a pot of gold. From the information in the reams of notes, the careful charts and the dog-eared research books, he thought he'd found it.

In the panelled study, a single light shot a beam across a durable oak desk. The light fell over a hand— narrow, slender, without the affectation of rings or polish. Yet even bare, it remained an essentially feminine hand, the kind that could be pictured holding a porcelain cup or waving a feather fan. It was a surprisingly elegant hand for a woman who didn't consider herself elegant, delicate or particularly feminine. Kathleen Hardesty was, as her father had been, and as he'd directed her to be, a dedicated educator.

Minds were her concern—the expanding and the ful-filling of them. This included her own as well as every one of her students'. For as long as she could remem-ber, her father had impressed upon her the importance of education. He'd stressed the priority of it over every other aspect of life. Education was the cohesiveness that held civilization together. She grew up surrounded by the dusty smell of books and the quiet, placid tone of patient instruction.

She'd been expected to excel in school, and she had. She'd been expected to follow her father's path into ed-ucation. At twenty-eight, Kate was just finishing her first year at Yale as an assistant professor of English literature.

In the dim light of the quiet study, she looked the part. Her light brown hair was tidily secured at the nape of her neck with all the pins neatly tucked in. Her prac-tical tortoiseshell reading glasses seemed dark against her milk-pale complexion. Her high cheekbones gave her face an almost haughty look that was often dispelled by her warm, doe-brown eyes.

Though her jacket was draped over the back of her chair, the white blouse she wore was still crisp. Her cuffs were turned back to reveal delicate wrists and a slim Swiss watch on her left arm. Her earrings were tasteful gold studs given to Kate by her father on her twenty-first birthday, the only truly personal gift she could ever remember receiving from him.

Seven long years later, one short week after her father's funeral, Kate sat at his desk. The room still carried the scent of his cologne and a hint of the pipe tobacco he'd only smoked in that room.

She'd finally found the courage to go through his papers.

She hadn't known he was ill. In his early sixties, Hardesty had looked robust and strong. He hadn't told his daughter about his visits to the doctor, his check-ups, ECG results or the little pills he carried with him everywhere. She'd found his pills in his inside pocket after his fatal heart attack. Kate hadn't known his heart was weak because Hardesty never shared his shortcomings with anyone. She hadn't known about the charts and research papers in his desk; he'd never shared his dreams either.

Now that she was aware of both, Kate wasn't certain she ever really knew the man who'd raised her. The memory of her mother was dim; that was to be expected after more than twenty years. Her father had been alive just a week before.

Leaning back for a moment, she pushed her glasses up and rubbed the bridge of her nose between her thumb and forefinger. She tried, with only the desk lamp between herself and the dark, to think of her father in precise terms.

Physically, he'd been a tall, big man with a full head of steel-gray hair and a patient face. He had favored dark suits and white shirts. The only vanity she could remember had been his weekly manicures. But it wasn't a physical picture Kate struggled with now. As a father…

He was never unkind. In all her memories, Kate

couldn't remember her father ever raising his voice to her, ever striking her. He never had to, she thought with a sigh. All he had to do was express disappointment, disapproval, and that was enough.

He had been brilliant, tireless, dedicated. But all of that had been directed toward his vocation. As a father, Kate reflected... He'd never been unkind. That was all that would come to her, and because of it she felt a fresh wave of guilt and grief.

She hadn't disappointed him, that much she could cling to. He had told her so himself, in just those words, when she was accepted by the English Department at Yale. Nor had he expected her ever to disappoint him. Kate knew, though it had never been discussed, that her father wanted her to become head of the English Department within ten years. That had been the extent of his dream for her.

Had he ever realized just how much she'd loved him? She wondered as she shut her eyes, tired now from the hours of reading her father's handwriting. Had he ever known just how desperately she'd wanted to please him? If he'd just once said he was proud...

In the end, she hadn't had those few intense last moments with her father one reads about in books or sees in the movies. When she'd arrived at the hospital, he was already gone. There'd been no time for words. No time for tears.

Now she was on her own in the tidy Cape Cod house she'd shared with him for so long. The housekeeper would still come on Wednesday mornings, and the gardener would come on Saturdays to cut the grass. She alone would have to deal with the paperwork, the sorting, the shifting, the clearing out.

That could be done. Kate leaned back farther in her father's worn leather chair. It could be done because all of those things were practical matters. She dealt easily with the practical. But what about these papers she'd found? What would she do about the carefully drawn charts, the notebooks filled with information, directions, history, theory? In part, because she was raised to be logical, she considered filing them neatly away.

But there was another part, the part that enabled one to lose oneself in fantasies, in dreams, in the "perhapses" of life. This was the part that allowed Kate to lose herself totally in the possibilities of the written word, in the wonders of a book. The papers on her father's desk beckoned her.

He'd believed in it. She bent over the papers again. He'd believed in it or he never would have wasted his time documenting, searching, theorizing. She would never be able to discuss it with him. Yet, in a way, wasn't he telling her about it through his words?

Treasure. Sunken treasure. The stuff of fiction and Hollywood movies. Judging by the stack of papers and notebooks on his desk, Hardesty must have spent months, perhaps years, compiling information on the location of an English merchant ship lost off the coast of North Carolina two centuries before.

It brought Kate an immediate picture of Edward Teach—Blackbeard, the bloodthirsty pirate with the crazed superstitions and reign of terror. The stuff of romances, she thought. Of romance...

Ocracoke Island. The memory was sharp, sweet and painful. Kate had blocked out everything that had happened that summer four years before. Everything and everyone. Now, if she was to make a rational decision about what was to be done, she had to think of those long, lazy months on the remote Outer Banks of North Carolina.

She'd begun work on her doctorate. It had been a surprise when her father had announced that he planned to spend the summer on Ocracoke and invited her to accompany him. Of course, she'd gone, taking her portable typewriter, boxes of books, reams of paper. She hadn't expected to be seduced by white sand beaches and the call of gulls. She hadn't expected to fall desperately and insensibly in love.

Insensibly, Kate repeated to herself, as if in defense. She'd have to remember that was the most apt adjective. There'd been nothing sensible about her feelings for Ky Silver.

Even the name, she mused, was unique, unconventional, flashy. They'd been as suitable for each other as a peacock and a wren. Yet that hadn't stopped her from losing her head, her heart and her innocence during that balmy, magic summer.

She could still see him at the helm of the boat her father had rented, steering into the wind, laughing, dark hair flowing wildly. She could still remember that heady, weightless feeling when they'd gone scuba diving in the warm coastal waters. Kate had been too caught up in what was happening to herself to think about her father's sudden interest in boating and diving.

She'd been too swept away by her own feelings of astonishment that a man like Ky Silver should be attracted to someone like her to notice her father's preoccupation with currents and tides. There'd been too much excitement for her to realize that her father never bothered with fishing rods like the other vacationers.

But now her youthful fancies were behind her, Kate told herself. Now, she could clearly remember how many hours her father had closeted himself in his hotel room, reading book after book that he brought with him from the mainland library. He'd been researching even then. She was sure he'd continued that research in the following summers when she had refused to go back. Refused to go back, Kate remembered, because of Ky Silver.

Ky had asked her to believe in fairy tales. He asked her to give him the impossible. When she refused, frightened, he shrugged and walked away without a second look. She had never gone back to the white sand and gulls since then.

Kate looked down again at her father's papers. She had to go back now—go back and finish what her father had started. Perhaps, more than the house, the trust fund, the antique jewelry that had been her mother's, this was her father's legacy to her. If she filed those papers neatly away, they'd haunt her for the rest of her life.

She had to go back, Kate reaffirmed as she took off her glasses and folded them neatly on the blotter. And it was Ky Silver she'd have to go to. Her father's aspirations had drawn her away from Ky once; now, four years later, they were drawing her back.

But Dr. Kathleen Hardesty knew the difference between fairy tales and reality. Reaching in her father's desk drawer, she drew out a sheet of thick creamy stationery and began to write.

Ky let the wind buffet him as he opened the throttle. He liked speed in much the same way he liked a lazy afternoon in the hammock. They were two of the things that made life worthwhile. He was used to the smell of salt spray, but he still inhaled deeply. He was well accustomed to the vibration of the deck under his feet, but he still felt it. He wasn't a man to let anything go unnoticed or unappreciated.

He grew up in this quiet, remote little coastal town, and though he'd traveled and intended to travel more, he didn't plan to live anywhere else. It suited him—the freedom of the sea, and the coziness of a small community.

He didn't resent the tourists because he knew they helped keep the village alive, but he preferred the island in winter. Then the storms blew wild and cold, and only the hearty would brave the ferry across Hatteras Inlet.

He fished, but unlike the majority of his neighbors, he rarely sold what he caught. What he pulled out of the sea, he ate. He dove, occasionally collecting shells, but again, this was for his own pleasure. Often he took tourists out on his boat to fish or to scuba dive, because there were times he enjoyed the company. But there were afternoons, like this sparkling one, when he simply wanted the sea to himself.

He had always been restless. His mother had said that

he came into the world two weeks early because he grew impatient waiting. Ky turned thirty-two that spring, but was far from settled. He knew what he wanted—to live as he chose. The trouble was that he wasn't certain just what he wanted to choose.

At the moment, he chose the open sky and the endless sea. There were other moments when he knew that that wouldn't be enough.

But the sun was hot, the breeze cool and the shoreline was drawing near. The boat's motor was purring smoothly and in the small cooler was a tidy catch of fish he'd cook up for his supper that night. On a crystal, sparkling afternoon, perhaps it was enough.

From the shore he looked like a pirate might if there were pirates in the twentieth century. His hair was long enough to curl over his ears and well over the collar of a shirt had he worn one. It was black, a rich, true black that might have come from his Arapaho or Sicilian blood. His eyes were the deep, dark green of the sea on a cloudy day. His skin was bronzed from years in the sun, taut from the years of swimming and pulling in nets. His bone structure was also part of his heritage, sculpted, hard, defined.

When he smiled as he did now, racing the wind to shore, his face took on that reckless freedom women found irresistible. When he didn't smile, his eyes could turn as cold as a lion's before a leap. He discovered long ago that women found that equally irresistible.

Ky drew back on the throttle so that the boat slowed, rocked, then glided into its slip in Silver Lake Harbor.

With the quick, efficient movements of one born to the sea, he leaped onto the dock to secure the lines.

"Catch anything?"

Ky straightened and turned. He smiled, but absently, as one does at a brother seen almost every day of one's life. "Enough. Things slow at the Roost?"

Marsh smiled, and there was a brief flicker of family resemblance, but his eyes were a calm light brown and his hair was carefully styled. "Worried about your investment?"

Ky gave a half-shrug. "With you running things?"

Marsh didn't comment. They knew each other as intimately as men ever know each other. One was restless, the other calm. The opposition never seemed to matter. "Linda wants you to come up for dinner. She worries about you."

She would, Ky thought, amused. His sister-in-law loved to mother and fuss, even though she was five years younger than Ky. That was one of the reasons the restaurant she ran with Marsh was such a success— that, plus Marsh's business sense and the hefty investment and shrewd renovations Ky had made. Ky left the managing up to his brother and his sister-in-law. He didn't mind owning a restaurant, even keeping half an eye on the profit and loss, but he certainly had no interest in running one.

After the lines were secure, he wiped his palms down the hips of his cut-offs. "What's the special tonight?"

Marsh dipped his hands into his front pockets and rocked back on his heels. "Bluefish."

Grinning, Ky tossed back the lid of his cooler revealing his catch. "Tell Linda not to worry. I'll eat."

"That's not going to satisfy her." Marsh glanced at his brother as Ky looked out to sea. "She thinks you're alone too much."

"You're only alone too much if you don't like being alone." Ky glanced back over his shoulder. He didn't want to debate now, when the exhilaration of the speed and the sea were still upon him. But he'd never been a man to placate. "Maybe you two should think about having another baby, then Linda would be too busy to worry about big brothers."

"Give me a break. Hope's only eighteen months old."

"You've got to add nine to that," Ky reminded him carelessly. He was fond of his niece, despite—no, because she was a demon. "Anyway, it looks like the family lineage is in your hands."

"Yeah." Marsh shifted his feet, cleared his throat and fell silent. It was a habit he'd carried since childhood, one that could annoy or amuse Ky depending on his mood. At the moment, it was only mildly distracting.

Something was in the air. He could smell it, but he couldn't quite identify it. A storm brewing, he wondered? One of those hot, patient storms that seemed capable of brewing for weeks. He was certain he could smell it.

"Why don't you tell me what else is on your mind?" Ky suggested. "I want to get back to the house and clean these."

"You had a letter. It was put in our box by mistake."

It was a common enough occurrence, but by his

brother's expression Ky knew there was more. His sense of an impending storm grew sharper. Saying nothing, he held out his hand.

"Ky…" Marsh began. There was nothing he could say, just as there'd been nothing to say four years before. Reaching in his back pocket, he drew out the letter.

The envelope was made from heavy cream-colored paper. Ky didn't have to look at the return address. The handwriting and the memories it brought leaped out at him. For a moment, he felt his breath catch in his lungs as it might if someone had caught him with a blow to the solar plexus. Deliberately, he expelled it. "Thanks," he said, as if it meant nothing. He stuck the letter in his pocket before he picked up his cooler and gear.

"Ky—" Again Marsh broke off. His brother had turned his head, and the cool, half-impatient stare said very clearly— back off. "If you change your mind about dinner," Marsh said.

"I'll let you know." Ky went down the length of the dock without looking back.

He was grateful he hadn't bothered to bring his car down to the harbor. He needed to walk. He needed the fresh air and the exercise to keep his mind clear while he remembered what he didn't want to remember. What he never really forgot.

Kate. Four years ago she'd walked out of his life with the same sort of cool precision with which she'd walked into it. She had reminded him of a Victorian doll— a little prim, a little aloof. He'd never had much patience with neatly folded hands or haughty manners, yet almost from the first instant he'd wanted her.

At first, he thought it was the fact that she was so different. A challenge—something for Ky Silver to conquer. He enjoyed teaching her to dive, and watching the precise step-by-step way she learned. It hadn't been any hardship to look at her in a snug scuba suit, although she didn't have voluptuous curves. She had a trim, neat, almost boylike figure and what seemed like yards of thick, soft hair.

He could still remember the first time she took it down from its pristine knot. It left him breathless, hurting, fascinated. Ky would have touched it—touched her then and there if her father hadn't been standing beside her. But if a man was clever, if a man was determined, he could find a way to be alone with a woman.

Ky had found ways. Kate had taken to diving as though she'd been born to it. While her father had buried himself in his books, Ky had taken Kate out on the water—under the water, to the silent, dreamlike world that had attracted her just as it had always attracted him.

He could remember the first time he kissed her. They had been wet and cool from a dive, standing on the deck of his boat. He was able to see the lighthouse behind her and the vague line of the coast. Her hair had flowed down her back, sleek from the water, dripping with it. He'd reached out and gathered it in his hand.

"What are you doing?"

Four years later, he could hear that low, cultured, eastern voice, the curiosity in it. It took no effort for him to see the curiosity that had been in her eyes.

"I'm going to kiss you."

The curiosity had remained in her eyes, fascinating him. "Why?"

"Because I want to."

It was as simple as that for him. He wanted to. Her body had stiffened as he'd drawn her against him. When her lips parted in protest, he closed his over them. In the time it takes a heart to beat, the rigidity had melted from her body. She'd kissed him with all the young, stored-up passion that had been in her—passion mixed with innocence. He was experienced enough to recognize her innocence, and that too had fascinated him. Ky had, foolishly, youthfully and completely, fallen in love.

Kate had remained an enigma to him, though they shared impassioned hours of laughter and long, lazy talks. He admired her thirst for learning and she had a predilection for putting knowledge into neat slots that baffled him. She was enthusiastic about diving, but it hadn't been enough for her simply to be able to swim freely underwater, taking her air from tanks. She had to know how the tanks worked, why they were fashioned a certain way. Ky watched her absorb what he told her, and knew she'd retain it.

They had taken walks along the shoreline at night and she had recited poetry from memory. Beautiful words, Byron, Shelley, Keats. And he, who'd never been overly impressed by such things, had eaten it up because her voice had made the words somehow personal. Then she'd begin to talk about syntax, iambic pentameters, and Ky would find new ways to divert her.

For three months, he did little but think of her. For the first time, Ky had considered changing his lifestyle.

His little cottage near the beach needed work. It needed furniture. Kate would need more than milk crates and the hammock that had been his style. Because he'd been young and had never been in love before, Ky had taken his own plans for granted.

She'd walked out on him. She'd had her own plans, and he hadn't been part of them.

Her father came back to the island the following summer, and every summer thereafter. Kate never came back. Ky knew she had completed her doctorate and was teaching in a prestigious ivy league school where her father was all but a cornerstone. She had what she wanted. So, he told himself as he swung open the screen door of his cottage, did he. He went where he wanted, when he wanted. He called his own shots. His responsibilities extended only as far as he chose to extend them. To his way of thinking, that itself was a mark of success.

Setting the cooler on the kitchen floor, Ky opened the refrigerator. He twisted the top off a beer and drank half of it in one icy cold swallow. It washed some of the bitterness out of his mouth.

Calm now, and curious, he pulled the letter out of his pocket. Ripping it open, he drew out the single neatly written sheet.

Dear Ky,

You may or may not be aware that my father suffered a fatal heart attack two weeks ago. It was very sudden, and I'm currently trying to tie up the many details this involves.

In going through my father's papers, I find that

he had again made arrangements to come to the island this summer, and engage your services. I now find it necessary to take his place. For reasons which I'd rather explain in person, I need your help. You have my father's deposit. When I arrive in Ocracoke on the fifteenth, we can discuss terms.

If possible, contact me at the hotel, or leave a message. I hope we'll be able to come to a mutually agreeable arrangement. Please give my best to Marsh. Perhaps I'll see him during my stay.

Best,
Kathleen Hardesty

So the old man was dead. Ky set down the letter and lifted his beer again. He couldn't say he'd had any liking for Edwin Hardesty. Kate's father had been a stringent, humorless man. Still, he hadn't disliked him. Ky had, in an odd way, gotten used to his company over the past few summers. But this summer, it would be Kate.

Ky glanced at the letter again, then jogged his memory until he remembered the date. Two days, he mused. She'd be there in two days…to discuss terms. A smile played around the corners of his mouth but it didn't have anything to do with humor. They'd discuss terms, he agreed silently as he scanned Kate's letter again.

She wanted to take her father's place. Ky wondered if she'd realized, when she wrote that, just how ironic it was. Kathleen Hardesty had been obediently dogging her father's footsteps all her life. Why should that change after his death?

Had she changed? Ky wondered briefly. Would that fascinating aura of innocence and aloofness still cling to her? Or perhaps that had faded with the years. Would that rather sweet primness have developed into a rigidity? He'd see for himself in a couple of days, he realized, but tossed the letter onto the counter rather than into the trash.

So, she wanted to engage his services, he mused. Leaning both hands on either side of the sink, he looked out the window in the direction of the water he could smell, but not quite see. She wanted a business arrangement—the rental of his boat, his gear and his time. He felt the bitterness well up and swallowed it as cleanly as he had the beer. She'd have her business arrangement. And she'd pay. He'd see to that.

Ky left the kitchen with his catch still in the cooler. The appetite he'd worked up with salt spray and speed had vanished.

Kate pulled her car onto the ferry to Ocracoke and set the brake. The morning was cool and very clear. Even so, she was tempted to simply lean her head back and close her eyes. She wasn't certain what impulse had pushed her to drive from Connecticut rather than fly, but now that she'd all but reached her destination, she was too weary to analyze.

In the bucket seat beside her was her briefcase, and inside, all the papers she'd collected from her father's desk. Perhaps once she was in the hotel on the island, she could go through them again, understand them better. Perhaps the feeling that she was doing the right thing would come back. Over the past few days she'd lost that sense.

The closer she came to the island, the more she began to think she was making a mistake. Not to the island, Kate corrected ruthlessly—the closer she came to Ky. It was a fact, and Kate knew it was imperative to face facts so that they could be dealt with logically.

She had a little time left, a little time to calm the feelings that had somehow gotten stirred up during the drive south. It was foolish, and somehow it helped Kate to remind herself of that. She wasn't a woman returning to a lover, but a woman hoping to engage a diver in a very specific venture. Past personal feelings wouldn't enter into it because they were just that. Past.

The Kate Hardesty who'd arrived on Ocracoke four years ago had little to do with the Dr. Kathleen Hardesty who was going there now. She wasn't young, inexperienced or impressionable. Those reckless, wild traits of Ky's wouldn't appeal to her now. They wouldn't frighten her. They would be, if Ky agreed to her terms, business partners.

Kate felt the ferry move beneath her as she stared through the windshield. Yes, she thought, unless Ky had changed a great deal, the prospect of diving for treasure would appeal to his sense of adventure.

She knew enough about diving in the technical sense to be sure she'd find no one better equipped for the job. It was always advisable to have the best. More relaxed and less weary, Kate stepped out of her car to stand at the rail. From there she could watch the gulls swoop and the tiny uninhabited islands pass by. She felt a sense of homecoming, but pushed it away. Connecticut was home. Once Kate did what she came for, she'd go back.

The water swirled behind the boat. She couldn't hear it over the motor, but looking down she could watch the wake. One island was nearly imperceptible under a flock of big, brown pelicans. It made her smile, pleased to see the odd, awkward-looking birds again. They passed the long spit of land, where fishermen parked trucks and tried their luck, near the point where bay met sea. She could watch the waves crash and foam where there was no shore, just a turbulent marriage of waters. That was something she hadn't forgotten, though she hadn't seen it since she left the island. Nor had she forgotten just how treacherous the current was along that verge.

Excitement. She breathed deeply before she turned back to her car. The treacherous was always exciting.

When the ferry docked, she had only a short wait before she could drive her car onto the narrow black-top. The trip to town wouldn't take long, and it wasn't possible to lose your way if you stayed on the one long road. The sea battered on one side, the sound flowed smoothly on the other—both were deep blue in the late morning light.

Her nerves were gone, at least that's what she told herself. It had just been a case of last-minute jitters—very normal. She was prepared to see Ky again, speak to him, work with him if they could agree on the terms.

With the windows down, the soft, moist air blew around her. It was soothing. She'd almost forgotten just how soothing air could be, or the sound of water lapping constantly against sand. It was right to come.

When she saw the first faded buildings of the village, she felt a wave of relief. She was here. There was no turning back now.

The hotel where she had stayed that summer with her father was on the sound side of the island. It was small and quiet. If the service was a bit slow by northern standards, the view made up for it.

Kate pulled up in front and turned off the ignition. Self-satisfaction made her sigh. She'd taken the first step and was completely prepared for the next.

Then as she stepped out of the car, she saw him. For an instant, the confident professor of English literature vanished. She was only a woman, vulnerable to her own emotions.

Oh God, he hasn't changed. Not at all. As Ky came closer, she could remember every kiss, every murmur, every crazed storm of their loving. The breeze blew his hair back from his face so that every familiar angle and plane was clear to her. With the sun warm on her skin, bright in her eyes, she felt the years spin back, then forward again. He hadn't changed.

He hadn't expected to see her yet. Somehow he thought she'd arrive that afternoon. Yet he found it necessary to go by the Roost that morning knowing the restaurant was directly across from the hotel where she'd be staying.

She was here, looking neat and a bit too thin in her tailored slacks and blouse. Her hair was pinned up so that the soft femininity of her neck and throat were revealed. Her eyes seemed too dark against her pale skin—skin Ky knew would turn golden slowly under the summer sun.

She looked the same. Soft, prim, calm. Lovely. He ignored the thud in the pit of his stomach as he stepped in front of her. He looked her up and down with the arrogance that was so much a part of him. Then he grinned because he had an overwhelming urge to strangle her.

"Kate. Looks like my timing's good."

She was almost certain she couldn't speak and was therefore determined to speak calmly. "Ky, it's nice to see you again."

"Is it?"

Ignoring the sarcasm, Kate walked around to her trunk and released it. "I'd like to get together with you as soon as possible. There are some things I want to show you, and some business I'd like to discuss."

"Sure, always open for business."

He watched her pull two cases from her trunk, but didn't offer to help. He saw there was no ring on her hand—but it wouldn't have mattered.

"Perhaps we can meet this afternoon then, after I've settled in." The sooner the better, she told herself. They would establish the purpose, the ground rules and the payment. "We could have lunch in the hotel."

"No, thanks," he said easily, leaning against the side of her car while she set her cases down. "You want me, you know where to find me. It's a small island."

With his hands in the pockets of his jeans, he walked away from her. Though she didn't want to, Kate remembered that the last time he'd walked away, they'd stood in almost the same spot.

Picking up her cases, she headed for the hotel, perhaps a bit too quickly.

Chapter 2

She knew where to find him. If the island had been double in size, she'd still have known where to find him. Kate acknowledged that Ky hadn't changed. That meant if he wasn't out on his boat, he would be at home, in the small, slightly dilapidated cottage he owned near the beach. Because she felt it would be a strategic error to go after him too soon, she dawdled over her unpacking.

But there were memories even here, where she'd spent one giddy, whirlwind night of love with Ky. It had been the only time they were able to sleep together through the night, embracing each other in the crisp hotel sheets until the first light of dawn crept around the edges of the window shades. She remembered how reckless she'd felt during those few stolen hours, and how dull the morning had seemed because it brought them to an end.

Now she could look out the same window she had stood by then, staring out in the same direction she'd stared out then when she watched Ky walk away. She remembered the sky had been streaked with a rose color before it had brightened to a pure, pale blue.

Then, with her skin still warm from her lover's touch and her mind glazed with lack of sleep and passion, Kate had believed such things could go on forever. But of course they couldn't. She had seen that only weeks later. Passion and reckless nights of loving had to give way to responsibilities, obligations.

Staring out the same window, in the same direction, Kate could feel the sense of loss she'd felt that long ago dawn without the underlying hope that they'd be together again. And again.

They wouldn't be together again, and there'd been no one else since that one heady summer. She had her career, her vocation, her books. She had had her taste of passion.

Turning away, she busied herself by rearranging everything she'd just arranged in her drawers and closet. When she decided she'd stalled in her hotel room long enough, Kate started out. She didn't take her car. She walked, just as she always walked to Ky's home.

She told herself she was over the shock of seeing him again. It was only natural that there be some strain, some discomfort. She was honest enough to admit that it would have been easier if there'd been only strain and discomfort, and not that one sharp quiver of pleasure. Kate acknowledged it, now that it had passed.

No, Ky Silver hadn't changed, she reminded herself.

He was still arrogant, self-absorbed and cocky. Those traits might have appealed to her once, but she'd been very young. If she were wise, she could use those same traits to persuade Ky to help her. Yes, those traits, she thought, and the tempting offer of a treasure hunt. Even at her most pessimistic, she couldn't believe Ky would refuse. It was his nature to take chances.

This time she'd be in charge. Kate drew in a deep breath of warm air that tasted of sea. Somehow she felt it would steady her. Ky was going to find she was no longer naive, or susceptible to a few careless words of affection.

With her briefcase in hand, Kate walked through the village. This too was the same, she thought. She was glad of it. The simplicity and solitude still appealed to her. She enjoyed the dozens of little shops, the restaurants and small inns tucked here and there, all somehow using the harbor as a central point, the lighthouse as a landmark. The villagers still made the most of their notorious one-time resident and permanent ghost, Blackbeard. His name or face was lavishly displayed on store signs.

She passed the harbor, unconsciously scanning for Ky's boat. It was there, in the same slip he'd always used—clean lines, scrubbed deck, shining hardware. The flying bridge gleamed in the afternoon light and looked the same she remembered. Reckless, challenging. The paint was fresh and there was no film of salt spray on the bridge windows. However careless Ky had been about his own appearance or his home, he'd always pampered his boat.

The *Vortex*. Kate studied the flamboyant lettering on the stern. He could pamper, she thought again, but he also expected a lot in return. She knew the speed he could urge out of the secondhand cabin cruiser he'd lovingly reconstructed himself. Nothing could block the image of the days she'd stood beside him at the helm. The wind had whipped her hair as he'd laughed and pushed for speed, and more speed. Her heart thudded, her pulse raced until she was certain nothing and no one could catch them. She'd been afraid, of him, of the rush of wind—but she'd stayed with both. In the end, she'd left both.

He enjoyed the demanding, the thrilling, the frightening. Kate gripped the handle of her briefcase tighter. Isn't that why she came to him? There were dozens of other experienced divers, many, many other experts on the coastal waters of the Outer Banks. There was only one Ky Silver.

"Kate? Kate Hardesty?"

At the sound of her name, Kate turned and felt the years tumble back again. "Linda!" This time there was no restraint. With an openness she showed to very few, Kate embraced the woman who dashed up to her. "It's wonderful to see you." With a laugh, she drew Linda away to study her. The same chestnut hair cut short and pert, the same frank, brown eyes. It seemed very little had changed on the island. "You look wonderful."

"When I looked out the window and saw you, I could hardly believe it. Kate, you've barely changed at all." With her usual candor and lack of pretension, Linda took a quick, thorough survey. It was quick only because she did things quickly, but it wasn't subtle. "You're too thin," she decided. "But that might be jealousy."

"You still look like a college freshman," Kate returned. "That is jealousy."

As swiftly as the laugh had come, Linda sobered. "I'm sorry about your father, Kate. These past weeks must've been difficult for you."

Kate heard the sincerity, but she'd already tied up her grief and stored it away. "Ky told you?"

"Ky never tells me anything," Linda said with a sniff. In an unconscious move, she glanced in the direction of his boat. It was in its slip and Kate had been walking north—in the direction of Ky's cottage. There could be only one place she could have been going. "Marsh did. How long are you going to stay?"

"I'm not sure yet." She felt the weight of her briefcase. Dreams held the same weight as responsibilities. "There are some things I have to do."

"One of the things you have to do is have dinner at the Roost tonight. It's the restaurant right across from your hotel."

Kate looked back at the rough wooden sign. "Yes, I noticed it. Is it new?"

Linda glanced over her shoulder with a self-satisfied nod. "By Ocracoke standards. We run it."

"We?"

"Marsh and I." With a beaming smile, Linda held out her left hand. "We've been married for three years." Then she rolled her eyes in a habit Kate remembered. "It only took me fifteen years to convince him he couldn't live without me."

"I'm happy for you." She was, and if she felt a pang, she ignored it. "Married and running a restaurant. My father never filled me in on island gossip."

"We have a daughter too. Hope. She's a year and a half old and a terror. For some reason, she takes after Ky." Linda sobered again, laying a hand lightly on Kate's arm. "You're going to see him now." It wasn't a question; she didn't bother to disguise it as one.

"Yes." *Keep it casual,* Kate ordered herself. Don't let the questions and concern in Linda's eyes weaken you. There were ties between Linda and Ky, not only newly formed family ones, but the older tie of the island. "My father was working on something. I need Ky's help with it."

Linda studied Kate's calm face. "You know what you're doing?"

"Yes." She didn't show a flicker of unease. Her stomach slowly wrapped itself in knots. "I know what I'm doing."

"Okay." Accepting Kate's answer, but not satisfied, Linda dropped her hand. "Please come by—the restaurant or the house. We live just down the road from Ky. Marsh'll want to see you, and I'd like to show off Hope—and our menu," she added with a grin. "Both are outstanding."

"Of course I'll come by." On impulse, she took both of Linda's hands. "It's really good to see you again. I know I didn't keep in touch, but—"

"I understand." Linda gave her hands a quick

squeeze. "That was yesterday. I've got to get back, the lunch crowd's pretty heavy during the season." She let out a little sigh, wondering if Kate was as calm as she seemed. And if Ky were as big a fool as ever. "Good luck," she murmured, then dashed across the street again.

"Thanks," Kate said under her breath. She was going to need it.

The walk was as beautiful as she remembered. She passed the little shops with their display windows showing handmade crafts or antiques. She passed the blue-and-white clapboard houses and the neat little streets on the outskirts of town with their bleached green lawns and leafy trees.

A dog raced back and forth on the length of his chain as she wandered by, barking at her as if he knew he was supposed to but didn't have much interest in it. She could see the tower of the white lighthouse. There'd been a keeper there once, but those days were over. Then she was on the narrow path that led to Ky's cottage.

Her palms were damp. She cursed herself. If she had to remember, she'd remember later, when she was alone. When she was safe.

The path was as it had been, just wide enough for a car, sparsely graveled, lined with bushes that always grew out a bit too far. The bushes and trees had always had a wild, overgrown look that suited the spot. That suited him.

Ky had told her he didn't care much for visitors. If he wanted company, all he had to do was go into town where he knew everyone. That was typical of Ky Silver, Kate mused. If I want you, I'll let you know. Otherwise, back off.

He'd wanted her once.... Nervous, Kate shifted the briefcase to her other hand. Whatever he wanted now, he'd have to hear her out. She needed him for what he was best at—diving and taking chances.

When the house came into view, she stopped, staring. It was still small, still primitive. But it no longer looked as though it would keel over on its side in a brisk wind.

The roof had been redone. Obviously Ky wouldn't need to set out pots and pans during a rain any longer. The porch he'd once talked vaguely about building now ran the length of the front, sturdy and wide. The screen door that had once been patched in a half a dozen places had been replaced by a new one. Yet nothing looked new, she observed. It just looked right. The cedar had weathered to silver, the windows were untrimmed but gleaming. There was, much to her surprise, a spill of impatiens in a long wooden planter.

She'd been wrong, Kate decided as she walked closer. Ky Silver had changed. Precisely how, and precisely how much, she had yet to find out.

She was nearly to the first step when she heard sounds coming from the rear of the house. There was a shed back there, she remembered, full of boards and tools and salvage. Grateful that she didn't have to meet him in the house, Kate walked around the side to the tiny backyard. She could hear the sea and knew it was less than a two-minute walk through high grass and sand dunes.

Did he still go down there in the evenings? she wondered. Just to look, he'd said. Just to smell. Sometimes he'd pick up driftwood or shells or whatever small treasures the sea gave up to the sand. Once he'd given her a small smooth shell that fit into the palm of her hand—very white with a delicate pink center. A woman with her first gift of diamonds could not have been more thrilled.

Shaking the memories away, she went into the shed. It was as tall as the cottage and half as wide. The last time she'd been there, it'd been crowded with planks and boards and boxes of hardware. Now she saw the hull of a boat. At a worktable with his back to her, Ky sanded the mast.

"You've built it." The words came out before she could stop them, full of astonished pleasure. How many times had he told her about the boat he'd build one day? It had seemed to Kate it had been his only concrete ambition. Mahogany on oak, he'd said. A seventeen-foot sloop that would cut through the water like a dream. He'd have bronze fastenings and teak on the deck. One day he'd sail the inner coastal waters from Ocracoke to New England. He'd described the boat so minutely that she'd seen it then just as clearly as she saw it now.

"I told you I would." Ky turned away from the mast and faced her. She, in the doorway, had the sun at her back. He was half in shadow.

"Yes." Feeling foolish, Kate tightened her grip on the briefcase. "You did."

"But you didn't believe me." Ky tossed aside the sandpaper. Did she have to look so neat and cool, and impossibly lovely? A trickle of sweat ran down his back. "You always had a problem seeing beyond the moment."

Reckless, impatient, compelling. Would he always bring those words to her mind? "You always had a problem dealing with the moment," she said.

His brow lifted, whether in surprise or derision she couldn't be sure. "Then it might be said *we* always had a problem." He walked to her, so that the sun slanting through the small windows fell over him, then behind him. "But it didn't always seem to matter." To satisfy himself that he still could, Ky reached out and touched her face. She didn't move, and her skin was as soft and cool as he remembered. "You look tired Kate."

The muscles in her stomach quivered, but not her voice. "It was a long trip."

His thumb brushed along her cheekbone. "You need some sun."

This time she backed away. "I intend to get some."

"So I gathered from your letter." Pleased that she'd retreated first, Ky leaned against the open door. "You wrote that you wanted to talk to me in person. You're here. Why don't you tell me what you want?"

The cocky grin might have made her melt once. Now it stiffened her spine. "My father was researching a project. I intend to finish it."

"So?"

"I need your help."

Ky laughed and stepped past her into the sunlight. He needed the air, the distance. He needed to touch her again. "From your tone, there's nothing you hate more than asking me for it."

"No." She stood firm, feeling suddenly strong and bitter. "Nothing."

There was no humor in his eyes as he faced her again. The expression in them was cold and flat. She'd seen it before. "Then let's understand each other before we start. You left the island and me, and took what I wanted."

He couldn't make her cringe now as he once had with only that look. "What happened four years ago has nothing to do with today."

"The hell it doesn't." He came toward her again so that she took an involuntary step backward. "Still afraid of me?" he asked softly.

As it had a moment ago, the question turned the fear to anger. "No," she told him, and meant it. "I'm not afraid of you, Ky. I've no intention of discussing the past, but I will agree that I left the island and you. I'm here now on business. I'd like you to hear me out. If you're interested, we'll discuss terms, nothing else."

"I'm not one of your students, professor." The drawl crept into his voice, as it did when he let it. "Don't instruct."

She curled her fingers tighter around the handle of her briefcase. "In business, there are always ground rules."

"Nobody agreed to let you make them."

"I made a mistake," Kate said quietly as she fought for control. "I'll find someone else."

She'd taken only two steps away when Ky grabbed her arm. "No, you won't." The stormy look in his eyes made her throat dry. She knew what he meant. She'd never find anyone else that could make her feel as he made her feel, or want as he made her want. Deliberately, Kate removed his hand from her arm.

"I came here on business. I've no intention of fighting with you over something that doesn't exist any longer."

"We'll see about that." How long could he hold on? Ky wondered. It hurt just to look at her and to feel her withdrawing with every second that went by. "But for now, why don't you tell me what you have in that businesslike briefcase, professor."

Kate took a deep breath. She should have known it wouldn't be easy. Nothing was ever easy with Ky. "Charts," she said precisely. "Notebooks full of research, maps, carefully documented facts and precise theories. In my opinion, my father was very close to pinpointing the exact location of the *Liberty,* an English merchant vessel that sank, stores intact, off the North Carolina coast two hundred and fifty years ago."

He listened without a comment or a change of expression from beginning to end. When she finished, Ky studied her face for one long moment. "Come inside," he said and turned toward the house. "Show me what you've got."

His arrogance made her want to turn away and go back to town exactly as she'd come. There were other divers, others who knew the coast and the waters as well as Ky did. Kate forced herself to calm down, forced herself to think. There were others, but if it was a choice between the devil she knew and the unknown, she had no choice. Kate followed him into the house.

This, too, had changed. The kitchen she remembered had had a paint splattered floor, with the only usable counter space being a tottering picnic table. The floor had been stripped and varnished, the cabinets redone, and scrubbed butcher block counters lined the sink. He had put in a skylight so that the sun spilled down over the picnic table, now re-worked and re-painted, with benches along either side.

"Did you do all of this yourself?"

"Yeah. Surprised?"

So he didn't want to make polite conversation. Kate set her briefcase on the table. "Yes. You always seemed content that the walls were about to cave in on you."

"I was content with a lot of things, once. Want a beer?"

"No." Kate sat down and drew the first of her father's notebooks out of her briefcase. "You'll want to read these. It would be unnecessary and time-consuming for you to read every page, but if you'd look over the ones I've marked, I think you'll have enough to go by."

"All right." Ky turned from the refrigerator, beer in hand. He sat, watching her over the rim as he took the first swallow, then he opened the notebook.

Edwin Hardesty's handwriting was very clear and precise. He wrote down his facts in didactic, unromantic terms. What could have been exciting was as dry as a thesis, but it was accurate. Ky had no doubt of that.

The *Liberty* had been lost, with its stores of sugar, tea, silks, wine and other imports for the colonies. Hardesty had listed the manifest down to the last piece of hardtack. When it had left England, the ship had also been carrying gold. Twenty-five thousand in coins of the realm. Ky glanced up from the notebook to see Kate watching him.

"Interesting," he said simply, and turned to the next page she marked.

There'd been only three survivors who'd washed up on the island. One of the crew had described the storm that had sunk the *Liberty,* giving details on the height of the waves, the splintering wood, the water gushing into the hole. It was a grim, grisly story which Hardesty had recounted in his pragmatic style, complete with footnotes. The crewman had also given the last known location of the ship before it had gone down. Ky didn't require Hardesty's calculations to figure the ship had sunk two-and-a-half miles off the coast of Ocracoke.

Going from one notebook to another, Ky read through Hardesty's well-drafted theories, his clear to-the-point documentations, corroborated and recorroborated. He scanned the charts, then studied them with more care. He remembered the man's avid interest in diving, which had always seemed inconsistent with his precise lifestyle.

So he'd been looking for gold, Ky mused. All these years the man had been digging in books and looking for gold. If it had been anyone else, Ky might have dismissed it as another fable. Little towns along the coast were full of stories about buried treasure. Edward Teach had used the shallow waters of the inlets to frustrate and outwit the crown until his last battle off the shores of Ocracoke. That alone kept the dreams of finding sunken treasures alive.

But it was Dr. Edwin J. Hardesty, Yale professor, an unimaginative, humorless man who didn't believe there was time to be wasted on the frivolous, who'd written these notebooks.

Ky might still have dismissed it, but Kate was sitting across from him. He had enough adventurous blood in him to believe in destinies.

Setting the last notebook aside, he picked up his beer again. "So, you want to treasure hunt."

She ignored the humor in his voice. With her hands folded on the table, she leaned forward. "I intend to follow through with what my father was working on."

"Do you believe it?"

Did she? Kate opened her mouth and closed it again. She had no idea. "I don't believe that all of my father's time and research should go for nothing. I want to try. As it happens, I need you to help me do it. You'll be compensated."

"Will I?" He studied the liquid left in the beer bottle with a half smile. "Will I indeed?"

"I need you, your boat and your equipment for a month, maybe two. I can't dive alone because I just don't know the waters well enough to risk it, and I don't have the time to waste. I have to be back in Connecticut by the end of August."

"To get more chalk dust under your fingernails."

She sat back slowly. "You have no right to criticize my profession."

"I'm sure the chalk's very exclusive at Yale," Ky commented. "So you're giving yourself six weeks or so to find a pot of gold."

"If my father's calculations are viable, it won't take that long."

"If," Ky repeated. Setting down his bottle, he leaned forward. "I've got no timetable. You want six weeks of my time, you can have it. For a price."

"Which is?"

"A hundred dollars a day and fifty percent of whatever we find."

Kate gave him a cool look as she slipped the notebooks back into her briefcase. "Whatever I was four years ago, Ky, I'm not a fool now. A hundred dollars a day is outrageous when we're dealing with monthly rates. And fifty percent is out of the question." It gave her a certain satisfaction to bargain with him. This made it business, pure and simple. "I'll give you fifty dollars a day and ten percent."

With the maddening half grin on his face he swirled the beer in the bottle. "I don't turn my boat on for fifty a day."

She tilted her head a bit to study him. Something tore inside him. She'd often done that whenever he said something she wanted to think over. "You're more mercenary than you once were."

"We've all got to make a living, professor." Didn't she feel anything? he thought furiously. Wasn't she suffering just a little, being in the house where they'd made love their first and last time? "You want a service," he said quietly, "you pay for it. Nothing's free. Seventy-five a day and twenty-five percent. We'll say it's for old-times' sake."

"No, we'll say it's for business' sake." She made

herself extend her hand, but when his closed over it, she regretted the gesture. It was callused, hard, strong. Kate knew how his hand felt skimming over her skin, driving her to desperation, soothing, teasing, seducing.

"We have a deal." Ky thought he could see a flash of remembrance in her eyes. He kept her hand in his knowing she didn't welcome his touch. Because she didn't. "There's no guarantee you'll find your treasure."

"That's understood."

"Fine. I'll deduct your father's deposit from the total."

"All right." With her free hand, she clutched at her briefcase. "When do we start?"

"Meet me at the harbor at eight tomorrow." Deliberately, he placed his other free hand over hers on the leather case. "Leave this with me. I want to look over the papers some more."

"There's no need for you to have them," Kate began, but his hands tightened on hers.

"If you don't trust me with them, you take them along." His voice was very smooth and very quiet. At its most dangerous. "And find yourself another diver."

Their gazes locked. Her hands were trapped and so was she. Kate knew there would be sacrifices she'd have to make. "I'll meet you at eight."

"Fine." He released her hands and sat back. "Nice doing business with you, Kate."

Dismissed, she rose. Just how much had she sacrificed already? she wondered. "Goodbye."

He lifted and drained his half-finished beer when the screen shut behind her. Then he made himself sit there until he was certain that when he rose and walked to the window she'd be out of sight. He made himself sit there until the air flowing through the screens had carried her scent away.

Sunken ships and deep-sea treasure. It would have excited him, captured his imagination, enthusiasm and interest if he hadn't had an overwhelming urge to just get in his boat and head toward the horizon. He hadn't believed she could still affect him that way, that much, that completely. He'd forgotten that just being within touching distance of her tied his stomach in knots.

He'd never gotten over her. No matter what he filled his life with over the past four years, he'd never gotten over the slim, intellectual woman with the haughty face and doe's eyes.

Ky sat, staring at the briefcase with her initials stamped discreetly near the handle. He'd never expected her to come back, but he'd just discovered he'd never accepted the fact that she'd left him. Somehow, he'd managed to deceive himself through the years. Now, seeing her again, he knew it had just been a matter of pure survival and nothing to do with truth. He'd had to go on, to pretend that that part of his life was behind him, or he would have gone mad.

She was back now, but she hadn't come back to him. A business arrangement. Ky ran his hand over the smooth leather of the case. She simply wanted the best diver she knew and was willing to pay for him. Fee for services, nothing more, nothing less. The past meant little or nothing to her.

Fury grew until his knuckles whitened around the

bottle. He'd give her what she paid for, he promised himself. And maybe a bit extra.

This time when she went away, he wouldn't be left feeling like an inadequate fool. She'd be the one who would have to go on pretending for the rest of her life. This time when she went away, he'd be done with her. God, he'd have to be.

Rising quickly, he went out to the shed. If he stayed inside, he'd give in to the need to get very, very drunk.

Chapter 3

Kate had the water in the tub so hot that the mirror over the white pedestal sink was fogged. Oil floated on the surface, subtly fragrant and soothing. She'd lost track of how long she lay there—soaking, recharging. The next irrevocable step had been taken. She'd survived. Somehow during her discussion with Ky in his kitchen she had fought back the memories of laughter and passion. She couldn't count how many meals they'd shared there, cooking their catch, sipping wine.

Somehow during the walk back to her hotel, she'd overcome the need to weep. Tomorrow would be just a little easier. Tomorrow, and every day that followed. She had to believe it.

His animosity would help. His derision toward her kept Kate from romanticizing what she had to tell herself had never been more than a youthful summer fling.

Perspective. She'd always been able to stand back and align everything in its proper perspective.

Perhaps her feelings for Ky weren't as dead as she had hoped or pretended they were. But her emotions were tinged with bitterness. Only a fool asked for more sorrow. Only a romantic believed that bitterness could ever be sweet. It had been a long time since Kate had been a romantic fool. Even so, they would work together because both had an interest in what might be lying on the sea floor.

Think of it. Two hundred and fifty years. Kate closed her eyes and let her mind drift. The silks and sugar would be gone, but would they find brass fittings deep in corrosion after two-and-a-half centuries? The hull would be covered with fungus and barnacles, but how much of the oak would still be intact? Might the log have been secured in a waterproof hold and still be legible? It could be donated to a museum in her father's name. It would be something—the last something she could do for him. Perhaps then she'd be able to lay all her ambiguous feelings to rest.

The gold, Kate thought as she rose from the tub, the gold would survive. She wasn't immune to the lure of it. Yet she knew it would be the hunt that would be exciting, and somehow fulfilling. If she found it...

What would she do? Kate wondered. She dropped the hotel towel over the rod before she wrapped herself in her robe. Behind her, the mirror was still fogged with steam from the water that drained slowly from the tub. Would she put her share tidily in some conservative investments? Would she take a leisurely trip to the Greek islands to see what Byron had seen and fallen in love with there? With a laugh, Kate walked through to the other room to pick up her brush. Strange, she hadn't thought beyond the search yet. Perhaps that was for the best, it wasn't wise to plan too far ahead.

You always had a problem seeing beyond the moment.

Damn him! With a sudden fury, Kate slammed the brush onto the dresser. She'd seen beyond the moment. She'd seen that he'd offered her no more than a tentative affair in a run-down beach shack. No guarantees, no commitment, no future. She only thanked God she'd had enough of her senses left to understand it and to walk away from what was essentially nothing at all. She'd never let Ky know just how horribly it had hurt to walk away from nothing at all.

Her father had been right to quietly point out the weaknesses in Ky, and her obligation to herself and her chosen profession. Ky's lack of ambition, his careless attitude toward the future weren't qualities, but flaws. She'd had a responsibility, and by accepting it had given herself independence and satisfaction.

Calmer, she picked up her brush again. She was dwelling on the past too much. It was time to stop. With the deft movements of habit, she secured her hair into a sleek twist. From this time on, she'd think only of what was to come, not what had, or might have been.

She needed to get out.

With panic just under the surface, Kate pulled a dress out of her closet. It no longer mattered that she was tired, that all she really wanted to do was to crawl into bed and let her mind and body rest. Nerves wouldn't permit it. She'd go across the street, have a drink with Linda and Marsh. She'd see their baby, have a long, extravagant dinner. When she came back to the hotel, alone, she'd make certain she'd be too tired for dreams.

Tomorrow, she had work to do.

Because she dressed quickly, Kate arrived at the Roost just past six. What she saw, she immediately approved of. It wasn't elegant, but it was comfortable. It didn't have the dimly lit, cathedral feel of so many of the restaurants she'd dined in with her father, with colleagues, back in Connecticut. It was relaxed, welcoming, cozy.

There were paintings of ships and boats along the stuccoed walls, of armadas and cutters. Throughout the dining room was other sailing paraphernalia—a ship's compass with its brass gleaming, a colorful spinnaker draped behind the bar with the stools in front of it shaped like wooden kegs. There was a crow's nest spearing toward the ceiling with ferns spilling out and down the mast.

The room was already half full of couples and families, the bulk of whom Kate identified as tourists. She could hear the comforting sound of cutlery scraping lightly over plates. There was the smell of good food and the hum of mixed conversations.

Comfortable, she thought again, but definitely well organized. Waiters and waitresses in sailor's denims moved smoothly, making every second count without looking rushed. The window opened out to a full evening view of Silver Lake Harbor. Kate turned her back on it because she knew her gaze would fall on the *Vortex* or its empty slip.

Tomorrow was soon enough for that. She wanted one night without memories.

"Kate."

She felt the hands on her shoulders and recognized the voice. There was a smile on her face when she turned around. "Marsh, I'm so glad to see you."

In his quiet way, he studied her, measured her and saw both the strain and the relief. In the same way, he'd had a crush on her that had faded into admiration and respect before the end of that one summer. "Beautiful as ever. Linda said you were, but it's nice to see for myself."

She laughed, because he'd always been able to make her feel as though life could be honed down to the most simple of terms. She'd never questioned why that trait had made her relax with Marsh and tingle with Ky.

"Several congratulations are in order, I hear. On your marriage, your daughter and your business."

"I'll take them all. How about the best table in the house?"

"No less than I expected." She linked her arm through his. "Your life agrees with you," she decided as he led her to a table by the window. "You look happy."

"Look and am." He lifted a hand to brush hers. "We were sorry to hear about your father, Kate."

"I know. Thank you."

Marsh sat across from her and fixed her with eyes so much calmer, so much softer than his brother's. She'd always wondered why the man with the dreamer's eyes had been so practical while Ky had been the real dreamer. "It's tragic, but I can't say I'm sorry it brought you back to the island. We've missed you." He paused, just long enough for effect. "All of us."

Kate picked up the square carmine-colored napkin and ran it through her hands. "Things change," she said deliberately. "You and Linda are certainly proof of that. When I left, you thought she was a bit of a nuisance."

"That hasn't changed," he claimed and grinned. He glanced up at the young, ponytailed waitress. "This is Cindy, she'll take good care of you, Miss Hardesty—" He looked back at Kate with a grin. "I guess I should say Dr. Hardesty."

"Miss'll do," Kate told him. "I've taken the summer off."

"Miss Hardesty's a guest, a special one," he added, giving the waitress a smile. "How about a drink before you order? Or a bottle of wine?"

"Piesporter," the reply came from a deep, masculine voice.

Kate's fingers tightened on the linen, but she forced herself to look up calmly to meet Ky's amused eyes.

"The professor has a fondness for it."

"Yes, Mr. Silver."

Before Kate could agree or disagree, the waitress had dashed off.

"Well, Ky," Marsh commented easily. "You have a way of making the help come to attention."

With a shrug, Ky leaned against his brother's chair. If the three of them felt the air was suddenly tighter, each concealed it in their own way. "I had an urge for scampi."

"I can recommend it," Marsh told Kate. "Linda and the chef debated the recipe, then babied it until they reached perfection."

Kate smiled at Marsh as though there were no dark, brooding man looking down at her. "I'll try it. Are you going to join me?"

"I wish I could. Linda had to run home and deal with some crisis—Hope has a way of creating them and browbeating the babysitter—but I'll try to get back for coffee. Enjoy your dinner." Rising, he sent his brother a cool, knowing look, then walked away.

"Marsh never completely got over that first case of adulation," Ky commented, then took his brother's seat without invitation.

"Marsh has always been a good friend." Kate draped the napkin over her lap with great care. "Though I realize this is your brother's restaurant, Ky, I'm sure you don't want my company for dinner any more than I want yours."

"That's where you're wrong." He sent a quick, dashing smile at the waitress as she brought the wine. He didn't bother to correct Kate's assumption on the Roost's ownership. Kate sat stone-faced, her manners too good to allow her to argue, while Cindy opened the bottle and poured the first sip for Ky to taste.

"It's fine," he told her. "I'll pour." Taking the bottle, he filled Kate's glass to within half an inch of the rim. "Since we've both chosen the Roost tonight, why don't we have a little test?"

Kate lifted her glass and sipped. The wine was cool and dry. She remembered the first bottle they'd shared—sitting on the floor of his cottage the night she gave him her innocence. Deliberately, she took another swallow. "What kind of test?"

"We can see if the two of us can share a civilized meal in public. That was something we never got around to before."

Kate frowned as he lifted his glass. She'd never seen Ky drink from a wineglass. The few times they had indulged in wine, it had been drunk out of one of the half a dozen water glasses he'd owned. The stemware seemed too delicate for his hand, the wine too mellow for the look in his eye.

No, they'd never eaten dinner in public before. Her father would have exuded disapproval for socializing with someone he'd considered an employee. Kate had known it, and hadn't risked it.

Things were different now, she told herself as she lifted her own glass. In a sense, Ky was now her employee. She could make her own judgments. Recklessly, she toasted him. "To a profitable arrangement then."

"I couldn't have said it better myself." He touched the rim of his glass to hers, but his gaze was direct and uncomfortable. "Blue suits you," he said, referring to her dress, but not taking his eyes off hers. "The deep midnight blue that makes your skin look like something that should be tasted very, very carefully."

She stared at him, stunned at how easily his voice could take on that low, intimate tone that had always made the blood rush out of her brain. He'd always been able to make words seem something dark and secret. That had been one of his greatest skills, one she had never been prepared for. She was no more prepared for it now.

"Would you care to order now?" The waitress stopped beside the table, cheerful, eager to please.

Ky smiled when Kate remained silent. "We're having scampi. The house dressing on the salads will be fine." He leaned back, glass in hand, still smiling. But the smile on his lips didn't connect with his eyes. "You're not drinking your wine. Maybe I should've asked if your taste has changed over the years."

"It's fine." Deliberately she sipped, then kept the glass in her hand as though it would anchor her. "Marsh looks well," she commented. "I was happy to hear about him and Linda. I always pictured them together."

"Did you?" Ky lifted his glass toward the lowering evening light slanting through the window. He watched the colors spear through the wine and glass and onto Kate's hand. "He didn't. But then…" Shifting his gaze, he met her eyes again. "Marsh always took more time to make up his mind than me."

"Recklessness," she continued as she struggled just to breathe evenly, "was always more your style than your brother's."

"But you didn't come to my brother with your charts and notes, did you?"

"No." With an effort she kept her voice and her eyes level. "I didn't. Perhaps I decided a certain amount of recklessness had its uses."

"Find me useful, do you, Kate?"

The waitress served the salads but didn't speak this time. She saw the look in Ky's eyes.

So had Kate. "When I'm having a job done, I've found that it saves a considerable amount of time and trouble to find the most suitable person." With forced calm, she set down her wine and picked up her fork. "I wouldn't have come back to Ocracoke for any other reason." She tilted her head, surprised by the quick surge of challenge that rushed through her. "Things will be simpler for both of us if that's clear up front."

Anger moved through him, but he controlled it. If they were playing word games, he had to keep his wits. She'd always been clever, but now it appeared the cleverness was glossed over with sophistication. He remembered the innocent, curious Kate with a pang. "As I recall, you were always one for complicating rather than simplifying. I had to explain the purpose, history and mechanics of every piece of equipment before you'd take the first dive."

"That's called caution, not complication."

"You'd know more about caution than I would. Some people spend half their lives testing the wind." He drank deeply of the wine. "I'd rather ride with it."

"Yes." This time it was she who smiled with her lips only. "I remember very well. No plans, no ties, tomorrow the wind might change."

"If you're anchored in one spot too long, you can become like those trees out there." He gestured out the window where a line of sparse junipers bent away from the sea. "Stunted."

"Yet you're still here, where you were born, where you grew up."

Slowly Ky poured her more wine. "The island's too isolated, the life a bit too basic for some. I prefer it to those structured little communities with their parties and country clubs."

Kate looked like she belonged in such a place, Ky thought as he fought against the frustrated desire that ebbed and flowed inside him. She belonged in an elegant silk suit, holding a Dresden cup and discussing an obscure eighteenth-century English poet. Was that why she could still make him feel rough and awkward and too full of longings?

If they could be swept back in time, he'd have stolen her, taken her out to open sea and kept her there. They would have traveled from port to exotic port. If having her meant he could never go home again, then he'd have sailed until his time was up. But he would have had her. Ky's fingers tightened around his glass. By God, he would have had her.

The main course was slipped in front of him discreetly. Ky brought himself back to the moment. It wasn't the eighteenth century, but today. Still, she had brought him the past with the papers and maps. Perhaps they'd both find more than they'd bargained for.

"I looked over the things you left with me."

"Oh?" She felt a quick tingle of excitement but speared the first delicate shrimp as though it were all that concerned her.

"Your father's research is very thorough."

"Of course."

Ky let out a quick laugh. "Of course," he repeated, toasting her. "In any case, I think he might have been on the right track. You do realize that the section he narrowed it down to goes into a dangerous area."

Her brows drew together, but she continued to eat. "Sharks?"

"Sharks are a little difficult to confine to an area," he said easily. "A lot of people forget that the war came this close in the forties. There are still mines all along the coast of the Outer Banks. If we're going down to the bottom, it'd be smart to keep that in mind."

"I've no intention of being careless."

"No, but sometimes people look so far ahead they don't see what's under their feet."

Though he'd eaten barely half of his meal, Ky picked up his wine again. How could he eat when his whole system was aware of her? He couldn't stop himself from wondering what it would be like to pull those confining pins out of her hair as he'd done so often in the past. He couldn't prevent the memory from springing up about what it had been like to bundle her into his arms and just hold her there with her body fitting so neatly against his. He could picture those long, serious looks she'd give him just before passion would start to take over, then the freedom he could feel racing through her in those last heady moments of love-making.

How could it have been so right once and so wrong now? Wouldn't her body still fit against his? Wouldn't her hair flow through his hands as it fell—that quiet brown that took on such fascinating lights in the sun. She'd always murmur his name after passion was spent, as if the sound alone sustained her. He wanted to hear her say it, just once more, soft and breathless while they were tangled together, bodies still warm and pulsing. He wasn't sure he could resist it.

Absently Ky signaled for coffee. Perhaps he didn't want to resist it. He needed her. He'd forgotten just how sharp and sure a need could be. Perhaps he'd take her. He didn't believe she was indifferent to him—certain things never fade completely. In his own time, in his own way, he'd take what he once had from her. And pray it would be enough this time.

When he looked back at her, Kate felt the warning signals shiver through her. Ky was a difficult man to understand. She knew only that he'd come to some decision and that it involved her. Grateful for the warming effects of the coffee, she drank. She was in charge this time, she reminded herself, every step of the way and she'd make him aware of it. There was no time like the present to begin.

"I'll be at the harbor at eight," she said briskly. "I'll require tanks, of course, but I brought my own wet suit. I'd appreciate it if you'd have my briefcase and its contents on board. I believe we'd be wise to spend between six and eight hours out a day."

"Have you kept up with your diving?"

"I know what to do."

"I'd be the last to argue that you had the best teacher." He tilted his cup back in a quick, impatient gesture Kate found typical of him. "But if you're rusty, we'll take it slow for a day or two."

"I'm a perfectly competent diver."

"I want more than competence in a partner."

He saw the flare in her eyes and his need sharpened. It was a rare and arousing thing to watch her controlled and reasonable temperament heat up. "We're not partners. You're working for me."

"A matter of viewpoint," Ky said easily. He rose, deliberately blocking her in. "We'll be putting in a full day tomorrow, so you'd better go catch up on all the sleep you've been missing lately."

"I don't need you to worry about my health, Ky."

"I worry about my own," he said curtly. "You don't go under with me unless you're rested and alert. You come to the harbor in the morning with shadows under your eyes, you won't make the first dive." Furiously she squashed the urge to argue with the reasonable. "If you're sluggish, you make mistakes," Ky said briefly. "A mistake you make can cost me. That logical enough for you, professor?"

"It's perfectly clear." Bracing herself for the brush of bodies, Kate rose. But bracing herself didn't stop the jolt, not for either of them.

"I'll walk you back."

"It's not necessary."

His hand curled over her wrist, strong and stubborn. "It's civilized," he said lazily. "You were always big on being civilized."

Until you'd touch me, she thought. No, she wouldn't remember that, not if she wanted to sleep tonight. Kate merely inclined her head in cool agreement. "I want to thank Marsh."

"You can thank him tomorrow." Ky dropped the waitress's tip on the table. "He's busy."

She started to protest, then saw Marsh disappear into what must have been the kitchen. "All right." Kate moved by him and out into the balmy evening air.

The sun was low, though it wouldn't set for nearly an hour. The clouds to the west were just touched with mauve and rose. When she stepped outside, Kate decided there were more people in the restaurant than there were on the streets.

A charter fishing boat glided into the harbor. Some of the tourists would be staying on the island, others would be riding back across Hatteras Inlet on one of the last ferries of the day.

She'd like to go out on the water now, while the light was softening and the breeze was quiet. Now, she thought, while others were coming in and the sea would stretch for mile after endless empty mile.

Shaking off the mood, she headed for the hotel. What she needed wasn't a sunset sail but a good solid night's sleep. Daydreaming was foolish, and tomorrow too important.

The same hotel. Ky glanced up at her window. He already knew she had the same room. He'd walked her there before, but then she'd have had her arm through his in that sweet way she had of joining them together. She'd have looked up and laughed at him over something that had happened that day. And she'd have kissed him, warm, long and lingeringly before the door would close behind her.

Because her thoughts had run the same gamut, Kate

turned to him while they were still outside the hotel. "Thank you, Ky." She made a business out of shifting her purse strap on her arm. "There's no need for you to go any further out of your way."

"No, there isn't." He'd have something to take home with him that night, he thought with sudden, fierce impatience. And he'd leave her something to take up to the room where they'd had one long, glorious night. "But then we've always looked at needs from different angles." He cupped his hand around the back of her neck, holding firm as he felt her stiffen.

"Don't." She didn't back away. Kate told herself she didn't back away because to do so would make her seem vulnerable. And she was, feeling those long hard fingers play against her skin again.

"I think this is something you owe me," he told her in a voice so quiet it shivered on the air. "Maybe something I owe myself."

He wasn't gentle. That was deliberate. Somewhere inside him was a need to punish for what hadn't been— or perhaps what had. The mouth he crushed on hers hungered, the arms he wrapped around her demanded. If she'd forgotten, he thought grimly, this would remind her. And remind her.

With her arms trapped between them, he could feel her hands ball into tight fists. Let her hate him, loathe him. He'd rather that than cool politeness.

But God she was sweet. Sweet and as delicate as one of the frothy waves that lapped and spread along the shoreline. Dimly, distantly, he knew he could drown in her without a murmur or complaint.

She wanted it to be different. Oh, how she wanted it to be different so that she'd feel nothing. But she felt everything.

The hard, impatient mouth that had always thrilled and bemused her—it was the same. The lean restless body that fit so unerringly against her—no different. The scent that clung to him, sea and salt—hadn't changed. Always when he kissed her, there'd been the sounds of water or wind or gulls. That, too, remained constant. Behind them boats rocked gently in their slips, water against wood. A gull resting on pilings let out a long, lonely call. The light dimmed as the sun dropped closer to the sea. The flood of past feelings rose up to merge and mingle with the moment.

She didn't resist him. Kate had told herself she wouldn't give him the satisfaction of a struggle. But the command to her brain not to respond was lost in the thin clouds of dusk. She gave because she had to. She took because she had no choice.

His tongue played over hers and her fists uncurled until Kate's palms rested against his chest. So warm, so hard, so familiar. He kissed as he always had, with complete concentration, no inhibitions and little patience.

Time tumbled back and she was young and in love and foolish. Why, she wondered while her head swam, should that make her want to weep?

He had to let her go or he'd beg. Ky could feel it rising in him. He wasn't fool enough to plead for what was already gone. He wasn't strong enough to accept that he had to let go again. The tug-of-war going on inside him was fierce enough to make him moan. On the sound he pulled away from her, frustrated, infuriated, bewitched.

Taking a moment, he stared down at her. Her look was the same, he realized—that half surprised, half speculative look she'd given him after their first kiss. It disoriented him. Whatever he'd sought to prove, Ky knew now he'd only proven that he was still as much enchanted with her as he'd ever been. He bit back an oath, instead, giving her a half salute as he walked away.

"Get eight hours of sleep," he ordered without turning around.

Chapter 4

Some mornings the sun seemed to rise more slowly than others, as if nature wanted to show off her particular majesty just a bit longer. When she'd gone to bed, Kate had left her shades up knowing that the morning light would awaken her before the travel alarm beside her bed rang.

She took the dawn as a gift to herself, something individual and personal. Standing at the window, she watched it bloom. The first quiet breeze of morning drifted through the screen to run over her hair and face, through the thin material of her nightshirt, cool and promising. While she stood, Kate absorbed the colors, the light and the silent thunder of day breaking over water.

The lazy contemplation was far different from her structured routine of the past months and years. Morn-

ings had been a time to dress, a time to run over her
schedule and notes for the day's classes over two cups
of coffee and a quick breakfast. She never had time to
give herself the dawn, so she took it now.

She slept better than she'd expected, lulled by the
quiet, exhausted by the days of traveling and the strain
on her emotions. There'd been no dreams to haunt her
from the time she'd turned back the sheets until the first
light had fallen over her face. Then she rose quickly.
There'd be no dreams now.

Kate let the morning wash over her with all its new
promises, its beginnings. Today was the start. Everything, from the moment she'd taken out her father's
papers until she'd seen Ky again, had been a prelude.
Even the brief, torrid embrace of the night before had
been no more than a ghost of the past. Today was the
real beginning.

She dressed and went out into the morning.

Breakfast was impossible. The excitement she'd so
meticulously held off was beginning to strain for freedom. The feeling that what she was doing was right
was back with her. Whatever it took, whatever it cost
her, she'd look for the gold her father had dreamed of.
She'd follow his directions. If she found nothing, she'd
have looked anyway.

In looking, Kate had come to believe she'd lay all
her personal ghosts to rest.

Ky's kiss. It had been aching, disturbing as it had always been. She'd been absorbed, just as she'd always
been. Though she knew she had to face both Ky and
the past, she hadn't known it would be so frighteningly

easy to go back—back to that dark, dreamy world where only he had taken her.

Now that she knew, now that she'd faced even that, Kate had to prepare to fight the wind.

He'd never forgiven her, she realized, for saying no. For bruising his pride. She'd gone back to her world when he'd asked her to stay in his. Asked her to stay, Kate remembered, without offering anything, not even a promise. If he'd given her that, no matter how casual or airy the promise might have been, she wouldn't have gone. She wondered if he knew that.

Perhaps he thought if he could make her lose herself to him again, the scales would be even. She wouldn't lose. Kate stuck her hands into the pockets of her brief pleated shorts. No, she didn't intend to lose. If he had pressed her last night, if he'd known just how weakened she'd been by that one kiss…

But he wouldn't know, she told herself. She wouldn't weaken again. For the summer, she'd make the treasure her goal and her one ambition. She wouldn't leave the island empty-handed this time.

He was already on board the *Vortex*. Kate could see him stowing gear, his hair tousled by the breeze that flowed in from the sea. With only cut-offs and a sleeveless T-shirt between him and the sun she could see the muscles coil and relax, the skin gleam.

Magnificent. She felt the dull ache deep in her stomach and tried to rationalize it away. After all, a well-honed masculine build should make a woman respond. It was natural. One could even call it impersonal, Kate decided. As she started down the dock she wished she could believe it.

He didn't see her. A fishing boat already well out on the water had caught his attention. For a moment, she stopped, just watching him. Why was it she could always sense the restlessness in him? There was movement in him even when he was still, sound even when he was silent. What was it he saw when he looked out over the sea? Challenge? Romance?

He was a man who always seemed poised for action, for doing. Yet he could sit quietly and watch the waves as if there were nothing more important than that endless battle between earth and water.

Just now he stood on the deck of his boat, hands on hips, watching the tubby fishing vessel putt toward the horizon. It was something he'd seen countless times, yet he stopped to take it in again. Kate looked where Ky looked and wished she could see what he was seeing.

Quietly she went forward, her deck shoes making no sound, but he turned, eyes still intense. "You're early," he said, and with no more greeting reached out a hand to help her on board.

"I thought you might be as anxious to start as I am."

Palm met palm, rough against smooth. Both of them broke contact as soon as possible.

"It should be an easy ride." He looked back to sea, toward the boat, but this time he didn't focus on it. "The wind's coming in from the north, no more than ten knots."

"Good." Though it wouldn't have mattered to her

nor, she thought, to him, if the wind had been twice as fast. This was the morning to begin.

She could sense the impatience in him, the desire to be gone and doing. Wanting to make things as simple as possible Kate helped Ky cast off, then walked to the stern. That would keep the maximum distance between them. They didn't speak. The engine roared to life, shattering the calm. Smoothly, Ky maneuvered the small cruiser out of the harbor, setting up a small wake that caused the water to lap against pilings. He kept the same steady even speed while they sailed through the shallows of Ocracoke Inlet. Looking back, Kate watched the distance between the boat and the village grow.

The dreamy quality remained. The last thing she saw was a child walking down a pier with a rod cocked rakishly over his shoulder. Then she turned her face to the sea.

Warm wind, glaring sun. Excitement. Kate hadn't been sure the feelings would be the same. But when she closed her eyes, letting the dull red light glow behind her lids, the salty mist touch her face, she knew this was a love that had remained constant, one that had waited for her.

Sitting perfectly still, she could feel Ky increase the speed until the boat was eating its way through the water as sleekly as a cat moves through the jungle. With her eyes closed, she enjoyed the movement, the speed, the sun. This was a thrill that had never faded. Tasting it again, she understood that it never would.

She'd been right, Kate realized, the hunt would be

much more exciting than the final goal. The hunt, and
no matter how cautious she was, the man at the helm.

He'd told himself he wouldn't look back at her. But he
had to—just once. Eyes closed, a smile playing around
her mouth, hair dancing around her face where the wind
nudged it from the pins. It brought back a flash of memory—to the first time he'd seen her like that and realized
he had to have her. She looked calm, totally at peace.
He felt there was a war raging inside him that he had
no control over.

Even when he turned back to sea again Ky could
see her, leaning back against the stern, absorbing what
wind and water offered. In defense, he tried to picture
her in a classroom, patiently explaining the intricacies
of *Don Juan* or *Henry IV*. It didn't help. He could only
imagine her sitting behind him, soaking up sun and
wind as if she'd been starved for it.

Perhaps she had been. Though she didn't know what
direction Ky's thoughts had taken, Kate realized she'd
never been further away from the classroom or the demands she placed on herself there than she was at this
moment. She was part teacher, there was no question
of that, but she was also, no matter how she'd tried to
banish it, part dreamer.

With the sun and the wind on her skin, she was too
exhilarated to be frightened by the knowledge, too content to worry. It was a wild, free sensation to experience
again something known, loved, then lost.

Perhaps... Perhaps it was too much like the one frenzied kiss she'd shared with Ky the night before, but she
needed it. It might be a foolish need, even a danger-

ous one. Just once, only this once, she told herself, she wouldn't question it.

Steady, strong, she opened her eyes again. Now she could watch the sun toss its diamonds on the surface of the water. They rippled, enticing, enchanting. The fishing boat Ky had watched move away from the island before them was anchored, casting its nets. A purse seiner, she remembered. Ky had explained the wide, weighted net to her once and how it was often used to haul in menhaden.

She wondered why he'd never chosen that life, where he could work and live on the water day after day. But not alone, she recalled with a ghost of a smile. Fishermen were their own community, on the sea and off it. It wasn't often Ky chose to share himself or his time with anyone. There were times, like this one, when she understood that perfectly.

Whether it was the freedom or the strength that was in her, Kate approached him without nerves. "It's as beautiful as I remember."

He dreaded having her stand beside him again. Now, however, he discovered the tension at the base of his neck had eased. "It doesn't change much." Together they watched the gulls swoop around the fishing boat, hoping for easy pickings. "Fishing's been good this year."

"Have you been doing much?"

"Off and on."

"Clamming?"

He had to smile when he remembered how she'd looked, jeans rolled up to her knees, bare feet full of sand as he'd taught her how to dig. "Yeah."

She, too, remembered, but her only memories were of warm days, warm nights. "I've often wondered what it's like on the island in winter."

"Quiet."

She took the single careless answer with a nod. "I've often wondered why you preferred that."

He turned to her, measuring. "Have you?"

Perhaps that had been a mistake. Since it had already been made, Kate shrugged. "It would be foolish of me to say I hadn't thought of the island or you at all during the last four years. You've always made me curious."

He laughed. It was so typical of her to put things that way. "Because all your tidy questions weren't answered. You think too much like a teacher, Kate."

"Isn't life a multiple choice?" she countered. "Maybe two or three answers would fit, but only one's ultimately right."

"No, only one's ultimately wrong." He saw her eyes take on that thoughtful, considering expression. She was, he knew, weighing the pros and cons of his statement. Whether she agreed or not, she'd consider all the angles. "You haven't changed either," he murmured.

"I thought the same of you. We're both wrong. Neither of us have stayed the same. That's as it should be." Kate looked away from him, further east, then gave a quick cry of pleasure. "Oh, look!" Without thinking, she put her hand on his arm, slender fingers gripping taut muscle. "Dolphins."

She watched them, a dozen, perhaps more, leap and dive in their musical pattern. Pleasure was touched with envy. To move like that, she thought, from water to air and back to water again. It was a freedom that might drive a man mad with the glory of it. But what a madness...

"Fantastic, isn't it?" she murmured. "To be part of the air and the sea. I'd nearly forgotten."

"How much?" Ky studied her profile until he could have etched the shape of it on the wind. "How much have you nearly forgotten?"

Kate turned her head, only then realizing just how close they stood. Unconsciously, she'd moved nearer to him when she'd seen the dolphins. Now she could see nothing but his face, inches from hers, feel nothing but the warm skin beneath her hand. His question, the depth of it, seemed to echo off the surface of the water to haunt her.

She stepped back. The drop before her was very deep and torn with riptides. "All that was necessary," she said simply. "I'd like to look over my father's charts. Did you bring them on board?"

"Your briefcase is in the cabin." His hands gripped the wheel tightly, as though he were fighting against a storm. Perhaps he was. "You should be able to find your way below."

Without answering, Kate walked around him to the short steep steps that led belowdecks.

There were two narrow bunks with the spreads taut enough to bounce a coin if one was dropped. The galley just beyond would have all the essentials, she knew, in small, efficient scale. Everything would be in its place, as tidy as a monk's cell.

Kate could remember lying with Ky on one of the

pristine bunks, flushed with passion while the boat swayed gently in the current and the music from his radio played jazz.

She gripped the leather of her case as if the pain in her fingers would help fight off the memories. To fight everything off entirely was too much to expect, but the intensity eased. Carefully she unfolded one of her father's charts and spread it on the bunk.

Like everything her father had done, the chart was precise and without frills. Though it had certainly not been his field, Hardesty had drawn a chart any sailor would have trusted.

It showed the coast of North Carolina, Pamlico Sound and the Outer Banks, from Manteo to Cape Lookout. As well as the lines of latitude and longitude, the chart also had the thin crisscrossing lines that marked depth.

Seventy-six degrees north by thirty-five degrees east. From the markings, that was the area her father had decided the *Liberty* had gone down. That was southeast of Ocracoke by no more than a few miles. And the depth… Yes, she decided as she frowned over the chart, the depth would still be considered shallow diving. She and Ky would have the relative freedom of wet suits and tanks rather than the leaded boots and helmets required for deep-sea explorations.

X marks the spot, she thought, a bit giddy, but made herself fold the chart with the same care she'd used to open it. She felt the boat slow then heard the resounding silence when the engines shut off. A fresh tremor of anticipation went through her as she climbed the steps into the sunlight again.

Ky was already checking the tanks though she knew he would have gone over all the equipment thoroughly before setting out. "We'll go down here," he said as he rose from his crouched position. "We're about half a mile from the last place your father went in last summer."

In one easy motion he pulled off his shirt. Kate knew he was self-aware, but he'd never been self-conscious. Ky had already stripped down to brief bikini trunks before she turned away for her own gear.

If her heart was pounding, it was possible to tell herself it was in anticipation of the dive. If her throat was dry, she could almost believe it was nerves at the thought of giving herself to the sea again. His body was hard and brown and lean, but she was only concerned with his skill and his knowledge. And he, she told herself, was only concerned with his fee and his twenty-five percent of the find.

She wore a snug tank suit under her shorts that clung to subtle curves and revealed long, slender legs that Ky knew were soft as water, strong as a runner's. He began to pull on the thin rubber wet suit. They were here to look for gold, to find a treasure that had been lost. Some treasures, he knew, could never be recovered.

As he thought of it, Ky glanced up to see Kate draw the pins from her hair. It fell, soft and slow, over, then past her shoulders. If she'd shot a dart into his chest, she couldn't have pierced his heart more accurately. Swearing under his breath, Ky lifted the first set of tanks.

"We'll go down for an hour today."

"But—"

"An hour's more than enough," he interrupted without sparing her a glance. "You haven't worn tanks in four years."

Kate slipped into the set he offered her, securing the straps until they were snug, but not tight. "I didn't tell you that."

"No, but you'd sure as hell have told me if you had." The corner of his mouth lifted when she remained silent. After attaching his own tanks, Ky climbed over the side onto the ladder. She could either argue, he figured, or she could follow.

To clear his mask, he spat into it, rubbed, then reached down to rinse it in salt water. Pulling it over his eyes and nose, Ky dropped into the sea. It took less than ten seconds before Kate plunged into the water beside him. He paused a moment, to make certain she didn't flounder or forget to breathe, then he headed for greater depth.

No, she wouldn't forget to breathe, but the first breath was almost a sigh as her body submerged. It was as thrilling to her as it had been the first time, this incredible ability to stay beneath the ocean's surface and breathe air.

Kate looked up to see the sun spearing through the water, and held out a hand to watch the watery light play on her skin. She could have stayed there, she realized, just reveling in it. But with a curl of her body and a kick, she followed Ky into depth and dimness.

Ky saw a school of menhaden and wondered if they'd

end up in the net of the fishing boat he'd watched that morning. When the fish swerved in a mass and rushed past him, he turned to Kate again. She'd been right when she'd told him she knew what to do. She swam as cleanly and as competently as ever.

He expected her to ask him how he intended to look for the *Liberty,* what plan he'd outlined. When she hadn't, Ky had figured it was for one of two reasons. Either she didn't want to have any in-depth conversation with him at the moment, or she'd already reasoned it out for herself. It seemed more likely to be the latter, as her mind was also as clean and competent as ever.

The most logical method of searching seemed to be a semi-circular route around Hardesty's previous dives. Slowly and methodically, they would widen the circle. If Hardesty had been right, they'd find the *Liberty* eventually. If he'd been wrong…they'd have spent the summer treasure hunting.

Though the tanks on her back reminded Kate not to take the weightless freedom for granted, she thought she could stay down forever. She wanted to touch—the water, the sea grass, the soft, sandy bottom. Reaching out toward a school of bluefish she watched them scatter defensively then regroup. She knew there were times when, as a diver moved through the dim, liquid world, he could forget the need for the sun. Perhaps Ky had been right in limiting the dive. She had to be careful not to take what she found again for granted.

The flattened disklike shape caught Ky's attention. Automatically, he reached for Kate's arm to stop her forward progress. The stingray that scuttled along the bottom looking for tasty crustaceans might be amusing to watch, but it was deadly. He gauged this one to be as long as he was tall with a tail as sharp and cruel as a razor. They'd give it a wide berth.

Seeing the ray reminded Kate that the sea wasn't all beauty and dreams. It was also pain and death. Even as she watched, the stingray struck out with its whiplike tail and caught a small, hapless bluefish. Once, then twice. It was nature, it was life. But she turned away. Through the protective masks, her eyes met Ky's.

She expected to see derision for an obvious weakness, or worse, amusement. She saw neither. His eyes were gentle, as they were very rarely. Lifting a hand, he ran his knuckles down her cheek, as he'd done years before when he'd chosen to offer comfort or affection. She felt the warmth, it reflected in her eyes. Then, as quickly as the moment had come, it was over. Turning, Ky swam away, gesturing for her to follow.

He couldn't afford to be distracted by those glimpses of vulnerability, those flashes of sweetness. They had already done him in once. Top priority was the job they'd set out to do. Whatever other plans he had, Ky intended to be in full control. When the time was right, he'd have his fill of Kate. That he promised himself. He'd take exactly what he felt she owed him. But she wouldn't touch his emotions again. When he took her to bed, it would be with cold calculation.

That was something else he promised himself.

Though they found no sign of the *Liberty*, Ky saw wreckage from other ships—pieces of metal, rusted, covered with barnacles. They might have been from a sub or a battleship from World War II. The sea absorbed what remained in her.

He was tempted to swim farther out, but knew it would take twenty minutes to return to the boat. Circling around, he headed back, overlapping, double-checking the area they'd just covered.

Not quite a needle in a haystack, Ky mused, but close. Two centuries of storms and currents and sea quakes. Even if they had the exact location where the *Liberty* had sunk, rather than the last known location, it took calculation and guesswork, then luck to narrow the field down to a radius of twenty miles.

Ky believed in luck much the same way he imagined Hardesty had believed in calculation. Perhaps with a mixture of the two, he and Kate would find what was left of the *Liberty*.

Glancing over, he watched Kate gliding beside him. She was looking everywhere at once, but Ky didn't think her mind was on treasure or sunken ships. She was, as she'd been that summer before, completely enchanted with the sea and the life it held. He wondered if she still remembered all the information she'd demanded of him before the first dive. What about the physiological adjustments to the body? How was the CO_2 absorbed? What about the change in external pressure?

Ky felt a flash of humor as they started to ascend. He was dead sure Kate remembered every answer he'd given her, right down to the decimal point in pounds of pressure per square inch.

The sun caught her as she rose toward the surface, slowly. It shone around and through her hair, giving her an ethereal appearance as she swam straight up, legs kicking gently, face tilted toward sun and surface. If there were mermaids, Ky knew they'd look as she did—slim, long, with pale loose hair free in the water. A man could only hold on to a mermaid if he accepted the world she lived in as his own. Reaching out, he caught the tip of her hair in his fingers just before they broke the surface together.

Kate came up laughing, letting her mouthpiece fall and pushing her mask up. "Oh, it's wonderful! Just as I remembered." Treading water, she laughed again and Ky realized it was a sound he hadn't heard in four years. But he remembered it exactly.

"You looked like you wanted to play more than you wanted to look for sunken ships." He grinned at her, enjoying her pleasure and the ease of a smile he'd never expected to see again.

"I did." Almost reluctant, she reached out for the ladder to climb on board. "I never expected to find anything the first time down, and it was so wonderful just to dive again." She stripped off her tanks then checked the valves herself before she set them down. "Whenever I go down I begin to believe I don't need the sun anymore. Then when I come up it's warmer and brighter than I remember."

With the adrenaline still flowing, she peeled off her flippers, then her mask, to stand, face lifted toward the sun. "There's nothing else exactly like it."

"Skin diving." Ky tugged down the zipper of his wet suit. "I tried some in Tahiti last year. It's incredible being in that clear water with no equipment but a mask and flippers, and your own lungs."

"Tahiti?" Surprised and interested, Kate looked back as Ky stripped off the wet suit. "You went there?"

"Couple of weeks late last year." He dropped the wet suit in the big plastic can he used for storing equipment before rinsing.

"Because of your affection for islands?"

"And grass skirts."

The laughter bubbled out again. "I'm sure you'd look great in one."

He'd forgotten just how quick she could be when she relaxed. Because the gesture appealed, Ky reached over and gave her hair a quick tug. "I wish I'd taken snapshots." Turning, he jogged down the steps into the cabin.

"Too busy ogling the natives to put them on film for posterity?" Kate called out as she dropped down on the narrow bench on the starboard side.

"Something like that. And, of course, trying to pretend I didn't notice the natives ogling me."

She grinned. "People in grass skirts," she began then let out a muffled shout as he tossed a peach in her direction. Catching it cleanly, Kate smiled at him before she bit into the fruit.

"Still have good reflexes," Ky commented as he came up the last step.

"Especially when I'm hungry." She touched her tongue to her palm where juice dribbled. "I couldn't eat this morning, I was too keyed up."

He held out one of two bottles of cold soda he'd taken from the refrigerator. "About the dive?"

"That and…" Kate broke off, surprised that she was talking to him as if it had been four years before.

"And?" Ky prompted. Though his tone was casual, his gaze had sharpened.

Aware of it, Kate rose, turning away to look back over the stern. She saw nothing there but sky and water. "It was the morning," she murmured. "The way the sun came up over the water. All that color." She shook her head and water dripped from the ends of her hair onto the deck. "I haven't watched a sunrise in a very long time."

Making himself relax again, Ky leaned back, biting into his own peach as he watched her. "Why?"

"No time. No need."

"Do they both mean the same thing to you?"

Restless, she moved her shoulders. "When your life revolves around schedules and classes, I suppose one equals the other."

"That's what you want? A daily timetable?"

Kate looked back over her shoulder, meeting his eyes levelly. How could they ever understand each other? she wondered. Her world was as foreign to him as his to her. "It's what I've chosen."

"One of your multiple choices of life?" Ky countered, giving a short laugh before he tilted his bottle back again.

"Maybe, or maybe some parts of life only have one choice." She turned completely around, determined not to lose the euphoria that had come to her with the dive. "Tell me about Tahiti, Ky. What's it like?"

"Soft air, soft water. Blue, green, white. Those are

the colors that come to mind, then outrageous splashes of red and orange and yellow."

"Like a Gauguin painting."

The length of the deck separated them. Perhaps that made it easier for him to smile. "I suppose, but I don't think he'd have appreciated all the hotels and resorts. It isn't an island that's been left to itself."

"Things rarely are."

"Whether they should be or not."

Something in the way he said it, in the way he looked at her, made Kate think he wasn't speaking of an island now, but of something more personal. She drank, cooling her throat, moistening her lips. "Did you scuba?"

"Some. Shells and coral so thick I could've filled a boat with them if I'd wanted. Fish that looked like they should've been in an aquarium. And sharks." He remembered one that had nearly caught him half a mile out. Remembering made him grin. "The waters off Tahiti are anything but boring."

Kate recognized the look, the recklessness that would always surface just under his skill. Perhaps he didn't look for trouble, but she thought he'd rarely sidestep it. No, she doubted they'd ever fully understand each other, if they had a lifetime.

"Did you bring back a shark's tooth necklace?"

"I gave it to Hope." He grinned again. "Linda won't let her have it yet."

"I should think not. Does it feel odd, being an uncle?"

"No. She looks like me."

"Ah, the male ego."

Ky shrugged, aware that he had a healthy share and

was comfortable with it. "I get a kick out of watching her run Marsh and Linda in circles. There's not much entertainment on the island."

She tried to imagine Ky being entertained by something as tame as a baby girl. She failed. "It's strange," Kate said after a moment. "Coming back to find Marsh and Linda married and parents. When I left Marsh treated Linda like his little sister."

"Didn't your father keep you up on progress on the island?"

The smile left her eyes. "No."

Ky lifted a brow. "Did you ask?"

"No."

He tossed his empty bottle into a small barrel. "He hadn't told you anything about the ship either, about why he kept coming back to the island year after year."

She tossed her drying hair back from her face. It hadn't been put in the tone of a question. Still, she answered because it was simpler that way. "No, he never mentioned the *Liberty* to me."

"That doesn't bother you?"

The ache came, but she pushed it aside. "Why should it?" she countered. "He was entitled to his own life, his privacy."

"But you weren't."

She felt the chill come and go. Crossing the deck, Kate dropped her bottle beside Ky's before reaching for her shirt. "I don't know what you mean."

"You know exactly what I mean." He closed his hand over hers before she could pull the shirt on. Because it would've been cowardly to do otherwise, she lifted her head and faced him. "You know," he said again, quietly. "You just aren't ready to say it out loud yet."

"Leave it alone, Ky." Her voice trembled, and though it infuriated her, she couldn't prevent it. "Just leave it."

He wanted to shake her, to make her admit, so that he could hear, that she'd left him because her father had preferred it. He wanted her to say, perhaps sob, that she hadn't had the strength to stand up to the man who had shaped and molded her life to suit his values and wants.

With an effort, he relaxed his fingers. As he had before, Ky turned away with something like a shrug. "For now," he said easily as he went back to the helm. "Summer's just beginning." He started the engine before turning around for one last look. "We both know what can happen during a summer."

Chapter 5

"The first thing you have to understand about Hope," Linda began, steadying a vase the toddler had jostled, "is that she has a mind of her own."

Kate watched the chubby black-haired Hope climb onto a wing-backed chair to examine herself in an ornamental mirror. In the fifteen minutes Kate had been in Linda's home, Hope hadn't been still a moment. She was quick, surprisingly agile, with a look in her eyes that made Kate believe she knew exactly what she wanted and intended to get it, one way or the other. Ky had been right. His niece looked like him, in more ways than one.

"I can see that. Where do you find the energy to run a restaurant, keep a home and manage a fireball?"

"Vitamins." Linda sighed. "Lots and lots of vitamins. Hope, don't put your fingers on the glass."

"Hope!" the toddler cried out, making faces at herself in the mirror. "Pretty, pretty, pretty."

"The Silver ego," Linda commented. "It never tarnishes."

With a chuckle, Kate watched Hope crawl backward out of the chair, land on her diaper-padded bottom and begin to systematically destroy the tower of blocks she'd built a short time before. "Well, she is pretty. It only shows she's smart enough to know it."

"It's hard for me to argue that point, except when she's spread toothpaste all over the bathroom floor." With a contented sigh, Linda sat back on the couch. She enjoyed having Monday afternoons off to play with Hope and catch up on the dozens of things that went by the wayside when the restaurant demanded her time. "You've been here over a week now, and this is the first time we've been able to talk."

Kate bent over to ruffle Hope's hair. "You're a busy woman."

"So are you."

Kate heard the question, not so subtly submerged in the statement, and smiled. "You know I didn't come back to the island to fish and wade, Linda."

"All right, all right, the heck with being tactful." With a mother's skill, she kept her antenna honed on her active toddler and leaned toward Kate. "What *are* you and Ky doing out on his boat every day?"

With Linda, evasions were neither necessary nor advisable. "Looking for treasure," Kate said simply.

"Oh." Expressing only mild surprise, Linda saved a budding African violet from her daughter's curious fingers. "Blackbeard's treasure." She handed Hope a rubber duck in lieu of the plant. "My grandfather still tells stories about it. Pieces of eight, a king's ransom and bottles of rum. I always figured that it was buried on land."

Amused at the way Linda could handle the toddler without breaking rhythm, Kate shook her head. "No, not Blackbeard's."

There were dozens of theories and myths about where the infamous pirate had hidden his booty, and fantastic speculation on just how rich the trove was. Kate had never considered them any more than stories. Yet, she supposed, in her own way, she was following a similar fantasy.

"My father'd been researching the whereabouts of an English merchant ship that sank off the coast here in the eighteenth century."

"Your father?" Instantly Linda's attention sharpened. She couldn't conceive of the Edwin Hardesty she remembered from summers past as a treasure searcher. "That's why he kept coming to the island every summer? I could never figure out why…" She broke off, grimaced, then plunged ahead. "I'm sorry, Kate, but he never seemed the type to take up scuba diving as a hobby, and I never once saw him with a fish. He certainly managed to keep what he was doing a secret."

"Yes, even from me."

"You didn't know?" Linda glanced over idly as Hope began to beat on a plastic bucket with a wooden puzzle piece.

"Not until I went through his papers a few weeks ago. I decided to follow through on what he'd started."

"And you came to Ky."

"I came to Ky." Kate smoothed the material of her thin summer skirt over her knees. "I needed a boat, a diver, preferably an islander. He's the best."

Linda's attention shifted from her daughter to Kate. There was simple understanding there, but it didn't completely mask impatience. "Is that the only reason you came to Ky?"

Needs rose up to taunt her. Memories washed up in one warm wave. "Yes, that's the only reason."

Linda wondered why Kate should want her to believe what Kate didn't believe herself. "What if I told you he's never forgotten you?"

Kate shook her head quickly, almost frantically. "Don't."

"I love him." Linda rose to distract Hope who'd discovered tossing blocks was more interesting than stacking them. "Even though he's a frustrating, difficult man. He's Marsh's brother." She set Hope in front of a small army of stuffed animals before she turned and smiled. "He's my brother. And you were the first mainlander I was ever really close to. It's hard for me to be objective."

It was tempting to pour out her heart, her doubts. Too tempting. "I appreciate that, Linda. Believe me, what was between Ky and me was over a long time ago. Lives change."

Making a neutral sound, Linda sat again. There were some people you didn't press. Ky and Kate were both the same in that area, however diverse they were otherwise. "All right. You know what I've been doing the past four years." She sent a long-suffering look in Hope's direction. "Tell me what your life's been like."

"Quieter."

Linda laughed. "A small border war would be quieter than life in this house."

"Earning my doctorate as early as I did took a lot of concentrated effort." She'd needed that one goal to keep herself level, to keep herself...calm. "When you're teaching as well it doesn't leave much time for anything else." Shrugging, she rose. It sounded so staid, she realized. So dull. She'd wanted to learn, she'd wanted to teach, but in and of itself, it sounded hollow.

There were toys spread all over the living room, tiny pieces of childhood. A tie was tossed carelessly over the back of a chair next to a table where Linda had dropped her purse. Small pieces of a marriage. Family. She wondered, with a panic that came and went quickly, how she would ever survive the empty house back in Connecticut.

"This past year at Yale has been fascinating and difficult." Was she defending or explaining? Kate wondered impatiently. "Strange, even though my father taught, I didn't realize that being a teacher is just as hard and demanding as being a student."

"Harder," Linda declared after a moment. "You have to have the answers."

"Yes." Kate crouched down to look at Hope's collection of stuffed animals. "I suppose that's part of the appeal, though. The challenge of either knowing the answer or reasoning it out, then watching it sink in."

"Hoping it sinks in?" Linda ventured.

Kate laughed again. "Yes, I suppose that's it. When it does, that's the most rewarding aspect. Being a mother can't be that much different. You're teaching every day."

"Or trying to," Linda said dryly.

"The same thing."

"You're happy?"

Hope squeezed a bright pink dragon then held it out for Kate. Was she happy? Kate wondered as she obliged by cuddling the dragon in turn. She'd been aiming for achievement, she supposed, not happiness. Her father had never asked that very simple, very basic question. She'd never taken the time to ask herself. "I want to teach," she answered at length. "I'd be unhappy if I couldn't."

"That's a roundabout way of answering without answering at all."

"Sometimes there isn't any yes or no."

"Ky!" Hope shouted so that Kate jolted, whipping her head around to the front door.

"No." Linda noted the reaction, but said nothing. "She means the dragon. He gave it to her, so it's Ky."

"Oh." She wanted to swear but managed to smile as she handed the baby back her treasured dragon. It wasn't reasonable that just his name should make her hands unsteady, her pulse unsteady, her thoughts unsteady. "He wouldn't pick the usual, would he?" she asked carelessly as she rose.

"No." She gave Kate a very direct, very level look. "His tastes have always run to the unique."

Amusement helped to relax her. Kate's brow rose as she met the look. "You don't give up, do you?"

"Not on something I believe in." A trace of stubbornness came through. The stubbornness, Kate mused, that had kept her determinedly waiting for Marsh to fall in love with her. "I believe in you and Ky," Linda continued. "You two can make a mess of it for as long as you want, but I'll still believe in you."

"You haven't changed," Kate said on a sigh. "I came back to find you a wife, a mother and the owner of a restaurant, but you haven't changed at all."

"Being a wife and mother only makes me more certain that what I believe is right." She had her share of arrogance, too, and used it. "We don't own the restaurant," she added as an afterthought.

"No?" Surprised, Kate looked up again. "But I thought you said the Roost was yours and Marsh's."

"We run it," Linda corrected. "And we do have a twenty percent interest." Sitting back, she gave Kate a pleased smile. There was nothing she liked better than to drop small bombs in calm water and watch the ripples. "Ky owns the Roost."

"Ky?" Kate couldn't have disguised the astonishment if she'd tried. The Ky Silver she thought she knew hadn't owned anything but a boat and a shaky beach cottage. He hadn't wanted to. Buying a restaurant, even a small one on a remote island took more than capital. It took ambition.

"Apparently he didn't bother to mention it."

"No." He'd had several opportunities, Kate recalled, the night they'd had dinner. "No, he didn't. It doesn't seem characteristic," she murmured. "I can picture him buying another boat, a bigger boat or a faster boat, but I can't imagine him buying a restaurant."

"I guess it surprised everyone except Marsh—but then Marsh knows Ky better than anyone. A couple of weeks before we were married, Ky told us he'd bought the place and intended to remodel. Marsh was ferrying over to Hatteras every day to work, I was helping out in my aunt's craft shop during the season. When Ky asked if we wanted to buy in for twenty percent and take over as managers, we jumped at it." She smiled, pleased, and perhaps relieved. "It wasn't a mistake for any of us."

Kate remembered the homey atmosphere, the excellent seafood, the fast service. No, it hadn't been a mistake, but Ky... "I just can't picture Ky in business, not on land anyway."

"Ky knows the island," Linda said simply. "And he knows what he wants. To my way of thinking, he just doesn't always know how to get it."

Kate was going to avoid that area of speculation. "I'm going to take a walk down to the beach," she decided. "Would you like to come?"

"I'd love to, but—" With a gesture of her hand Linda indicated why Hope had been quiet for the last few minutes. With her arm hooked around her dragon, she was sprawled over the rest of the animals, sound asleep.

"It's either stop or go with her, isn't it?" Kate observed with a laugh.

"The nice thing is that when she stops, so can I." Expertly Linda gathered up Hope, cradling her daughter

on her shoulder. "Have a nice walk, and stop into the
Roost tonight if you have the chance."

"I will." Kate touched Hope's head, the thick, dark,
disordered hair that was so much like her uncle's. "She's
beautiful, Linda. You're very lucky."

"I know. It's something I don't ever forget."

Kate let herself out of the house and walked along the
quiet street. Clouds were low, making the light gloomy,
but the rain held off. She could taste it in the breeze, the
clean freshness of it, mixed with the faintest hint of the
sea. It was in that direction she walked.

On an island, she'd discovered, you were much more
drawn to the water than to the land. It was the one thing
she'd understood completely about Ky, the one thing
she'd never questioned.

It had been easier to avoid going to the beach in Connecticut, though she'd always loved the rocky, windy
New England coast. She'd been able to resist it, knowing what memories it would bring back. Pain. Kate had
learned there were ways of avoiding pain. But here,
knowing you could reach the edge of land by walking
in any direction, she couldn't resist. It might have been
wiser to walk to the sound, or the inlet. She walked to
the sea.

It was warm enough that she needed no more than
the sheer skirt and blouse, breezy enough so that the
material fluttered around her. She saw two men, caps
low over foreheads, their rods secured in the sand, talking together while they sat on buckets and waited for a
strike. Their voices didn't carry above the roar and thunder of surf, but she knew their conversation would deal

with bait and lures and yesterday's catch. She wouldn't disturb them, nor they her. It was the way of the islander to be friendly enough, but not intrusive.

The water was as gray as the sky, but she didn't mind. Kate had learned not just to accept its moods but to appreciate the contrasts of each one. When the sea was like this, brooding, with threats of violence on the surface, that meant a storm. She found it appealed to a restlessness in herself she rarely acknowledged.

Whitecaps tossed with systematic fever. The spray rose high and wide. The cry of gulls didn't seem lonely or plaintive now, but challenging. No, a gray gloomy sky meeting a gray sea was anything but dull. It teamed with energy. It boiled with life.

The wind tugged at her hair, loosening pins. She didn't notice. Standing just away from the edge of the surf, Kate faced wind and sea with her eyes wide. She had to think about what she'd just discovered about Ky. Perhaps what she had been determined not to discover about herself.

Thinking there, alone in the gray threatening light before a storm, was what Kate felt she needed. The constant wind blowing in from the east would keep her head clear. Maybe the smells and sounds of the sea would remind her of what she'd had and rejected, and what she'd chosen to have.

Once she'd had a powerful force that had held her swirling, breathless. That force was Ky, a man who could pull on your emotions, your senses, by simply being. The recklessness had attracted her once, the tough arrogance combined with unexpected gentleness.

What she saw as his irresponsibility had disturbed her. Kate sensed that he was a man who would drift through life when she'd been taught from birth to seek out a goal and work for it to the exclusion of all else. It was that very different outlook on life that set them poles apart.

Perhaps he had decided to take on some responsibility in his life with the restaurant, Kate decided. If he had she was glad of it. But it couldn't make any difference. They were still poles apart.

She chose the calm, the ordered. Success was satisfaction in itself when success came from something loved. Teaching was vital to her, not just a job, not even a profession. The giving of knowledge fed her. Perhaps for a moment in Linda's cozy, cluttered home it hadn't seemed like enough. Not quite enough. Still, Kate knew if you wished for too much, you often received nothing at all.

With the wind whipping at her face she watched the rain begin far out to sea in a dark curtain. If the past had been a treasure she'd lost, no chart could take her back. In her life, she'd been taught only one direction.

Ky never questioned his impulses to walk on the beach. He was a man who was comfortable with his own mood swings, so comfortable, he rarely noticed them. He hadn't deliberately decided to stop work on his boat at a certain time. He simply felt the temptation of sea and storm and surrendered to it.

Ky watched the seas as he made his way up and over the hill of sand. He could have found his way without faltering in the dark, with no moon. He'd stood on shore and watched the rain at sea before, but repetition didn't lessen the pleasure. The wind would bring it to the island, but there was still time to seek shelter if shelter were desired. More often than not, Ky would let the rain flow over him while the waves rose and fell wildly.

He'd seen his share of tropical storms and hurricanes. While he might find them exhilarating, he appreciated the relative peace of a summer rain. Today he was grateful for it. It had given him a day away from Kate.

They had somehow reached a shaky, tense coexistence that made it possible for them to be together day after day in a relatively small space. The tension was making him nervy; nervy enough to make a mistake when no diver could afford to make one.

Seeing her, being with her, knowing she'd withdrawn from him as a person was infinitely more difficult than being apart from her. To Kate, he was only a means to an end, a tool she used in the same way he imagined she used a textbook. If that was a bitter pill, he felt he had only himself to blame. He'd accepted her terms. Now all he had to do was live with them.

He hadn't heard her laugh again since the first dive. He missed that, Ky discovered, every bit as much as he missed the taste of her lips, the feel of her in his arms. She wouldn't give him any of it willingly, and he'd nearly convinced himself he didn't want her any other way.

But at night, alone, with the sound of the surf in his head, he wasn't sure he'd survive another hour. Yet he had to. It was the fierce drive for survival that had gotten him through the past years. Her rejection had eaten away at him, then it had pushed him to prove something to himself. Kate had been the reason for his risking every penny he'd had to buy the Roost. He'd needed something tangible. The Roost had given him that, in much the same way the charter boat he'd recently bought gave him a sense of worth he once thought was unnecessary.

So he owned a restaurant that made a profit, and a boat that was beginning to justify his investment. It had given his innate love of risk an outlet. It wasn't money that mattered, but the dealing, the speculation, the possibilities. A search for sunken treasure wasn't much different.

What was she looking for really? Ky wondered. Was the gold her objective? Was she simply looking for an unusual way to spend her holiday? Was she still trying to give her father the blind devotion he'd expected all her life? Was it the hunt? Watching the wall of rain move slowly closer, Ky found of all the possibilities he wanted it to be the last.

With perhaps a hundred yards between them, both Kate and Ky looked out to the sea and the rain without being aware of each other. He thought of her and she of him, but the rain crept closer and time slipped by. The wind grew bolder. Both of them could admit to the restlessness that churned inside them, but neither could acknowledge simple loneliness.

Then they turned to walk back up the dunes and saw each other.

Kate wondered how long he'd been there, and how, when she could feel the waves of tension and need, she

hadn't known the moment he'd stepped onto the beach.
Her mind, her body—always so calm and cooperative—
sprang to fevered life when she saw him. Kate knew she
couldn't fight that, only the outcome. Still, she wanted
him. She told herself that just wanting was asking for
disaster, but that didn't stop the need. If she ran from
him now she'd admit defeat. Instead, Kate took the first
step across the sand toward him.

The thin white cotton of her skirt flapped around
her, billowing, then clinging to the slender body he already knew. Her skin seemed very pale, her eyes very
dark. Again Ky thought of mermaids, of illusions and
of foolish dreams.

"You always liked the beach before a storm," Kate
said when she reached him. She couldn't smile though
she told herself she would. She wanted, though she told
herself she wouldn't.

"It won't be much longer." He hooked his thumbs
into the front pockets of his jeans. "If you didn't bring
your car, you're going to get wet."

"I was visiting Linda." Kate turned her head to look
back at the rain. No, it wouldn't be much longer. "It
doesn't matter," she murmured. "Storms like this are
over just as quickly as they begin." Storms like this, she
thought, and like others. "I met Hope. You were right."

"About what?"

"She looks like you." This time she did manage to
smile, though the tension was balled at the base of her
neck. "Did you know she named a doll after you?"

"A dragon's not a doll," Ky corrected. His lips
curved. He could resist a great deal, be apathetic about

a great deal more, but he found it virtually impossible to do either when it came to his niece. "She's a great kid. Hell of a sailor."

"You take her out on your boat?"

He heard the astonishment and shrugged it away. "Why not? She likes the water."

"I just can't picture you..." Breaking off, Kate turned back to the sea again. No, she couldn't picture him entertaining a child with toy dragons and boat rides, just as she couldn't picture him in the business world with ledgers and accountants. "You surprise me," she said a bit more casually. "About a lot of things."

He wanted to reach out and touch her hair, wrap those loose blowing ends around his finger. He kept his hands in his pockets. "Such as?"

"Linda told me you own the Roost."

He didn't have to see her face to know it would hold that thoughtful, considering expression. "That's right, or most of it anyway."

"You didn't mention it when we were having dinner there."

"Why should I?" She didn't have to see him to know he shrugged. "Most people don't care who owns a place as long as the food's good and the service is quick."

"I guess I'm not most people." She said it quietly, so quietly the words barely carried over the sound of the waves. Even so, Ky tensed.

"Why would it matter to you?"

Before she could think, she turned back, her eyes full of emotion. "Because it all matters. The whys, the hows. Because so much has changed and so much is the same. Because I want…" Breaking off, she took a step back. The look in her eyes turned to panic just before she started to dash away.

"What?" Ky demanded, grabbing her arm. "What do you want?"

"I don't know!" she shouted, unaware that it was the first time she'd done so in years. "I don't know what I want. I don't understand why I don't."

"Forget about understanding." He pulled her closer, holding her tighter when she resisted—or tried to. "Forget everything that's not here and now." The nights of restlessness and frustration already had his mercurial temperament on edge. Seeing her when he hadn't expected to made his emotions teeter. "You walked away from me once, but I won't crawl for you again. And you," he added with his eyes suddenly dark, his face suddenly close, "you damn well won't walk away as easily this time, Kate. Not this time."

With his arms wrapped around her he held her against him. His lips hovered above hers, threatening, promising. She couldn't tell. She didn't care. It was their taste she wanted, their pressure, no matter how harsh, how demanding. No matter what the consequence. Intellect and emotion might battle, and the battle might be eternal. Yet as she stood there crushed against him, feeling the wind whip at both of them, she already knew what the inevitable outcome would be.

"Tell me what you want, Kate." His voice was low, but as demanding as a shout. "Tell me what you want— now."

Now, she thought. If there could only be just now.

She started to shake her head, but his breath feathered over her skin. That alone made future and past fade into insignificance.

"You," she heard herself murmur. "Just you." Reaching up she drew his face down to hers.

A wild passionate wind, a thunderous surf, the threat of rain just moments away. She felt his body—hard and confident against hers. She tasted his lips—soft, urgent. Over the thunder in her head and the thunder to the east, she heard her own moan. She wanted, as long as the moment lasted.

His tongue tempted; she surrendered to it. He dove deep and took all, then more. It might never be enough. With no hesitation, Kate met demand with demand, heat with heat. While mouth sought mouth, her hands roamed his face, teaching what she hadn't forgotten, reacquainting her with the familiar.

His skin was rough with a day's beard, the angle of cheek and jaw, hard and defined. As her fingers inched up she felt the soft brush of his hair blown by the wind. The contrast made her tremble before she dove her fingers deeper.

She could make him blind and deaf with needs. Knowing it, Ky couldn't stop it. The way she touched him, so sure, so sweet while her mouth was molten fire. Desire boiled in him, rising so quickly he was weak with it before his mind accepted what his body couldn't deny. He held her closer, hard against soft, rough against smooth, flame against flame.

Through the thin barrier of her blouse he felt her flesh warm to his touch. He knew the skin here would be delicate, as fragile as the underside of a rose. The scent would be as sweet, the taste as honeyed. Memories, the moment, the dream of more, all these combined to make him half mad. He knew what it would be like to have her, and knowing alone aroused. He felt her now, and feeling made him irrational.

He wanted to take her right there, next to the sea, while the sky opened up and poured over them.

"I want you." With his face buried against her neck he searched for all the places he remembered. "You know how much. You always knew."

"Yes." Her head was spinning. Every touch, every taste added speed to the whirl. Whatever doubts she'd had, Kate had never doubted the want. She hadn't always understood it, the intensity of it, but she'd never doubted it. It was pulling at her now—his, hers—the mutual, mindless passion they'd always been able to ignite in one another. She knew where it would lead—to dark, secret places full of sound and velocity. Not the eye of the hurricane, never the calm with him, but full fury from beginning to end. She knew where it would lead, and knew there'd be glory and freedom. But Ky had spoken no less than the truth when he'd said she wouldn't walk away so easily this time. It was that truth that made her reach for reason, when it would have been so simple to reach for madness.

"We can't." Breathless, she tried to turn in his arms. "Ky, *I* can't." This time when she took his face in her hands it was to draw it away from hers. "This isn't right for me."

Fury mixed with passion. It showed in his eyes, in

the press of his fingers on her arms. "It's right for you. It's never been anything but right for you."

"No." She had to deny it, she had to mean it, because he was so persuasive. "No, it's not. I've always been attracted to you. It'd be ridiculous for me to try to pretend otherwise, but this isn't what I want for myself."

His fingers tightened. If they brought her pain neither of them acknowledged it. "I told you to tell me what you wanted. You did."

As he spoke the sky opened, just as he'd imagined. Rain swept in from the sea, tasting of salt, the damp wind and mystery. Instantly drenched, they stood just as they were, close, distant, with his hands firm on her arms and hers light on his face. She felt the water wash over her body, watched it run over his. It stirred her. She couldn't say why, she wouldn't give in to it.

"At that moment I did want you, I can't deny it."

"And now?" he demanded.

"I'm going back to the village."

"Damn it, Kate, what else do you want?"

She stared at him through the rain. His eyes were dark, stormy as the sea that raged behind him. Somehow he was more difficult to resist when he was like this, volatile, on edge, not quite controlled. She felt desire knot in her stomach, and swim in her head. That was all, Kate told herself. That was all it had ever been. Desire without understanding. Passion without future. Emotion without reason.

"Nothing you can give me," she whispered, knowing she'd have to dig for the strength to walk away, dig for it even to take the first step. "Nothing we can give to each other." Dropping her hands she stepped back. "I'm going back."

"You'll come back to me," Ky said as she took the first steps from him. "And if you don't," he added in a tone that made her hesitate, "it won't make any difference. We'll finish what's been started again."

She shivered, but continued to walk. *Finish what's been started again.* That was what she most feared.

Chapter 6

The storm passed. In the morning the sea was calm and blue, sprinkled with diamonds of sunlight from a sky where all clouds had been whisked away. It was true that rain freshened things—the air, grass, even the wood and stone of buildings.

The day was perfect, the wind calm. Kate's nerves rolled and jumped.

She'd committed herself to the project. It was her agreement with Ky that forced her to go to the harbor as she'd been doing every other morning. It made her climb on deck when she wanted nothing more than to pack and leave the island the way she'd come. If Ky could complete the agreement after what had passed between them on the beach, so could she.

Perhaps he sensed the fatigue she was feeling, but he made no comment on it. They spoke only when necessary as he headed out to open sea. Ky stood at the helm, Kate at the stern. Still, even the roar of the engine didn't disguise the strained silence. Ky checked the boat's compass, then cut the engines. Silence continued, thunderously.

With the deck separating them, each began to don their equipment—wet suits, the weight belts that would give them neutral buoyancy in the water, headlamps to light the sea's dimness, masks for sight. Ky checked his depth gauge and compass on his right wrist, then the luminous dial of the watch on his left while Kate attached the scabbard for her diver's knife onto her leg just below the knee.

Without speaking, they checked the valves and gaskets on the tanks, then strapped them on, securing buckles. As was his habit, Ky went into the water first, waiting until Kate joined him. Together they jackknifed below the surface.

The familiar euphoria reached out for her. Each time she dived, Kate expected the underwater world to become more commonplace. Each time it was still magic. She acknowledged what made it possible for her to join creatures of the sea—the regulator with its mouthpiece and hose that brought her air from the tanks on her back, the mask that gave her visibility. She knew the importance of every gauge. She acknowledged the technology, then put it in the practical side of her brain while she simply enjoyed.

They swam deeper, keeping in constant visual contact. Kate knew Ky often dived alone, and that doing so was always a risk. She also knew that no matter how much anger and resentment he felt toward her, she could trust him with her life.

She relied on Ky's instincts as much as his ability. It was his expertise that guided her now, perhaps more than her father's careful research and calculations. They were combing the very edge of the territory her father had mapped out, but Kate felt no discouragement. If she hadn't trusted Ky's skill and instincts, she would never have come back to Ocracoke.

They were going deeper now than they had on their other dives. Kate equalized by letting a tiny bit of air into her suit. Feeling the "squeeze" on her eardrums at the change in pressure, she relieved it carefully. A damaged eardrum could mean weeks without being able to dive.

When Ky signaled for her to switch on her headlamp she obeyed without question. Excitement began to rise.

The sunlight was fathoms above them. The world here never saw it. Sea grass swayed in the current. Now and then a fish, curious and brave enough, would swim along beside them only to vanish in the blink of an eye at a sudden movement.

Ky swam smoothly through the water, using his feet to propel him at a steady pace. Their lamps cut through the murk, surprising more fish, illuminating rock formations that had existed under the sea for centuries. Kate discovered shapes and faces in them.

No, she could never dive alone, Kate decided as Ky slowed his pace to keep rhythm with her more meandering one. It was so easy for her to lose her sense of time and direction. Air came into her lungs with a simple drawing of breath as long as the tanks held oxygen, but the gauges on her wrist only worked if she remembered to look at them.

Even mortality could be forgotten in enchantment. And enchantment could too easily lead to a mistake. It was a lesson she knew, but one that could slip away from her. The timelessness, the freedom was seductive. The feeling was somehow as sensual as the timeless freedom felt in a lover's arms. Kate knew this pleasure could be as dangerous as a lover, but found it as difficult to resist.

There was so much to see, to touch. Crustaceans of different shapes, sizes and hues. They were alive here in their own milieu, so different from when they washed up helplessly on the beach for children to collect in buckets. Fish swam in and out of waving grass that would be limp and lifeless on land. Unlike dolphins or man, some creatures would never know the thrill of both air and water.

Her beam passed over another formation, crusted with barnacles and sea life. She nearly passed it, but curiosity made her turn back so that the light skimmed over it a second time. Odd, she thought, how structured some of the shapes could be. It almost looked like…

Hesitating, using her arms to reverse her progress, Kate turned in the water to play her light over the shape from end to end. Excitement rose so quickly she grabbed Ky's arm in a grip strong enough to make him stop to search for a defect in her equipment. With a shake of her head Kate warded him off, then pointed.

When their twin lights illuminated the form on the

ocean floor, Kate nearly shouted with the discovery. It wasn't a shelf of rock. The closer they swam toward it the more apparent that became. Though it was heavily corroded and covered with crustaceans, the shape of the cannon remained recognizable.

Ky swam around the barrel. When he removed his knife and struck the cannon with the hilt the metallic sound rang out strangely. Kate was certain she'd never heard anything more musical. Her laughter came out in a string of bubbles that made Ky look in her direction and grin.

They'd found a corroded cannon, he thought, and she was as thrilled as if they'd found a chest full of doubloons. And he understood it. They'd found something perhaps no one had seen for two centuries. That in itself was a treasure.

With a movement of his hand he indicated for her to follow, then they began to swim slowly east. If they'd found a cannon, it was likely they'd find more.

Reluctant to leave her initial discovery, Kate swam with him, looking back as often as she looked ahead. She hadn't realized the excitement would be this intense. How could she explain what it felt like to discover something that had lain untouched on the sea floor for more than two centuries? Who would understand more clearly, she wondered, her colleagues at Yale or Ky? Somehow she felt her colleagues would understand intellectually, but they would never understand the exhilaration. Intellectual pleasure didn't make you giddy enough to want to turn somersaults.

How would her father have felt if he'd found it? She

wished she knew. She wished she could have given him that one instant of exultation, perhaps shared it with him as they'd so rarely shared anything. He'd only known the planning, the theorizing, the bookwork. With one long look at that ancient weapon, she'd known so much more.

When Ky stopped and touched her shoulders, her emotions were as mixed as her thoughts. If she could have spoken she'd have told him to hold her, though she wouldn't have known why. She was thrilled, yet running through the joy was a thin shaft of sorrow— for what was lost, she thought. For what she'd never be able to find again.

Perhaps he knew something of what moved her. They couldn't communicate with words, but he touched her cheek—just a brush of his finger over her skin. It was more comforting to her than a dozen soft speeches.

She understood then that she'd never stopped loving him. No matter how many years, how many miles had separated them, what life she had she'd left with him. The time in between had been little more than existence. It was possible to live with emptiness, even to be content with it until you had that heady taste of life again.

She might have panicked. She might have run if she hadn't been trapped there, fathoms deep in the midst of a discovery. Instead, she accepted the knowledge, hoping that time would tell her what to do.

He wanted to ask her what was going through her mind. Her eyes were full of so many emotions. Words would have to wait. Their time in the sea was almost up. He touched her face again and waited for the smile.

When she gave it to him, Ky pointed at something behind her that he had just noticed moments before.

An oaken plank, old, splintered and bumpy with parasites. For the second time Ky removed his knife and began to pry the board from its bed. Silt floated up thinly, cutting visibility before it settled again. Replacing his knife, Ky gave the thumbs-up signal that meant they'd surface. Kate shook her head indicating that they should continue to search, but Ky merely pointed to his watch, then again to the surface.

Frustrated with the technology that allowed her to dive, but also forced her to seek air again, Kate nodded.

They swam west, back toward the boat. When she passed the cannon again, Kate felt a quick thrill of pride. She'd found it. And the discoveries were only beginning.

The moment her head was above water, she started to laugh. "We found it!" She grabbed the ladder with one hand as Ky began to climb up, placing his find and his tanks on the deck first. "I can't believe it, after hardly more than a week. It's incredible, that cannon lying down there all these years." Water ran down her face but she didn't notice. "We have to find the hull, Ky." Impatient, she released her tanks and handed them up to him before she climbed aboard.

"The chances are good—eventually."

"Eventually?" Kate tossed her wet hair out of her eyes. "We found this in just over a week." She indicated the board on the deck. She crouched over it, just wanting to touch. "We found the *Liberty*."

"We found a wreck," he corrected. "It doesn't have to be the *Liberty*."

"It is," she said with a determination that caused his brow to lift. "We found the cannon and this just on the edge of the area my father had charted. It all fits too well."

"Regardless of what wreck it is, it's undocumented. You'll get your name in the books, professor."

Annoyed, she rose. They stood facing each other on either side of the plank they'd lifted out of the sea. "I don't care about having my name in the books."

"Your father's name then." He unzipped his wet suit to let his skin dry.

She remembered her feelings after spotting the cannon, how Ky had seemed to understand them. Could they only be kind to each other, only be close to each other, fathoms under the surface? "Is there something wrong with that?"

"Only if it's an obsession. You always had a problem with your father."

"Because he didn't approve of you?" she shot back.

His eyes took on that eerily calm, almost flat expression that meant his anger was lethal. "Because it mattered too much to you what he approved of."

That stung. The truth often did. "I came here to finish my father's project," she said evenly. "I made that clear from the beginning. You're still getting your fee."

"You're still following directions. His directions." Before she could retort, he turned toward the cabin. "We'll eat and rest before we go back under."

With an effort, she held on to her temper. She wanted

to dive again, badly. She wanted to find more. Not for her father's approval, Kate thought fiercely. Certainly not for Ky's. She wanted this for herself. Pulling down the zipper of her wet suit, she went down the cabin steps.

She'd eat because strength and energy were vital to a diver. She'd rest for the same reason. Then, she determined, she'd go back to the wreck and find proof that it was the *Liberty*.

Calmer, she watched Ky go through a small cupboard. "Peanut butter?" she asked when she saw the jar he pulled out.

"Protein."

Her laugh helped her to relax again. "Do you still eat it with bananas?"

"It's still good for you."

Though she wrinkled her nose at the combination, she reminded herself that beggars couldn't be choosers. "When we find the treasure," she said recklessly, "I'll buy you a bottle of champagne."

Their fingers brushed as he handed her the first sandwich. "I'll hold you to it." He picked up his own sandwich and a quart of milk. "Let's eat on deck."

He wasn't certain if he wanted the sun or the space, but it wasn't any easier to be with her in that tiny cabin than it had been the first time, or the last. Taking her assent for granted, Ky went up the stairs again, without looking back. Kate followed.

"It might be good for you," Kate commented as she took the first bite, "but it still tastes like something you give five-year-olds when they scrape their knees."

"Five-year-olds require a lot of protein."

Giving up, Kate sat cross-legged on the deck. The sun was bright, the movement of the boat gentle. She wouldn't let his digs get to her, nor would she dig back. They were in this together, she reminded herself. Tension and sniping wouldn't help them find what they sought.

"It's the *Liberty,* Ky," she murmured, looking at the plank again. "I know it is."

"It's possible." He stretched out with his back against the port side. "But there are a lot of wrecks, unidentified and otherwise, all through these waters. Diamond Shoals is a graveyard."

"Diamond Shoals is fifty miles north."

"And the entire coastline along these barrier islands is full of littoral currents, rip currents and shifting sand ridges. Two hundred years ago they didn't have modern navigational devices. Hell, they didn't even have the lighthouses until the nineteenth century. I couldn't even give you an educated guess as to how many ships went down from the time Columbus set out until World War II."

Kate took another bite. "We're only concerned with one ship."

"Finding one's no big problem," he returned. "Finding a specific one's something else. Last year, after a couple of hurricanes breezed through, they found wrecks uncovered on the beach on Hatteras. There are plenty of houses on the island that were built from pieces of wreckage like that." He pointed to the plank with the remains of his sandwich.

Kate frowned at the board again. "It could be the *Liberty* just as easily as it couldn't."

"All right." Appreciating her stubbornness, Ky grinned. "But whatever it is, there might be treasure. Anything lost for more than two hundred years is pretty much finders keepers."

She didn't want to say that it wasn't any treasure she wanted. Just the *Liberty*'s. From what he said before, Kate was aware he already understood that. It was simply different for him. She took a long drink of cold milk. "What do you plan to do with your share?"

With his eyes half closed, he shrugged. He could do as he pleased now, a cache of gold wouldn't change that. "Buy another boat, I imagine."

"With what two-hundred-year-old gold would be worth today, you'd be able to buy a hell of a boat."

He grinned, but kept his eyes shaded. "I intend to. What about you?"

"I'm not sure." She wished she had some tangible goal for the money, something exciting, even fanciful. It just didn't seem possible to think beyond the hunt yet. "I thought I might travel a bit."

"Where?"

"Greece maybe. The islands."

"Alone?"

The food and the motion of the boat lulled her. She made a neutral sound as she shut her eyes.

"Isn't there some dedicated teacher you'd take with you? Someone you could discuss the Trojan War with?"

"Mmm, I don't want to go to Greece with a dedicated teacher."

"Someone else?"

"There's no one."

Sitting on the deck with her face lifted, her hair blowing, she looked like a finely crafted piece of porcelain. Something a man might look at, admire, but not touch. When her eyes were open, hot, her skin flushed with passion, he burned for her. When she was like this, calm, distant, he ached. He let the needs run through him because he knew there was no stopping them.

"Why?"

"Hmm?"

"Why isn't there anyone?"

Lazily she opened her eyes. "Anyone?"

"Why don't you have a lover?"

The sleepy haze cleared from her eyes instantly. He saw her fingers tense on the dark blue material that stretched snugly over her knees. "It's none of your business whether I do or not."

"You've just told me you don't."

"I told you there's no one I'd travel with," she corrected, but when she started to rise, he put a hand on her shoulder.

"It's the same thing."

"No, it's not, but it's still none of your business, Ky, any more than your personal life is mine."

"I've had women," he said easily. "But I haven't had a lover since you left the island."

She felt the pain and the pleasure sweep up through her. It was dangerous to dwell on the sensation. As dangerous as it was to lose yourself deep under the ocean.

"Don't." She lifted her hand to remove his from her shoulder. "This isn't good for either of us."

"Why?" His fingers linked with hers. "We want each other. We both know the rules this time around."

Rules. No commitment, no promises. Yes, she understood them this time, but like mortality during a dive, they could easily be forgotten. Even now, with his eyes on hers, her fingers caught in his, the structure of those rules became dimmer and dimmer. He would hurt her again. There was never any question of that. Somehow, in the past twenty-four hours, it had become a matter of *how* she would deal with the pain, not *if.*

"Ky, I'm not ready." Her voice was low, not pleading, but plainly vulnerable. Though she wasn't aware of it, there was no defense she could put to better use.

He drew her up so that they were both standing, touching only hand to hand. Though she was tall, her slimness made her appear utterly fragile. It was that and the way she looked at him, with her head tilted back so their eyes could meet, that prevented him from taking what he was determined to have, without questions, without her willingness. Ruthlessly, that was how he told himself he wanted to take her, even though he knew he couldn't.

"I'm not a patient man."

"No."

He nodded, then released her hand while he still could. "Remember it," he warned before he turned to go to the helm. "We'll take the boat east, over the wreck and dive again."

An hour later they found a piece of rigging, broken

and corroded, less than three yards from the cannon. By hand signals, Ky indicated that they'd start a stockpile of the salvage. Later they'd come back with the means of bringing it up. There were more planks, some too big for a man to carry up, some small enough for Kate to hold in one hand.

When she found a pottery bowl, miraculously unbroken, she realized just what an archaeologist must feel after hours of digging when he unearths a fragment of another era. Here it was, cupped in her hand, a simple bowl, covered with silt, covered with age. Someone had eaten from it once, a seaman, relaxing briefly below deck, perhaps on his first voyage across the Atlantic to the New World. His last journey in any event, Kate mused as she turned the bowl over in her hand.

The rigging, the cannon, the planks equaled ship. The bowl equaled man.

Though she put the bowl with the other pieces of their find, she intended to take it up with her on this dive. Whatever other artifacts they found could go to a museum, but the first, she'd keep.

They found pieces of glass that might have come from bottles that held whiskey, chunks of crockery that hadn't survived intact like the bowl. Bits of cups, bowls, plates littered the sea floor.

The galley, she decided. They must have found the galley. Over the years, the water pressure would have simply disintegrated the ship until it was all pieces spread on and under the floor of the ocean. It would, in essence, have become part of the sea, a home for the creatures and plant life that dwelt there.

But they'd found the galley. If they could find something, just one thing with the ship's name inscribed on it, they'd be certain.

Diligently, using her knife as a digging tool, Kate worked at the floor of the sea. It wasn't a practical way to search, but she saw no harm in trying her luck. They'd found crockery, glass, the unbroken bowl. Even as she glanced up she saw Ky examining what might have been half a dinner plate.

When she unearthed a long wooden ladle, Kate found that her excitement increased. They *had* found the galley, and in time, she'd prove to Ky that they'd found the *Liberty*.

Engrossed in her find, she turned to signal to Ky and moved directly into the path of a stingray.

He saw it. Ky was no more than a yard from Kate when the movement of the ray unearthing itself from its layer of sand and silt had caught his eye. His movement was pure reflex, done without thought or plan. He was quick. But even as he grabbed Kate's hand to swing her back behind him, out of range, the wicked, saw-toothed tail lashed out.

Her scream was muffled by the water, but the sound went through Ky just as surely as the stingray's poison went through Kate. Her body went stiff against his, rigid in pain and shock. The ladle she'd found floated down, out of her grip, until it landed silently on the bottom.

He knew what to do. No rational diver goes down unless he has a knowledge of how to handle an emergency. Still, Ky felt a moment of panic. This wasn't just another diver, it was Kate. Before his mind could clear, her stiffened body went limp against him. Then he acted.

Cool, almost mechanically, he tilted her head back with the chin carry to keep her air passage open. He held her securely, pressing his chest into her tanks, keeping his hand against her rib cage. It ran through his mind that it was best she'd fainted. Unconscious she wouldn't struggle as she might had she been awake and in pain. It was best she'd fainted because he couldn't bear to think of her in pain. He kicked off for the surface.

On the rise he squeezed her, hard, forcing expanding air out of her lungs. There was always the risk of embolism. They were going up faster than safety allowed. Even while he ventilated his own lungs, Ky kept a lookout. She would bleed, and blood brought sharks.

The minute they surfaced, Ky released her weight belt. Supporting her with his arm wrapped around her, his hand grasping the ladder, Ky unhooked his tanks, slipped them over the side of the boat, then removed Kate's. Her face was waxy, but as he pulled the mask from her face she moaned. With that slight sound of life some of the blood came back to his own body. With her draped limply over his shoulder, he climbed the ladder onto the *Vortex*.

He laid her down on the deck, and with hands that didn't hesitate, began to pull the wet suit from her. She moaned again when he drew the snug material over the wound just above her ankle, but she didn't reach the surface of consciousness. Grimly, Ky examined the laceration the ray had caused. Even through the protection of her suit, the tail had penetrated deep into her skin. If Ky had only been quicker…

Cursing himself, Ky hurried to the cabin for the first-aid kit.

As consciousness began to return, Kate felt the ache swimming up from her ankle to her head. Spears of pain shot through her, sharp enough to make her gasp and struggle, as if she could move away from it and find ease again.

"Try to lie still."

The voice was gentle and calm. Kate balled her hands into fists and obeyed it. Opening her eyes, she stared up at the pure blue sky. Her mind whirled with confusion, but she stared at the sky as though it were the only tangible thing in her life. If she concentrated, she could rise above the hurt. The ladle. Opening her hand she found it empty, she'd lost the ladle. For some reason it seemed vital that she have it.

"We found the galley." Her voice was hoarse with anguish, but her one hand remained open and limp. "I found a ladle. They'd have used it for spooning soup into that bowl. The bowl—it wasn't even broken. Ky…" Her voice weakened with a new flood of sensation as memory began to return. "It was a stingray. I wasn't watching for it, it just seemed to be there. Am I going to die?"

"No!" His answer was sharp, almost angry. Bending over her, he placed both hands on her shoulders so that she'd look directly into his face. He had to be sure she understood everything he said. "It was a stingray," he confirmed, not adding that it had been a good ten feet long. "Part of the spine's broken off, lodged just above your ankle."

He watched her eyes cloud further, part pain, part fear. His hands tightened on her shoulders. "It's not in deep. I can get it out, but it'll hurt like hell."

She knew what he was saying. She could stay as she was until he got her back to the doctor on the island, or she could trust him to treat her now. Though her lips trembled, she kept her eyes on his and spoke clearly.

"Do it now."

"Okay." He continued to stare at her, into the eyes that were glazed with shock. "Hang on. Don't try to be brave. Scream as much as you want but try not to move. I'll be quick." Bending farther, he kissed her hard. "I promise."

Kate nodded, then concentrating on the feeling of his lips against hers, shut her eyes. He was quick. Within seconds she felt the hurt rip through her, over the threshold she thought she could bear and beyond.... She pulled in air to scream, but went back under the surface into liquid dimness.

Ky let the blood flow freely onto the deck for a moment, knowing it would wash away some of the poison. His hands had been rock steady when he'd pulled the spine from her flesh. His mind had been cold. Now with her blood on his hands, they began to shake. Ignoring them, and the icy fear of seeing Kate's smooth skin ripped and raw, Ky washed the wound, cleansed it, bound it. Within the hour, he'd have her to a doctor.

With unsteady fingers, he checked the pulse at the base of her neck. It wasn't strong, but it was steady. Lifting an eyelid with his thumb, he checked her pupils. He didn't believe she was in shock, she'd simply escaped from the pain. He thanked God for that.

On a long breath he let his forehead rest against hers, only for a moment. He prayed that she'd remain unconscious until she was safely under a doctor's care.

He didn't take the time to wash her blood from his hands before he took the helm. Ky whipped the boat around in a quick circle and headed full throttle back to Ocracoke.

Chapter 7

As she started to float toward consciousness, Kate focused, drifted, then focused again. She saw the whirl of a white ceiling rather than the pure blue arc of sky. Even when the mist returned she remembered the hurt and thrashed out against it. She couldn't face it a second time. Yet she found as she rose closer to the surface that she didn't have the will to fight against it. That brought fear. If she'd had the strength, she might have wept.

Then she felt a cool hand on her cheek. Ky's voice pierced the last layers of fog, low and gentle. "Take it easy, Kate. You're all right now. It's all over."

Though her breath hitched as she inhaled, Kate opened her eyes. The pain didn't come. All she felt was his hand on her cheek, all she saw was his face. "Ky." When she said his name, Kate reached for his hand, the one solid thing she was sure of. Her own voice frightened her. It was hardly more than a wisp of air.

"You're going to be fine. The doctor took care of you." As he spoke, Ky rubbed his thumb over her knuckles, establishing a point of concentration, and kept his other hand lightly on her cheek, knowing that contact was important. He'd nearly gone mad waiting for her to open her eyes again. "Dr. Bailey, you remember. You met him before."

It seemed vital that she should remember so she forced her mind to search back. She had a vague picture of a tough, weathered old man who looked more suited to the sea than the examining room. "Yes. He likes…likes ale and flounder."

He might have laughed at her memory if her voice had been stronger. "You're going to be fine, but he wants you to rest for a few more days."

"I feel…strange." She lifted a hand to her own head as if to assure herself it was still there.

"You're on medication, that's why you're groggy. Understand?"

"Yes." Slowly she turned her head and focused on her surroundings. The walls were a warm ivory, not the sterile white of a hospital. The dark oak trim gleamed dully. On the hardwood floor lay a single rug, its muted Indian design fading with age. It was the only thing Kate recognized. The last time she'd been in Ky's bedroom only half the drywall had been in place and one of the windows had had a long, thin crack in the bottom pane. "Not the hospital," she managed.

"No." He stroked her head, needing to touch as much

as to check for her fever that had finally broken near dawn. "It was easier to bring you here after Bailey took care of you. You didn't need a hospital, but neither of us liked the idea of your being in a hotel right now."

"Your house," she murmured, struggling to concentrate her strength. "This is your bedroom, I remember the rug."

They'd made love on it once. That's what Ky remembered. With an effort, he kept his hands light. "Are you hungry?"

"I don't know." Basically, she felt nothing. When she tried to sit up, the drug spun in her head, making both the room and reality reel away. That would have to stop, Kate decided while she waited for the dizziness to pass. She'd rather have some pain than that helpless, weighted sensation.

Without fuss, Ky moved the pillows and shifted her to a sitting position. "The doctor said you should eat when you woke up. Just some soup." Rising he looked down on her, in much the same way, Kate thought, as he'd looked at a cracked mast he was considering mending. "I'll fix it. Don't get up," he added as he walked to the door. "You're not strong enough yet."

As he went into the hall he began to swear in a low, steady stream.

Of course she wasn't strong enough, he thought with a last vicious curse. She was pale enough to fade into the sheets she lay on. No resistance, that's what Bailey had said. Not enough food, not enough sleep, too much strain. If he could do nothing else, Ky determined as he pulled open a kitchen cupboard, he could do something about that. She was going to eat, and lie flat on her back until the doctor said otherwise.

He'd known she was weak, that was the worst of it. Ky dumped the contents of a can into a pot then hurled the empty container into the trash. He'd seen the strain on her face, the shadows under her eyes, he'd heard the traces of fatigue come and go in her voice, but he'd been too wrapped up in his own needs to do anything about it.

With a flick of the wrist, he turned on the burner under the soup, then the burner under the coffee. God, he needed coffee. For a moment he simply stood with his fingers pressed against his eyes waiting for his system to settle.

He couldn't remember ever spending a more frantic twenty-four hours. Even after the doctor had checked and treated her, even when Ky had brought her home and she'd been fathoms deep under the drug, his nerves hadn't eased. He'd been terrified to leave the room for more than five minutes at a time. The fever had raged through her, though she'd been unaware. Most of the night he'd sat beside her, bathing away the sweat and talking to her, though she couldn't hear.

Through the night he'd existed on coffee and nerves. With a half laugh he reached for a cup. It looked like that wasn't going to change for a while yet.

He knew he still wanted her, knew he still felt something for her, under the bitterness and anger. But until he'd seen her lying unconscious on the deck of his boat, with her blood on his hands, he hadn't realized that he still loved her.

He'd known what to do about the want, even the bitterness, but now, faced with love, Ky hadn't a clue. It didn't seem possible for him to love someone so frail, so calm, so…different than he. Yet the emotion he'd once felt for her had grown and ripened into something so solid he couldn't see any way around it. For now, he'd concentrate on getting her on her feet again. He poured the soup into a bowl and carried it upstairs.

It would have been an easy matter to close her eyes and slide under again. Too easy. Willing herself to stay awake, Kate concentrated on Ky's room. There were a number of changes here as well, she mused. He'd trimmed the windows in oak, giving them a wide sill where he'd scattered the best of his shells. A piece of satiny driftwood stood, beautiful as a piece of sculpture. There was a paneled closet door with a faceted glass knob where there'd once been a rod, a round-backed rattan chair where there'd been packing crates.

Only the bed was the same, she mused. The wide four-poster had been his mother's. She knew he'd given the rest of his family's furniture to Marsh. Ky had told her once he'd felt no need or desire for it, but he kept the bed. He was born there, unexpectedly, during a night in which the island had been racked by a storm.

And they'd made love there, Kate remembered as she ran her fingers over the sheets. The first time, and the last.

Stopping the movement of her fingers, she looked over as Ky came back into the room. Memories had to be pushed aside. "You've done a lot of work in here."

"A bit." He set the tray over her lap as he sat on the edge of the bed.

As the scent of the soup reached her, Kate shut her eyes. Just the aroma seemed to be enough. "It smells wonderful."

"The smell won't put any meat on you."

She smiled, and opened her eyes again. Then before she'd realized it, Ky had spoon-fed her the first bite. "It tastes wonderful too." Though she reached for the spoon, he dipped it into the bowl himself then held it to her lips. "I can do it," she began, then was forced to swallow more broth.

"Just eat." Fighting off waves of emotion he spoke briskly. "You look like hell."

"I'm sure I do," she said easily. "Most people don't look their best a couple of hours after being stung by a stingray."

"Twenty-four," Ky corrected as he fed her another spoon of soup.

"Twenty-four what?"

"Hours." Ky slipped in another spoonful when her eyes widened.

"I've been unconscious for twenty-four hours?" She looked to the window and the sunlight as if she could find some means of disproving it.

"You slipped in and out quite a bit before Bailey gave you the shot. He said you probably wouldn't remember." *Thank God,* Ky added silently. Whenever she'd fought her way back to consciousness, she'd been in agony. He could still hear her moans, feel the way she'd clutched him. He never knew a person could suffer physically

for another's pain the way he'd suffered for hers. Even
now it made his muscles clench.

"That must've been some shot he gave me."

"He gave you what you needed." His eyes met hers.
For the first time Kate saw the fatigue in them, and
the anger.

"You've been up all night," she murmured. "Haven't
you had any rest at all?"

"You needed to be watched," he said briefly. "Bailey wanted you to stay under, so you'd sleep through
the worst of the pain, and so you'd just sleep period."
His voice changed as he lost control over the anger. He
couldn't prevent the edge of accusation from showing,
partly for her, partly for himself. "The wound wasn't
that bad, do you understand? But you weren't in any
shape to handle it. Bailey said you've been well on the
way to working yourself into exhaustion."

"That's ridiculous. I don't—"

Ky swore at her, filling her mouth with more soup.
"Don't tell me it's ridiculous. I had to listen to him. I
had to look at you. You don't eat, you don't sleep, you're
going to fall down on your face."

There was too much of the drug in her system to
allow her temper to bite. Instead of annoyance, her
words came out like a sigh. "I didn't fall on my face."

"Only a matter of time." Fury was coming too
quickly. Though his fingers tightened on the spoon, Ky
held it back. "I don't care how much you want to find the
treasure, you can't enjoy it if you're flat on your back."

The soup was warming her. As much as her pride
urged her to refuse, her system craved the food. "I won't

be," she told him, not even aware that her words were beginning to slur. "We'll dive again tomorrow, and I'll prove it's the *Liberty*."

He started to swear at her, but one look at the heavy eyes and the pale cheeks had him swallowing the words. "Sure." He spooned in more soup knowing she'd be asleep again within moments.

"I'll give the ladle and the rigging and the rest to a museum." Her eyes closed. "For my father."

Ky set the tray on the floor. "Yes, I know."

"It was important to him. I need...I just need to give him something." Her eyes fluttered open briefly. "I didn't know he was ill. He never told me about his heart, about the pills. If I'd known..."

"You couldn't have done any more than you did." His voice was gentle again as he shifted the pillows down.

"I loved him."

"I know you did."

"I could never seem to make the people I love understand what I need. I don't know why."

"Rest now. When you're well, we'll find the treasure."

She felt herself sinking into warmth, softness, the dark. "Ky." Kate reached out and felt his fingers wrap around hers. With her eyes closed, it was all the reality she needed.

"I'll stay," he murmured, brushing the hair from her cheek. "Just rest."

"All those years..." He could feel her fingers relaxing in his as she slipped deeper. "I never forgot you. I never stopped wanting you. Not ever..."

He stared down at her as she slept. Her face was utterly peaceful, pale as marble, soft as silk. Unable to resist, he lifted her fingers to his own cheek, just to feel her flesh against his. He wouldn't think about what she'd said now. He couldn't. The strain of the last day had taken a toll on him as well. If he didn't get some rest, he wouldn't be able to care for her when she woke again.

Rising, Ky pulled down the shades, and took off his shirt. Then he lay down next to Kate in the big four-poster bed and slept for the first time in thirty-six hours.

The pain was a dull, consistent throb, not the silvery sharp flash she remembered, but a gnawing ache that wouldn't pass. When it woke her, Kate lay still, trying to orient herself. Her mind was clearer now. She was grateful for that, even though with the drug out of her system she was well aware of the wound. It was dark, but the moonlight slipped around the edges of the shades Ky had drawn. She was grateful for that too. It seemed she'd been a prisoner of the dark for too long.

It was night. She prayed it was only hours after she'd last awoken, not another full day later. She didn't want that quick panic at the thought of losing time again. Because she needed to be certain she was in control this time, she went over everything she remembered.

The pottery bowl, the ladle, then the stingray. She closed her eyes a moment, knowing it would be a very long time before she forgot what it had felt like to be struck with that whiplike tail. She remembered waking up on the deck of the *Vortex,* the pure blue sky overhead, and the strong, calm way Ky had spoken to her before he'd pulled out the spine. That pain, the horror of that one instant was very clear. Then, there was nothing else.

She remembered nothing of the journey back to the island, or of Dr. Bailey's ministrations or of being transported to Ky's home. Her next clear image was of waking in his bedroom, of dark oak trim on the windows, wide sills with shells set on them.

He'd fed her soup—yes, that was clear, but then things started to become hazy again. She knew he'd been angry, though she couldn't remember why. At the moment, it was more important to her that she could put events in some sort of sequence.

As she lay in the dark, fully awake and finally aware, she heard the sound of quiet, steady breathing beside her. Turning her head, Kate saw Ky beside her, hardly more than a silhouette with the moonlight just touching the skin of his chest so that she could see it rise and fall.

He'd said he would stay, she remembered. And he'd been tired. Abruptly Kate remembered there'd been fatigue in his eyes as well as temper. He'd been caring for her.

A mellow warmth moved through her, one she hadn't felt in a very long time. He had taken care of her, and though it had made him angry, he'd done it. And he'd stayed. Reaching out, she touched his cheek.

Though the gesture was whisper light, Ky awoke immediately. His sleep had been little more than a half doze so that he could recharge his system yet be aware of any sign that Kate needed attention. Sitting up, he shook his head to clear it.

He looked like a boy caught napping. For some reason the gesture moved Kate unbearably. "I didn't mean to wake you," she murmured.

He reached for the lamp beside the bed and turned it on low. Though his body revolted against the interruption, his mind was fully awake. "Pain?"

"No."

He studied her face carefully. The glazed look from the drug had left her eyes, but the color hadn't returned. "Kate."

"All right. Some."

"Bailey left some pills."

As he started to rise, Kate reached for him again. "No, I don't want anything. It makes me groggy."

"It takes away the pain."

"Not now, Ky, please. I promise I'll tell you if it gets bad."

Because her voice was close to desperate he made himself content with that. At the moment, she looked too fragile to argue with. "Are you hungry?"

She smiled, shaking her head. "No. It must be the middle of the night. I was only trying to orient myself." She touched him again, in gratitude, in comfort. "You should sleep."

"I've had enough. Anyway, you're the patient."

Automatically, he put his hand to her forehead to check for fever. Touched, Kate laid hers over it. She felt the quick reflexive tensing of his fingers.

"Thank you." When he would have removed his hand, she linked her fingers with his. "You've been taking good care of me."

"You needed it," he said simply and much too swiftly.

He couldn't allow her to stir him now, not when they were in that big, soft bed surrounded by memories.

"You haven't left me since it happened."

"I had no place to go."

His answer made her smile. Kate reached up her free hand to touch his cheek. There had been changes, she thought, many changes. But so many things had stayed the same. "You were angry with me."

"You haven't been taking care of yourself." He told himself he should move away from the bed, from Kate, from everything that weakened him there.

He stayed, leaning over her, one hand caught in hers. Her eyes were dark, soft in the dim light, full of the sweetness and innocence he remembered. He wanted to hold her until there was no more pain for either of them, but he knew, if he pressed his body against hers now, he wouldn't stop. Again he started to move, pulling away the hand that held hers. Again Kate stopped him.

"I would've died if you hadn't gotten me up."

"That's why it's smarter to dive with a partner."

"I might still have died if you hadn't done everything you did."

He shrugged this off, too aware that the fingers on his face were stroking lightly, something she had done in the past. Sometimes before they'd made love, and often afterward, when they'd talked in quiet voices, she'd stroke his face, tracing the shape of it as though she'd needed to memorize it. Perhaps she, too, sometimes awoke in the middle of the night and remembered too much.

Unable to bear it, Ky put his hand around her wrist

and drew it away. "The wound wasn't that bad," he said simply.

"I've never seen a stingray that large." She shivered and his hand tightened on her wrist.

"Don't think about it now. It's over."

Was it? she wondered as she lifted her head and looked into his eyes. Was anything ever really over? For four years she'd told herself there were joys and pains that could be forgotten, absorbed into the routine that was life as it had to be lived. Now, she was no longer sure. She needed to be. More than anything else, she needed to be sure.

"Hold me," she murmured.

Was she trying to make him crazy? Ky wondered. Did she want him to cross the border, that edge he was trying so desperately to avoid? It took most of the strength he had left just to keep his voice even. "Kate, you need to sleep now. In the morning—"

"I don't want to think about the morning," she murmured. "Only now. And now I need you to hold me." Before he could refuse, she slipped her arms around his waist and rested her head on his shoulder.

She felt his hesitation, but not his one vivid flash of longing before his arms came around her. On a long breath Kate closed her eyes. Too much time had passed since she'd had this, the gentleness, the sweetness she'd experienced only with Ky. No one else had ever held her with such kindness, such simple compassion. Somehow, she never found it odd that a man could be so reckless and arrogant, yet kind and compassionate at the same time.

Perhaps she'd been attracted to the recklessness, but it had been the kindness she had fallen in love with. Until now, in the quiet of the deep night, she hadn't understood. Until now, in the security of his arms, she hadn't accepted what she wanted.

Life as it had to be lived, she thought again. Was taking what she so desperately needed part of that?

She was so slender, so soft beneath the thin nightshirt. Her hair lay over his skin, loose and free, its color muted in the dim light. He could feel her palms against his back, those elegant hands that had always made him think more of an artist than a teacher. Her breathing was quiet, serene, as he knew it was when she slept. The light scent of woman clung to the material of the nightshirt.

Holding her didn't bring the pain he'd expected but a contentment he'd been aching for without realizing it. The tension in his muscles eased, the knot in his stomach vanished. With his eyes closed, he rested his cheek on her hair. It seemed like a lifetime since he'd known the pleasure of quiet satisfaction. She'd asked him to hold her, but had she known he needed to be held just as badly?

Kate felt him relax degree by degree and wondered if it had been she who'd caused the tension in him, and she who'd ultimately released it. Had she hurt him more than she'd realized? Had he cared more than she'd dared to believe? Or was it simply that the physical need never completely faded? It didn't matter, not tonight.

Ky was right. She knew the rules this time around. She wouldn't expect more than he offered. Whatever he offered was much, much more than she'd had in the long, dry years without him. In turn, she could give what she ached to give. Her love.

"It's the same for me as it always was," she murmured. Then, tilting her head back, she looked at him. Her hair streamed down her back, her eyes were wide and honest. He felt the need slam into him like a fist.

"Kate—"

"I never expected to feel the same way when I came back," she interrupted. "I don't think I'd have come. I wouldn't have had the courage."

"Kate, you're not well." He said it very slowly, as if he had to explain to them both. "You've lost blood, had a fever. It's taken a lot out of you. It'd be best, I think, if you tried to sleep now."

She felt no fever now. She felt cool and light and full of needs. "That day on the beach during the storm, you said I'd come to you." Kate brought her hands up his back until they reached his shoulders. "Even then I knew you were right. I'm coming to you now. Make love with me, Ky, here, in the bed where you loved me that first time."

And the last, he remembered, fighting back a torrent of desire. "You're not well," he managed a second time.

"Well enough to know what I want." She brushed her lips over his chin where his beard grew rough with neglect. So long…that was all that would come clearly to her. It had been so long. Too long. "Well enough to know what I need. It's always been you." Her fingers tightened on his shoulders, her lips inches from his. "It's only been you."

Perhaps moving away from her was the answer. But some answers were impossible. "Tomorrow you may be sorry."

She smiled in her calm, quiet way that always moved him. "Then we'll have tonight."

He couldn't resist her. The warmth. He didn't want to hurt her. The softness. The need building inside him threatened to send them both raging even though he knew she was still weak, still fragile. He remembered how it had been the first time, when she'd been innocent. He'd been so careful, though he had never felt the need to care before, and hadn't since. Remembering that, he laid her back.

"We'll have tonight," he repeated and touched his lips to hers.

Sweet, fresh, clean. Those words went through his head, those sensations went through his system as her lips parted for his. So he lingered over her kiss, enjoying with tenderness what he'd once promised himself to take ruthlessly. His mouth caressed, without haste, without pressure. Tasting, just tasting, while the hunger grew.

Her hands reached for his face, fingers stroking, the rough, the smooth. She could hear her own heart beat in her head, feel the slow, easy pleasure that came in liquid waves. He murmured to her, lovely, quiet words that made her thrill when she felt them formed against her mouth. With his tongue he teased hers in long, lazy sweeps until she felt her mind cloud as it had under the drug. Then when she felt the first twinge of desperation, he kissed her with an absorbed patience that left her weak.

He felt it—that initial change from equality to submission that had always excited him. The aggression would come later, knocking the breath from him, taking him to the edge. He knew that too. But for the moment, she was soft, yielding.

He slid his hands over the nightshirt, stroking, lingering. The material between his flesh and hers teased them both. She moved to his rhythm, glorying in the steady loss of control. He took her deeper with a touch, still deeper with a taste. She dove, knowing the full pleasure of ultimate trust. Wherever he took her, she wanted to go.

With a whispering movement he took his hand over the slender curve of her breast. She was soft, the material smooth, making her hardening nipple a sensuous contrast. He loitered there while her breathing grew unsteady, reveling in the changes of her body. Lingering over each separate button of her nightshirt, Ky unfastened them, then slowly parted the material, as if he were unveiling a priceless treasure.

He'd never forgotten how lovely she was, how exciting delicacy could be. Now that he had her again, he allowed himself the time to look, to touch carefully, all the while watching the contact of his lean, tanned hand against her pale skin. With tenderness he felt seldom and demonstrated rarely, he lowered his mouth, letting his lips follow the progress his fingers had already begun.

She was coming to life under him. Kate felt her blood

begin to boil as though it had lain dormant in her veins for years. She felt her heart begin to thump as though it had been frozen in ice until that moment. She heard her name as only he said it. As only he could.

Sensations? Could there be so many of them? Could she have known them all once, experienced them all once, then lived without them? A whisper, a sigh, the brush of a fingertip along her skin. The scent of a man touched by the sea, the taste of her lover lingering on her lips. The glow of soft lights against closed lids. Time faded. No yesterday. No tomorrow.

She could feel the slick material of the nightshirt slide away, then the warm, smooth sheets beneath her back. The skim of his tongue along her rib cage incited a thrill that began in her core and exploded inside her head.

She remembered the dawn breaking slowly over the sea. Now she knew the same magnificence inside her own body. Light and warmth spread through her, gradually, patiently, until she was glowing with a new beginning.

He hadn't known he could hold such raging desire in check and still feel such complete pleasure, such whirling excitement. He was aware of every heightening degree of passion that worked through her. He understood the changing, rippling thrill she felt if he used more pressure here, a longer taste there. It brought him a wild sense of power, made only more acute by the knowledge that he must harness it. She was fluid. She was silk. And then with a suddenness that sent him reeling, she was fire.

Her body arched on the first tumultuous crest. It ripped through her like a madness. Greedy, ravenous for more, she began to demand what he'd only hinted at. Her hands ran over him, nearly destroying his control in a matter of seconds. Her mouth was hot, hungry, and sought his with an urgency he couldn't resist. Then she rained kisses over his face, down his throat until he gripped the sheets with his hands for fear of crushing her too tightly and bruising her skin.

She touched him with those slender, elegant fingers so that the blood rushed fast and furious into his head. "You make me crazy," he murmured.

"Yes." She could do no more than whisper, but her eyes opened. "Yes."

"I want to watch you go up," he said softly as he slid into her. "I want to see what making love with me does to you."

She arched again, the moan inching out of her as she experienced a second wild peak. He saw her eyes darken, cloud as he took her slowly, steadily toward the verge between passion and madness. He watched the color come into her cheeks, saw her lips tremble as she spoke his name. Her hands gripped his shoulders, but neither of them knew her short, tapered nails dug into his skin.

They moved together, neither able to lead, both able to follow. As pleasure built, he never took his eyes from her face.

All sensation focused into one. They were only one. With a freedom that reaches perfection only rarely, they gave perfection to each other.

Chapter 8

She was sleeping soundly when Ky woke. Ky observed a hint of color in her cheeks and was determined to see that it stayed there. The touch of his hand to her hair was gentle but proprietary. Her skin was cool and dry, her breathing quiet but steady.

What she'd given him the night before had been offered with complete freedom, without shadows of the past, with none of the bitter taste of regret. It was something else he intended to keep constant.

No, he wasn't going to allow her to withdraw from him again. Not an inch. He'd lost her four years ago, or perhaps he'd never really had her—not in the way he'd believed, not in the way he'd taken for granted. But this time, Ky determined, it would be different.

In his own way, he needed to take care of her. Her fragility drew that from him. In another way, he needed a partner on equal terms. Her strength offered him that. For reasons he never completely understood, Kate was exactly what he'd always wanted.

Clumsiness, arrogance, inexperience, or perhaps a combination of all three made him lose her once. Now that he had a second chance, he was going to make sure it worked. With a little more time, he might figure out how.

Rising, he dressed in the shaded light of the bedroom, then left her to sleep.

When she woke slowly, Kate was reluctant to surface from the simple pleasure of a dream. The room was dim, her mind was hazy with sleep and fantasy. The throb in her leg came as a surprise. How could there be pain when everything was so perfect? With a sigh, she reached for Ky and found the bed empty.

The haze vanished immediately, as did all traces of sleep and the pretty edge of fantasy. Kate sat up, and though the movement jolted the pain in her leg, she stared at the empty space beside her.

Had that been a dream as well? she wondered. Tentatively, she reached out and found the sheets cool. All a fantasy brought on by medication and confusion? Unsure, unsteady, she pushed the hair away from her face. Was it possible that she'd imagined it all—the gentleness, the sweetness, the passion?

She'd needed Ky. That hadn't been a dream. Even now she could feel the dull ache in her stomach that came from need. Had the need caused her to fantasize all that strange, stirring beauty during the night?

The bed beside her was empty, the sheets cool. She was alone.

The pleasure she awoke with drained, leaving her empty, leaving her grateful for the pain that was her only grip on reality. She wanted to weep, but found she hadn't the energy for tears.

"So you're up."

Ky's voice made her whip her head around. Her nerves were strung tight. He walked into the bedroom carrying a tray, wearing an easy smile.

"That saves me from having to wake you up to get some food into you." Before he approached the bed, he went to both windows and drew up the shades. Light poured into the room and the warm breeze that had been trapped behind the shades rushed in to ruffle the sheets. Feeling it, she had to control a shudder. "How'd you sleep?"

"Fine." The awkwardness was unexpected. Kate folded her hands and sat perfectly still. "I want to thank you for everything you've done."

"You've already thanked me once. It wasn't necessary then or now." Because her tone had put him on guard, Ky stopped next to the bed to take a good long look at her. "You're hurting."

"It's not bad."

"This time you take a pill." After setting the tray on her lap, he walked to the dresser and picked up a small bottle. "No arguments," he said, anticipating her refusal.

"Ky, it's really not bad." When had he offered her a pill before? The struggle to remember brought only more frustration. "There's barely any pain."

"Any pain's too much." He sat on the bed, and putting the pill into her palm curled her hand over it with his own. "When it's you."

With her fingers curled warmly under his, she knew. Elation came so quietly she was afraid to move and chase it away. "I didn't dream it, did I?" she whispered.

"Dream what?" He kissed the back of her hand before he handed her the glass of juice.

"Last night. When I woke up, I was afraid it had all been a dream."

He smiled and, bending, touched his lips to hers. "If it was, I had the same dream." He kissed her again, with humor in his eyes. "It was wonderful."

"Then it doesn't matter whether it was a dream or not."

"Oh, no, I prefer reality."

With a laugh, she started to drop the pill on the tray, but he stopped her. "Ky—"

"You're hurting," he said again. "I can see it in your eyes. Your medication wore off hours ago, Kate."

"And kept me unconscious for an entire day."

"This is mild, just to take the edge off. Listen—" His hand tightened on hers. "I had to watch you in agony."

"Ky, don't."

"No, you'll do it for me if not for yourself. I had to watch you bleed and faint and drift in and out of consciousness." He ran his hand down her hair, then cupped her face so she'd look directly into his eyes. "I can't tell you what it did to me because I don't know how to describe it. I know I can't watch you in pain anymore."

In silence, she took the pill and drained the glass

of juice. For him, as he said, not for herself. When she swallowed the medication, Ky tugged at her hair. "It hardly has more punch than an aspirin, Kate. Bailey said he'd give you something stronger if you needed it, but he'd rather you go with this."

"It'll be fine. It's really more uncomfortable than painful." It wasn't quite the truth, nor did he believe her, but they both let it lie for the moment. Each of them moved cautiously, afraid to spoil what might have begun to bloom again. Kate glanced down at the empty juice glass. The cold, fresh flavor still lingered on her tongue. "Did Dr. Bailey say when I could dive again?"

"Dive?" Ky's brows rose as he uncovered the plate of bacon, eggs and toast. "Kate, you're not even getting up out of bed for the rest of the week."

"Out of bed?" she repeated. "A week?" She ignored the overloaded plate of food as she gaped at him. "Ky, I was stung by a stingray, not attacked by a shark."

"You were stung by a stingray," he agreed. "And your system was so depleted Bailey almost sent you to a hospital. I realize things might've been rough on you since your father died, but you haven't helped anything by not taking care of yourself."

It was the first time he'd mentioned her father's death, and Kate noted he still expressed no sympathy. "Doctors tend to fuss," she began.

"Bailey doesn't," he interrupted. The anger came back and ran along the edge of his words. "He's a tough, cynical old goat, but he knows his business. He told me that you'd apparently worked yourself right to the edge of exhaustion, that your resistance was nil and that you were a good ten pounds underweight." He held out the fork. "We're going to do something about that, professor. Starting now."

Kate looked down at what had to be four large eggs, scrambled, six slices of bacon and four pieces of toast. "I can see you intend to," she murmured.

"I'm not having you sick." He took her hand again and his grip was firm. "I'm going to take care of you, Kate, whether you like it or not."

She looked back at him in her calm, considering way. "I don't know if I do like it," she decided. "But I suppose we'll both find out."

Ky dipped the fork into the eggs. "Eat."

A smile played at the corners of her mouth. She'd never been pampered in her life and thought it might be entirely too easy to get used to it. "All right, but this time I'll feed myself."

She already knew she'd never finish the entire meal, but for his sake, and the sake of peace, she was determined to deal with half of it. That had been precisely his strategy. If he'd have brought her a smaller portion, she'd have eaten half of that, and have eaten less. He knew her better than either one of them fully realized.

"You're still a wonderful cook," she commented, breaking a piece of bacon in half. "Much better than I."

"If you're good, I might broil up some flounder tonight."

She remembered just how exquisitely he prepared fish. "How good?"

"As good as it takes." He accepted the slice of toast she offered him but dumped on a generous slab of jam.

"Maybe I'll beg some of the hot fudge cake from the Roost."

"Looks like I'll have to be on my best behavior."

"That's the idea."

"Ky…" She was already beginning to poke at her eggs. Had eating always been quite such an effort? "About last night, what happened—"

"Should never have stopped," he finished.

Her lashes swept up, and her eyes were quiet and candid. "I'm not sure."

"I am," he countered. Taking her face in his hands, he kissed her, softly, with only a hint of passion. But the hint was a promise of much more. "Let it be enough for now, Kate. If it has to get complicated, let's wait until other things are a little more settled."

Complicated. Were commitments complicated, the future, promises? She looked down at her plate knowing she simply didn't have the strength to ask or to answer. Not now. "In a way I feel as though I'm slipping back—to that summer four years ago. And yet…"

"It's like a step forward."

Kate looked at him again, but this time reached out. He'd always understood. Though he said little, though his way was sometimes rough, he'd always understood. "Yes. Either way it's a little unnerving."

"I've never liked smooth water. You get a better ride with a few waves."

"Perhaps." She shook her head. Slipping back, stepping forward, it hardly mattered. Either way, she was moving toward him. "Ky, I can't eat any more."

"I figured." Easily, he picked up an extra fork from

the tray and began eating the cooling eggs himself. "It's still probably more than you eat for breakfast in a week."

"Probably," she agreed in a murmur, realizing just how well he'd maneuvered her. Kate lay back against the propped-up pillows, annoyed that she was growing sleepy again. No more medication, she decided silently as Ky polished off their joint breakfast. If she could just avoid that, and go out for a little while, she'd be fine. The trick would be to convince Ky.

Kate looked toward the window, and the sunshine. "I don't want to lose a week's time going over the wreck."

He didn't have to follow the direction of her gaze to follow the direction of her thoughts. "I'll be going down," he said easily. "Tomorrow, the next day anyway." Sooner, he thought to himself, depending on how Kate mended.

"Alone?"

He caught the tone as he bit into the last piece of bacon. "I've gone down alone before."

She would have protested, stating how dangerous it was, if she'd believed it would have done any good. Ky did a great deal alone because that was how he preferred it. Instead, Kate chose another route.

"We're looking for the *Liberty* together, Ky. It isn't a one-man operation."

He sent her a long, quiet look before he picked up the coffee she hadn't touched. "Afraid I'll take off with the treasure?"

"Of course not." She wouldn't allow her emotions to get in the way. "If I hadn't trusted your integrity," she said evenly, "I wouldn't have shown you the chart in the first place."

"Fair enough," he allowed with a nod. "So if I continue to dive while you're recuperating, we won't lose time."

"I don't want to lose you either." It was out before she could stop it. Swearing lightly, Kate looked toward the window again. The sky was the pale blue sometimes seen on summer mornings.

Ky merely sat for a moment while the pleasure of her words rippled through him. "You'd worry about me?"

Angry, Kate turned back. He looked so smug, so infuriatingly content. "No, I wouldn't worry. God usually makes a point of looking after fools."

Grinning, he set the tray on the floor beside the bed. "Maybe I'd like you to worry, a little."

"Sorry I can't oblige you."

"Your voice gets very prim when you're annoyed," he commented. "I like it."

"I'm not prim."

He ran a hand down her loosened hair. No, she looked anything but prim at the moment. Soft and feminine, but not prim. "Your voice is. Like one of those pretty, lacy ladies who used to sit in parlors eating finger sandwiches."

She pushed his hand aside. He wouldn't get around her with charm. "Perhaps I should shout instead."

"Like that too, but more…" He kissed one cheek, then the other. "I like to see you smile at me. The way you smile at nobody else."

Her skin was already beginning to warm. No, he

might not get around her with charm, but...he'd distract her from her point if she wasn't careful. "I'd be bored, that's all. If I have to sit here, hour after hour with nothing to do."

"I've got lots of books." He slipped her nightshirt down her shoulder then kissed her bare skin with the lightest of touches. "Probably lay my hands on some crossword puzzles, too."

"Thanks a lot."

"There's a copy of Byron downstairs."

Despite her determination not to, Kate looked toward him again. "Byron?"

"I bought it after you left. The words are wonderful." He had the three buttons undone with such quick expertise, she never noticed. "But I could always hear the way you'd say them. I remember one night on the beach, when the moon was full on the water. I don't remember the name of the poem, but I remember how it started, and how it sounded when you said it. 'It is the hour'," he began, then smiled at her.

"'It is the hour'," Kate continued, "'when from the boughs the nightingale is heard/It is the hour when lovers' vows seem sweet in every whisper'd word/And gentle winds, and waters near make music to the lonely ear'..." She trailed off, remembering even the scent of that night. "You were never very interested in Byron's technique."

"No matter how hard you tried to explain it to me."

Yes, he was distracting her. Kate was already finding it difficult to remember what point she'd been trying to make. "He was one of the leading poets of his day."

"Hmm." Ky caught the lobe of her ear between his teeth.

"He had a fascination for war and conflict, and yet he had more love affairs in his poems than Shelley or Keats."

"How about out of his poems?"

"There too." She closed her eyes as his tongue began to do outrageous things to her nervous system. "He used humor, satire as well as a pure lyrical style. If he'd ever completed *Don Juan...*" She trailed off with a sigh that edged toward a moan.

"Did I interrupt you?" Ky brushed his fingers down her thigh. "I really love to hear you lecture."

"Yes."

"Good." He traced her lips with his tongue. "I just thought maybe I could give you something to do for a while." He skimmed his hand over her hip then up to the side of her breast. "So you won't be bored by staying in bed. Want to tell me more about Byron?"

With a long quiet breath, she wound her arms around his neck. The point she'd been trying to make didn't seem important any longer. "No, but I might like staying in bed after all, even without the crossword puzzles."

"You'll relax." He said it softly, but the command was unmistakable. She might have argued, but the kiss was long and lingering, leaving her slow and helplessly yielding.

"I don't have a choice," she murmured. "Between the medication and you."

"That's the idea." He'd love her, Ky thought, but so gently she'd have nothing to do but feel. Then she'd sleep. "There are things I want from you." He lifted his head until their eyes met. "Things I need from you."

"You never tell me what they are."

"Maybe not." He laid his forehead on hers. Maybe he just didn't know how to tell her. Or how to ask. "For now, what I want is to see you well." Again he lifted his head, and his eyes focused on hers. "I'm not an unselfish man, Kate. I want that just as much for myself as I want it for you. I fully intended to have you back in my bed, but I didn't want it for you. I fully intended to have you back in my bed, but I didn't care to have you unconscious here first."

"Whatever you intended, I make my own choices." Her hands slid up his shoulders to touch his face. "I chose to make love with you then. I choose to make love with you now."

He laughed and pressed her palm to his lips. "Professor, you think I'd have given you a choice? Maybe we don't know each other as well as we should at this point, but you should know that much."

Thoughtfully, she ran her thumb down his cheekbone. It was hard, elegantly defined. Somehow it suited him in the same way the unshaven face suited him. But did she? Kate wondered. Were they, despite all their differences, right for each other?

It seemed when they were like this, there was no question of suitability, no question of what was right or wrong. Each completed the other. Yet there had to be more. No matter how much each of them denied it on the surface, there had to be more. And ultimately, there had to be a choice.

"When you take what isn't offered freely, you have nothing." She felt the rough scrape of his unshaven face on her palm and the thrill went through her system. "If I give, you have whatever you need without asking."

"Do I?" he murmured before he touched his lips to hers again. "And you? What do you have?"

She closed her eyes as her body drifted on a calm, quiet plane of pleasure. "What I need."

For how long? The question ran through his mind, prodding against his contentment. But he didn't ask. There'd be a time, he knew, for more questions, for the hundreds of demands he wanted to make. For ultimatums. Now she was sleepy, relaxed in the way he wanted her to be.

With no more words he let her body drift, stroking gently, letting her system steep in the pleasure he could give. With no one else could he remember asking so little for himself and receiving so much. She was the hinge that could open or close the door on the better part of him.

He listened to her sigh as he touched her. The second was a kind of pure contentment that mirrored his own feelings. It seemed neither of them required any more.

Kate knew it shouldn't be so simple. It had never been simple with anyone else, so that in the end she'd never given herself to anyone else. Only with Ky had she ever known that full excitement that left her free. Only with Ky had she ever known the pure ease that felt so right.

They'd been apart four years, yet if it had been forty,

she would have recognized his touch in an instant. That touch was all she needed to make her want him.

She remembered the demands and fire that had always been threaded through their lovemaking before. It had been the excitement she'd craved even while it had baffled her. Now there was patience touched with a consideration she didn't know he was capable of.

Perhaps if she hadn't loved him already, she would have fallen in love at that moment when the sun filtered through the windows and his hands were on her skin. She wanted to give him the fire, but his hands kept it banked. She wanted to meet any demands, but he made none. Instead, she floated on the clouds he brought to her.

Though the heat smoldered inside him, she kept him sane. Just by her pliancy. Though passion began to take over, she kept him calm. Just by her serenity. He'd never looked for serenity in his life. It had simply come to him, as Kate had. He'd never understood what it meant to be calm, but he had known the emptiness and the chaos of living without it.

Without urgency or force, he slipped inside her. Slowly, with a sweetness that made her weak, he gave her the ultimate gift. Passion, fulfillment, with the softer emotions covering a need that seemed insatiable.

Then she slept, and he left her to her dreams.

When she awoke again, Kate wasn't groggy, but weak. Even as sleep cleared, a sense of helpless annoyance went though her. It was midafternoon. She didn't need a clock, the angle of the sunlight that slanted through the window across from the bed told her what time it was. More hours had been lost without her knowledge. And where was Ky?

Kate groped for her nightshirt and slipped into it. If he followed his pattern, he'd be popping through the door with a loaded lunch tray and a pill. Not this time, Kate determined as she eased herself out of bed. Nothing else was going into her system that made her lose time.

But as she stood, the dregs of the medication swam in her head. Reflexively, she nearly sat again before she stopped herself. Infuriated, she gripped the bedpost, breathed deeply then put her weight on her injured foot. It took the pain to clear her head.

Pain had its uses, she thought grimly. After she'd given the hurt a moment to subside, it eased into a throb. That could be tolerated, she told herself and walked to the mirror over Ky's dresser.

She didn't like what she saw. Her hair was listless, her face washed-out and her eyes dull. Swearing, she put her hands to her cheeks and rubbed as though she could force color into them. What she needed, Kate decided, was a hot shower, a shampoo and some fresh air. Regardless of what Ky thought, she was going to have them.

Taking a deep breath, she headed for the door. Even as she reached for the knob, it opened.

"What're you doing up?"

Though they were precisely the words she'd expected, Kate had expected them from Ky, not Linda. "I was just—"

"Do you want Ky to skin me alive?" Linda demanded, backing Kate toward the bed with a tray of steaming soup in her hand. "Listen, you're supposed to rest and eat, then eat and rest. Orders."

Realizing abruptly that she was retreating, Kate held her ground. "Whose?"

"Ky's. And," she continued before Kate could retort, "Dr. Bailey's."

"I don't have to take orders from either of them."

"Maybe you don't," Linda agreed dryly. "But I don't argue with a man who's protecting his woman, or with the man who poked a needle into my bottom when I was three. Both of them can be nasty. Now lie down."

"Linda..." Though she knew the sigh sounded long suffering, Kate couldn't prevent it. "I've a cut on my leg. I've been in bed for something like forty-eight hours straight. If I don't have a shower and a breath of air soon, I'm going to go crazy."

A smile tugged at Linda's mouth that she partially concealed by nibbling on her lower lip. "A bit grumpy, are we?"

"I can be more than a bit." This time the sigh was simply bad tempered. "Look at me!" Kate demanded, tugging on her hair. "I feel as though I've just crawled out from under a rock."

"Okay. I know how I felt after I'd delivered Hope. After I'd had my cuddle with her I wanted a shower and shampoo so bad I was close to tears." She set the tray on the table beside the bed. "You can have ten minutes in the shower, then you can eat while I change your bandage. But Ky made me swear I'd make you eat every bite." She put her hands on her hips. "So that's the deal."

"He's overreacting," Kate began. "It's absurd. I don't need to be babied this way."

"Tell me that when you don't look like I could blow you over. Now come on, I'll give you a hand in the shower."

"No, damn it, I'm perfectly capable of taking a shower by myself." Ignoring the pain in her leg, she stormed out of the room, slamming the door at her back. Linda swallowed a laugh and sat down on the bed to wait.

Fifteen minutes later, refreshed and thoroughly ashamed of herself, Kate came back in. Wrapped in Ky's robe, she rubbed a towel over her hair. "Linda—"

"Don't apologize. If I'd been stuck in bed for two days, I'd snap at the first person who gave me trouble. Besides—" Linda knew how to play her cards "—if you're really sorry you'll eat all your soup, so Ky won't yell at me."

"All right." Resigned, Kate sat back in the bed and took the tray on her lap. She swallowed the first bite of soup and stifled her objection as Linda began to fiddle with her bandage. "It's wonderful."

"The seafood chowder's one of our specialties. Oh, honey." Linda's eyes darkened with concern after she removed the gauze. "This must've hurt like hell. No wonder Ky's been frantic."

Drumming up her courage, Kate leaned over enough to look at the wound. There was no inflammation as she'd feared, no puffiness. Though the slice was six inches in length, it was clean. Her stomach muscles unknotted. "It's not so bad," she murmured. "There's no infection."

"Look, I've been caught by a stingray, a small one. I probably had a cut half an inch across and I cried like a baby. Don't tell me it's not so bad."

"Well, I slept through most of it." She winced, then deliberately relaxed her muscles.

Linda narrowed her eyes as she studied Kate's face. "Ky said you should have a pill if there was any pain when you woke."

"If you want to do me a favor, you can dump them out." Calmly, Kate ate another spoonful of soup. "I really hate to argue with him, or with you, but I'm not taking any more pills and losing any more time. I appreciate the fact that he wants to pamper me. It's unexpectedly sweet, but I can only take it so far."

"He's worried about you. He feels responsible."

"For my carelessness?" With a shake of her head, Kate concentrated on finishing the soup. "It was an accident, and if there's blame, it's mine. I was so wrapped up in looking for salvage I didn't take basic precautions. I practically bumped into the ray." With an effort, she controlled a shudder. "Ky acted much more quickly than I. He'd already started to pull me out of range. If he hadn't, things would have been much more serious."

"He loves you."

Kate's fingers tightened on the spoon. With exaggerated care, she set it back on the tray. "Linda, there's a vast difference between concern, attraction, even affection and love."

Linda simply nodded in agreement. "Yes. I said Ky loves you."

She managed to smile and pick up the tea that had been cooling beside the soup. "*You* said," Kate returned simply. "*Ky* hasn't."

"Well neither did Marsh until I was ready to strangle him, but that didn't stop me."

"I'm not you." Kate lay back against the pillows, grateful that most of the weakness and the weariness had passed. "And Ky isn't Marsh."

Impatient, Linda rose and swirled around the room. "People who complicate simple things make me so mad!"

Smiling, Kate sipped her tea. "Others simplify the complicated."

With a sniff, Linda turned back. "I've known Ky Silver all my life. I watched him bounce around from one cute girl to the next, then one attractive woman to another until I lost count. Then you came along." Stopping, she leaned against the bedpost. "It was as if someone had hit him over the head with a blunt instrument. You dazed him, Kate, almost from the first minute. You fascinated him."

"Dazing, fascinating." Kate shrugged while she tried to ignore the ache in her heart. "Flattering, I suppose, but neither of those things equals love."

The stubborn line came and went between Linda's brows. "I don't believe love comes in an instant, it grows. If you could have seen the way Ky was after you left four years ago, you'd know—"

"Don't tell me about four years ago," Kate interrupted. "What happened four years ago is over. Ky and I are two different people today, with different expectations. This time…" She took a deep breath. "This time when it ends, I won't be hurt because I know the limits."

"You've just gotten back together and you're already talking about endings and limitations!" Dragging a hand through her hair, Linda came forward to sit on the edge of the bed. "What's wrong with you? Don't you know how to wish anymore? How to dream?"

"I was never very good at either. Linda…" She hesitated, wanting to choose her phrasing carefully. "I don't want to expect any more from Ky than what he can easily give. After August, I know we'll each go back to our separate worlds—there's no bridge between them. Maybe I was meant to come back so we could make up for whatever pain we caused each other before. This time I want to leave still being friends. He's…" She hesitated again because this phrasing was even more important. "He's always been a very important part of my life."

Linda waited a moment, then narrowed her eyes. "That's about the dumbest thing I've ever heard."

Despite herself, Kate laughed. "Linda—"

Holding up her hands, she shook her head and cut Kate off. "No, I can't talk about it anymore, I get too mad and I'm supposed to be taking care of you." She let out her breath on a huff as she removed Kate's tray. "I just can't understand how anyone so smart could be so stupid, but the more I think about it the more I can see that you and Ky deserve each other."

"That sounds more like an insult than a compliment."

"It was."

Kate pushed her tongue against her teeth to hold back a smile. "I see."

"Don't look so smug just because you've made me so angry I don't want to talk about it anymore." She drew her shoulders back. "I might just give Ky a piece of my mind when he gets home."

"That's his problem," Kate said cheerfully. "Where'd he go?"

"Diving."

Amusement faded. "Alone?"

"There's no use worrying about it." Linda spoke briskly as she cursed herself for not thinking of a simple lie. "He dives alone ninety percent of the time."

"I know." But Kate folded her hands, preparing to worry until he returned.

Chapter 9

"I'm going with you."

The sunlight was strong, the scent of the ocean pure. Through the screen the sound of gulls from a quarter of a mile away could be heard clearly. Ky turned from the stove where he poured the last cup of coffee and eyed Kate as she stood in the doorway.

She'd pinned her hair up and had dressed in thin cotton pants and a shirt, both of which were baggy and cool. It occured to him that she looked more like a student than a college professor.

He knew enough of women and their illusions to see that she'd added color to her cheeks. She hadn't needed blusher the evening before when he'd returned from the wreck. Then she had been angry, and passionate. He nearly smiled as he lifted his cup.

"You wasted your time getting dressed," he said easily. "You're going back to bed."

Kate disliked stubborn people, people who demanded their own way flatly and unreasonably. At that moment, she decided they were *both* stubborn. "No." On the surface she remained as calm as he was while she walked into the kitchen. "I'm going with you."

Unlike Kate, Ky never minded a good argument. Preparing for one, he leaned back against the stove. "I don't take down a diver against doctor's orders."

She'd expected that. With a shrug, she opened the refrigerator and took out a bottle of juice. She knew she was being bad tempered, and though it was completely out of character, she was enjoying the experience. The simple truth was that she had to do something or go mad.

As far as she could remember, she'd never spent two more listless days. She had to move, think, feel the sun. It might have been satisfying to stomp her feet and demand, but, she thought, fruitless. If she had to compromise to get her way, then compromise she would.

"I can rent a boat and equipment and go down on my own." With the glass in hand, she turned, challenging. "You can't stop me."

"Try me."

It was said simply, quietly, but she'd seen the flare of anger in his eyes. *Better,* she thought. *Much better.* "I've a right to do precisely as I choose. We both know it." Perhaps her leg was uncomfortable, but as to the rest of her body, it was charged up and ready to move. Nor was there anything wrong with her mind. Kate had plotted her strategy very well. After all, she thought grimly, there'd certainly been enough time to think it through.

"We both know you're not in any shape to dive." His first urge was to carry her back to bed, his second to shake her until she rattled. Ky did neither, only drank his coffee and watched her over the rim. A power struggle wasn't something he'd expected, but he wouldn't back away from it. "You're not stupid, Kate. You know you can't go down yet, and you know I won't let you."

"I've rested for two days. I feel fine." As she walked toward him she was pleased to see him frown. He understood she had a mind of her own, and that he had to deal with it. The truth was, she was stronger than either of them had expected her to be. "As far as diving goes, I'm willing to leave that to you for the next couple of days, but…" She paused, wanting to be certain he knew she was negotiating, not conceding. "I'm going out on the *Vortex* with you. And I'm going out this morning."

He lifted a brow. She'd never intended to dive, but she'd used it as a pressure point to get what she wanted. He couldn't blame her. Ky remembered recovering from a broken leg when he was fourteen. The pain was vague in his mind now, but the boredom was still perfectly clear. "You'll lie down in the cabin when you're told."

She smiled and shook her head. "I'll lie down in the cabin if I need to."

He took her chin in his hand and squeezed. "Damn right you will. Okay, let's go. I want an early start."

Once he was resigned, Ky moved quickly. She could either keep up, or be left behind. Within minutes he parked his car near his slip at Silver Lake Harbor and was boarding the *Vortex*. Content, Kate took a seat beside him at the helm and prepared to enjoy the sun and the wind. Already she felt the energy begin to churn.

"I've done a chart of the wreck as of yesterday's dive," he told her as he maneuvered out of the harbor.

"A chart?" Automatically she pushed at her hair as she turned toward him. "You didn't show me."

"Because you were asleep when I finished it."

"I've been asleep ninety percent of the time," she mumbled.

As he headed out to sea, Ky laid a hand on her shoulder. "You look better, Kate, no shadows. No strain. That's more important."

For a moment, just a moment, she pressed her cheek against his hand. Few women could resist such soft concern, and yet…she didn't want his concern to cloud their reason for being together. Concern could turn to pity. She needed him to see her as a partner, as equal. As long as she was his lover, it was vital that they meet on the same ground. Then when she left… When she left there'd be no regrets.

"I don't need to be pampered anymore, Ky."

His shoulders moved as he glanced at the compass. "I enjoyed it."

She was resisting being cared for. He understood it, appreciated it and regretted it. There had been something appealing about seeing to her needs, about having her depend on him. He didn't know how to tell her he wanted her to be well and strong just as much as he wanted her to turn to him in times of need.

Somehow, he felt their time together had been too short for him to speak. He didn't deal well with caution.

As a diver, he knew its importance, but as a man... As a man he fretted to go with his instincts, with his impulses.

His fingers brushed her neck briefly before he turned to the wheel. He'd already decided he'd have to approach his relationship with Kate as he'd approach a very deep, very dangerous dive—with an eye on currents, pressure and the unexpected.

"That chart's in the cabin," he told her as he cut the engine. "You might want to look it over while I'm down."

She agreed with a nod, but the restlessness was already on her as Ky began to don his equipment. She didn't want to make an issue of his diving alone. He wouldn't listen to her in any case; if anything came of it, it would only be an argument. In silence she watched him check his tanks. He'd be down for an hour. Kate was already marking time.

"There are cold drinks in the galley." He adjusted the strap of his mask before climbing over the side. "Don't sit in the sun too long."

"Be careful," she blurted out before she could stop herself.

Ky grinned, then was gone with a quiet splash.

Though she ran over to the side, Kate was too late to watch him dive. For a long time after, she simply leaned over the boat, staring at the water's surface. She imagined Ky going deeper, deeper, adjusting his pressure, moving out with power until he'd reached the bottom and the wreck.

He'd brought back the bowl and ladle the evening before. They sat on the dresser in his bedroom while the broken rigging and pieces of crockery were stored downstairs. Thus far he'd done no more than gather what they'd already found together, but today, Kate thought with a twinge of impatience, he'd extend the search. Whatever he found, he'd find alone.

She turned away from the water, frustrated that she was excluded. It occurred to her that all her life she'd been an onlooker, someone who analyzed and explained the action rather than causing it. This search had been her first opportunity to change that, and now she was back to square one.

Stuffing her hands in her pockets, Kate looked up at the sky. There were clouds to the west, but they were thin and white. Harmless. She felt too much like that herself at the moment—something unsubstantial. Sighing, she went below deck. There was nothing to do now but wait.

Ky found two more cannons and sent up buoys to mark their position. It would be possible, if he didn't find something more concrete, to salvage the cannons and have them dated by an expert. Though he swam from end to end, searching carefully, he knew it was unlikely he'd find a date stamp through the layers of corrosion. But in time... Satisfied, he swam north.

If he accomplished nothing else on this dive, he wanted to establish the size of the site. With luck it would be fairly small, perhaps no bigger than a football field. However, there was always the chance that the wreckage could be scattered over several square miles. Before they brought in a salvage ship, he wanted to take a great deal of care with the preliminary work.

They would need tools. A metal detector would be invaluable. Thus far, they'd done no more than find a wreck, no matter how certain Kate was that it was the *Liberty*. For the moment he had no way to determine the origin of the ship, he had to find cargo. Once he'd found that, perhaps treasure would follow.

Once he'd found the treasure... Would she leave? Would she take her share of the gold and the artifacts and drive home?

Not if he could help it, Ky determined as he shone his headlamp over the sea floor. When the search was over and they'd salvaged what could be salvaged from the sea, it would be time to salvage what they'd once had—what had perhaps never truly been lost. If they could find what had been buried for centuries, they could find what had been buried for four years.

He couldn't find much without tools. Most of the ship—or what remained of it—was buried under silt. On another dive, he'd use the prop-wash, the excavation device he'd constructed in his shop. With that he could blow away inches of sediment at a time—a slow but safe way to uncover artifacts. But someone would have to stay on board to run it.

He thought of Kate and rejected the idea immediately. Though he had no doubt she could handle the technical aspect—it would only have to be explained to her once—she'd never go for it. Ky began to think it was time they enlisted Marsh.

He knew his air time was almost up and he'd have to surface for fresh tanks. Still, he lingered near the bottom, searching, prodding. He wanted to take something up for Kate, something tangible that would put the enthusiasm back in her eyes.

It took him more than half of his allotted time to find

it, but when Ky held the unbroken bottle in his hand, he knew Kate's reaction would be worth the effort. It was a common bottle, not priceless crystal, but he could see no mold marks, which meant it had been hand blown. Crust was weathered over it in layers, but Ky took the time to carefully chip some away, from the bottom only. If the date wasn't on the bottom, he'd need the crust to have the bottle dated. Already he was thinking of the Corning Glass Museum and their rate of success.

Then he saw the date, and with a satisfied grin placed the find in the goodie bag on his belt. With his air supply running short, he started toward the surface.

His hour was up. Or so nearly up, Kate thought, that he should have surfaced already if he'd allowed himself any safety factor. She paced from port to starboard and back again. Would he always risk his own welfare to the limit?

She'd long since given up sitting quietly in the cabin, going over the makeshift chart Ky had begun. She'd found a book on shipwrecks that Ky had obviously purchased recently, and though it had also been among her father's research books, she'd skimmed through it again.

It gave a detailed guide to identifying and excavating a wreck, listed common mistakes and hazards. She found it difficult to read about hazards while Ky was alone beneath the surface. Still, even the simple language of the book couldn't disguise the adventure. For perhaps half the time Ky had been gone, she'd lost herself in it. Spanish galleons, Dutch merchant ships, English frigates.

She'd found the list of wrecks off North Carolina

alone extensive. But these, she'd thought, had already been located, documented. The adventure there was over. One day, because of the chain her father had started and she'd continued, the *Liberty* would be among them.

Fretfully, Kate waited for Ky to surface. She thought of her father. He'd pored over this same book as well— planning, calculating. Yet his calculations hadn't taken him beyond the initial stage. If he'd shared his goal with her, would he have taken her on his summer quests? She'd never know, because she'd never been given the choice.

She was making her own choices now, Kate mused. Her first had been to return to Ocracoke, accepting the consequences. Her next had been to give herself to Ky without conditions. Her last, she thought as she stared down at the quiet water, would be to leave him again. Yet, in reality, perhaps she'd still been given no choice. It was all a matter of currents. She could only swim against them for so long.

Relief washed over her when she spotted the flow of bubbles. Ky grabbed the bottom rung of the ladder as he pushed up his mask. "Waiting for me?"

Relief mixed with annoyance for the time she'd spent worrying about him. "You cut it close."

"Yeah, a little." He passed up his tanks. "I had to stop and get you a present."

"It's not a joke, Ky." Kate watched him come over the side, agile, lean and energetic. "You'd be furious with me if I'd cut my time that close."

"Leave it up to Linda to fuss," he advised as he pulled down the zipper of his wet suit. "She was born that way." Then he grabbed her, crushing her against him so that she felt the excitement he'd brought up with him. His mouth closed over hers, tasting of salt from the sea. Because he was wet, her clothes clung to him, binding them together for the brief instant he held her. But when he would have released her, she held fast, drawing the kiss out into something that warmed his cool skin.

"I worry about you, Ky." For one last moment, she held on fiercely. "Damn it, is that what you want to hear?"

"No." He took her face in his hands and shook his head. "No."

Kate broke away, afraid she'd say too much, afraid she'd say things neither of them were ready to hear. She knew the rules this time. She groped for something calm, something simple. "I suppose I got a bit frantic waiting up here. It's different when you're down."

"Yeah." What did she want from him? he wondered. Why was it that every time she started to show her concern for him, she clammed up? "I've got some more things to add to the chart."

"I saw the buoys you sent up." Kate moistened her lips and relaxed, muscle by muscle.

"Two more cannons. From the size of them, I'd say she was a fairly small ship. It's unlikely she was constructed for battle."

"She was a merchant ship."

"Maybe. I'm going to take the metal detector down and see what I come up with. From the stuff we've found, I don't think she's buried too deep."

Kate nodded. Delve into business, keep the personal

aspect light. "I'd like to send off a piece of the planking and some of the glass to be analyzed. I think we'll have more luck with the glass, but it doesn't hurt to cover all the angles."

"No, it doesn't. Don't you want your present?"

At ease again, she smiled. "I thought you were joking. Did you bring me a shell?"

"I thought you'd like this better." Reaching into his bag, Ky brought out the bottle. "It's too bad it's not still corked. We could've had wine with peanut butter."

"Oh, Ky, it's not damaged!" Thrilled, she reached out for it, but he pulled it back out of reach and grinned.

"Bottoms up," he told her and turned the bottle upside down.

Kate stared at the smeared bottom of the bottle. "Oh, God," she whispered. "It's dated. 1749." Gingerly, she took the bottle in both hands. "The year before the *Liberty* sank."

"It's another ship, maybe," Ky reminded her. "But it does narrow down the time element."

"Over two hundred years," she murmured. "Glass, it's so breakable, so vulnerable, and yet it survived two centuries." Her eyes lit with enthusiasm as she looked back at him. "Ky, we should be able to find out where the bottle was made."

"Probably, but most glass bottles found on wrecks from the seventeenth and eighteenth century were manufactured in England anyway. It wouldn't prove the ship was English."

She let out a huff of breath, but her energy hadn't dimmed. "You've been doing your research."

"I don't go into any project until I know the angles."
Ky knelt down to check the fresh tanks.

"You're going back down now?"

"I want to get as much mapped out as I can before
we start dealing with too much equipment."

She'd done enough homework herself to know that
the most common mistake of the modern-day salvor
was in failing to map out a site. Yet she couldn't stem
her impatience. It seemed so time-consuming when
they could be concentrating on getting under the layers of silt.

It seemed to her that she and Ky had changed positions somehow. She'd always been the cautious one,
proceeding step by logical step, while he'd taken the
risks. Struggling with the impotence of having to wait
and watch, she stood back while he strapped on the
fresh tanks. As she watched, Ky picked up a brass rod.

"What's that for?"

"It's the base for this." He held out a device that re-
sembled a compass. "It's called an azimuth circle. It's
a cheap, effective way to map out the site. I drive this
into the approximate center of the wreck so that it be-
comes the datum point, align the circle with the mag-
netic north, then I use a length of chain to measure the
distance to the cannons, or whatever I need to map.
After I get it set, I'll be back up for the metal detector."

Frustration built again. He was doing all the work
while she simply stood still. "Ky, I feel fine. I could
help if—"

"No." He didn't bother to argue or list reasons. He
simply went over the side and under.

It was midafternoon when they started back. Ky

spent the last hour at sea adding to the chart, putting in the information he'd gathered that day. He'd brought more up in his goodie bag—a tankard, spoons and forks that might have been made of iron. It seemed they had indeed found the galley. Kate decided she'd begin a detailed list of their finds that evening. If it was all she could do at the moment, she'd do it with pleasure.

Her mood had lifted a bit since she'd caught three good-size bluefish while Ky had been down at the wreck the second time. No matter how much Ky argued, she fully intended to cook them herself and eat them sitting at the table, not lying in bed.

"Pretty pleased with yourself, aren't you?"

She gave him a cool smile. They were cruising back toward Silver Lake Harbor and though she felt a weariness, it was a pleasant feeling, not the dragging fatigue of the past days. "Three bluefish in that amount of time's a very respectable haul."

"No argument there. Especially since I intend to eat half of them."

"I'm going to grill them."

"Are you?"

She met his lifted brow with a neutral look. "I caught, I cook."

Ky kept the boat at an even speed as he studied her. She looked a bit tired, but he thought he could convince her to take a nap if he claimed he wanted one himself. She was healing quickly. And she was right. He couldn't pamper her. "I could probably bring myself to start the charcoal for you."

"Fair enough. I'll even let you clean them."

He laughed at the bland tone and ruffled her hair until the pins fell out.

"Ky!" Automatically, Kate reached up to repair the damage.

"Wear it up in the school room," he advised, tossing some of the pins overboard. "I find it difficult to resist you when your hair's down and just a bit mussed."

"Is that so?" She debated being annoyed, then decided there were more productive ways to pass the time. Kate let the wind toss her hair as she moved closer to him so that their bodies touched. She smiled at the quick look of surprise in his eyes as she slipped both hands under his T-shirt. "Why don't you turn off the engine and show me what happens when you stop resisting?"

For all her generosity and freedom in lovemaking, she'd never been the initiator. Ky found himself both baffled and aroused as she smiled up at him, her hands stroking slowly over his chest. "You know what happens when I stop resisting," he murmured.

She gave a low, quiet laugh. "Refresh my memory." Without waiting for an answer, she drew back on the throttle herself until the boat was simply idling. "You didn't make love with me last night." Her hands slid around and up his back.

"You were sleeping." She was seducing him in the middle of the afternoon, in the middle of the ocean. He found he wanted to savor the new experience as much as he wanted to bring it to fruition.

"I'm not sleeping now." Rising on her toes, she brushed her lips over his, lightly, temptingly. She felt his heartbeat race against her body and reveled in a sense of power she'd never explored. "Or perhaps you're in a hurry to get back, and uh, clean fish."

She was taunting him. Why had he never seen the witch in her before? Ky felt his stomach knot with need, but when he drew her closer, she resisted. Just slightly. Just enough to torment. "If I make love with you now, I won't be gentle."

She kept her lips inches from his. "Is that a warning?" she whispered. "Or a promise?"

He felt the first tremor move through him and was astonished. Not even for her had he ever trembled. Not even for her. The need grew, stretching restlessly, recklessly. "I'm not sure you know what you're doing, Kate."

Nor did she, but she smiled because it no longer mattered. Only the outcome mattered. "Come down to the cabin with me and we'll both find out." She slipped away from him and without a word disappeared below deck.

His hand wasn't steady when he reached for the key to turn off the engines. He needed a moment, perhaps a bit more, to regain the control he'd held so carefully since they'd become lovers again. Ever since he'd had her blood on his hands, he had a tremendous fear of hurting her. Since he'd had a taste of her again, he had an equal fear of driving her away. Caution was a strain, but he'd kept it in focus with sheer will. As Ky started down the steps, he told himself he'd continue to be cautious.

She'd unbuttoned her blouse but hadn't removed it. When he came into the narrow cabin with her, Kate smiled. She was afraid, though she hardly knew why. But over the fear was a heady sense of power and strength that fought for full release. She wanted to take him to the edge, to push him to the limits of passion. At that moment, she was certain she could.

When he came no closer to her, Kate stepped forward and pulled his shirt over his head. "Your skin's gold," she murmured. "It's always excited me." Taking her pleasure slowly, she ran her hands up his sides, feeling the quiver she caused. "You've always excited me."

Her hands were steady, her pulse throbbed as she unsnapped his cut-offs. With her eyes on his, she slowly, slowly, undressed him. "No one's ever made me want the way you make me want."

He had to stop her and take control again. She couldn't know the effect of those long, fragile fingers when they brushed easily over his skin, or how her calm eyes made him rage inside.

"Kate..." He took her hands in his and bent to kiss her. But she turned her head, meeting his neck with warm lips that sent a spear of fire up his spine.

Then her body was pressed against his, flesh meeting flesh where her blouse parted. Her mouth trailed over his chest, her hands down his back to his hips. He felt the fury of desire whip through him as though it had sharp, hungry teeth.

So he forgot control, gentleness, vulnerability. She drove him to forget. She intended to.

They were tangled on the narrow bunk, her blouse halfway down her back and parted so that her breasts pushed into his chest, driving him mad with their firm, subtle curves. She nipped at his lips, demanding, pushing for more, still more. Waves of passion overtook them.

His need was incendiary. She was like a flame, impossible to hold, searing here, singeing there until his body was burning with needs and fierce fantasies.

Her hands were swift, sending sharp gasping pleasure everywhere at once until he wasn't sure he could take it anymore. Yet he no longer thought of stopping her. Less of stopping himself.

His hands gripped her with an urgency that made her moan from the sheer strength in them. She wanted his strength now—mindless strength that would carry them both to a place they'd never gone before. And she was leading. The knowledge made her laugh aloud as she tasted his skin, his lips, his tongue.

She slid down his body, feeling each jolt of pleasure as it shot through him. There could be no slow, lingering loving now. They'd pushed each other beyond reason. The air here was dark and thin and whirling with sound. Kate drank it in.

When he found her moist, hot and ready she let him take her over peak after shuddering peak, knowing as he drove her, she drove him. Her body was filled with sensations that came and went like comets, slipped away and burst on her again, and again. Through the thunder in her head she heard herself say his name, clear and quick.

On the sound, she took him into her and welcomed the madness.

Chapter 10

She was wrong.

Kate had thought she'd be ready, even anxious to dive again. There hadn't been a day during her recuperation that she hadn't thought of going down. Every time Ky had brought back an artifact, she was thrilled with the discovery and frustrated with her own lack of participation. Like a schoolgirl approaching summer, she'd begun to count the days.

Now, a week after the accident, Kate stood on the deck of the *Vortex* with her mouth dry and her hands trembling as she pulled on her wet suit. She could only be grateful that Ky was already over the side, hooking up his home-rigged prop-wash to the boat's propeller. Drafted to the crew, Marsh stood at the stern watching his brother. With Linda's eager support, he'd agreed to give Ky a few hours a day of his precious free time while he was needed.

Kate took the moment she had alone to gather her thoughts and her nerve.

It was only natural to be anxious about diving after the experience she'd had. Kate told herself that was logical. But it didn't stop her hands from trembling as she zipped up her suit. She could equate it with falling off a horse and having to mount again. It was psychological. But it didn't ease the painful tension in her stomach.

Trembling hands and nerves. With or without them, she told herself as she hooked on her weight belt, she was going down. Nothing, not even her own fears, was going to stop her from finishing what she'd begun.

"He's got it," Marsh called out when Ky signaled him.

"I'll be ready." Kate picked up the cloth bag she'd use to bring up small artifacts. With luck, and if the prop-wash did its job, she knew they'd soon need more sophisticated methods to bring up the salvage.

"Kate."

She didn't look up, but continued to hook on the goodie bag. "Yes?"

"You know it's only natural that you'd be nervous going down." Marsh touched a hand to her shoulder, but she busied herself by strapping on her diving knife. "If you want a little more time, I'll work with Ky and you can run the wash."

"No." She said it too quickly, then cursed herself. "It's all right, Marsh." With forced calm she hung the underwater camera she'd purchased only the day before around her neck. "I have to take the first dive sometime."

"It doesn't have to be now."

She smiled at him again thinking how calm, how steady he appeared when compared to Ky. This was the sort of man it would have made sense for her to be attracted to. Confused emotions made no sense. "Yes, it does. Please." She put her hand on his arm before he could speak again. "Don't say anything to Ky."

Did she think he'd have to? Marsh wondered as he inclined his head in agreement. Unless he was way off the mark, Marsh was certain Ky knew every expression, every gesture, every intonation of her voice.

"Let's run it a couple of minutes at full throttle." Ky climbed over the side, dripping and eager. "With the depth and the size of the prop, we're going to have to test the effect. There might not be enough power to do us any good."

In agreement, Marsh went to the helm. "Are you thinking about using an air lift?"

Ky's only answer was a noncommittal grunt. He had thought of it. The metal tube with its stream of compressed air was a quick, efficient way to excavate on silty bottoms. They might get away with the use of a small air lift, if it became necessary. But perhaps the prop-wash would do the job well enough. Either way, he was thinking more seriously about a bigger ship, with more sophisticated equipment and more power. As he saw it, it all depended on what they found today.

He picked up one last piece of equipment—a small

powerful spear gun. He'd take no more chances with Kate.

"Okay, slow it down to the minimum," he ordered. "And keep it there. Once Kate and I are down, we don't want the prop-wash shooting cannonballs around."

Kate stopped the deep breathing she was using to ease tension. Her voice was cool and steady. "Would it have that kind of power?"

"Not at this speed." Ky adjusted his mask then took her hand. "Ready?"

"Yes."

Then he kissed her, hard. "You've got guts, professor," he murmured. His eyes were dark, intense as they passed over her face. "It's one of the sexiest things about you." With this he was over the side.

He knew. Kate gave a quiet unsteady sigh as she started down the ladder. He knew she was afraid, and that had been his way of giving her support. She looked up once and saw Marsh. He lifted his hand in salute. Throat dry, nerves jumping, Kate let the sea take her.

She felt a moment's panic, a complete disorientation the moment she was submerged. It ran through her head that down here, she was helpless. The deeper she went, the more vulnerable she became. Choking for air, she kicked back toward the surface and the light.

Then Ky had her hands, holding her to him, holding her under. His grip was firm, stilling the first panic. Feeling the wild race of her pulse, he held on during her first resistance.

Then he touched her cheek, waiting until she'd calmed enough to look at him. In his eyes she saw strength and challenge. Pride alone forced her to fight her way beyond the fear and meet him, equal to equal.

When she'd regulated her breathing, accepting that her air came through the tanks on her back, he kissed the back of her hand. Kate felt the tension give. She wouldn't be helpless, she reminded herself. She'd be careful.

With a nod, she pointed down, indicating she was ready to dive. Keeping hands linked, they started toward the bottom.

The whirlpool action created by the wash of the prop had already blasted away some of the sediment. At first glance Ky could see that if the wreck was buried under more than a few feet, they'd need something stronger than his homemade apparatus and single prop engine. But for now, it would do. Patience, which came to him only with deliberate effort, was more important at this stage than speed. With the wreck, he thought, and—he glanced over at the woman beside him—with a great deal more. He had to take care not to hurry.

It was still working, blowing away some of the overburden at a rate Ky figured would equal an inch per minute. He and Kate alone couldn't deal with any more speed. He watched the swirl of water and sediment while she swam a few feet away to catalog one of the cannons on film. When she came closer, he grinned as she placed the camera in front of her face again. She was relaxed, her initial fear forgotten. He could see it simply in the way she moved. Then she let the camera fall so they could begin the search again.

Kate saw something solid wash away from the hole

being created by the whirl of water. Grabbing it up, she found herself holding a candlestick. In her excitement, she turned it over and over in her hand.

Silver? she wondered with a rush of adrenaline. Had they found their first real treasure? It was black with oxidation, so it was impossible to be certain what it was made of. Still, it thrilled her. After days and days of only waiting, she was again pursuing the dream.

When she looked up, Ky was already gathering the uncovered items and laying them in the mesh basket. There were more candleholders, more tableware, but not the plain unglazed pottery they'd found before. Kate's pulse began to drum with excitement while she meticulously snapped pictures. They'd be able to find a hallmark, she was certain of it. Then they'd know if they had indeed found a British ship. Ordinary seamen didn't use silver, or even pewter table service. They'd uncovered more than the galley now. And they were just beginning.

When Ky found the first piece of porcelain he signaled to her. True, the vase—if that's what it once had been—had suffered under the water pressure and the years. It was broken so that only half of the shell remained, but so did the manufacturer's mark.

When Kate read it, she gripped Ky's arm. *Whieldon.* English. The master potter who'd trained the likes of Wedgwood. Kate cupped the broken fragment in her hands as though it were alive. When she lifted her eyes to Ky's they were filled with triumph.

Fretting against her inability to speak, Kate pointed to the mark again. Ky merely nodded and indicated the basket. Though she was loath to part with it, Kate found herself even more eager to discover more. She settled the porcelain in the mesh. When she swam back, Ky's hands were filled with other pieces. Some were hardly more than shards, others were identifiable as pieces left from bowls or lids.

No, it didn't prove it was a merchant ship, Kate told herself as she gathered what she could herself. So far, it only proved that the officers and perhaps some passengers had eaten elegantly on their way to the New World. English officers, she reminded herself. In her mind they'd taken the identification that far.

The force of the wash sent an object shooting up. Ky reached out for it and found a crusted, filthy pot he guessed would have been used for tea or coffee. Perhaps it was cracked under the layers, but it held together in his hands. He tapped on his tank to get Kate's attention.

She knew it was priceless the moment she saw it. Stemming impatience, she signaled for Ky to hold it out as she lifted the camera again. Obliging, he crossed his legs like a genie and posed.

It made her giggle. They'd perhaps just found something worth thousands of dollars, but he could still act silly. Nothing was too serious for Ky. As she brought him into frame, Kate felt the same foolish pleasure. She'd known the hunt would be exciting, perhaps rewarding, but she'd never known it would be fun. She swam forward and reached for the pot herself.

Running her fingers over it, she could detect some kind of design under the crust. Not ordinary pottery, she was sure. Not utility-ware. She held something elegant, something well crafted.

He understood its worth as well as she. Taking it from her, Ky indicated they would bring it and the rest of the morning's salvage to the surface. Pointing to his watch he showed her that their tanks were running low.

She didn't argue. They'd come back. The *Liberty* would wait for them. Each took a handle of the mesh basket and swam leisurely toward the surface.

"Do you know how I feel?" Kate demanded the moment she could speak.

"Yes." Ky gripped the ladder with one hand and waited for her to unstrap her tanks and slip them over onto the deck. "I know just how you feel."

"The teapot." Breathing fast, she hauled herself up the ladder. "Ky, it's priceless. It's like finding a perfectly formed rose inside a mass of briars." Before he could answer, she was laughing and calling out to Marsh. "It's fabulous! Absolutely fabulous."

Marsh cut the engine then walked over to help them. "You two work fast." Bending he touched a tentative finger to the pot. "God, it's all in one piece."

"We'll be able to date it as soon as it's cleaned. But look." Kate drew out the broken vase. "This is the mark of an English potter. English," she repeated, turning to Ky. "He trained Wedgwood, and Wedgwood didn't begin manufacturing until the 1760s, so—"

"So this piece more than likely came from the era we're looking for," Ky finished. "*Liberty* or not," he continued, crouching down beside her. "It looks like you've found yourself an eighteenth-century wreck that's probably of English origin and certainly hasn't been recorded before." He took one of her hands between both of his. "Your father would've been proud of you."

Stunned, she stared at him. Emotions raced through her with such velocity she had no way of controlling or channeling them. The hand holding the broken vase began to tremble. Quickly, she set it down in the basket again and rose.

"I'm going below," she managed and fled.

Proud of her. Kate put a hand over her mouth as she stumbled into the cabin. His pride, his love. Wasn't it all she'd really ever wanted from her father? Was it possible she could only gain it after his death?

She drank in deep gulps of air and struggled to level her emotions. No, she wanted to find the *Liberty,* she wanted to bring her father's dream to reality, have his name on a plaque in a museum with the artifacts they'd found. She owed him that. But she'd promised herself she'd find the *Liberty* for herself as well. For herself.

It was her choice, her first real decision to come in from the sidelines and act on her own. For herself, Kate thought again as she brought the first surge of emotion under control.

"Kate?"

She turned, and though she thought she was perfectly calm, Ky could see the turmoil in her eyes. Unsure how to handle it, he spoke practically.

"You'd better get out of that suit."

"But we're going back down."

"Not today." To prove his point he began to strip out of his own suit just as Marsh started the engines.

Automatically, she balanced herself as the boat turned. "Ky, we've got two more sets of tanks. There's no reason for us to go back when we're just getting started."

"Your first dive took most of the strength you've built up. If you want to dive tomorrow, you've got to take it slow today."

Her anger erupted so quickly, it left them both astonished. "The hell with that!" she exploded. "I'm sick to death of being treated as if I don't know my own limitations or my own mind and body."

Ky walked into the galley and picked up a can of beer. With a flick of his wrist, air hissed out. "I don't know what you're talking about."

"I lay in bed for the better part of a week because of pressure from you and Linda and anyone else who came around me. I'm not tolerating this any longer."

With one hand, he pushed dripping hair from his forehead as he lifted the can. "You're tolerating exactly what's necessary until I say differently."

"You say?" she tossed back. Cheeks flaming, she strode over to him. "I don't have to do what you say, or what anyone says. Not anymore. It's about time you remember just who's in charge of this salvage operation."

His eyes narrowed. "In charge?"

"I hired you. Seventy-five a day and twenty-five percent. Those were the terms. There was nothing in there about you running my life."

He abruptly went still. For a moment, all that could

be heard over the engines was her angry breathing. *Dollars and percents,* he thought with a deadly sort of calm. *Just dollars and percents.* "So that's what it comes down to?"

Too overwrought to see beyond her own anger, she continued to lash out. "We made an agreement. I fully intend to see that you get everything we arranged, but I won't have you telling me when I can go down. I won't have you judging when I'm well and when I'm not. I'm sick to death of being dictated to. And I won't be—not by you, not by anyone. Not any longer."

The metal of the can gave under his fingers. "Fine. You do exactly what you want, professor. But while you're about it, get yourself another diver. I'll send you a bill." Ky went up the cabin steps the way he came down. Quickly and without a sound.

With her hands gripped together, Kate sat down on the bunk and waited until she heard the engines stop again. She refused to think. Thinking hurt. She refused to feel. There was too much to feel. When she was certain she was in control, she stood and went up on deck.

Everything was exactly as she'd left it—the wire basket filled with bits of porcelain and tableware, her nearly depleted tanks. Ky was gone. Marsh walked over from the stern where he'd been waiting for her.

"You're going to need a hand with these."

Kate nodded and pulled a thigh length T-shirt over her tank suit. "Yes. I want to take everything back to my room at the hotel. I have to arrange for shipping."

"Okay." But instead of reaching down for the basket, he took her arm. "Kate, I don't like to give advice."

"Good." Then she swore at her own rudeness. "I'm sorry, Marsh. I'm feeling a little rough at the moment."

"I can see that, and I know things aren't always smooth for you and Ky. Look, he has a habit of closing himself up, of not saying everything that's on his mind. Or worse," Marsh added. "Of saying the first thing that comes to mind."

"He's perfectly free to do so. I came here for the specific purpose of finding and excavating the *Liberty*. If Ky and I can't deal together on a business level, I have to do without his help."

"Listen, he has a few blind spots."

"Marsh, you're his brother. Your allegiance is with him as it should be."

"I care about both of you."

She took a deep breath, refusing to let the emotion surface and carry her with it. "I appreciate that. The best thing you can do for me now, perhaps for both of us, is to tell me where I can rent a boat and some equipment. I'm going back out this afternoon."

"Kate."

"I'm going back out this afternoon," she repeated. "With or without your help."

Resigned, Marsh picked up the mesh basket. "All right, you can use mine."

It took the rest of the morning for Kate to arrange everything, including the resolution of a lengthy argument with Marsh. She refused to let him come with her, ending by saying she'd simply rent a boat and do without his assistance altogether. In the end, she stood at the helm of his boat alone and headed out to sea.

She craved the solitude. Almost in defiance, she pushed the throttle forward. If it was defiance, she didn't care, any more than she cared whom she was defying. It was vital to do this one act for herself.

She refused to think about Ky, about why she'd exploded at him. If her words had been harsh, they'd also been necessary. She comforted herself with that. For too long, for a lifetime, she'd been influenced by someone else's opinion, someone else's expectations.

Mechanically, she stopped the engines and put on her equipment, checking and rechecking as she went. She'd never gone down alone before. Even that seemed suddenly a vital thing to do.

With a last look at her compass, she took the mesh basket over the side.

As she went deep, a thrill went through her. She was alone. In acres and acres of sea, she was alone. The water parted for her like silk. She was in control, and her destiny was her own.

She didn't rush. Kate found she wanted that euphoric feeling of being isolated under the sea where only curious fish bothered to give her a passing glance. Ultimately, her only responsibility here was to herself. Briefly, she closed her eyes and floated. At last, only to herself.

When she reached the site, she felt a new surge of pride. This was something she'd done without her father. She wouldn't think of the whys or the hows now, but simply the triumph. For two centuries, it had waited.

And now, *she'd* found it. She circled the hole the prop-wash had created and began to fan using her hand.

Her first find was a dinner plate with a flamboyant floral pattern around the rim. She found one, then half a dozen, two of which were intact. On the back was the mark of an English potter. There were cups as well, dainty, exquisite English china that might have graced the table of a wealthy colonist, might have become a beloved heirloom, if nature hadn't interfered. Now they looked like something out of a horror show—crusted, misshapen with sea life. They couldn't have been more beautiful to her.

As she continued to fan, Kate nearly missed what appeared to be a dark sea shell. On closer examination she saw it was a silver coin. She couldn't make out the currency, but knew it didn't matter. It could just as easily be Spanish, as she'd read that Spanish currency had been used by all European nations with settlements in the New World.

The point was, it was a coin. The first coin. Though it was silver, not gold, and unidentifiable at the moment, she'd found it by herself.

Kate started to slip it into her goodie bag when her arm was jerked back.

The thrill of fear went wildly from her toes to her throat. The spear gun was on board the *Vortex*. She had no weapon. Before she could do more than turn in defense, she was caught by the shoulders with Ky's furious hands.

Terror died, but the anger in his eyes only incited her own. Damn him for frightening her, for interfering. Shaking him away, Kate signaled for him to leave. With one arm, he encircled her waist and started for the surface.

Only once did she even come close to breaking away from him. Ky simply banded his arm around her again, more tightly, until she had a choice between submitting or cutting off her own air.

When they broke the surface, Kate drew in breath to shout, but even in this, she was out-maneuvered.

"Idiot!" he shouted at her, dragging her to the ladder. "One day off your back and you jump into forty feet of water by yourself. I don't know why in hell I ever thought you had any brains."

Breathless, she heaved her tanks over the side. When she was on solid ground again, she intended to have her say. For now, she'd let him have his.

"I take my eyes off you for a couple hours and you go off half-cocked. If I'd murdered Marsh, it would have been on your head."

To her further fury, Kate saw that she'd boarded the *Vortex*. Marsh's boat was nowhere in sight.

"Where's the *Gull?*" she demanded.

"Marsh had the sense to tell me what you were doing." The words came out like bullets as he stripped off his gear. "I didn't kill him because I needed him to come out with me and take the *Gull* back." He stood in front of her, dripping, and as furious as she'd ever seen him. "Don't you have any more sense than to dive out here alone?"

She tossed her head back. "Don't you?"

Infuriated, he grabbed her and started to peel the

wet suit from her himself. "We're not talking about me, damn it. I've been diving since I was six. I know the currents."

"*I* know the currents."

"And I haven't been flat on my back for a week."

"I was flat on my back for a week because you were overreacting." She struggled away from him, and because the wet suit was already down to her waist, peeled it off. "You've no right to tell me when and where I can dive, Ky. Superior strength gives you no right to drag me up when I'm in the middle of salvaging."

"The hell with what I have a right to do." Grabbing her again, he shook her with more violence than he'd ever shown her. A dozen things might have happened to her in the thirty minutes she'd been down. A dozen things he knew too well. "I make my own rights. You're not going down alone if I have to chain you up to stop it."

"You told me to get another diver," she said between her teeth. "Until I do, I dive alone."

"You threw that damn business arrangement in my face. Percentages. Lousy percentages and a daily rate. Do you know how that made me feel?"

"No!" she shouted, pushing him away. "No, I don't know how that made you feel. I don't know how anything makes you feel. You don't tell me." Dragging both hands through her dripping hair she walked away. "We agreed to the terms. That's all I know."

"That was before."

"Before what?" she demanded. Tears brimmed for

no reason she could name, but she blinked them back again. "Before I slept with you?"

"Damn it, Kate." He was across the deck, backing her into the rail before she could take a breath. "Are you trying to get at me for something I did or didn't do four years ago? I don't even know what it is. I don't know what you want from me or what you don't want and I'm sick of trying to outguess you."

"I don't want to be pushed into a corner," she told him fiercely. "That's what I don't want. I don't want to be expected to fall in passively with someone else's plans for me. That's what I don't want. I don't want it assumed that I simply don't have any personal goals or wishes of my own. Or any basic competence of my own. *That's* what I don't want!"

"Fine." They were both losing control, but he no longer gave a damn. Ky ripped off his wet suit and tossed it aside. "You just remember something, lady. I don't expect anything of you and I don't assume. Once maybe, but not anymore. There was only one person who ever pushed you into a corner and it wasn't me." He hurled his mask across the deck where it bounced and smacked into the side. "I'm the one who let you go."

She stiffened. Even with the distance between them he could see her eyes frost over. "I won't discuss my father with you."

"You caught on real quick though, didn't you?"

"You resented him. You—"

"I?" Ky interrupted. "Maybe you better look at yourself, Kate."

"I loved him," she said passionately. "All my life I tried to show him. You don't understand."

"How do you know that I don't understand?" he exploded. "Don't you know I can see what you're feeling every time we find something down there? Do you think I'm so blind I don't see that you're hurting because *you* found it, not him? Don't you think it tears me apart to see that you punish yourself for not being what you think he wanted you to be? And I'm tired," he continued as her breath started to hitch. "Damn tired of being compared to and measured by a man you loved without ever being close to him."

"I don't." She covered her face, hating the weakness but powerless against it. "I don't do that. I only want…"

"What?" he demanded. "What do you want?"

"I didn't cry when he died," she said into her hands. "I didn't cry, not even at the funeral. I owed him tears, Ky. I owed him something."

"You don't owe him anything you didn't already give him over and over again." Frustrated, he dragged a hand through his hair before he went to her. "Kate." Because words seemed useless, he simply gathered her close.

"I didn't cry."

"Cry now," he murmured. He pressed his lips to the top of her head. "Cry now."

So she did, desperately, for what she'd never been able to quite touch, for what she'd never been able to quite hold. She'd ached for love, for the simple companionship of understanding. She wept because it was too late for that now from her father. She wept because she wasn't certain she could ask for love again from anyone else.

Ky held her, lowering her onto the bench as he cradled her in his lap. He couldn't offer her words of comfort. They were the most difficult words for him to come by. He could only offer her a place to weep, and silence.

As the tears began to pass, she kept her face against his shoulder. There was such simplicity there, though it came from a man of complications. Such gentleness, though it sprang from a restless nature. "I couldn't mourn for him before," she murmured. "I'm not sure why."

"You don't have to cry to mourn."

"Maybe not," she said wearily. "I don't know. But it's true, what you said. I've wanted to do all this for him because he'll never have the chance to finish what he started. I don't know if you can understand, but I feel if I do this I'll have done everything I could. For him, and for myself."

"Kate." Ky tipped back her head so he could see her face. Her eyes were puffy, rimmed with red. "I don't have to understand. I just have to love you."

He felt her stiffen in his arms and immediately cursed himself. Why was it he never said things to her the way they should be said? Sweetly, calmly, softly. She was a woman who needed soft words, and he was a man who always struggled with them.

She didn't move, and for a long, long moment, they stayed precisely as they were.

"Do you?" she managed after a moment.

"Do I what?"

Would he make her drag it from him? "Love me?"

"Kate." Frustrated, he drew away from her. "I don't know how else to show you. You want bouquets of flowers, bottles of French champagne, poems? Damn it, I'm not made that way."

"I want a straight answer."

He let out a short breath. Sometimes her very calmness drove him to distraction. "I've always loved you. I've never stopped."

That went through her, sharp, hot, with a mixture of pain and pleasure she wasn't quite sure how to deal with. Slowly, she rose out of his arms, and walking across the deck, looked out to sea. The buoys that marked the site bobbed gently. Why were there no buoys in life to show you the way?

"You never told me."

"Look, I can't even count the number of women I've said it to." When she turned back with her brow raised, he rose, uncomfortable. "It was easy to say it to them because it didn't mean anything. It's a hell of a lot harder to get the words out when you mean them, and when you're afraid someone's going to back away from you the minute you do."

"I wouldn't have done that."

"You backed away, you went away for four years, when I asked you to stay."

"You asked me to stay," she reminded him. "You asked me not to go back to Connecticut, but to move in with you. Just like that. No promises, no commitment, no sign that you had any intention of building a life with me. I had responsibilities."

"To do what your father wanted you to do."

She swallowed that. It was true in its way. "All right, yes. But you never said you loved me."

He came closer. "I'm telling you now."

She nodded, but her heart was in her throat. "And I'm not backing away. I'm just not sure I can take the next step. I'm not sure you can either."

"You want a promise."

She shook her head, not certain what she'd do if indeed he gave her one. "I want time, for both of us. It seems we both have a lot of thinking to do."

"Kate." Impatient, he came to her, taking her hands. They trembled. "Some things you don't have to think about. Some things you can think about too much."

"You've lived your life a certain way a long time, and I mine," she said quickly. "Ky, I've just begun to change—to feel the change. I don't want to make a mistake, not with you. It's too important. With time—"

"We've lost four years," he interrupted. He needed to resolve something, he discovered, and quickly. "I can't wait any longer to hear it if it's inside you."

Kate let out the breath she'd been holding. If he could ask, she could give. It would be enough. "I love you, Ky. I never stopped either. I never told you when I should have."

He felt the weight drain from his body as he cupped her face. "You're telling me now."

It was enough.

Chapter 11

Love. Kate had read hundreds of poems about that one phenomenon. She'd read, analyzed and taught from countless novels where love was the catalyst to all action, all emotion. With her students, she'd dissected innumerable lines from books, plays and verse that all led back to that one word.

Now, for perhaps the first time in her life, it was offered to her. She found it had more power than could possibly be taught. She found she didn't understand it.

Ky hadn't Byron's way with words, or Keat's romantic phrasing. What he'd said, he'd said simply. It meant everything. She still didn't understand it.

She could, in her own way, understand her feelings. She'd loved Ky for years, since that first revelation one summer when she'd come to know what it meant to want to fully share oneself with another.

But what, she wondered, did Ky find in her to love? It wasn't modesty that caused her to ask herself this question, but the basic practicality she'd grown up with. Where there was an effect, there was a cause. Where there was reaction, there was action. The world ran on this principle. She'd won Ky's love—but how?

Kate had no insecurity about her own intelligence. Perhaps, if anything, she overrated her mind, and it was this that caused her to underrate her other attributes.

He was a man of action, of restless and mercurial nature. She, on the other hand, considered herself almost blandly level. While she thrived on routine, Ky thrived on the unexpected. Why should he love her? Yet he did.

If she accepted that, it was vital to come to a resolution. Love led to commitment. It was there that she found the wall solid, without footholds.

He lived on a remote island because he was basically a loner, because he preferred moving at his own pace, in his own time. She was a teacher who lived by a day-to-day schedule. Without the satisfaction of giving knowledge, she'd stagnate. In the structured routine of a college town, Ky would go mad.

Because she could find no compromise, Kate opted to do what she'd decided to do in the beginning. She'd ride with the current until the summer was over. Perhaps by then, an answer would come.

They spoke no more of percentages. Kate quietly dropped the notion of keeping her hotel room. These, she told herself, were small matters when so much more hung in the balance during her second summer with Ky.

The days went quickly with her and Ky working together with the prop-wash or by hand. Slowly, painstakingly, they uncovered more salvage. The candlesticks had turned out to be pewter, but the coin had been Spanish silver. Its date had been 1748.

In the next two-week period, they uncovered much more—a heavy intricately carved silver platter, more china and porcelain, and in another area dozens of nails and tools.

Kate documented each find on film, for practical and personal reasons. She needed the neat, orderly way of keeping track of the salvage. She wanted to be able to look back on those pictures and remember how she felt when Ky held up a crusted teacup or an oxidized tankard. She'd be able to look and remember how he'd played an outstaring game with a large lazy bluefish. And lost.

More than once Ky had suggested the use of a larger ship equipped for salvage. They discussed it, and its advantages, but they never acted on it. Somehow, they both felt they wanted to move slowly, working basically with their own hands until there came a time when they had to make a decision.

The cannons and the heavier pieces of ship's planking couldn't be brought up without help, so these they left to the sea for the time being. They continued to use tanks, rather than changing to a surface-supplied source of air, so they had to surface and change gear every hour or so. A diving rig would have saved time—but that wasn't their goal.

Their methods weren't efficient by professional salvor standards, but they had an unspoken agreement. Stretch time. Make it last.

The nights they spent together in the big four-poster, talking of the day's finds, or of tomorrow's, making love, marking time. They didn't speak of the future that loomed after the summer's end. They never talked of what they'd do the day after the treasure was found.

The treasure became their focus, something that kept them from reaching out when the other wasn't ready.

The day was fiercely hot as they prepared to dive. The sun was baking. It was mid-July. She'd been in Ocracoke for a month. For all her practicality, Kate told herself it was an omen. Today was the turning point of summer.

Even as she pulled the wet suit up to her waist, sweat beaded on her back. She could almost taste the cool freshness of the water. The sun glared on her tanks as she lifted them, bouncing off to spear her eyes.

"Here." Taking them from her, Ky strapped them onto her back, checking the gauges himself. "The water's going to feel like heaven."

"Yeah." Marsh tipped up a quart bottle of juice. "Think of me baking up here while you're having all the fun."

"Keep the throttle low, brother," Ky said with a grin as he climbed over the side. "We'll bring you a reward."

"Make it something round and shiny with a date stamped on it," Marsh called back, then winked at Kate as she started down the ladder. "Good luck."

She felt the excitement as the water lapped over her ankles. "Today, I don't think I need it."

The noise of the prop-wash disturbed the silence of the water, but not the mystery. Even with technology and equipment, the water remained an enigma, part beauty, part danger. They went deeper and deeper until they reached the site with the scoops in the silt caused by their earlier explorations.

They'd already found what they thought had been the officers' and passengers' quarters, identifying it by the discovery of a snuff box, a silver bedside candle-holder and Ky's personal favorite—a decorated sword. The few pieces of jewelry they'd found indicated a personal cache rather than cargo.

Though they fully intended to excavate in the area of the cache, it was the cargo they sought. Using the passengers' quarters and the galley as points of reference, they concentrated on what should have been the stern of the ship.

There were ballast rocks to deal with. This entailed a slow, menial process that required moving them by hand to an area they'd already excavated. It was time consuming, unrewarding and necessary. Still, Kate found something peaceful in the mindless work, and something fascinating about the ability to do it under fathoms of water with basically little effort. She could move a ballast pile as easily as Ky, whereas on land, she would have tired quickly.

Reaching down to clear another area, Ky's fingers brushed something small and hard. Curious, he fanned aside a thin layer of silt and picked up what at first looked like a tab on a can of beer. As he brought it closer, he saw it was much more refined, and though there were layers of crust on the knob of the circle, he felt his heart give a quick jerk.

He'd heard of diamonds in the rough, but he'd never thought to find one by simply reaching for it. He was no expert, but as he painstakingly cleaned what he could from the stone, he judged it to be at least two carats. With a tap on Kate's shoulder, he got her attention.

It gave him a great deal of pleasure to see her eyes widen and to hear the muffled sound of her surprise. Together, they turned it over and over again. It was dull and dirty, but the gem was there.

They were finding bits and pieces of civilization. Perhaps a woman had worn the ring while dining with the captain on her way to America. Perhaps some British officer had carried it in his vest pocket, waiting to give it to the woman he'd hoped to marry. It might have belonged to an elderly widow, or a young bride. The mystery of it, and its tangibility, were more precious than the stone itself. It was…lasting.

Ky held it out to her, offering. Their routine had fallen into a finders-keepers arrangement, in that whoever found a particular piece carried it in their own bag to the surface where everything was carefully cataloged on film and paper. Kate looked at the small, water-dulled piece of the past in Ky's fingers.

Was he offering her the ring because it was a woman's fancy, or was he offering her something else? Unsure, she shook her head, pointing to the bag on his belt. If he were asking her something, she needed it to be done with words.

Ky dropped the ring into his bag, secured it, then went back to work.

He thought he understood her, in some ways. In other ways, Ky found she was as much a mystery as the sea. What did she want from him? If it was love, he'd given her that. If it was time, they were both running out of it. He wanted to demand, was accustomed to demanding, yet she blocked his ability with a look.

She said she'd changed—that she was just beginning to feel in control of her life. He thought he understood that, as well as her fierce need for independence. And yet... He'd never known anything but independence. He, too, had changed. He needed her to give him the boundaries and the borders that came with dependence. His for her, and hers for him. Was the timing wrong again? Would it ever be right?

Damn it, he wanted her, he thought as he heaved another rock out of his way. Not just for today, but for tomorrow. Not tied against him, but bound to him. Why couldn't she understand that?

She loved him. It was something she murmured in the night when she was sleepy and caught close against him. She wasn't a woman to use words unless they had meaning. Yet with the love he offered and the love she returned, she'd begun to hold something back from him, as though he could have only a portion of her, but not all. Edged with frustration, he cleared more ballast. He needed, and would have, all.

Marriage? Was he thinking of marriage? Kate found

herself flustered and uneasy. She'd never expected Ky to look for that kind of commitment, that kind of permanency. Perhaps she'd misread him. After all, it was difficult to be certain of someone's intention, yet she knew just how clearly Ky and she had been able to communicate underwater.

There was so much to consider, so many things to weigh. He wouldn't understand that, Kate mused. Ky was a man who made decisions in an instant and took the consequences. He wouldn't think about all the variables, all the what-ifs, all the maybes. She had to think about them all. She simply knew no other way.

Kate watched the silt and sand blowing away, causing a cuplike indentation to form on the ocean floor. Outside influences, she mused. They could eat away at the layers and uncover the core, but sometimes what was beneath couldn't stand up to the pressure.

Is that what would happen between her and Ky? How would their relationship hold up under the pressure of variant lifestyles—the demands of her profession and the free-wheeling tone of his? Would it stay intact, or would it begin to sift away, layer by layer? How much of herself would he ask her to give? And in loving, how much of herself would she lose?

It was a possibility she couldn't ignore, a threat she needed to build a solid defense against. Time. Perhaps time was the answer. But summer was waning.

The force of the wash made a small object spin up, out of the layer of silt and into the water. Kate grabbed at it and the sharp edge scraped her palm. Curious, she turned it over for examination. A buckle? she wondered.

The shape seemed to indicate it, and she could just make out a fastening. Even as she started to hold it out for Ky another, then another was pushed off the ocean bed.

Shoe buckles, Kate realized, astonished. Dozens of them. No, she realized as more and more began to twist up in the water's spin and reel away. Hundreds. With a quick frenzy, she began to gather what she could. More than hundreds, she discovered as her heart thudded. There were thousands of them, literally thousands.

She held a buckle in her hand and looked at Ky in triumph. They'd found the cargo. There'd been shoe buckles on the manifest of the *Liberty*. Five thousand of them. Nothing but a merchantman carried something like that in bulk.

Proof. She waved the buckle, her arm sweeping out in slow motion to take in the swarm of them swirling away from the wash and dropping again. Proof, her mind shouted out. The cargo-hold was beneath them. And the treasure. They had only to reach it.

Ky took her hands and nodded, knowing what was in her mind. Beneath his fingers he could feel the race of her pulse. He wanted that for her, the excitement, the thrill that came from discovering something only half believed in. She brought the back of his hand to her cheek, her eyes laughing, buckles spinning around them. Kate wanted to laugh until she was too weak to stand. Five thousand shoe buckles would guide them to a chest of gold.

Kate saw the humor in his eyes and knew Ky's thoughts ran along the same path as hers. He pointed to himself, then thumbs up. With a minimum of signaling, he told Kate that he would surface to tell Marsh to shut off the engines. It was time to work by hand.

Excited, she nodded. She wanted only to begin. Resting near the bottom, Kate watched Ky go up and out of sight. Oddly, she found she needed time alone. She'd shared the heady instant of discovery with Ky, and now she needed to absorb it.

The *Liberty* was beneath her, the ship her father had searched for. The dream he'd kept close, carefully researching, meticulously calculating, but never finding.

Joy and sorrow mixed as she gathered a handful of the buckles and placed them carefully in her bag. For him. In that moment she felt she'd given him everything she'd always needed to.

Carefully, and this time for personal reasons rather than the catalog, she began to shoot pictures. Years from now, she thought. Years and years from now, she'd look at a snapshot of swirling silt and drifting pieces of metal, and she'd remember. Nothing could ever take that moment of quiet satisfaction from her.

She glanced up at the sudden silence. The wash had stilled. Ky had reached the surface. Silt and the pieces of crusted, decorated metal began to settle again without the agitation of the wash. The sea was a world without sound, without movement.

Kate looked down at the scoop in the ocean floor. They were nearly there. For a moment she was tempted to begin to fan and search by herself, but she'd wait for Ky. They began together, and they'd finish together. Content, she watched for his return.

When Kate saw the movement above her, she started

to signal. Her hand froze in place, then her arm, her shoulder and the rest of her body, degree by degree. It came smoothly through the water, sleek and silent. Deadly.

The noise of the prop-wash had kept the sea life away. Now the abrupt quiet brought out the curious. Among the schools of harmless fish glided the long bulletlike shape of a shark.

Kate was still, hardly daring to breathe as she feared even the trail of bubbles might attract him. He moved without haste, apparently not interested in her. Perhaps he'd already hunted successfully that day. But even with a full belly, a shark would attack what annoyed his uncertain temper.

She gauged him to be ten feet in length. Part of her mind registered that he was fairly small for what she recognized as a tiger shark. They could easily double that length. But she knew the jaws, those large sickle-shaped teeth, would be strong, merciless and fatal.

If she remained still, the chances were good that he would simply go in search of more interesting waters. Isn't that what she'd read sitting cozily under lamplight at her own desk? Isn't that what Ky had told her once when they'd shared a quiet lunch on his boat? All that seemed so remote, so unreal now, as she looked above and saw the predator between herself and the surface.

It was movement that attracted them, she reminded herself as she forced her mind to function. The movement a swimmer made with kicking feet and sweeping arms.

Don't panic. She forced herself to breathe slowly. No

sudden moves. She forced her nervous hands to form tight, still fists.

He was no more than ten feet away. Kate could see the small black eyes and the gentle movement of his gills. Breathing shallowly, she never took her eyes from his. She had only to be perfectly still and wait for him to swim on.

But Ky. Kate's mouth went dry as she looked toward the direction where Ky had disappeared moments before. He'd be coming back, any minute, unaware of what was lurking near the bottom. Waiting. Cruising.

The shark would sense the disturbance in the water with the uncanny ability the hunter had. The kick of Ky's feet, the swing of his arms would attract the shark long before Kate would have a chance to warn him of any danger.

He'd be unaware, helpless, and then… Her blood seemed to freeze. She'd heard of the sensation but now she experienced it. Cold seemed to envelop her. Terror made her head light. Kate bit down on her lip until pain cleared her thoughts. She wouldn't stand by idly while Ky came blindly into a death trap.

Glancing down, she saw the spear gun. It was over five feet away and unloaded for safety. Safety, she thought hysterically. She'd never loaded one, much less shot one. And first, she'd have to get to it. There'd only be one chance. Knowing she'd have no time to settle her nerves, Kate made her move.

She kept her eyes on the shark as she inched slowly toward the gun. At the moment, he seemed to be merely cruising, not particularly interested in anything. He never even glanced her way. Perhaps he would move on before Ky came back, but she needed the weapon. Fingers shaking, she gripped the butt of the gun. Time seemed to crawl. Her movements were so slow, so measured, she hardly seemed to move at all. But her mind whirled.

Even as she gripped the spear she saw the shape that glided down from the surface. The shark turned lazily to the left. To Ky.

No! her mind screamed as she rammed the spear into position. Her only thought that of protecting what she loved. Kate swam forward without hesitation, taking a path between Ky and the shark. She had to get close.

Her mind was cold now, with fear, with purpose. For the second time, she saw those small, deadly eyes. This time, they focused on her. If she'd never seen true evil before, Kate knew she faced it now. This was cruelty, and a death that wouldn't come easily.

The shark moved toward her with a speed that made her heart stop. His jaws opened. There was a black, black cave behind them.

Ky dove quickly, wanting to get back to Kate, wanting to search for what had brought them back together. If it was the treasure she needed to settle her mind, he'd find it. With it, they could open whatever doors they needed to open, lock whatever needed to be locked. Excitement drummed through him as he dove deeper.

When he spotted the shark, he pulled up short. He'd felt that deep primitive fear before, but never so sharply. Though it was less than useless against such a predator, he reached for his diver's knife. He'd left Kate alone. Cold-bloodedly, he set for the attack.

Like a rocket, Kate shot up between himself and the shark. Terror such as he'd never known washed over him. Was she mad? Was she simply unaware? Giving no time to thought, Ky barreled through the water toward her.

He was too far away. He knew it even as the panic hammered into him. The shark would be on her before he was close enough to sink the knife in.

When he saw what she held in her hand, and realized her purpose he somehow doubled his speed. Everything was in slow motion, and yet it seemed to happen in the blink of an eye. He saw the gaping hole in the shark's mouth as it closed in on Kate. For the first time in his life, prayers ran through him like water.

The spear shot out, sinking deep through the shark's flesh. Instinctively, Kate let herself drop as the shark came forward full of anger and pain. He would follow her now, she knew. If the spear didn't work, he would be on her in moments.

Ky saw blood gush from the wound. It wouldn't be enough. The shark jerked as if to reject the spear, and slowed his pace. Just enough. Teeth bared, Ky fell on its back, hacking with the knife as quickly as the water would allow. The shark turned, furious. Using all his strength, Ky turned with it, forcing the knife into the underbelly and ripping down. It ran through his mind that he was holding death, and it was as cold as the poets said.

From a few feet away, Kate watched the battle. She was numb, body and mind. Blood spurted out to dissipate in the water. Letting the empty gun fall, she too reached for her knife and swam forward.

But it was over. One instant the fish and Ky were as one form, locked together. Then they were separate as the body of the shark sank lifelessly toward the bottom. She saw the eyes one last time.

Her arm was gripped painfully. Limp, Kate allowed herself to be dragged to the surface. Safe. It was the only clear thought her mind could form. He was safe.

Too breathless to speak, Ky pulled her toward the ladder, tanks and all. He saw her slip near the top and roll onto the deck. Even as he swung over himself, he saw two fins slice through the water and disappear below where the blood drew them.

"What the hell—" Jumping up from his seat, Marsh ran across the deck to where Kate still lay, gasping for air.

"Sharks." Ky cut off the word as he knelt beside her. "I had to bring her up fast. Kate." Ky reached a hand beneath her neck, lifting her up as he began to take off her tanks. "Are you dizzy? Do you have any pain— your knees, elbows?"

Though she was still gasping for air, she shook her head. "No, no, I'm all right." She knew he worried about decompression sickness and tried to steady herself to reassure him. "Ky, we weren't that deep after—when we came up."

He nodded, grimly acknowledging that she was winded, not incoherent. Standing, he pulled off his mask and heaved it across the deck. Temper helped alleviate the helpless shaking. Kate merely drew her knees up and rested her forehead on them.

"Somebody want to fill me in?" Marsh asked, glancing from one to the other. "I left off when Ky came up raving about shoe buckles."

"Cargo-hold," Kate murmured. "We found it."

"So Ky said." Marsh glanced at his brother whose knuckles were whitening against the rail as he looked out to sea. "Run into some company down there?"

"There was a shark. A tiger."

"She nearly got herself killed," Ky explained. Fury was a direct result of fear, and just as deadly. "She swam right in front of him." Before Marsh could make any comment, Ky turned on Kate. "Did you forget everything I taught you?" he demanded. "You manage to get a doctorate but you can't remember that you're supposed to minimize your movements when a shark's cruising? You know that arm and leg swings attract them, but you swim in front of him, flailing around as though you wanted to shake hands—holding a damn spear gun that's just as likely to annoy him as do any real damage. If I hadn't been coming down just then, he'd have torn you to pieces."

Kate lifted her head slowly. Whatever emotion she'd felt up to that moment was replaced by an anger so deep it overshadowed everything. Meticulously she removed her flippers, her mask and her weight belt before she rose. "If you hadn't been coming down just then," she said precisely, "there'd have been no reason for me to swim in front of him." Turning, she walked to the steps and down into the cabin.

For a full minute there was utter silence on deck. Above, a gull screeched, then swerved west. Knowing there'd be no more dives that day, Marsh went to the helm. As he glanced over he saw the deep stain of blood on the water's surface.

"It's customary," he began with his back to his brother, "to thank someone when they save your life." Without waiting for a comment, he switched on the engine.

Shaken, Ky ran a hand through his hair. Some of the shark's blood had stained his fingers. Standing still, he stared at it.

Not through carelessness, he thought with a jolt. It had been deliberate. Kate had deliberately put herself in the path of the shark. For him. She'd risked her life to save him. He ran both hands over his face before he started below deck.

He saw her sitting on a bunk with a glass in her hand. A bottle of brandy sat at her feet. When she lifted the glass to her lips her hand shook lightly. Beneath the tan the sun had given her, her face was drawn and pale. No one had ever put him first so completely, so unselfishly. It left him without any idea of what to say.

"Kate…"

"I'm not in the mood to be shouted at right now," she told him before she drank again. "If you need to vent your temper, you'll have to save it."

"I'm not going to shout." Because he felt every bit as unsteady as she did, he sat beside her and lifted the bottle, drinking straight from it. The brandy ran hot and strong through him. "You scared the hell out of me."

"I'm not going to apologize for what I did."

"I should thank you." He drank again and felt the

nerves in his stomach ease. "The point is, you had no business doing what you did. Nothing but blind luck kept you from being torn up down there."

Turning her head, she stared at him. "I should've stayed safe and sound on the bottom while you dealt with the shark—with your diver's knife."

He met the look levelly. "Yes."

"And you'd have done that, if it'd been me?"

"That's different."

"Oh." Glass in hand, she rose. She took a moment to study him, that raw-boned, dark face, the dripping hair that needed a trim, the eyes that reflected the sea. "Would you care to explain that little piece of logic to me?"

"I don't have to explain it, it just is." He tipped the bottle back again. It helped to cloud his imagination which kept bringing images of what might have happened to her.

"No, it just isn't, and that's one of your major problems."

"Kate, have you any idea what could have happened if you hadn't lucked out and hit a vital spot with that spear?"

"Yes." She drained her glass and felt some of the edge dull. The fear might come back again unexpectedly, but she felt she was strong enough to deal with it. And the anger. No matter how it slashed at her, she would put herself between him and danger again. "I understand perfectly. Now, I'm going up with Marsh."

"Wait a minute." He stood to block her way. "Can't you see that I couldn't stand it if anything happened to you? I want to take care of you. I need to keep you safe."

"While you take all the risks?" she countered. "Is that supposed to be the balance of our relationship, Ky? You man, me woman? I bake bread, you hunt the meat?"

"Damn it, Kate, it's not as basic as that."

"It's just as basic as that," she tossed back. The color had come back to her face. Her legs were steady again. And she would be heard. "You want me to be quiet and content—and amenable to the way you choose to live. You want me to do as you say, bend to your will, and yet I know how you felt about my father."

It didn't seem she had the energy to be angry any longer. She was just weary, bone weary from slamming herself up against a wall that didn't seem ready to budge.

"I spent all my life doing what it pleased him to have me do," she continued in calmer tones. "No waves, no problems, no rebellion. He gave me a nod of approval, but no true respect and certainly no true affection. Now, you're asking me to do the same thing again with you." She felt no tears, only that weariness of spirit. "Why do you suppose the only two men I've ever loved should want me to be so utterly pliant to their will? Why do you suppose I lost both of them because I tried so hard to do just that?"

"No." He put his hands on her shoulders. "No, that's not true. It's not what I want from you or for you. I just want to take care of you."

She shook her head. "What's the difference, Ky?" she whispered. "What the hell's the difference?" Pushing past him, Kate went out on deck.

Chapter 12

Because in her quiet, immovable way Kate had demanded it, Ky left her alone. Perhaps it was for the best as it gave him time to think and to reassess what he wanted.

He realized that because of his fear for her, because of his need to care for her, he'd hurt her and damaged their already tenuous relationship.

On a certain level, she'd hit the mark in her accusations. He did want her to be safe and cared for while he sweated and took the risks. It was his nature to protect what he loved—in Kate's case, perhaps too much. It was also his nature to want other wills bent to his. He wanted Kate, and was honest enough to admit that he'd already outlined the terms in his own mind.

Her father's quiet manipulating had infuriated Ky and yet, he found himself doing the same thing. Not so quietly, he admitted, not nearly as subtly, but he was doing the same thing. Still, it wasn't for the same reasons. He wanted Kate to be with him, to align herself to him. It was as simple as that. He was certain, if she'd just let him, that he could make her happy.

But he never fully considered that she'd have demands or terms of her own. Until now, Ky hadn't thought how he'd adjust to them.

The light of dawn was quiet as Ky added the finishing touches to the lettering on his sailboat. For most of the night, he'd worked in the shed, giving Kate her time alone, and himself the time to think. Now that the night was over, only one thing remained clear. He loved her. But it had come home to him that it might not be enough. Though impatience continued to push at him, he reined it in. Perhaps he had to leave it to her to show him what would be.

For the next few days, they would concentrate on excavating the cargo that had sunk two centuries before. The longer they searched, the more the treasure became a symbol for him. If he could give it to her, it would be the end of the quest for both of them. Once it was over, they'd both have what they wanted. She, the fulfillment of her father's dream, and he, the satisfaction of seeing her freed from it.

Ky closed the shed doors behind him and headed back for the house. In a few days, he thought with a glance over his shoulder, he'd have something else to give her. Something else to ask her.

He was still some feet away from the house when he

smelled the morning scents of bacon and coffee drifting through the kitchen windows. When he entered, Kate was standing at the stove, a long T-shirt over her tank suit, her feet bare, her hair loose. He could see the light dusting of freckles over the bridge of her nose, and the pale soft curve of her lips.

His need to gather her close rammed into him with such power, he had to stop and catch his breath. "Kate—"

"I thought since we'd be putting in a long day we should have a full breakfast." She'd heard him come in, sensed it. Because it made her knees weak, she spoke briskly. "I'd like to get an early start."

He watched her drop eggs into the skillet where the white began to sizzle and solidify around the edges. "Kate, I'd like to talk to you."

"I've been thinking we might consider renting a salvage ship after all," she interrupted, "and perhaps hiring another couple of divers. Excavating the cargo's going to be very slow work with just the two of us. It's certainly time we looked into lifting bags and lines."

Long days in the sun had lightened her hair. There were shades upon shades of variation so that as it flowed it reminded him of the smooth soft pelt of a deer. "I don't want to talk business now."

"It's not something we can put off too much longer." Efficiently, she scooped up the eggs and slid them onto plates. "I'm beginning to think we should expedite the excavation rather than dragging it out for what may very well be several more weeks. Then, of course, if we're talking about excavating the entire site, it would be months."

"Not now." Ky turned off the burner under the skillet. Taking both plates from Kate, he set them on the table. "Look, I have to do something, and I'm not sure I'll do it very well."

Turning, Kate took silverware from the drawer and went to the table. "What?"

"Apologize." When she looked back at him in her cool, quiet way, he swore. "No, I won't do it well."

"It isn't necessary."

"Yes, it's necessary. Sit down." He let out a long breath as she remained standing. "Please," he added, then took a chair himself. Without a word, Kate sat across from him. "You saved my life yesterday." Even saying it aloud, he felt uneasy about it. "It was no less than that. I never could have taken that shark with my diver's knife. The only reason I did was because you'd weakened and distracted him."

Kate lifted her coffee and drank as though they were discussing the weather. It was the only way she had of blocking out images of what might have been. "Yes."

With a frustrated laugh, Ky stabbed at his eggs. "Not going to make it easy on me, are you?"

"No, I don't think I am."

"I've never been that scared," he said quietly. "Not for myself, certainly not for anyone else. I thought he had you." He looked up and met her calm, patient eyes. "I was still too far away to do anything about it. If…"

"Sometimes it's best not to think about the ifs."

"All right." He nodded and reached for her hand.

"Kate, realizing you put yourself in danger to protect me only made it worse somehow. The possibility of anything happening to you was bad enough, but the idea of it happening because of me was unbearable."

"You would've protected me."

"Yes, but—"

"There shouldn't be any buts, Ky."

"Maybe there shouldn't be," he agreed, "but I can't promise there won't be."

"I've changed." The fact filled her with an odd sense of power and unease. "For too many years I've channeled my own desires because I thought somehow that approval could be equated with love. I know better now."

"I'm not your father, Kate."

"No, but you also have a way of imposing your will on me. My fault to a point." Her voice was calm, level, as it was when she lectured her students. She hadn't slept while Ky had spent his hours in the shed. Like him, she'd spent her time in thought, in search for the right answers. "Four years ago, I had to give to one of you and deny the other. It broke my heart. Today, I know I have to answer to myself first." With her breakfast hardly touched, she took her plate to the sink. "I love you, Ky," she murmured. "But I have to answer to myself first."

Rising, he went to her and laid his hands on her shoulders. Somehow the strength that suddenly seemed so powerful in her both attracted him yet left him uneasy. "Okay." When she turned into his arms, he felt the world settle a bit. "Just let me know what the answer is."

"When I can." She closed her eyes and held tight. "When I can."

* * *

For three long days they dove, working away the silt to find new discoveries. With a small air lift and their own hands, they found the practical, the beautiful and the ordinary. They came upon more than eight thousand of the ten thousand decorated pipes on the *Liberty*'s manifest. At least half of them, to Kate's delight, had their bowls intact. They were clay, long-stemmed pipes with the bowls decorated with oak leaves or bunches of grapes and flowers. In a heady moment of pleasure, she snapped Ky's picture as he held one up to his lips.

She knew that at auction, they would more than pay for the investment she'd made. And, with them, the donation she'd make to a museum in her father's name was steadily growing. But more than this, the discovery of so many pipes on a wreck added force to their claim that the ship was English.

There were also snuff boxes, again thousands, leaving literally no doubt in her mind that they'd found the merchantman *Liberty*. They found tableware, some of it elegant, some basic utility-ware, but again in quantity. Their list of salvage grew beyond anything Kate had imagined, but they found no chest of gold.

They took turns hauling their finds to the surface, using an inverted plastic trash can filled with air to help them lift. Even with this, they stored the bulk of it on the sea floor. They were working alone again, without a need for Marsh to man the prop-wash. As it had been in the beginning, the project became a personal chore for only the two of them. What they found became a personal triumph. What they didn't find, a personal disappointment.

Kate delegated herself to deal with the snuff boxes, transporting them to the mesh baskets. Already, she was planning to clean several of them herself as part of the discovery. Beneath the layers of time there might be something elegant, ornate or ugly. She didn't believe it mattered what she found, as long as she found it.

Tea, sugar and other perishables the merchant ship had carried were long since gone without a trace. What she and Ky found now were the solid pieces of civilization that had survived centuries in the sea. A pipe meant for an eighteenth-century man had never reached the New World. It should have made her sad but, because it had survived, because she could hold it in her hand more than two hundred years later, Kate felt a quiet triumph. Some things last, whatever the odds.

Reaching down, she disturbed something that lay among the jumbled snuff boxes. Automatically, she jerked her hand back. Memories of the stingray and other dangers were still very fresh. When the small round object clinked against the side of a box and lay still, her heart began to pound. Almost afraid to touch, Kate reached for it. Between her fingers, she held a gold coin from another era.

Though she had read it was likely, she hadn't expected it to be as bright and shiny as the day it was minted. The pieces of silver they'd found had blackened, and other metal pieces had corroded, some of them crystalized almost beyond recognition. Yet, the gold, the small coin she'd plucked from the sea floor, winked back at her.

Its origin was English. The long-dead king stared out at her. The date was 1750.

"Ky!" Foolishly, she said his name. Though the sound was muffled and indistinguishable, he turned. Unable to wait, Kate swam toward him, clutching the coin. When she reached him, she took his hand and pressed the gold into his palm.

He knew at the moment of contact. He had only to look into her eyes. Taking her hand, he brought it to his lips. She'd found what she wanted. For no reason he could name, he felt empty. He pressed the coin back into her hand, closing her fingers over it tightly. The gold was hers.

Swimming beside her, Ky moved to the spot where Kate had found the coin. Together, they fanned, using all the patience each of them had stored. In the twenty minutes of bottom time they had left, they uncovered only five more coins. As if they were as fragile as glass, Kate placed them in her bag. Each took a mesh basket filled with salvage and surfaced.

"It's there, Ky." Kate let her mouthpiece drop as Ky hauled the first basket over the rail. "It's the *Liberty,* we've proven it."

"It's the *Liberty,*" he agreed, taking the second basket from her. "You've finished what your father started."

"Yes." She unhooked her tanks, but it was more than their weight she felt lifted from her shoulders. "I've finished." Digging into her bag, she pulled out the six bright coins. "These were loose. We still haven't found the chest. If it still exists."

He'd already thought of that, but not how he'd tell her his own theory. "They might have taken the chest to another part of the boat when the storm hit." It was a possibility; it had given them hope that the chest was still there.

Kate looked down. The glittery metal seemed to mock her. "It's possible they put the gold in one of the lifeboats when they manned them. The survivor's story wasn't clear after the ship began to break up."

"A lot of things are possible." He touched her cheek briefly before he started to strip off his gear. "With a little luck and a little more time, we might find it all."

She smiled as she dropped the coins back into her bag. "Then you could buy your boat."

"And you could go to Greece." Stripped down to his bathing trunks, Ky went to the helm. "We need to give ourselves the full twelve hours before we dive again, Kate. We've been calling it close as it is."

"That's fine." She made a business of removing her own suit. She needed the twelve hours, she discovered, for more than the practical reason of residual nitrogen.

They spoke little on the trip back. They should've been ecstatic. Kate knew it, and though she tried, she couldn't recapture that quick boost she'd felt when she picked up the first coin.

She discovered that if she'd had a choice she would have gone back weeks, to the time when the gold was a distant goal and the search was everything.

It took the rest of the day to transport the salvage

from the *Vortex* to Ky's house, to separate and catalog it. She'd already decided to contact the Park Service. Their advice in placing many of the artifacts would be invaluable. After taxes, she'd give her father his memorial. And, she mused, she'd give Ky whatever he wanted out of the salvage.

Their original agreement no longer mattered to her. If he wanted half, she'd give it. All she wanted, Kate realized, was the first bowl she'd found, the blackened silver coin and the gold one that had led her to the five other coins.

"We might think about investing in a small electrolytic reduction bath," Ky murmured as he turned what he guessed was a silver snuff box in his palm. "We could treat a lot of this salvage ourselves." Coming to a decision, he set the box down. "We're going to have to think about a bigger ship and equipment. It might be best to stop diving for the next couple of days while we arrange for it. It's been six weeks, and we've barely scratched the surface of what's down there."

She nodded, not entirely sure why she wanted to weep. He was right. It was time to move on, to expand. How could she explain to him, when she couldn't explain to herself, that she wanted nothing else from the sea? While the sun set, she watched him meticulously list the salvage.

"Ky…" She broke off because she couldn't find the words to tell him what moved through her. Sadness, emptiness, needs.

"What's wrong?"

"Nothing." But she took his hands as she rose. "Come

upstairs now," she said quietly. "Make love with me before the sun goes down."

Questions ran through him, but he told himself they could wait. The need he felt from her touched off his own. He wanted to give her, and to take from her, what couldn't be found anywhere else.

When they entered the bedroom it was washed with the warm, lingering light of the sun. The sky was slowly turning red as he lay beside her. Her arms reached out to gather him close. Her lips parted. Refusing to rush, they undressed each other. No boundaries. Flesh against flesh they lay. Mouth against mouth they touched.

Kisses—long and deep—took them both beyond the ordinary world of place and time. Here, there were dozens of sensations to be felt, and no questions to be asked. Here, there was no past, no tomorrow, only the moment. Her body went limp under his, but her mouth hungered and sought.

No one else… No one else had ever taken her beyond herself so effortlessly. Never before had anyone made her so completely aware of her own body. A feathery touch along her skin drove pleasure through her with inescapable force.

The scent of sea still clung to both of them. As pleasure became liquid, they might have been fathoms under the ocean, moving freely without the strict rules of gravity. There were no rules here.

As his hands brought their emotions rising to the surface, so did hers for him. She explored the rippling muscles of his back, near the shoulders. Lingering there, she enjoyed just the feel of one of the subtle differences between them. His skin was smooth, but muscles bunched under it. His hands were gentle, but the palms were hard. He was lean, but there was no softness there.

Again and again she touched and tasted, needing to absorb him. Above all else, she needed to experience everything they'd ever had together this one time. They made love here, she remembered, that first time. The first time…and the last. Whenever she thought of him, she'd remember the quieting light of dusk and the distant sound of surf.

He didn't understand why he felt such restrained urgency from her, but he knew she needed everything he could give her. He loved her, perhaps not as gently as he could, but more thoroughly than ever before.

He touched. "Here," Ky murmured, using his fingertips to drive her up. As she gasped and arched, he watched her. "You're soft and hot."

He tasted. "And here…" With his tongue, he pushed her to the edge. As her hands gripped his, he groaned. Pleasure heaped upon pleasure. "You taste like temptation—sweet and forbidden. Tell me you want more."

"Yes." The word came out on a moan. "I want more."

So he gave her more.

Again and again, he took her up, watching the astonished pleasure on her face, feeling it in the arch of her body, hearing it in her quick breaths. She was helpless, mindless, his. He drove his tongue into her and felt her explode, wave after wave.

As she shuddered, he moved up her body, hands fast, mouth hot and open. Suddenly, on a surge of strength, she rolled on top of him. Within seconds, she'd devastated his claim to leadership. All fire, all speed, all woman, she took control.

Heedless, greedy, they moved over the bed. Murmurs were incoherent, care was forgotten. They took with only one goal in mind. Pleasure—sweet, forbidden pleasure.

Shaking, locked tight, they reached the goal together.

Dawn was breaking, clear and calm as Kate lay still, watching Ky sleep. She knew what she had to do for both of them, to both of them. Fate had brought them together a second time. It wouldn't bring them together again.

She'd bargained with Ky, offering him a share of gold for his skill. In the beginning, she'd believed that she wanted the treasure, needed it to give her all the options she'd never had before. That choice. Now, she knew she didn't want it at all. A hundred times more gold wouldn't change what was between her and Ky— what drew them to each other, and what kept them apart.

She loved him. She understood that, in his way, he loved her. Did that change the differences between them? Did that make her able and willing to give up her own life to suit his, or able and willing to demand that he do the same?

Their worlds were no closer together now than they'd been four years ago. Their desires no more in tune. With the gold she'd leave for him, he'd be able to do what he wanted with his life. She needed no treasure for that.

If she stayed… Unable to stop herself, Kate reached out to touch his cheek. If she stayed she'd bury herself for him. Eventually, she'd despise herself for it, and he'd resent her. Better that they take what they'd had for a few weeks than cover it with years of disappoinments.

The treasure was important to him. He'd taken risks for it, worked for it. She'd give her father his memorial. Ky would have the rest.

Quietly, still watching him sleep, she dressed.

It didn't take Kate long to gather what she'd come with. Taking her suitcase downstairs, she carefully packed what she'd take with her from the *Liberty*. In a box, she placed the pottery bowl wrapped in layers of newspaper. The coins, the blackened silver and the shiny gold, she zipped into a small pouch. With equal care, she packed the film she'd taken during their days under the ocean.

What she'd designated for the museum she'd already marked. Leaving the list on the table, she left the house.

She told herself it would be cleaner if she left no note, yet she found herself hesitating. How could she make him understand? After putting her suitcase in her car, she went back into the house. Quietly, she took the five gold coins upstairs and placed them on Ky's dresser. With a last look at him as he slept, she went back out again.

She'd have a final moment with the sea. In the quiet air of morning, Kate walked over the dunes.

She'd remember it this way—empty, endless and full of sound. Surf foamed against the sand, white on white. What was beneath the surface would always call her— the memories of peace, of excitement, of sharing both with Ky. Only a summer, she thought. Life was made of four seasons, not one.

Day was strengthening, and her time was up. Turning, she scanned the island until she saw the tip of the lighthouse. Some things lasted, she thought with a smile. She'd learned a great deal in a few short weeks. She was her own woman at last. She could make her own way. As a teacher, she told herself that knowledge was precious. But it made her ache with loneliness. She left the empty sea behind her.

Though she wanted to, Kate deliberately kept herself from looking at the house as she walked back to her car. She didn't need to see it again to remember it. If things had been different... Kate reached for the door handle of her car. Her fingers were still inches from it when she was spun around.

"What the hell're you doing?"

Facing Ky, she felt her resolve crumble, then rebuild. He was barely awake, and barely dressed. His eyes were heavy with sleep, his hair disheveled from it. All he wore was a pair of ragged cut-offs. She folded her hands in front of her and hoped her voice would be strong and clear.

"I had hoped to be gone before you woke."

"Gone?" His eyes locked on hers. "Where?"

"I'm going back to Connecticut."

"Oh?" He swore he wouldn't lose his temper. Not this time. This time, it might be fatal for both of them. "Why?"

Her nerves skipped. The question had been quiet enough, but she knew that cold, flat expression in his eyes. The wrong move, and he'd leap. "You said it yourself yesterday, Ky, when we came up from the last dive. I've done what I came for."

He opened his hand. Five coins shone in the morning sun. "What about this?"

"I left them for you." She swallowed, no longer certain how long she could speak without showing she was breaking in two. "The treasure isn't important to me. It's yours."

"Damn generous of you." Turning over his hand, he dropped the coins into the sand. "That's how much the gold means to me, professor."

She stared at the gold on the ground in front of her. "I don't understand you."

"*You* wanted the treasure," he tossed at her. "It never mattered to me."

"But you said," she began, then shook her head. "When I first came to you, you took the job because of the treasure."

"I took the job because of you. You wanted the gold, Kate."

"It wasn't the money." Dragging a hand through her hair, she turned away. "It was never the money."

"Maybe not. It was your father."

She nodded because it was true, but it no longer hurt. "I finished what he started, and I gave myself something. I don't want any more coins, Ky."

"Why are you running away from me again?"

Slowly, she turned back. "We're four years older than we were before, but we're the same people."

"So?"

"Ky, when I went away before, it was partially because of my father, because I felt I owed him my loyalty. But if I'd thought you'd wanted me. *Me*," she repeated, placing her palm over her heart, "not what you wanted me to be. If I'd thought that, and if I'd thought you and I could make a future together, I wouldn't have gone. I wouldn't be leaving now."

"What the hell gives you the right to decide what I want, what I feel?" He whirled away from her, too furious to remain close. "Maybe I made mistakes, maybe I just assumed too much four years ago. Damn it, I paid for it, Kate, every day from the time you left until you came back. I've done everything I could to be careful this time around, not to push, not to assume. Then I wake up and find you leaving without a word."

"There aren't any words, Ky. I've always given you too many of them, and you've never given me enough."

"You're better with words than I am."

"All right, then I'll use them. I love you." She waited until he turned back to her. The restlessness was on him again. He was holding it off with sheer will. "I've always loved you, but I think I know my own limitations. Maybe I know yours too."

"No, you think too much about limitations, Kate, and not enough about possibilities. I let you walk away from me before. It's not going to be so easy this time."

"I have to be my own person, Ky. I won't live the rest of my life as I've lived it up to now."

"Who the hell wants you to?" he exploded. "Who the hell wants you to be anything but what you are? It's about time you stopped equating love with responsibility and started looking at the other side of it. It's sharing, giving and taking and laughing. If I ask you to give part of yourself to me, I'm going to give part of myself right back."

Unable to stop himself he took her arms in his hands, just holding, as if through the contact he could make his words sink in.

"I don't want your constant devotion. I don't want you to be obliged to me. I don't want to go through life thinking that whatever you do, you do because you want to please me. Damn it, I don't want that kind of responsibility."

Without words, she stared at him. He'd never said anything to her so simply, so free of half meanings. Hope rose in her. Yet still, he was telling her only what he didn't want. Once he gave her the flip side of that coin hope could vanish.

"Tell me what you do want."

He had only one answer. "Come with me a minute." Taking her hand, he drew her toward the shed. "When I started this, it was because I'd always promised myself I would. Before long, the reasons changed." Turning the latch, he pulled the shed doors open.

For a moment, she saw nothing. Gradually, her eyes adjusted to the dimness and she stepped inside. The boat was nearly finished. The hull was sanded and sealed and painted, waiting for Ky to take it outside and attach the mast. It was lovely, clean and simple. Just looking at it, Kate could imagine the way it would flow with the wind. Free, light and clever.

"It's beautiful, Ky. I always wondered…" She broke off as she read the name printed boldly on the stern.

Second Chance.

"That's all I want from you," Ky told her, pointing to the two words. "The boat's yours. When I started it, I thought I was building it for me. But I built it for you, because I knew it was one dream you'd share with me. I only want what's printed on it, Kate. For both of us." Speechless, she watched him lean over the starboard side and open a small compartment. He drew out a tiny box.

"I had this cleaned. You wouldn't take it from me before." Opening the lid, he revealed the diamond he'd found, sparkling now in a simple gold setting. "It didn't cost me anything and it wasn't made especially for you. It's just something I found among a bunch of rocks."

When she started to speak, he held up a hand. "Hold on. You wanted words, I haven't finished with them yet. I know you have to teach, I'm not asking you to give it up. I am asking that you give me one year here on the island. There's a school here, not Yale, but people still have to be taught. A year, Kate. If it isn't what you want after that, I'll go back with you."

Her brows drew together. "Back? To Connecticut? You'd live in Connecticut?"

"If that's what it takes."

A compromise…she thought, baffled. Was he offering to adjust his life for hers? "And if that isn't right for you?"

"Then we'll try someplace else, damn it. We'll find someplace in between. Maybe we'll move half a dozen times in the next few years. What does it matter?"

What did it matter? she wondered as she studied him.

He was offering her what she'd waited for all of her life. Love without chains.

"I want you to marry me." He wondered if that simple statement shook her as much as it did him. "Tomorrow isn't soon enough, but if you'll give me the year, I can wait."

She nearly smiled. He'd never wait. Once he had her promise of the year, he'd subtly and not so subtly work on her until she found herself at the altar. It was nearly tempting to make him go through the effort.

Limitations? Had she spoken of limitations? Love had none.

"No," she decided aloud. "You only get the year if I get the ring. And what goes with it."

"Deal." He took her hand quickly as though she might change her mind. "Once it's on, you're stuck, professor." Pulling the ring from the box he slipped it onto her finger. Swearing lightly, he shook his head. "It's too big."

"It's all right. I'll keep my hand closed for the next fifty years or so." With a laugh, she went into his arms. All doubts vanished. They'd make it, she told herself. South, north or anywhere in between.

"We'll have it sized," he murmured, nuzzling into her neck.

"Only if they can do it while it's on my finger." Kate closed her eyes. She'd just found everything. Did he know it? "Ky, about the *Liberty,* the rest of the treasure."

He tilted her face up to kiss her. "We've already found it."

* * * * *

THE WELCOMING

For my friend Catherine Coulter,
because she's always good for a laugh.

Chapter 1

Everything he needed was in the backpack slung over his shoulders. Including his .38. If things went well he would have no use for it.

Roman drew a cigarette out of the crumpled pack in his breast pocket and turned away from the wind to light it. A boy of about eight raced along the rail of the ferry, cheerfully ignoring his mother's calls. Roman felt a tug of empathy for the kid. It was cold, certainly. The biting wind off Puget Sound was anything but spring-like. But it was one hell of a view. Sitting in the glass-walled lounge would be cozier, but it was bound to take something away from the experience.

The kid was snatched by a blonde woman with pink cheeks and a rapidly reddening nose. Roman listened to them grumble at each other as she dragged the boy back inside. Families, he thought, rarely agreed on anything.

Turning away, he leaned over the rail, lazily smoking as the ferry steamed by clumpy islands.

They had left the Seattle skyline behind, though the mountains of mainland Washington still rose up to amaze and impress the viewer. There was an aloneness here, despite the smattering of hardy passengers walking the slanting deck or bundling up in the patches of sunlight along wooden benches. He preferred the city, with its pace, its crowds, its energy. Its anonymity. He always had. For the life of him, he couldn't understand where this restless discontent he felt had come from, or why it was weighing so heavily on him.

The job. For the past year he'd been blaming it on the job. The pressure was something he'd always accepted, even courted. He'd always thought life without it would be bland and pointless. But just lately it hadn't been enough. He moved from place to place, taking little away, leaving less behind.

Time to get out, he thought as he watched a fishing boat chug by. Time to move on. And do what? he wondered in disgust, blowing out a stream of smoke. He could go into business for himself. He'd toyed with that notion a time or two. He could travel. He'd already been around the world, but it might be different to do it as a tourist.

Some brave soul came out on deck with a video camera. Roman turned, shifted, eased out of range. It was in all likelihood an unnecessary precaution; the move was instinctive. So was the watchfulness, and so was the casual stance, which hid a wiry readiness.

No one paid much attention to him, though a few of the women looked twice.

He was just over average height, with the taut, solid build of a lightweight boxer. The slouchy jacket and worn jeans hid well-tuned muscles. He wore no hat and his thick black hair flew freely away from his tanned, hollow-cheeked face. It was unshaven, tough-featured. The eyes, a pale, clear green, might have softened the go-to-hell appearance, but they were intense, direct and, at the moment, bored.

It promised to be a slow, routine assignment.

Roman heard the docking call and shifted his pack. Routine or not, the job was his. He would get it done, file his report, then take a few weeks to figure out what he wanted to do with the rest of his life.

He disembarked with the smattering of other walking passengers. There was a wild, sweet scent of flowers now that competed with the darker scent of the water. The flowers grew in free, romantic splendor, many with blossoms as big as his fist. Some part of him appreciated their color and their charm, but he rarely took the time to stop and smell the roses.

Cars rolled off the ramp and cruised toward home or a day of sightseeing. Once the car decks were unloaded, the new passengers would board and set off for one of the other islands or for the longer, colder trip to British Columbia.

Roman pulled out another cigarette, lit it and took a casual look around—at the pretty, colorful gardens, the charming white hotel and restaurant, the signs that gave information on ferries and parking. It was all a matter of timing now. He ignored the patio café, though he would have dearly loved a cup of coffee, and wound his way to the parking area.

He spotted the van easily enough, the white-and-blue American model with Whale Watch Inn painted on the side. It was his job to talk himself onto the van and into the inn. If the details had been taken care of on this end, it would be routine. If not, he would find another way.

Stalling, he bent down to tie his shoe. The waiting cars were being loaded, and the foot passengers were already on deck. There were no more than a dozen vehicles in the parking area now, including the van. He was taking another moment to unbutton his jacket when he saw the woman.

Her hair was pulled back in a braid, not loose as it had been in the file picture. It seemed to be a deeper, richer blond in the sunlight. She wore tinted glasses, big-framed amber lenses that obscured half of her face, but he knew he wasn't mistaken. He could see the delicate line of her jaw, the small, straight nose, the full, shapely mouth.

His information was accurate. She was five-five, a hundred and ten pounds, with a small, athletic build. Her dress was casual—jeans, a chunky cream-colored cable-knit sweater over a blue shirt. The shirt would match her eyes. The jeans were tucked into suede ankle boots, and a pair of slim crystal earrings dangled at her ears.

She walked with a sense of purpose, keys jingling in one hand, a big canvas bag slung over her other shoulder. There was nothing flirtatious about the walk, but a man would notice it. Long, limber strides, a subtle swing at the hips, head up, eyes ahead.

Yeah, a man would notice, Roman thought as he flicked the cigarette away. He figured she knew it.

He waited until she reached the van before he started toward her.

Charity stopped humming the finale of Beethoven's *Ninth,* looked down at her right front tire and swore. Because she didn't think anyone was watching, she kicked it, then moved around to the back of the van to get the jack.

"Got a problem?"

She jolted, nearly dropped the jack on her foot, then whirled around.

A tough customer. That was Charity's first thought as she stared at Roman. His eyes were narrowed against the sun. He had one hand hooked around the strap of his backpack and the other tucked in his pocket. She put her own hand on her heart, made certain it was still beating, then smiled.

"Yes. I have a flat. I just dropped a family of four off for the ferry, two of whom were under six and candidates for reform school. My nerves are shot, the plumbing's on the fritz in unit 6, and my handyman just won the lottery. How are you?"

The file hadn't mentioned that she had a voice like café au lait, the rich, dark kind you drank in New Orleans. He noted that, filed it away, then nodded toward the flat. "Want me to change it?"

Charity could have done it herself, but she wasn't one to refuse help when it was offered. Besides, he could probably do it faster, and he looked as though he could use the five dollars she would give him.

"Thanks." She handed him the jack, then dug a lemon drop out of her bag. The flat was bound to eat up the time she'd scheduled for lunch. "Did you just come in on the ferry?"

"Yeah." He didn't care for small talk, but he used it, and her friendliness, as handily as he used the jack. "I've been doing some traveling. Thought I'd spend some time on Orcas, see if I can spot some whales."

"You've come to the right place. I saw a pod yesterday from my window." She leaned against the van, enjoying the sunlight. As he worked, she watched his hands. Strong, competent, quick. She appreciated someone who could do a simple job well. "Are you on vacation?"

"Just traveling. I pick up odd jobs here and there. Know anyone looking for help?"

"Maybe." Lips pursed, she studied him as he pulled off the flat. He straightened, keeping one hand on the tire. "What kind of work?"

"This and that. Where's the spare?"

"Spare?" Looking into his eyes for more than ten seconds was like being hypnotized.

"Tire." The corner of his mouth quirked slightly in a reluctant smile. "You need one that isn't flat."

"Right. The spare." Shaking her head at her own foolishness, she went to get it. "It's in the back." She turned and bumped into him. "Sorry."

He put one hand on her arm to steady her. They stood

for a moment in the sunlight, frowning at each other. "It's all right. I'll get it."

When he climbed into the van, Charity blew out a long, steadying breath. Her nerves were more ragged than she'd have believed possible. "Oh, watch out for the—" She grimaced as Roman sat back on his heels and peeled the remains of a cherry lollipop from his knee. Her laugh was spontaneous and as rich as her voice. "Sorry. A souvenir of Orcas Island from Jimmy 'The Destroyer' MacCarthy, a five-year-old delinquent."

"I'd rather have a T-shirt."

"Yes, well, who wouldn't?" Charity took the sticky mess from him, wrapped it in a tattered tissue and dropped it into her bag. "We're a family establishment," she explained as he climbed out with the spare. "Mostly everyone enjoys having children around, but once in a while you get a pair like Jimmy and Judy, the twin ghouls from Walla Walla, and you think about turning the place into a service station. Do you like children?"

He glanced up as he slipped the tire into place. "From a safe distance."

She laughed appreciatively at his answer. "Where are you from?"

"St. Louis." He could have chosen a dozen places. He couldn't have said why he'd chosen to tell the truth. "But I don't get back much."

"Family?"

"No."

The way he said it made her stifle her innate curiosity. She wouldn't invade anyone's privacy any more than she would drop the lint-covered lollipop on the ground. "I was born right here on Orcas. Every year I tell myself I'm going to take six months and travel. Anywhere." She shrugged as he tightened the last of the lug nuts. "I never seem to manage it. Anyway, it's beautiful here. If you don't have a deadline, you may find yourself staying longer than you planned."

"Maybe." He stood up to replace the jack. "If I can find some work, and a place to stay."

Charity didn't consider it an impulse. She had studied, measured and considered him for nearly fifteen minutes. Most job interviews took little more. He had a strong back and intelligent—if disconcerting—eyes, and if the state of his pack and his shoes was any indication he was down on his luck. As her name implied, she had been taught to offer people a helping hand. And if she could solve one of her more immediate and pressing problems at the same time...

"You any good with your hands?" she asked him.

He looked at her unable to prevent his mind from taking a slight detour. "Yeah. Pretty good."

Her brow—and her blood pressure—rose a little when she saw his quick survey. "I mean with tools. Hammer, saw, screwdriver. Can you do any carpentry, household repairs?"

"Sure." It was going to be easy, almost too easy. He wondered why he felt the small, unaccustomed tug of guilt.

"Like I said, my handyman won the lottery, a big one. He's gone to Hawaii to study bikinis and eat poi. I'd wish him well, except we were in the middle of renovating the west wing. Of the inn," she added, pointing to the logo on the van. "If you know your way around two-by-fours and drywall I can give you room and board and five an hour."

"Sounds like we've solved both our problems."

"Great." She offered a hand. "I'm Charity Ford."

"DeWinter." He clasped her hand. "Roman DeWinter."

"Okay, Roman." She swung her door open. "Climb aboard."

She didn't look gullible, Roman thought as he settled into the seat beside her. But then, he knew—better than most—that looks were deceiving. He was exactly where he wanted to be, and he hadn't had to resort to a song and dance. He lit a cigarette as she pulled out of the parking lot.

"My grandfather built the inn in 1938," she said, rolling down her window. "He added on to it a couple of times over the years, but it's still really an inn. We can't bring ourselves to call it a resort, even in the brochures. I hope you're looking for remote."

"That suits me."

"Me too. Most of the time." Talkative guy, she mused with a half smile. But that was all right. She could talk enough for both of them. "It's early in the season yet, so we're a long way from full." She cocked her elbow on the opened window and cheerfully took over the bulk of the conversation. The sunlight played on her earrings and refracted into brilliant colors. "You should have plenty of free time to knock around. The view from Mount Constitution's really spectacular. Or, if you're into it, the hiking trails are great."

"I thought I might spend some time in B.C."

"That's easy enough. Take the ferry to Sidney. We do pretty well with tour groups going back and forth."

"We?"

"The inn. Pop—my grandfather—built a half-dozen cabins in the sixties. We give a special package rate to tour groups. They can rent the cabins and have breakfast and dinner included. They're a little rustic, but the tourists really go for them. We get a group about once a week. During the season we can triple that."

She turned onto a narrow, winding road and kept the speed at fifty.

Roman already knew the answers, but he knew it might seem odd if he didn't ask the questions. "Do you run the inn?"

"Yeah. I've worked there on and off for as long as I can remember. When my grandfather died a couple of years ago I took over." She paused a moment. It still hurt; she supposed it always would. "He loved it. Not just the place, but the whole idea of meeting new people every day, making them comfortable, finding out about them."

"I guess it does pretty well."

She shrugged. "We get by." They rounded a bend where the forest gave way to a wide expanse of blue water. The curve of the island was clear, jutting out and tucking back in contrasting shades of deep green and brown. A few houses were tucked high in the cliffs beyond. A boat with billowing white sails ran with the wind, rippling the glassy water. "There are views like this all around the island. Even when you live here they dazzle you."

"And scenery's good for business."

She frowned a little. "It doesn't hurt," she said, and glanced back at him. "Are you really interested in seeing whales?"

"It seemed like a good idea since I was here."

She stopped the van and pointed to the cliffs. "If you've got patience and a good set of binoculars, up there's a good bet. We've spotted them from the inn, as I said. Still, if you want a close look, your best bet's out on a boat." When he didn't comment, she started the van again. He was making her jittery, she realized. He seemed to be looking not at the water or the forest but at her.

Roman glanced at her hands. Strong, competent, no-nonsense hands, he decided, though the fingers were beginning to tap a bit nervously on the wheel. She continued to drive fast, steering the van easily through the switchbacks. Another car approached. Without slackening speed, Charity lifted a hand in a salute.

"That was Lori, one of our waitresses. She works an early shift so she can be home when her kids get back from school. We usually run with a staff of ten, then add on five or six part-time during the summer."

They rounded the next curve, and the inn came into view. It was exactly what he'd expected, and yet it was more charming than the pictures he'd been shown. It was white clapboard, with weathered blue trim around arched and oval windows. There were fanciful turrets, narrow walkways and a wide skirting porch. A sweep of lawn led directly to the water, where a narrow, rickety dock jutted out. Tied to it was a small motorboat that swung lazily in the current.

A mill wheel turned in a shallow pond at the side of the inn, slapping the water musically. To the west, where the trees began to thicken, he could make out one of the cabins she had spoken of. Flowers were everywhere.

"There's a bigger pond out back." Charity drove around the side and pulled into a small graveled lot that was already half full. "We keep the trout there. The trail takes you to cabins 1, 2 and 3. Then it forks off to 4, 5 and 6." She stepped out and waited for him to join her. "Most everyone uses the back entrance. I can show you around the grounds later, if you like, but we'll get you settled in first."

"It's a nice place." He said it almost without thinking, and he meant it. There were two rockers on the square back porch, and an adirondack chair that needed its white paint freshened. Roman turned to study the view a guest would overlook from the empty seat. Part forest, part water, and very appealing. Restful. Welcoming. He thought of the pistol in his backpack. Appearances, he thought again, were deceiving.

With a slight frown, Charity watched him. He didn't seem to be looking so much as absorbing. It was an odd thought, but she would have sworn if anyone were to ask him to describe the inn six months later he would be able to, right down to the last pinecone.

Then he turned to her, and the feeling remained, more personal now, more intense. The breeze picked up, jingling the wind chimes that hung from the eaves.

"Are you an artist?" she asked abruptly.

"No." He smiled, and the change in his face was quick and charming. "Why?"

"Just wondering." You'd have to be careful of that smile, Charity decided. It made you relax, and she doubted he was a man it was wise to relax around.

The double glass doors opened up into a large, airy room that smelled of lavender and woodsmoke. There were two long, cushiony sofas and a pair of overstuffed chairs near a huge stone fireplace where logs crackled. Antiques were scattered throughout the room—a desk and chair with a trio of old inkwells, an oak hatrack, a buffet with glossy carved doors. Tucked into a corner was a spinet with yellowing keys and the pair of wide arched windows that dominated the far wall made the water seem part of the room's decor. At a table near them, two women were playing a leisurely game of Scrabble.

"Who's winning today?" Charity asked.

Both looked up. And beamed. "It's neck and neck." The woman on the right fluffed her hair when she spotted Roman. She was old enough to be his grandmother, but she slipped her glasses off and straightened her thin shoulders. "I didn't realize you were bringing back another guest, dear."

"Neither did I." Charity moved over to add another log to the fire. "Roman DeWinter, Miss Lucy and Miss Millie."

His smile came again, smoothly. "Ladies."

"DeWinter." Miss Lucy put on her glasses to get a better look. "Didn't we know a DeWinter once, Millie?"

"Not that I recall." Millie, always ready to flirt, continued to beam at Roman, though he was hardly more than a myopic blur. "Have you been to the inn before, Mr. DeWinter?"

"No, ma'am. This is my first time in the San Juans."

"You're in for a treat." Millie let out a little sigh. It was really too bad what the years did. It seemed only yesterday that handsome young men had kissed her hand and asked her to go for a walk. Today they called her ma'am. She went wistfully back to her game.

"The ladies have been coming to the inn longer than I can remember," Charity told Roman as she led the way down a hall. "They're lovely, but I should warn you about Miss Millie. I'm told she had quite a reputation in her day, and she still has an eye for an attractive man."

"I'll watch my step."

"I get the impression you usually do." She took out a set of keys and unlocked the door. "This leads to the west wing." She started down another hall, brisk, businesslike. "As you can see, renovations were well under way before George hit the jackpot. The trim's been stripped." She gestured to the neat piles of wood along the freshly painted wall. "The doors need to be refinished yet, and the original hardware's in that box."

After taking off her sunglasses, she dropped them into her bag. He'd been right. The collar of her shirt matched her eyes almost exactly. He looked into them as she examined George's handiwork.

"How many rooms?"

"There are two singles, a double and a family suite in this wing, all in varying stages of disorder." She skirted a door that was propped against a wall, then walked into a room. "You can take this one. It's as close to being finished as I have in this section."

It was a small, bright room. Its window was bordered with stained glass and looked out over the mill wheel. The bed was stripped, and the floors were bare and in need of sanding. Wallpaper that was obviously new covered the walls from the ceiling down to a white chair rail. Below that was bare drywall.

"It doesn't look like much now," Charity commented.

"It's fine." He'd spent time in places that made the little room look like a suite at the Waldorf.

Automatically she checked the closet and the adjoining bath, making a mental list of what was needed. "You can start in here, if it'll make you more comfortable. I'm not particular. George had his own system. I never understood it, but he usually managed to get things done."

He hooked his thumbs in the front pockets of his jeans. "You got a game plan?"

"Absolutely."

Charity spent the next thirty minutes taking him through the wing and explaining exactly what she wanted. Roman listened, commenting little, and studied the setup. He knew from the blueprints he'd studied that the floor plan of this section mirrored that of the east wing. His position in it would give him easy access to the main floor and the rest of the inn.

He'd have to work, he mused as he looked at the half-finished walls and the paint tarps. He considered it a small bonus. Working with his hands was something he enjoyed and something he'd had little time for in the past.

She was very precise in her instructions. A woman who knew what she wanted and intended to have it. He appreciated that. He had no doubt that she was very good at what she did, whether it was running an inn... or something else.

"What's up there?" He pointed to a set of stairs at the end of the hallway.

"My rooms. We'll worry about them after the guest quarters are done." She jingled the keys as her thoughts went off in a dozen directions. "So, what do you think?"

"About what?"

"About the work."

"Do you have tools?"

"In the shed, the other side of the parking area."

"I can handle it."

"Yes." Charity tossed the keys to him. She was certain he could. They were standing in the octagonal parlor of the family suite. It was empty but for stacks of material and tarps. And it was quiet. She noticed all at once that they were standing quite close together and that she couldn't hear a sound. Feeling foolish, she took a key off her ring.

"You'll need this."

"Thanks." He tucked it in his pocket.

She drew a deep breath, wondering why she felt as though she'd just taken a long step with her eyes closed. "Have you had lunch?"

"No."

"I'll show you down to the kitchen. Mae'll fix you

up." She started out, a little too quickly. She wanted to escape from the sensation that she was completely alone with him. And helpless. Charity moved her shoulders restlessly. A stupid thought, she told herself. She'd never been helpless. Still, she felt a breath of relief when she closed the door behind them.

She took him downstairs, through the empty lobby and into a large dining room decorated in pastels. There were small milk-glass vases on each table, with a handful of fresh flowers in each. Big windows opened onto a view of the water, and as if carrying through the theme, an aquarium was built into the south wall.

She stopped there for a moment, hardly breaking stride, scanning the room until she was satisfied that the tables were properly set for dinner. Then she pushed through a swinging door into the kitchen.

"And I say it needs more basil."

"I say it don't."

"Whatever you do," Charity murmured under her breath, "don't agree with either of them. Ladies," she said, using her best smile. "I brought you a hungry man."

The woman guarding the pot held up a dripping spoon. The best way to describe her was wide—face, hips, hands. She gave Roman a quick, squint-eyed survey. "Sit down, then," she told him, jerking a thumb in the direction of a long wooden table.

"Mae Jenkins, Roman DeWinter."

"Ma'am."

"And Dolores Rumsey." The other woman was holding a jar of herbs. She was as narrow as Mae was wide.

After giving Roman a nod, she began to ease her way toward the pot.

"Keep away from that," Mae ordered, "and get the man some fried chicken."

Muttering, Dolores stalked off to find a plate.

"Roman's going to pick up where George left off," Charity explained. "He'll be staying in the west wing."

"Not from around here." Mae looked at him again, the way he imagined a nanny would look at a small, grubby child.

"No."

With a sniff, she poured him some coffee. "Looks like you could use a couple of decent meals."

"You'll get them here," Charity put in, playing peace-maker. She winced only a little when Dolores slapped a plate of cold chicken and potato salad in front of Roman.

"Needed more dill." Dolores glared at him, as if she were daring him to disagree. "She wouldn't listen."

Roman figured the best option was to grin at her and keep his mouth full. Before Mae could respond, the door swung open again.

"Can a guy get a cup of coffee in here?" The man stopped and sent Roman a curious look.

"Bob Mullins, Roman DeWinter. I hired him to fin-ish the west wing. Bob's one of my many right hands."

"Welcome aboard." He moved to the stove to pour himself a cup of coffee, adding three lumps of sugar as Mae clucked her tongue at him. The sweet tooth didn't seem to have an effect on him. He was tall, perhaps six-two, and he couldn't weigh more than 160. His light brown hair was cut short around his ears and swept back from his high forehead.

"You from back east?" Bob asked between sips of coffee.

"East of here."

"Easy to do." He grinned when Mae flapped a hand to move him away from her stove.

"Did you get that invoice business straightened out with the greengrocer?" Charity asked.

"All taken care of. You got a couple of calls while you were out. And there's some papers you need to sign."

"I'll get to it." She checked her watch. "Now." She glanced over at Roman. "I'll be in the office off the lobby if there's anything you need to know."

"I'll be fine."

"Okay." She studied him for another moment. She couldn't quite figure out how he could be in a room with four other people and seem so alone. "See you later."

Roman took a long, casual tour of the inn before he began to haul tools into the west wing. He saw a young couple who had to be newlyweds locked in an embrace near the pond. A man and a young boy played one-on-one on a small concrete basketball court. The ladies, as he had come to think of them, had left their game to sit on the porch and discuss the garden. Looking exhausted, a family of four pulled up in a station wagon, then trooped toward the cabins. A man in a fielder's cap walked down the pier with a video camera on his shoulder.

There were birds trilling in the trees, and there was

the distant sound of a motorboat. He heard a baby crying halfheartedly, and the strains of a Mozart piano sonata.

If he hadn't pored over the data himself he would have sworn he was in the wrong place.

He chose the family suite and went to work, wondering how long it would take him to get into Charity's rooms.

There was something soothing about working with his hands. Two hours passed, and he relaxed a little. A check of his watch had him deciding to take another, unnecessary trip to the shed. Charity had mentioned that wine was served in what she called the gathering room every evening at five. It wouldn't hurt for him to get another, closer look at the inn's guests.

He started out, then stopped by the doorway to his room. He'd heard something, a movement. Cautious, he eased inside the door and scanned the empty room.

Humming under her breath, Charity came out of the bath, where she'd just placed fresh towels. She unfolded linens and began to make the bed.

"What are you doing?"

Muffling a scream, she stumbled backward, then eased down on the bed to catch her breath. "My God, Roman, don't do that."

He stepped into the room, watching her with narrowed eyes. "I asked what you were doing."

"That should be obvious." She patted the pile of linens with her hand.

"You do the housekeeping, too?"

"From time to time." Recovered, she stood up and

smoothed the bottom sheet on the bed. "There's soap and towels in the bath," she told him, then tilted her head. "Looks like you can use them." She unfolded the top sheet with an expert flick. "Been busy?"

"That was the deal."

With a murmur of agreement, she tucked up the corners at the foot of the bed the way he remembered his grandmother doing. "I put an extra pillow and blanket in the closet." She moved from one side of the bed to the other in a way that had him watching her with simple male appreciation. He couldn't remember the last time he'd seen anyone make a bed. It stirred thoughts in him that he couldn't afford. Thoughts of what it might be like to mess it up again—with her.

"Do you ever stop?"

"I've been known to." She spread a white wedding-ring quilt on the bed. "We're expecting a tour tomorrow, so everyone's a bit busy."

"Tomorrow?"

"Mmm. On the first ferry from Sidney." She fluffed his pillows, satisfied. "Did you—"

She broke off when she turned and all but fell against him. His hands went to her hips instinctively as hers braced against his shoulders. An embrace—unplanned, unwanted and shockingly intimate.

She was slender beneath the long, chunky sweater, he realized, even more slender than a man might expect. And her eyes were bluer than they had any right to be, bigger, softer. She smelled like the inn, smelled of that welcoming combination of lavender and woodsmoke.

Drawn to it, he continued to hold her, though he knew he shouldn't.

"Did I what?" His fingers spread over her hips, drawing her just a fraction closer. He saw the dazed confusion in her eyes; her reaction tugged at him.

She'd forgotten everything. She could only stare, almost stupefied by the sensations that spiked through her. Involuntarily her fingers curled into his shirt. She got an impression of strength, a ruthless strength with the potential for violence. The fact that it excited her left her speechless.

"Do you want something?" he murmured.

"What?"

He thought about kissing her, about pressing his mouth hard on hers and plunging into her. He would enjoy the taste, the momentary passion. "I asked if you wanted something." Slowly he ran his hands up under her sweater to her waist.

The shock of heat, the press of fingers, brought her back. "No." She started to back away, found herself held still, and fought her rising panic. Before she could speak again, he had released her. Disappointment. That was an odd reaction, she thought, when you'd just missed getting burned.

"I was—" She took a deep breath and waited for her scattered nerves to settle. "I was going to ask if you'd found everything you needed."

His eyes never left hers. "It looks like it."

She pressed her lips together to moisten them. "Good. I've got a lot to do, so I'll let you get back."

He took her arm before she could step away. Maybe it

wasn't smart, but he wanted to touch her again. "Thanks for the towels."

"Sure."

He watched her hurry out, knowing her nerves were as jangled as his own. Thoughtfully he pulled out a cigarette. He couldn't remember ever having been thrown off balance so easily. Certainly not by a woman who'd done nothing more than look at him. Still, he made a habit of landing on his feet.

It might be to his advantage to get close to her, to play on the response he'd felt from her. Ignoring a wave of self-disgust, he struck a match.

He had a job to do. He couldn't afford to think about Charity Ford as anything more than a means to an end.

He drew smoke in, cursing the dull ache in his belly.

Chapter 2

It was barely dawn, and the sky to the east was fantastic. Roman stood near the edge of the narrow road, his hands tucked in his back pockets. Though he rarely had time for them, he enjoyed mornings such as this, when the air was cool and sparkling clear. A man could breathe here, and if he could afford the luxury he could empty his mind and simply experience.

He'd promised himself thirty minutes, thirty solitary, soothing minutes. The blooming sunlight pushed through the cloud formations, turning them into wild, vivid colors and shapes. Dream shapes. He considered lighting a cigarette, then rejected it. For the moment he wanted only the taste of morning air flavored by the sea.

There was a dog barking in the distance, a faint yap, yap, yap that only added to the ambience. Gulls, out for an early feeding, swooped low over the water, slicing the silence with their lonely cries. The fragrance of flowers, a celebration of spring, carried delicately on the quiet breeze.

He wondered why he'd been so certain he preferred the rush and noise of cities.

As he stood there he saw a deer come out of the trees and raise her head to scent the air. That was freedom, he thought abruptly. To know your place and to be content with it. The doe cleared the trees, picking her way delicately toward the high grass. Behind her came a gangly fawn. Staying upwind, Roman watched them graze.

He was restless. Even as he tried to absorb and accept the peace around him he felt the impatience struggling through. This wasn't his place. He had no place. That was one of the things that made him so perfect for his job. No roots, no family, no woman waiting for his return. That was the way he wanted it.

But he'd felt enormous satisfaction in doing the carpentry the day before, in leaving his mark on something that would last. All the better for his cover, he told himself. If he showed some skill and some care in the work he would be accepted more easily.

He was already accepted.

She trusted him. She'd given him a roof and a meal and a job, thinking he needed all three. She seemed to have no guile in her. Something had simmered between them the evening before, yet she had done nothing to provoke or prolong it. She hadn't—though he knew all females were capable of it from birth—issued a silent invitation that she might or might not have intended to keep.

She'd simply looked at him, and everything she felt had been almost ridiculously clear in her eyes.

He couldn't think of her as a woman. He couldn't think of her as ever being *his* woman.

He felt the urge for a cigarette again, and this time he deliberately suppressed it. If there was something you wanted that badly, it was best to pass it by. Once you gave in, you surrendered control.

He'd wanted Charity. For one brief, blinding instant the day before, he had craved her. A very serious error. He'd blocked the need, but it had continued to surface— when he'd heard her come into the wing for the night, when he'd listened to the sound of Chopin drifting softly down the stairway from her rooms. And again in the middle of the night, when he'd awakened to the deep country silence, thinking of her, imagining her.

He didn't have time for desires. In another place, at another time, they might have met and enjoyed each other for as long as enjoyments lasted. But now she was part of an assignment—nothing less, nothing more.

He heard the sound of running footsteps and tensed instinctively. The deer, as alert as he, lifted her head, then sprinted back into the trees with her young. His weapon was strapped just above his ankle, more out of habit than necessity, but he didn't reach for it. If he needed it it could be in his hand in under a second. Instead, he waited, braced, to see who was running down the deserted road at dawn.

Charity was breathing fast, more from the effort of keeping pace with her dog than from the three-mile run. Ludwig bounded ahead, tugged to the right, jerked to the left, tangled and untangled in the leash. It was a daily routine, one that both of them were accustomed to. She could have controlled the little golden cocker, but she didn't want to spoil his fun. Instead, she swerved with him, adjusting her pace from a flat-out run to an easy jog and back again.

She hesitated briefly when she saw Roman. Then, because Ludwig sprinted ahead, she tightened her grip on the leash and kept pace.

"Good morning," she called out, then skidded to a halt when Ludwig decided to jump on Roman's shins and bark at him. "He doesn't bite."

"That's what they all say." But he grinned and crouched down to scratch between the dog's ears. Ludwig immediately collapsed, rolled over and exposed his belly for rubbing. "Nice dog."

"A nice spoiled dog," Charity added. "I have to keep him fenced because of the guests, but he eats like a king. You're up early."

"So are you."

"I figure Ludwig deserves a good run every morning, since he's so understanding about being fenced."

To show his appreciation, Ludwig raced once around Roman, tangling his lead around his legs.

"Now if I could only get him to understand the concept of a leash." She stooped to untangle Roman and to control the now-prancing dog.

Her light jacket was unzipped, exposing a snug T-shirt darkened with sweat between her breasts. Her hair, pulled straight, almost severely, back from her face, accented her bone structure. Her skin seemed almost translucent as it glowed from her run. He had an urge to touch it, to see how it felt under his fingertips. And to see if that instant reaction would rush out again.

"Ludwig, be still a minute." She laughed and tugged at his collar.

In response, the dog jumped up and lapped at her face. "He listens well," Roman commented.

"You can see why I need the fence. He thinks he can play with everyone." Her hand brushed Roman's leg as she struggled with the leash.

When he took her wrist, both of them froze.

He could feel her pulse skip, then sprint. It was a quick, vulnerable response that was unbearably arousing. Though it cost him, he kept his fingers loose. He had only meant to stop her before she inadvertently found his weapon. Now they crouched, knee to knee, in the center of the deserted road, with the dog trying to nuzzle between them.

"You're trembling." He said it warily, but he didn't release her. "Do you always react that way when a man touches you?"

"No." Because it baffled her, she kept still and waited to see what would happen next. "I'm pretty sure this is a first."

It pleased him to hear it, and it annoyed him, because he wanted to believe it. "Then we'll have to be careful, won't we?" He released her, then stood up.

More slowly, because she wasn't sure of her balance, she rose. He was angry. Though he was holding on to his temper, it was clear enough to see in his eyes. "I'm not very good at being careful."

His gaze whipped back to hers. There was a fire in

it, a fire that raged and then was quickly and completely suppressed. "I am."

"Yes." The brief, heated glance had alarmed her, but Charity had always held her own. She tilted her head to study him. "I think you'd have to be, with that streak of violence you have to contend with. Who are you mad at, Roman?"

He didn't like to be read that easily. Watching her, he lowered a hand to pet Ludwig, who was resting his front paws on his knees. "Nobody at the moment," he told her, but it was a lie. He was furious—with himself.

She only shook her head. "You're entitled to your secrets, but I can't help wondering why you'd be angry with yourself for responding to me."

He took a lazy scan of the road, up, then down. They might have been alone on the island. "Would you like me to do something about it, here and now?"

He could, she realized. And he would. If he was pushed too far he would do exactly what he wanted, when he wanted. The frisson of excitement that passed through her annoyed her. Macho types were for other women, different women—not Charity Ford. Deliberately she looked at her watch.

"Thanks. I'm sure that's a delightful offer, but I have to get back and set up for breakfast." Struggling with the dog, she started off at what she hoped was a digni-fied walk. "I'll let you know if I can squeeze in, say, fifteen minutes later."

"Charity?"

She turned her head and aimed a cool look. "Yes?"

"Your shoe's untied."

She just lifted her chin and continued on.

Roman grinned at her back and tucked his thumbs in his pockets. Yes, indeed, the woman had one hell of a walk. It was too damn bad all around that he was beginning to like her.

He was interested in the tour group. It was a simple matter for Roman to loiter on the first floor, lingering over a second cup of coffee in the kitchen, passing idle conversation with the thick-armed Mae and the skinny Dolores. He hadn't expected to be put to work, but when he'd found himself with an armful of table linens he had made the best of it.

Charity, wearing a bright red sweatshirt with the inn's logo across the chest, meticulously arranged a folded napkin in a water glass. Roman waited a moment, watching her busy fingers smoothing and tapering the cloth.

"Where do you want these?"

She glanced over, wondering if she should still be annoyed with him, then decided against it. At the moment she needed every extra hand she could get. "On the tables would be a good start. White on the bottom, apricot on top, slanted. Okay?" She indicated a table that was already set.

"Sure." He began to spread the cloths. "How many are you expecting?"

"Fifteen on the tour." She held a glass up to the light and placed it on the table only after a critical inspection. "Their breakfast is included. Plus the guests already registered. We serve between seven-thirty and ten." She checked her watch, satisfied, then moved to another table. "We get some drop-ins, as well." After setting a chipped bread plate aside, she reached for another. "But it's lunch and dinner that really get hectic."

Dolores swooped in with a stack of china, then dashed out again when Mae squawked at her. Before the door had swung closed, the waitress they had passed on the road the day before rushed out with a tray of clanging silverware.

"Right," Roman murmured.

Charity rattled off instructions to the waitress, finished setting yet another table, then rushed over to a blackboard near the doorway and began to copy out the morning menu in a flowing, elegant hand.

Dolores, whose spiky red hair and pursed lips made Roman think of a scrawny chicken, shoved through the swinging door and set her fists on her skinny hips. "I don't have to take this, Charity."

Charity calmly continued to write. "Take what?"

"I'm doing the best that I can, and you know I told you I was feeling poorly."

Dolores was always feeling poorly, Charity thought as she added a ham-and-cheese omelet to the list. Especially when she didn't get her way. "Yes, Dolores."

"My chest's so tight that I can hardly take a breath."

"Um-hmm."

"Was up half the night, but I come in, just like always."

"And I appreciate it, Dolores. You know how much I depend on you."

"Well." Slightly mollified, Dolores tugged at her apron. "I guess I can be counted on to do my job, but you can just tell that woman in there—" She jerked a thumb toward the kitchen. "Just tell her to get off my back."

"I'll speak to her, Dolores. Just try to be patient. We're all a little frazzled this morning, with Mary Alice out sick again."

"Sick." Dolores sniffed. "Is that what they're calling it these days?"

Listening with only half an ear, Charity continued to write. "What do you mean?"

"Don't know why her car was in Bill Perkin's driveway all night again if she's sick. Now, with my condition—"

Charity stopped writing. Roman's brow lifted when he heard the sudden thread of steel in her voice. "We'll talk about this later, Dolores."

Deflated, Dolores poked out her lower lip and stalked back into the kitchen.

Storing her anger away, Charity turned to the waitress. "Lori?"

"Almost ready."

"Good. If you can handle the registered guests, I'll be back to give you a hand after I check the tour group in."

"No problem."

"I'll be at the front desk with Bob." Absently she pushed her braid behind her back. "If it gets too busy, send for me. Roman—"

"Want me to bus tables?"

She gave him a quick, grateful smile. "Do you know how?"

"I can figure it out."

"Thanks." She checked her watch, then rushed out. He hadn't expected to enjoy himself, but it was hard not to, with Miss Millie flirting with him over her raspberry preserves. The scent of baking—something rich, with apples and cinnamon—the quiet strains of classical music and the murmur of conversation made it almost impossible not to relax. He carried trays to and from the kitchen. The muttered exchanges between Mae and Dolores were more amusing than annoying.

So he enjoyed himself. And took advantage of his position by doing his job.

As he cleared the tables by the windows, he watched a tour van pull up to the front entrance. He counted heads and studied the faces of the group. The guide was a big man in a white shirt that strained across his shoulders. He had a round, ruddy, cheerful face that smiled continually as he piloted his passengers inside. Roman moved across the room to watch them mill around in the lobby.

They were a mix of couples and families with small children. The guide—Roman already knew his name was Block—greeted Charity with a hearty smile and then handed her a list of names.

Did she know that Block had done a stretch in Leavenworth for fraud? he wondered. Was she aware that the man she was joking with had escaped a second term only because of some fancy legal footwork?

Roman's jaw tensed as Block reached over and flicked a finger at Charity's dangling gold earring.

As she assigned cabins and dealt out keys, two of the group approached the desk to exchange money. Fifty for one, sixty for the other, Roman noted as Canadian bills were passed to Charity's assistant and American currency passed back.

Within ten minutes the entire group was seated in the dining room, contemplating breakfast. Charity breezed in behind them, putting on an apron. She flipped open a pad and began to take orders.

She didn't look as if she were in a hurry, Roman noted. The way she chatted and smiled and answered questions, it was as though she had all the time in the world. But she moved like lightning. She carried three plates on her right arm, served coffee with her left hand and cooed over a baby, all at the same time.

Something was eating at her, Roman mused. It hardly showed...just a faint frown between her eyes. Had something gone wrong that morning that he'd missed? If there was a glitch in the system, it was up to him to find it and exploit it. That was the reason he was here on the inside.

Charity poured another round of coffee for a table of four, joked with a bald man wearing a paisley tie, then made her way over to Roman.

"I think the crisis has passed." She smiled at him, but again he caught something.... Anger? Disappointment?

"Is there anything you don't do around here?"

"I try to stay out of the kitchen. The restaurant has a three-star rating." She glanced longingly at the coffeepot. There would be time for that later. "I want to thank you for pitching in this morning."

"That's okay." He discovered he wanted to see her smile. Really smile. "The tips were good. Miss Millie slipped me a five."

She obliged him. Her lips curved quickly, and whatever had clouded her eyes cleared for a moment. "She likes the way you look in a tool belt. Why don't you take a break before you start on the west wing?"

"All right."

She grimaced at the sound of glass breaking. "I didn't think the Snyder kid wanted that orange juice." She hurried off to clean up the mess and listen to the parents' apologies.

The front desk was deserted. Roman decided that Charity's assistant was either shut up in the side office or out hauling luggage to the cabins. He considered slipping behind the desk and taking a quick look at the books but decided it could wait. Some work was better done in the dark.

An hour later Charity let herself into the west wing. She'd managed to hold on to her temper as she'd passed the guests on the first floor. She'd smiled and chatted with an elderly couple playing Parcheesi in the gathering room. But when the door closed behind her she let loose with a series of furious, pent-up oaths. She wanted to kick something.

Roman stepped into a doorway and watched her stride down the hall. Anger had made her eyes dark and brilliant.

"Problem?"

"Yes," she snapped. She stalked half a dozen steps past him, then whirled around. "I can take incompetence, and even some degree of stupidity. I can even tolerate an occasional bout of laziness. But I won't be lied to."

Roman waited a beat. Her anger was ripe and rich,

but it wasn't directed at him. "All right," he said, and waited.

"She could have told me she wanted time off, or a different shift. I might have been able to work it out. Instead she lies, calling in sick at the last minute five days out of the last two weeks. I was worried about her." She turned again, then gave in and kicked a door. "I hate being made a fool of. And I *hate* being lied to."

It was a simple matter to put two and two together. "You're talking about the waitress…Mary Alice?"

"Of course." She spun around. "She came begging me for a job three months ago. That's our slowest time, but I felt sorry for her. Now she's sleeping with Bill Perkin— or I guess it's more accurate to say she's not getting any sleep, so she calls in sick. I had to fire her." She let out a breath with a sound like an engine letting off steam. "I get a headache whenever I have to fire anybody."

"Is that what was bothering you all morning?"

"As soon as Dolores mentioned Bill, I knew." Calmer now, she rubbed at the insistent ache between her eyes. "Then I had to get through the check-in and the break-fast shift before I could call and deal with her. She cried." She gave Roman a long, miserable look. "I knew she was going to cry."

"Listen, baby, the best thing for you to do is take some aspirin and forget about it."

"I've already taken some."

"Give it a chance to kick in." Before he realized what he was doing, he lifted his hands and framed her face. Moving his thumbs in slow circles, he massaged her temples. "You've got too much going on in there."

"Where?"

"In your head."

She felt her eyes getting heavy and her blood growing warm. "Not at the moment." She tilted her head back and let her eyes close. Moving on instinct, she stepped forward. "Roman…" She sighed a little as the ache melted out of her head and stirred in the very center of her. "I like the way you look in a tool belt, too."

"Do you know what you're asking for?"

She studied his mouth. It was full and firm, and it would certainly be ruthless on a woman's. "Not exactly." Perhaps that was the appeal, she thought as she stared up at him. She didn't know. But she felt, and what she felt was new and thrilling. "Maybe it's better that way."

"No." Though he knew it was a mistake, he couldn't resist skimming his fingers down to trace her jaw, then her lips. "It's always better to know the consequences before you take the action."

"So we're being careful again."

He dropped his hands. "Yeah."

She should have been grateful. Instead of taking advantage of her confused emotions he was backing off, giving her room. She wanted to be grateful, but she felt only the sting of rejection. He had started it, she thought. Again. And he had stopped it. Again. She was sick and tired of being jolted along according to his whims.

"You miss a lot that way, don't you, Roman? A lot of warmth, a lot of joy."

"A lot of disappointment."

"Maybe. I guess it's harder for some of us to live our

lives aloof from others. But if that's your choice, fine."
She drew in a deep breath. Her headache was coming
back, doubled. "Don't touch me again. I make it a habit
to finish whatever I start." She glanced into the room
behind them. "You're doing a nice job here," she said
briskly. "I'll let you get back to it."

He cursed her as he sanded the wood for the window
trim. She had no right to make him feel guilty just because he wanted to keep his distance. Noninvolvement
wasn't just a habit with him; it was a matter of survival.
It was self-indulgent and dangerous to move forward
every time you were attracted to a woman.

But it was more than attraction, and it was certainly
different from anything he'd felt before. Whenever he
was near her, his purpose became clouded with fantasies of what it would be like to be with her, to hold her,
to make love with her.

And fantasies were all they were, he reminded himself. If things went well he would be gone in a matter
of days. Before he was done he might very well destroy her life.

It was his job, he reminded himself.

He saw her, walking out to the van with those long,
purposeful strides of hers, the keys jingling in her hand.
Behind her were the newlyweds, holding hands, even
though each was carrying a suitcase.

She would be taking them to the ferry, he thought.
That would give him an hour to search her rooms.

He knew how to go through every inch of a room
without leaving a trace. He concentrated first on the obvious—the desk in the small parlor. It was common for

people to be careless in the privacy of their own homes. A slip of paper, a scribbled note, a name in an address book, were often left behind for the trained eye to spot.

It was an old desk, solid mahogany with a few rings and scratches. Two of the brass pulls were loose. Like the rest of the room, it was neat and well organized. Her personal papers—insurance documents, bills, correspondence—were filed on the left. Inn business took up the three drawers on the right.

He could see from a quick scan that the inn made a reasonable profit, most of which she funneled directly back into it. New linens, bathroom fixtures, paint. The stove Mae was so territorial about had been purchased only six months earlier.

She took a salary for herself, a surprisingly modest one. He didn't find, even after a more critical study, any evidence of her using any of the inn's finances to ease her own way.

An honest woman, Roman mused. At least on the surface.

There was a bowl of potpourri on the desk, as there was in every room in the inn. Beside it was a framed picture of Charity standing in front of the mill wheel with a fragile-looking man with white hair.

The grandfather, Roman decided, but it was Charity's image he studied. Her hair was pulled back in a ponytail, and her baggy overalls were stained at the knees. From gardening, Roman guessed. She was holding an armful of summer flowers. She looked as if she didn't have a care in the world, but he noted that her free arm was around the old man, supporting him.

He wondered what she had been thinking at that moment, what she had done the moment after the picture had been snapped. He swore at himself and looked away from the picture.

She left notes to herself: Return wallpaper samples. New blocks for toy chest. Call piano tuner. Get flat repaired.

He found nothing that touched on his reason for coming to the inn. Leaving the desk, he meticulously searched the rest of the parlor.

Then he went into the adjoining bedroom. The bed, a four-poster, was covered with a lacy white spread and plumped with petit-point pillows. Beside it was a beautiful old rocker, its arms worn smooth as glass. In it sat a big purple teddy bear wearing yellow suspenders.

The curtains were romantic priscillas. She'd left the windows open, and the breeze came through billowing them. A woman's room, Roman thought, unrelentingly feminine with its lace and pillows, its fragile scents and pale colors. Yet somehow it welcomed a man, made him wish, made him want. It made him want one hour, one night, in that softness, that comfort.

He crossed the faded handhooked rug and, burying his self-disgust, went through her dresser.

He found a few pieces of jewelry he took to be heirlooms. They belonged in a safe, he thought, annoyed with her. There was a bottle of perfume. He knew exactly how it would smell. It would smell the way her skin did. He nearly reached for it before he caught himself. Perfume wasn't of any interest to him. Evidence was.

A packet of letters caught his eye. From a lover? he wondered, dismissing the sudden pang of jealousy he felt as ridiculous.

The room was making him crazy, he thought as he carefully untied the slender satin ribbon. It was impossible not to imagine her there, curled on the bed, wearing something white and thin, her hair loose and the candles lit.

He shook himself as he unfolded the first letter. A room with a purple teddy bear wasn't seductive, he told himself.

The date showed him that they had been written when she had attended college in Seattle. From her grandfather, Roman realized as he scanned them. Every one. They were written with affection and humor, and they contained dozens of little stories about daily life at the inn. Roman put them back the way he'd found them.

Her clothes were casual, except for a few dresses hanging in the closet. There were sturdy boots, sneakers spotted with what looked like grass stains and two pairs of elegant heels on either side of fuzzy slippers in the shape of elephants. Like the rest of her rooms, they were meticulously arranged. Even in the closet he didn't find a trace of dust.

Besides an alarm clock and a pot of hand cream she had two books on her nightstand. One was a collection of poetry, the other a murder mystery with a gruesome cover. She had a cache of chocolate in the drawer and Chopin on her small portable stereo. There were candles, dozens of them, burned down to various heights. On one wall hung a seascape in deep, stormy blues and grays. On another was a collection of photos, most taken at the inn, many of her grandfather. Roman searched behind each one. He discovered that her paint was fading, nothing more.

Her rooms were clean. Roman stood in the center of the bedroom, taking in the scents of candle wax, potpourri and perfume. They couldn't have been cleaner if she'd known they were going to be searched. All he knew after an hour was that she was an organized woman who liked comfortable clothes and Chopin and had a weakness for chocolate and lurid paperback novels.

Why did that make her fascinating?

He scowled and shoved his hands in his pockets, struggling for objectivity as he had never had to struggle before. All the evidence pointed to her being involved in some very shady business. Everything he'd discovered in the last twenty-four hours indicated that she was an open, honest and hardworking woman.

Which did he believe?

He walked toward the door at the far end of the room. It opened onto a postage-stamp-size porch with a long set of stairs that led down to the pond. He wanted to open the door, to step out and breathe in the air, but he turned his back on it and went out the way he had come in.

The scent of her bedroom stayed with him for hours.

Chapter 3

"I told you that girl was no good."

"I know, Mae."

"I told you you were making a mistake taking her on like you did."

"Yes, Mae." Charity bit back a sigh. "You told me."

"You keep taking in strays, you're bound to get bit."

Charity resisted—just barely—the urge to scream. "So you've told me."

With a satisfied grunt, Mae finished wiping off her pride and joy, the eight-burner gas range. Charity might run the inn, but Mae had her own ideas about who was in charge. "You're too softhearted, Charity."

"I thought you said it was hardheaded."

"That too." Because she had a warm spot for her young employer, Mae poured a glass of milk and cut a generous slab from the remains of her double chocolate cake. Keeping her voice brisk, she set both on the table. "You eat this now. My baking always made you feel better as a girl."

Charity took a seat and poked a finger into the icing. "I would have given her some time off."

"I know." Mae rubbed her wide-palmed hand on Charity's shoulder. "That's the trouble with you. You take your name too seriously."

"I hate being made a fool of." Scowling, Charity took a huge bite of cake. Chocolate, she was sure, would be a better cure for her headache than an entire bottle of aspirin. Her guilt was a different matter. "Do you think she'll get another job? I know she's got rent to pay."

"Types like Mary Alice always land on their feet. Wouldn't surprise me if she moved in lock, stock and barrel with that Perkin boy, so don't you be worrying about the likes of her. Didn't I tell you she wouldn't last six months?"

Charity pushed more cake into her mouth. "You told me," she mumbled around it.

"Now then, what about this man you brought home?"

Charity took a gulp of her milk. "Roman DeWinter."

"Screwy name." Mae glanced around the kitchen, surprised and a little disappointed that there was nothing left to do. "What do you know about him?"

"He needed a job."

Mae wiped her reddened hands on the skirt of her apron. "I expect there's a whole slew of pickpockets, cat burglars and mass murderers who need jobs."

"He's not a mass murderer," Charity stated. She

thought she had better reserve judgment on the other occupations.

"Maybe, maybe not."

"He's a drifter." She shrugged and took another bite of the cake. "But I wouldn't say aimless. He knows where he's going. In any case, with George off doing the hula, I needed someone. He does good work, Mae."

Mae had determined that for herself with a quick trip into the west wing. But she had other things on her mind. "He looks at you."

Stalling, Charity ran a fingertip up and down the side of her glass. "Everyone looks at me. I'm always here."

"Don't play stupid with me, young lady. I powdered your bottom."

"Whatever that has to do with anything," Charity answered with a grin. "So he looks?" She moved her shoulders again. "I look back." When Mae arched her brows, Charity just smiled. "Aren't you always telling me I need a man in my life?"

"There's men and there's men," Mae said sagely. "This one's not bad on the eyes, and he ain't afraid of working. But he's got a hard streak in him. That one's been around, my girl, and no mistake."

"I guess you'd rather I spent time with Jimmy Loggerman."

"Spineless worm."

After a burst of laughter, Charity cupped her chin in her hands. "You were right, Mae. I do feel better."

Pleased, Mae untied the apron from around her ample girth. She didn't doubt that Charity was a sensible girl, but she intended to keep an eye on Roman herself. "Good. Don't cut any more of that cake or you'll be up all night with a bellyache."

"Yes'm."

"And don't leave a mess in my kitchen," she added as she tugged on a practical brown coat.

"No, ma'am. Good night, Mae."

Charity sighed as the door rattled shut. Mae's leaving usually signaled the end of the day. The guests would be tucked into their beds or finishing up a late card game. Barring an emergency, there was nothing left for Charity to do until sunrise.

Nothing to do but think.

Lately she'd been toying with the idea of putting in a whirlpool. That might lure a small percentage of the resortgoers. She'd priced a few solarium kits, and in her mind she could already see the sunroom on the inn's south side. In the winter guests could come back from hiking to a hot, bubbling tub and top off the day with rum punch by the fire.

She would enjoy it herself, especially on those rare winter days when the inn was empty and there was nothing for her to do but rattle around alone.

Then there was her long-range plan to add on a gift shop supplied by local artists and craftsmen. Nothing too elaborate, she thought. She wanted to keep things simple, in keeping with the spirit of the inn.

She wondered if Roman would stay around long enough to work on it.

It wasn't wise to think of him in connection with any of her plans. It probably wasn't wise to think of him at all. He was, as she had said herself, a drifter. Men like Roman didn't light in one spot for long.

She couldn't seem to stop thinking about him. Almost from the first moment she'd felt something. Attraction was one thing. He was, after all, an attractive man, in a tough, dangerous kind of way. But there was more. Something in his eyes? she wondered. In his voice? In the way he moved? She toyed with the rest of her cake, wishing she could pin it down. It might simply be that he was so different from herself. Taciturn, suspicious, solitary.

And yet…was it her imagination, or was part of him waiting, to reach out, to grab hold? He needed someone, she thought, though he was probably unaware of it.

Mae was right, she mused. She had always had a weakness for strays and a hard-luck story. But this was different. She closed her eyes for a moment, wishing she could explain, even to herself, why it was so very different.

She'd never experienced anything like the sensations that had rammed into her because of Roman. It was more than physical. She could admit that now. Still, it made no sense. Then again, Charity had always thought that feelings weren't required to make sense.

For a moment out on the deserted road this morning she'd felt emotions pour out of him. They had been almost frightening in their speed and power. Emotions like that could hurt…the one who felt them, the one who received them. They had left her dazed and aching—and wishing, she admitted.

She thought she knew what his mouth would taste

like. Not soft, not sweet, but pungent and powerful. When he was ready, he wouldn't ask, he'd take. It worried her that she didn't resent that. She had grown up knowing her own mind, making her own choices. A man like Roman would have little respect for a woman's wishes.

It would be better, much better, for them to keep their relationship—their short-term relationship, she added—on a purely business level. Friendly but careful. She let her chin sink into her hands again. It was a pity she had such a difficult time combining the two.

He watched her toy with the crumbs on her plate. Her hair was loose now and tousled, as if she had pulled it out of the braid and ran impatient fingers through it. Her bare feet were crossed at the ankles, resting on the chair across from her.

Relaxed. Roman wasn't sure he'd ever seen anyone so fully relaxed except in sleep. It was a sharp contrast to the churning energy that drove her during the day.

He wished she were in her rooms, tucked into bed and sleeping deeply. He'd wanted to avoid coming across her at all. That was personal. He needed her out of his way so that he could go through the office off the lobby. That was business.

He knew he should step back and keep out of sight until she retired for the night.

What was it about this quiet scene that was so appealing, so irresistible? The kitchen was warm and the scents of cooking were lingering, pleasantly overlaying those of pine and lemon from Mae's cleaning. There was a hanging basket over the sink that was almost choked with some leafy green plant. Every surface was scrubbed, clean and shiny. The huge refrigerator hummed.

She looked so comfortable, as if she were waiting for him to come in and sit with her, to talk of small, inconsequential things.

That was crazy. He didn't want any woman waiting for him, and especially not her.

But he didn't step back into the shadows of the dining room, though he could easily have done so. He stepped toward her, into the light.

"I thought people kept early hours in the country."

She jumped but recovered quickly. She was almost used to the silent way he moved. "Mostly. Mae was giving me chocolate and a pep talk. Want some cake?"

"No."

"Just as well. If you had I'd have taken another piece and made myself sick. No willpower. How about a beer?"

"Yeah. Thanks."

She got up lazily and moved to the refrigerator to rattle off a list of brands. He chose one and watched her pour it into a pilsner glass. She wasn't angry, he noted, though she had certainly been the last time they were together. So Charity didn't hold grudges. She wouldn't, Roman decided as he took the glass from her. She would forgive almost anything, would trust everyone and would give more than was asked.

"Why do you look at me that way?" she murmured.

He caught himself, then took a long, thirsty pull on the beer. "You have a beautiful face."

She lifted a brow when he sat down and pulled out a cigarette. After taking an ashtray from a drawer, she sat beside him. "I like to accept compliments whenever I get them, but I don't think that's the reason."

"It's reason enough for a man to look at a woman." He sipped his beer. "You had a busy night."

Let it go, Charity told herself. "Busy enough that I need to hire another waitress fast. I didn't get a chance to thank you for helping out with the dinner crowd."

"No problem. Lose the headache?"

She glanced up sharply. But, no, he wasn't making fun of her. It seemed, though she couldn't be sure why the impression was so strong, that his question was a kind of apology. She decided to accept it.

"Yes, thanks. Getting mad at you took my mind off Mary Alice, and Mae's chocolate cake did the rest." She thought about brewing some tea, then decided she was too lazy to bother. "So, how was your day?"

She smiled at him in an easy offer of friendship that he found difficult to resist and impossible to accept. "Okay. Miss Millie said the door to her room was sticking, so I pretended to sand it."

"And made her day."

He couldn't prevent the smile. "I don't think I've ever been ogled quite so completely before."

"Oh, I imagine you have." She tilted her head to study him from a new angle. "But, with apologies to your ego, in Miss Millie's case it's more a matter of nearsightedness than lust. She's too vain to wear her glasses in front of any male over twenty."

"I'd rather go on thinking she's leering at me," he

said. "She said she's been coming here twice a year since '52." He thought that over for a moment, amazed that anyone could return time after time to the same spot.

"She and Miss Lucy are fixtures here. When I was young I thought we were related."

"You been running this place long?"

"Off and on for all of my twenty-seven years." Smiling, she tipped back in her chair. She was a woman who relaxed easily and enjoyed seeing others relaxed. He seemed so now, she thought, with his legs stretched out under the table and a glass in his hand. "You don't really want to hear the story of my life, do you, Roman?"

He blew out a stream of smoke. "I've got nothing to do." And he wanted to hear her version of what he'd read in her file.

"Okay. I was born here. My mother had fallen in love a bit later in life than most. She was nearly forty when she had me, and fragile. There were complications. After she died, my grandfather raised me, so I grew up here at the inn, except for the periods of time when he sent me away to school. I loved this place." She glanced around the kitchen. "In school I pined for it, and for Pop. Even in college I missed it so much I'd ferry home every weekend. But he wanted me to see something else before I settled down here. I was going to travel some, get new ideas for the inn. See New York, New Orleans, Venice. I don't know...." Her words trailed off wistfully.

"Why didn't you?"

"My grandfather was ill. I was in my last year of college when I found out *how* ill. I wanted to quit, come home, but the idea upset him so much I thought it was better to graduate. He hung on for another three years, but it was…difficult." She didn't want to talk about the tears and the terror, or about the exhaustion of running the inn while caring for a near-invalid. "He was the bravest, kindest man I've ever known. He was so much a part of this place that there are still times when I expect to walk into a room and see him checking for dust on the furniture."

He was silent for a moment, thinking as much about what she'd left out as about what she'd told him. He knew her father was listed as unknown—a difficult obstacle anywhere, but especially in a small town. In the last six months of her grandfather's life his medical expenses had nearly driven the inn under. But she didn't speak of those things; nor did he detect any sign of bitterness.

"Do you ever think about selling the place, moving on?"

"No. Oh, I still think about Venice occasionally. There are dozens of places I'd like to go, as long as I had the inn to come back to." She rose to get him another beer. "When you run a place like this, you get to meet people from all over. There's always a story about a new place."

"Vicarious traveling?"

It stung, perhaps because it was too close to her own thoughts. "Maybe." She set the bottle at his elbow, then took her dishes to the sink. Even knowing that she was overly sensitive on this point didn't stop her from bristling. "Some of us are meant to be boring."

"I didn't say you were boring."

"No? Well, I suppose I am to someone who picks up and goes whenever and wherever he chooses. Simple, settled and naive."

"You're putting words in my mouth, baby."

"It's easy to do, *baby,* since you rarely put any there yourself. Turn off the lights when you leave."

He took her arm as she started by in a reflexive movement that he regretted almost before it was done. But it was done, and the sulky, defiant look she sent him began a chain reaction that raced through his system. There were things he could do with her, things he burned to do, that neither of them would ever forget.

"Why are you angry?"

"I don't know. I can't seem to talk to you for more than ten minutes without getting edgy. Since I normally get along with everyone, I figure it's you."

"You're probably right."

She calmed a little. It was hardly his fault that she had never been anywhere. "You've been around a little less than forty-eight hours and I've nearly fought with you three times. That's a record for me."

"I don't keep score."

"Oh, I think you do. I doubt you forget anything. Were you a cop?"

He had to make a deliberate effort to keep his face bland and fingers from tensing. "Why?"

"You said you weren't an artist. That was my first guess." She relaxed, though he hadn't removed his hand from her arm. Anger was something she enjoyed only in fast, brief spurts. "It's the way you look at people, as if you were filing away descriptions and any distinguishing marks. And sometimes when I'm with you I feel as though I should get ready for an interrogation. A writer, then? When you're in the hotel business you get pretty good at matching people with professions."

"You're off this time."

"Well, what are you, then?"

"Right now I'm a handyman."

She shrugged, making herself let it go. "Another trait of hotel people is respecting privacy, but if you turn out to be a mass murderer Mae's never going to let me hear the end of it."

"Generally I only kill one person at a time."

"That's good news." She ignored the suddenly very real anxiety that he was speaking the simple truth. "You're still holding my arm."

"I know."

So this was it, she thought, and struggled to keep her voice. "Should I ask you to let go?"

"I wouldn't bother."

She drew a deep, steadying breath. "All right. What do you want, Roman?"

"To get this out of the way, for both of us."

He rose. Her step backward was instinctive, and much more surprising to her than to him. "I don't think that's a good idea."

"Neither do I." With his free hand, he gathered up her hair. It was soft, as he'd known it would be. Thick and full and so soft that his fingers dived in and were lost. "But I'd rather regret something I did than something I didn't do."

"I'd rather not regret at all."

"Too late." He heard her suck in her breath as he yanked her against him. "One way or the other, we'll both have plenty to regret."

He was deliberately rough. He knew how to be gentle, though he rarely put the knowledge into practice. With her, he could have been. Perhaps because he knew that, he shoved aside any desire for tenderness. He wanted to frighten her, to make certain that when he let her go she would run, run away from him, because he wanted so badly for her to run to him.

Buried deep in his mind was the hope that he could make her afraid enough, repelled enough, to send him packing. If she did, she would be safe from him, and he from her. He thought he could accomplish it quickly. Then, suddenly, it was impossible to think at all.

She tasted like heaven. He'd never believed in heaven, but the flavor was on her lips, pure and sweet and promising. Her hand had gone to his chest in an automatic defensive movement. Yet she wasn't fighting him, as he'd been certain she would. She met his hard, almost brutal kiss with passion laced with trust.

His mind emptied. It was a terrifying experience for a man who kept his thoughts under such stringent control. Then it filled with her, her scent, her touch, her taste.

He broke away—for his sake now, not for hers. He was and had always been a survivor. His breath came fast and raw. One hand was still tangled in her hair, and his other was clamped tight on her arm. He couldn't let go. No matter how he chided himself to release her, to step back and walk away, he couldn't move. Staring at her, he saw his own reflection in her eyes.

He cursed her—it was a last quick denial—before he crushed his mouth to hers again. It wasn't heaven he was heading for, he told himself. It was hell.

She wanted to soothe him, but he never gave her the chance. As before, he sent her rushing into some hot, airless place where there was room only for sensation.

She'd been right. His mouth wasn't soft, it was hard and ruthless and irresistible. Without hesitation, without thought of self-preservation, she opened for him, greedily taking what was offered, selflessly giving what was demanded.

Her back was pressed against the smooth, cool surface of the refrigerator, trapped there by the firm, taut lines of his body. If it had been possible, she would have brought him closer.

His face was rough as it scraped against hers, and she trembled at the thrill of pleasure even that brought her. Desperate now, she nipped at his lower lip, and felt a new rush of excitement as he groaned and deepened an already bottomless kiss.

She wanted to be touched. She tried to murmur this new, compelling need against his mouth, but she managed only a moan. Her body ached. Just the anticipation of his hands running over her was making her shudder.

For a moment their hearts beat against each other in the same wild rhythm.

He tore away, aware that he had come perilously

close to a line he didn't dare cross. He could hardly breathe, much less think. Until he was certain he could do both, he was silent.

"Go to bed, Charity."

She stayed where she was, certain that if she took a step her legs would give away. He was still close enough for her to feel the heat radiating from his body. But she looked into his eyes and knew he was already out of reach.

"Just like that?"

Hurt. He could hear it in her voice, and he wished he could make himself believe she had brought it on herself. He reached for his beer but changed his mind when he saw that his hand was unsteady. Only one thing was clear. He had to get rid of her, quickly, before he touched her again.

"You're not the type for quick sex on the kitchen floor."

The color that passion had brought to her cheeks faded. "No. At least I never have been." After taking a deep breath, she stepped forward. She believed in facing facts, even unpleasant ones. "Is that all this would have been, Roman?"

His hand curled into a fist. "Yes," he said. "What else?"

"I see." She kept her eyes on his, wishing she could hate him. "I'm sorry for you."

"Don't be."

"You're in charge of your feelings, Roman, not mine. And I am sorry for you. Some people lose a leg or a hand or an eye. They either deal with that loss or become bitter. I can't see what piece of you is missing, Roman, but it's just as tragic." He didn't answer; she hadn't expected him to. "Don't forget the lights."

He waited until she was gone before he fumbled for a match. He needed time to gain control of his head—and his hands—before he searched the office. What worried him was that it was going to take a great deal longer to gain control of his heart.

Nearly two hours later he hiked a mile and a half to use the pay phone at the nearest gas station. The road was quiet, the tiny village dark. The wind had come up, and it tasted of rain. Roman hoped dispassionately that it would hold off until he was back at the inn.

He placed the call, waited for the connection.

"Conby."

"DeWinter."

"You're late."

Roman didn't bother to check his watch. He knew it was just shy of 3:00 a.m. on the East Coast. "Get you up?"

"Am I to assume that you've established yourself?"

"Yeah, I'm in. Rigging the handyman's lottery ticket cleared the way. Arranging the flat gave me the opening. Miss Ford is…trusting."

"So we were led to believe. Trusting doesn't mean she's not ambitious. What have you got?"

A bad case of guilt, Roman thought as he lit a match. A very bad case. "Her rooms are clean." He paused and held the flame to the tip of his cigarette. "There's a tour group in now, mostly Canadians. A few exchanged money. Nothing over a hundred."

The pause was very brief. "That's hardly enough to make the business worthwhile."

"I got a list out of the office. The names and addresses of the registered guests."

There was another, longer pause, and a rustling sound that told Roman that his contact was searching for writing materials. "Let me have it."

He read them off from the copy he'd made. "Block's the tour guide. He's the regular, comes in once a week for a one- or two-night stay, depending on the package."

"Vision Tours."

"Right."

"We've got a man on that end. You concentrate on Ford and her staff." Roman heard the faint *tap-tap-tap* of Conby's pencil against his pad. "There's no way they can be pulling this off without someone on the inside. She's the obvious answer."

"It doesn't fit."

"I beg your pardon?"

Roman crushed the cigarette under his boot heel. "I said it doesn't fit. I've watched her. I've gone through her personal accounts, damn it. She's got under three thousand in fluid cash. Everything else goes into the place for new sheets and soap."

"I see." The pause again. It was maddening. "I suppose our Miss Ford hasn't heard of Swiss bank accounts."

"I said she's not the type, Conby. It's the wrong angle."

"I'll worry about the angles, DeWinter. You worry about doing your job. I shouldn't have to remind you that it's taken us nearly a year to come close to pinning this thing down. The Bureau wants this wrapped quickly, and that's what I expect from you. If you have a personal problem with this, you'd better let me know now."

"No." He knew personal problems weren't permitted. "You want to waste time, and the taxpayers' money, it's all the same to me. I'll get back to you."

"Do that."

Roman hung up. It made him feel a little better to scowl at the phone and imagine Conby losing a good night's sleep. Then again, his kind rarely did. He'd wake some hapless clerk up at six and have the list run through the computer. Conby would drink his coffee, watch the *Today* show and wait in his comfortable house in the D.C. suburbs for the results.

Grunt work and dirty work were left to others.

That was the way the game was played, Roman reminded himself as he started the long walk back to the inn. But lately, just lately, he was getting very tired of the rules.

Charity heard him come in. Curious, she glanced at the clock after she heard the door close below. It was after one, and the rain had started nearly thirty minutes before with a gentle hissing that promised to gain strength through the night.

She wondered where he had been.

His business, she reminded herself as she rolled over

and tried to let the rain lull her to sleep. As long as he did his job, Roman DeWinter was free to come and go as he pleased. If he wanted to walk in the rain, that was fine by her.

How could he have kissed her like that and felt nothing?

Charity squeezed her eyes shut and swore at herself. It was her feelings she had to worry about, not Roman's. The trouble was, she always felt too much. This was one time she couldn't afford that luxury.

Something had happened to her when he'd kissed her. Something thrilling, something that had reached deep inside her and opened up endless possibilities. No, not possibilities, fantasies, she thought, shaking her head. If she were wise she would take that one moment of excitement and stop wanting more. Drifters made poor risks emotionally. She had the perfect example before her.

Her mother had turned to a drifter and had given him her heart, her trust, her body. She had ended up pregnant and alone. She had, Charity knew, pined for him for months. She'd died in the same hospital where her baby had been born, only days later. Betrayed, rejected and ashamed.

Charity had only discovered the extent of the shame after her grandfather's death. He'd kept the diary her mother had written. Charity had burned it, not out of shame but out of pity. She would always think of her mother as a tragic woman who had looked for love and had never found it.

But she wasn't her mother, Charity reminded herself as she lay awake listening to the rain. She was far, far less fragile. Love was what she had been named for, and she had felt its warmth all her life.

Now a drifter had come into her life.

He had spoken of regrets, she remembered. She was afraid that whatever happened—or didn't happen—between them, she would have them.

Chapter 4

The rain continued all morning, soft, slow, steady. It brought a chill, and a gloom that was no less appealing than the sunshine. Clouds hung over the water, turning everything to different shades of gray. Raindrops hissed on the roof and at the windows, making the inn seem all the more remote. Occasionally the wind gusted, rattling the panes.

At dawn Roman had watched Charity, bundled in a hooded windbreaker, take Ludwig out for his morning run. And he had watched her come back, dripping, forty minutes later. He'd heard the music begin to play in her room after she had come in the back entrance. She had chosen something quiet and floating with lots of violins this time. He'd been sorry when it had stopped and she had hurried down the hallway on her way to the dining room.

From his position on the second floor he couldn't hear the bustle in the kitchen below, but he could imagine it. Mae and Dolores would be bickering as waffle or muffin batter was whipped up. Charity would have grabbed a quick cup of coffee before rushing out to help the waitress set up tables and write the morning's menu.

Her hair would be damp, her voice calm as she smoothed over Dolores's daily complaints. She'd smell of the rain. When the early risers wandered down she would smile, greet them by name and make them feel as though they were sharing a meal at an old friend's house.

That was her greatest skill, Roman mused. Making a stranger feel at home.

Could she be as uncomplicated as she seemed? A part of him wanted badly to believe that. Another part of him found it impossible. Everyone had an angle, from the mailroom clerk dreaming of a desk job to the CEO wheeling another deal. She couldn't be any different.

He wouldn't have called the kiss they'd shared uncomplicated. There had been layers to it he couldn't have begun to peel away. It seemed contradictory that such a calm-eyed, smooth-voiced woman could explode with such towering passion. Yet she had. Perhaps her passion was as much a part of the act as her serenity.

It annoyed him. Just remembering his helpless response to her infuriated him. So he made himself dissect it further. If he was attracted to what she seemed to be, that was reasonable enough. He'd lived a solitary and often turbulent life. Though he had chosen to live that way, and certainly preferred it, it wasn't unusual that at some point he would find himself pulled toward a woman who represented everything he had never had. And had never wanted, Roman reminded himself as he tacked up a strip of molding.

He wasn't going to pretend he'd found any answers in Charity. The only answers he was looking for pertained to the job.

For now he would wait until the morning rush was over. When Charity was busy in her office, he would go down and charm some breakfast out of Mae. There was a woman who didn't trust him, Roman thought with a grin. There wasn't a naive bone in her sturdy body. And except for Charity there was no one, he was sure, who knew the workings of the inn better.

Yes, he'd put some effort into charming Mae. And he'd keep some distance between himself and Charity. For the time being.

"You're looking peaked this morning."

"Thank you very much." Charity swallowed a yawn as she poured her second cup of coffee. Peaked wasn't the word, she thought. She was exhausted right down to the bone. Her body wasn't used to functioning on three hours' sleep. She had Roman to thank for that, she thought, and shoved the just-filled cup aside.

"Sit." Mae pointed to the table. "I'll fix you some eggs."

"I haven't got time. I—"

"Sit," Mae repeated, waving a wooden spoon. "You need fuel."

"Mae's right," Dolores put in. "A body can't run on coffee. You need protein and carbohydrates." She set a blueberry muffin on the table. "Why, if I don't watch my protein intake I get weak as a lamb. 'Course, the doctor don't say, but I think I'm hydroglycemic."

"Hypoglycemic," Charity murmured.

"That's what I said." Dolores decided she liked the sound of it. At the moment, however, it was just as much fun to worry about Charity as it was to worry about herself. "She could use some nice crisp bacon with those eggs, Mae. That's what I think."

"I'm putting it on."

Outnumbered, Charity sat down. The two women could scrap for days, but when they had common cause they stuck together like glue.

"I'm not peaked," she said in her own defense. "I just didn't sleep well last night."

"A warm bath before bed," Mae told her as the bacon sizzled. "Not hot, mind you. Lukewarm."

"With bath salts. Not bubbles or oils," Dolores added as she plunked down a glass of juice. "Good old-fashioned bath salts. Ain't that right, Mae?"

"Couldn't hurt," Mae mumbled, too concerned about Charity to think of an argument. "You've been working too hard, girl."

"I agree," Charity said, because it was easiest that way. "The reason I don't have time for a long, leisurely breakfast is that I have to see about hiring a new waitress so I don't have to work so hard. I put an ad in this morning's paper, so the calls should be coming in."

"Told Bob to cancel the ad," Mae announced, cracking an egg into the pan.

"What? Why?" Charity started to rise. "Damn it,

Mae, if you think I'm going to take Mary Alice back after she—"

"No such thing, and don't you swear at me, young lady."

"Testy." Dolores clucked her tongue. "Happens when you work too hard."

"I'm sorry," Charity mumbled, managing not to grind her teeth. "But, Mae, I was counting on setting up interviews over the next couple of days. I want someone in by the end of the week."

"My brother's girl left that worthless husband of hers in Toledo and came home." Keeping her back to Charity, Mae set the bacon to drain, then poked at the eggs. "She's a good girl, Bonnie is. Worked here a couple of summers while she was in school."

"Yes, I remember. She married a musician who was playing at one of the resorts in Eastsound."

Mae scowled and began to scoop up the eggs. "Saxophone player," she said, as if that explained it all. "She got tired of living out of a van and came home a couple weeks back. Been looking for work."

With a sigh, Charity pushed a hand through her bangs. "Why didn't you tell me before?"

"You didn't need anyone before." Mae set the eggs in front of her. "You need someone now."

Charity glanced over as Mae began wiping off the stove. The cook's heart was as big as the rest of her. "When can she start?"

Mae's lips curved, and she cleared her throat and wiped at a spill with more energy. "Told her to come in this afternoon so's you could have a look at her. Don't expect you to hire her unless she measures up."

"Well, then." Charity picked up her fork. Pleased at the thought of having one job settled, she stretched out her legs and rested her feet on an empty chair. "I guess I've got time for breakfast after all."

Roman pushed through the door and almost swore out loud. The dining room was all but empty. He'd been certain Charity would be off doing one of the dozens of chores she took on. Instead, she was sitting in the warm, fragrant kitchen, much as she had been the night before. With one telling difference, Roman reflected. She wasn't relaxed now.

Her easy smile faded the moment he walked in. Slowly she slipped her feet off the chair and straightened her back. He could see her body tense, almost muscle by muscle. Her fork stopped halfway to her lips. Then she turned slightly away from him and continued to eat. It was, he supposed, as close to a slap in the face as she could manage.

He rearranged his idea about breakfast and gossip in the kitchen. For now he'd make do with coffee.

"Wondered where you'd got to," Mae said as she pulled bacon out of the refrigerator again.

"I didn't want to get in your way." He nodded toward the coffeepot. "I thought I'd take a cup up with me."

"You need fuel." Dolores busied herself arranging a place setting across from Charity. "Isn't that right, Mae? Man can't work unless he has a proper breakfast."

Mae poured a cup. "He looks like he could run on empty well enough."

It was quite true, Charity thought. She knew what time he'd come in the night before, and he'd been up and working when she'd left the wing to oversee the breakfast shift. He couldn't have gotten much more sleep than she had herself, but he didn't look any the worse for wear.

"Meals are part of your pay, Roman." Though her appetite had fled, Charity nipped off a bite of bacon. "I believe Mae has some pancake batter left over, if you'd prefer that to eggs."

It was a cool invitation, so cool that Dolores opened her mouth to comment. Mae gave her a quick poke and a scowl. He accepted the coffee Mae shoved at him and drank it black.

"Eggs are fine." But he didn't sit down. The welcoming feel that was usually so much a part of the kitchen was not evident. Roman leaned against the counter and sipped while Mae cooked beside him.

She wasn't going to feel guilty, Charity told herself, ignoring a chastising look from Dolores. After all, she was the boss, and her business with Roman was…well, just business. But she couldn't bear the long, strained silence.

"Mae, I'd like some petits fours and tea sandwiches this afternoon. The rain's supposed to last all day, so we'll have music and dancing in the gathering room." Because breakfast seemed less and less appealing, Charity pulled a notepad out of her shirt pocket. "Fifty sandwiches should do if we have a cheese tray. We'll set up an urn of tea, and one of hot chocolate."

"What time?"

"At three, I think. Then we can bring out the wine at five for anyone who wants to linger. You can have your niece help out."

She began making notes on the pad.

She looked tired, Roman thought. Pale and heavy-eyed and surprisingly fragile. She'd apparently pulled her hair back in a hasty ponytail when it had still been damp. Little tendrils had escaped as they'd dried. They seemed lighter than the rest, their color more delicate than rich. He wanted to brush them away from her temples and watch the color come back into her cheeks.

"Finish your eggs," Mae told her. Then she nodded at Roman. "Yours are ready."

"Thanks." He sat down, wishing no more fervently than Charity that he was ten miles away.

Dolores began to complain that the rain was making her sinuses swell.

"Pass the salt," Roman murmured.

Charity pushed it in his direction. Their fingers brushed briefly, and she snatched hers away.

"Thanks."

"You're welcome." Charity poked her fork into her eggs. She knew from experience that it would be difficult to escape from the kitchen without cleaning her plate, and she intended to do it quickly.

"Nice day," he said, because he wanted her to look at him again. She did, and pent-up anger was simmering in her eyes. He preferred it, he discovered, to the cool politeness that had been there.

"I like the rain."

"Like I said—" he broke open his muffin "—it's a nice day."

Dolores blew her nose heartily. Amusement curved the corners of Charity's mouth before she managed to suppress it. "You'll find the paint you need—wall, ceiling, trim—in the storage cellar. It's marked for the proper rooms."

"All right."

"The brushes and pans and rollers are down there, too. Everything's on the workbench on the right as you come down the stairs."

"I'll find them."

"Good. Cabin 4 has a dripping faucet."

"I'll look at it."

She didn't want him to be so damn agreeable, Charity thought. She wanted him to be as tense and out of sorts as she was. "The window sticks in unit 2 in the east wing."

He sent her an even look. "I'll unstick it."

"Fine." Suddenly she noticed that Dolores had stopped complaining and was gawking at her. Even Mae was frowning over her mixing bowl. The hell with it, Charity thought as she shoved her plate away. So she was issuing orders like Captain Bligh. She damn well felt like Captain Bligh.

She took a ring of keys out of her pocket. She'd just put them on that morning, having intended to see to the minor chores herself. "Make sure to bring these back to the office when you've finished. They're tagged for the proper doors."

"Yes, ma'am." Keeping his eyes on hers, he dropped the ring into his breast pocket. "Anything else?"

"I'll let you know." She rose, took her plate to the sink and stalked out.

"What got into her?" Dolores wanted to know. "She looked like she wanted to chew somebody's head off."

"She just didn't sleep well." More concerned than she wanted to let on, Mae set down the mixing bowl in which she'd been creaming butter and sugar. Because she felt like the mother of an ill-mannered child, she picked up the coffeepot and carried it over to Roman. "Charity's not feeling quite herself this morning," she told him as she poured him a second cup. "She's been overworked lately."

"I've got thick skin." But he'd felt the sting. "Maybe she should delegate more."

"Ha! That girl?" Pleased that he hadn't complained, she became more expansive. "It ain't in her. Feels responsible if a guest stubs his toe. Just like her grandpa." Mae added a stream of vanilla to the bowl and went back to her mixing. "Not a thing goes on around here she don't have a finger—more likely her whole hand— in. Except my cooking." Mae's wide face creased in a smile. "I shooed her out of here when she was a girl, and I can shoo her out of here today if need be."

"Girl can't boil water without scorching the pan," Dolores put in.

"She could if she wanted to," Mae said defensively, turning back to Roman with a sniff. "There's no need for her to cook when she's got me, and she's smart enough to know it. Everything else, though, from painting the porch to keeping the books, has to have her stamp on it. She's one who takes her responsibilities to heart."

Roman played out the lead she had offered him. "That's an admirable quality. You've worked for her a long time."

"Between Charity and her grandfather, I've worked at the inn for twenty-eight years come June." She jerked her head in Dolores's direction. "She's been here eight."

"Nine," Dolores said. "Nine years this month."

"It sounds like when people come to work here they stay."

"You got that right," Mae told him.

"It seems the inn has a loyal, hardworking staff."

"Charity makes it easy." Competently Mae measured out baking powder. "She was just feeling moody this morning."

"She did look a little tired," Roman said slowly, ignoring a pang of guilt. "Maybe she'll rest for a while today."

"Not likely."

"The housekeeping staff seems tight."

"She'll still find a bed to make."

"Bob handles the accounts."

"She'll poke her nose in the books and check every column." There was simple pride in her voice as she sifted flour into the bowl. "Not that she don't trust those who work for her," Mae added. "It would just make her heart stop dead to have a bill paid late or an order mixed up. Thing is, she'd rather blame herself than somebody else if a mistake's made."

"I guess nothing much gets by her."

"By Charity?" With a snicker, Mae plugged in her electric mixer. "She'd know if a napkin came back from the laundry with a stain on it. Watch where you sneeze," she added as Dolores covered her face with a tissue. "Drink some hot water with a squeeze of lemon."

"Hot tea with honey," Dolores said.

"Lemon. Honey'll clog your throat."

"My mother always gave me hot tea with honey," Dolores told her.

They were still arguing about it when Roman slipped out of the kitchen.

He spent most of his time closed off in the west wing. Working helped him think. Though he heard Charity pass in and out a few times, neither of them sought the other's company. He could be more objective, Roman realized, when he wasn't around her.

Mae's comments had cemented his observations and the information that had been made available to him. Charity Ford ran the inn from top to bottom. Whatever went on in it or passed through it was directly under her eye. Logically that meant that she was fully involved with, perhaps in charge of, the operation he had come to destroy.

And yet…what he had said to Conby the night before still held true. It didn't fit.

The woman worked almost around the clock to make the inn a success. He'd seen her do everything from potting geraniums to hauling firewood. And, unless she was an astounding actress, she enjoyed it all.

She didn't seem the type who would want to make

money the easy way. Nor did she seem the type who craved all the things easy money could buy. But that was instinct, not fact.

The problem was, Conby ran on facts. Roman had always relied heavily on instinct. His job was to prove her guilt, not her innocence. Yet, in less than two days, his priorities had changed.

It wasn't just a matter of finding her attractive. He had found other women attractive and had brought them down without a qualm. That was justice. One of the few things he believed in without reservation was justice.

With Charity he needed to be certain that his conclusions about her were based on more than the emotions she dragged out of him. Feelings and instincts were different. If a man in his position allowed himself to be swayed by feelings, he was useless.

Then what was it? No matter how long or how hard he thought it through, he couldn't pinpoint one specific reason why he was certain of her innocence. Because it was the whole of it, Roman realized. Her, the inn, the atmosphere that surrounded her. It made him want to believe that such people, such places, existed. And existed untainted.

He was getting soft. A pretty woman, big blue eyes, and he started to think in fairy tales. In disgust, he took the brushes and the paint pans to the sink to clean them. He was going to take a break, from work and from his own rambling thoughts.

In the gathering room, Charity was thinking just as reluctantly of him as she set a stack of records on the table between Miss Millie and Miss Lucy.

"What a lovely idea." Miss Lucy adjusted her glasses and peered at the labels. "A nice old-fashioned tea dance." From one of the units in the east wing came the unrelenting whine of a toddler. Miss Lucy sent a sympathetic glance in the direction of the noise. "I'm sure this will keep everyone entertained."

"It's hard for young people to know what to do with themselves on a rainy day. It makes them cross. Oh, look." Miss Millie held up a 45. "Rosemary Clooney. Isn't this delightful?"

"Pick out your favorites." Charity gave the room a distracted glance. How could she prepare for a party when all she could think of was the way Roman had looked at her across the breakfast table? "I'm depending on you."

The long buffet and a small server had been cleared off to hold the refreshments. If she could count on Mae—and she always had—they should be coming up from the kitchen shortly.

Would Roman come in? she wondered. Would he hear the music and slip silently into the room? Would he look at her until her heart started to hammer and she forgot there was anything or anyone but him?

She was going crazy, Charity decided. She glanced at her watch. It was a quarter to three. Word had been passed to all the guests, and with luck she would be ready for them when they began to arrive. The ladies were deep in a discussion of Perry Como. Leaving them to it, Charity began to tug on the sofa.

"What are you doing?"

A squeal escaped her, and she cursed Roman in the

next breath. "If you keep sneaking around I'm going to take Mae's idea of you being a cat burglar more seriously."

"I wasn't sneaking around. You were so busy huffing and puffing you didn't hear me."

"I wasn't huffing or puffing." She tossed her hair over her shoulder and glared at him. "But I am busy, so if you'd get out of my way—"

She waved a hand at him, and he caught it and held it. "I asked what you were doing."

She tugged, then tugged harder, struggling to control her temper. If he wanted to fight, she thought, she'd be happy to oblige him. "I'm knitting an afghan," she snapped. "What does it look like I'm doing? I'm moving the sofa."

"No, you're not."

She could, when the occasion called for, succeed in being haughty. "I beg your pardon?"

"I said you're not moving the sofa. It's too heavy."

"Thank you for your opinion, but I've moved it before." She lowered her voice when she noticed the interested glances the ladies were giving her. "And if you'd get the hell out of my way I'd move it again."

He stood where he was, blocking her. "You really do have to do everything yourself, don't you?"

"Meaning?"

"Where's your assistant?"

"The computer sprang a leak. Since Bob's better equipped to deal with that, he's playing with components and I'm moving furniture. Now—"

"Where do you want it?"

"I didn't ask you to—" But he'd already moved to the other end of the sofa.

"I said, where do you want it?"

"Against the side wall." Charity hefted her end and tried not to be grateful.

"What else?"

She smoothed down the skirt of her dress. "I've already given you a list of chores."

He hooked a thumb in his pocket as they stood on either side of the sofa. He had an urge to put his hand over her angry face and give it a nice hard shove. "I've finished them."

"The faucet in cabin 4?"

"It needed a new washer."

"The window in unit 2?"

"A little sanding."

She was running out of steam. "The painting?"

"The first coat's drying." He angled his head. "Want to check it out?"

She blew out a breath. It was difficult to be annoyed when he'd done everything she'd asked. "Efficient, aren't you, DeWinter?"

"That's right. Got your second wind?"

"What do you mean?"

"You looked a little tired this morning." He skimmed a glance over her. The dark plum-colored dress swirled down her legs. Little silver buttons ranged down from the high neck to the hem, making him wonder how long it would take him to unfasten them. There was silver at her ears, as well, a fanciful trio of columns he remembered having seen in her drawer. "You don't now," he added, bringing his eyes back to hers.

She started to breathe again, suddenly aware that she'd been holding her breath since he'd started his survey. Charity reminded herself that she didn't have time to let him—or her feelings for him—distract her.

"I'm too busy to be tired." Relieved, she signaled to a waitress who was climbing the steps with a laden tray. "Just set it on the buffet, Lori."

"Second load's right behind me."

"Great. I just need to—" She broke off when the first damp guests came through the back door. Giving up, she turned to Roman. If he was going to be in the way anyway, he might as well make himself useful. "I'd appreciate it if you'd roll up the rug and store it in the west wing. Then you're welcome to stay and enjoy yourself."

"Thanks. Maybe I will."

Charity greeted the guests, hung up their jackets, offered them refreshments and switched on the music almost before Roman could store the rug out of sight. Within fifteen minutes she had the group mixing and mingling.

She was made for this, he thought as he watched her. She was made for being in the center of things, for making people feel good. His place had always been on the fringe.

"Oh, Mr. DeWinter." Smelling of lilacs, Miss Millie offered him a cup and saucer. "You must have some tea. Nothing like tea to chase the blues away on a rainy day."

He smiled into her blurred eyes. If even she could

see that he was brooding, he'd better watch his step. "Thanks."

"I love a party," she said wistfully as she watched a few couples dance to a bluesy Clooney ballad. "Why, when I was a girl, I hardly thought of anything else. I met my husband at a tea like this. That was almost fifty years ago. We danced for hours."

He would never have considered himself gallant, but she was hard to resist. "Would you like to dance now?"

The faintest of blushes tinted her cheeks. "I'd love to, Mr. DeWinter."

Charity watched Roman lead Miss Millie onto the floor. Her heart softened. She tried to harden it again but found it was a lost cause. It was a sweet thing to do, she thought, particularly since he was anything but a sweet man. She doubted that teas and dreamy little old ladies were Roman's style, but Miss Millie would remember this day for a long time.

What woman wouldn't? Charity mused. To dance with a strong, mysterious man on a rainy afternoon was a memory to be pressed in a book like a red rose. It was undoubtedly fortunate he hadn't asked her. She had already stored away too many memories of Roman. With a sigh, she herded a group of children into the television room and pushed a Disney movie into the VCR.

Roman saw her leave. And he saw her come back.

"That was lovely," Miss Millie told him when the music had stopped.

"What?" Quickly he brought himself back. "My pleasure." Then he made her pleasure complete by kissing her hand. By the time she had walked over to sigh with her sister he had forgotten her and was thinking of Charity.

She was laughing as an older man led her onto the floor. The music had changed. It was up-tempo now, something brisk and Latin. A mambo, he thought. Or a merengue. He wouldn't know the difference. Apparently Charity knew well enough. She moved through the complicated, flashy number as if she'd been dancing all her life.

Her skirt flared, wrapped around her legs, then flared again as she turned. She laughed, her face level and close to her partner's as they matched steps. The first prick of jealousy infuriated Roman and made him feel like a fool. The man Charity was matching steps with was easily old enough to be her father.

By the time the music ended he had managed to suppress the uncomfortable emotion but another had sprung up to take its place. Desire. He wanted her, wanted to take her by the hand and pull her out of that crowded room into someplace dim and quiet where all they would hear was the rain. He wanted to see her eyes go big and unfocused the way they had when he'd kissed her. He wanted to feel the incredible sensation of her mouth softening and heating under his.

"It's an education to watch her, isn't it?"

Roman jerked himself back as Bob eased over to pluck a sandwich from the tray. "What?"

"Charity. Watching her dance is an education." He popped the tiny sandwich into his mouth. "She tried to teach me once, hoping I'd be able to entertain some of the ladies on occasions like this. Trouble is, I not only have two left feet, I have two left legs." He gave a cheerful shrug and reached for another sandwich.

"Did you get the computer fixed?"

"Yeah. Just a couple of minor glitches." The little triangle of bread disappeared. Roman caught a hint of nerves in the way Bob's knuckle tapped against the server. "I can't teach Charity about circuit boards and software any more than she can teach me the samba. How's the work going?"

"Well enough." He watched as Bob poured a cup of tea and added three sugars to it. "I should be done in two or three weeks."

"She'll find something else for you to do." He glanced over to where Charity and a new partner were dancing a fox-trot. "She's always got a new idea for this place. Lately she's been making noises about adding on a sunroom and putting in one of those whirlpool tubs."

Roman lit a cigarette. He was watching the guests now, making mental notes to pass on to Conby. There were two men who seemed to be alone, though they were chatting with other members of the tour group. Block stood by the doors, holding a plateful of sandwiches that he was dispatching with amazing ease and grinning at no one in particular.

"The inn must be doing well."

"Oh, it's stable." Bob turned his attention to the petits fours. "A couple of years ago things were a little rocky, but Charity would always find a way to keep the ship afloat. Nothing's more important to her."

Roman was silent for a moment. "I don't know much

about the hotel business, but she seems to know what she's doing."

"Inside and out." Bob chose a cake with pink frosting. "Charity *is* the inn."

"Have you worked for her long?"

"About two and a half years. She couldn't really afford me, but she wanted to turn things around, modernize the bookkeeping. Pump new life into the place, was what she said." Someone put on a jitterbug, and he grinned. "She did just that."

"Apparently."

"So you're from back east." Bob paused for a moment, then continued when Roman made no comment. "How long are you planning to stay?"

"As long as it takes."

He took a long sip of tea. "As long as what takes?"

"The job." Roman glanced idly toward the west wing. "I like to finish what I start."

"Yeah. Well…" He arranged several petits fours on a plate. "I'm going to go offer these to the ladies and hope they let me eat them."

Roman watched him pass Block and exchange a quick word with him before he crossed the room. Wanting time to think, Roman slipped back into the west wing.

It was still raining when he came back hours later. Music was playing, some slow, melodic ballad from the fifties. The room was dimmer now, lit only by the fire and a glass-globed lamp. It was empty, too, except for Charity, who was busy tidying up, humming along with the music.

"Party over?"

She glanced around, then went hurriedly back to stacking cups and plates. "Yes. You didn't stay long."

"I had work to do."

Because she wanted to keep moving, she switched to emptying ashtrays. She'd held on to her guilt long enough. "I was tired this morning, but that's no excuse for being rude to you. I'm sorry if I gave you the impression that you couldn't enjoy yourself for a few hours."

He didn't want to accept an apology that he knew he didn't deserve. "I enjoy the work."

That only made her feel worse. "Be that as it may, I don't usually go around barking orders. I was angry with you."

"Was?"

She looked up, and her eyes were clear and direct. "Am. But that's my problem. If it helps, I'm every bit as angry with myself for acting like a child because you didn't let things get out of hand last night."

Uncomfortable, he picked up the wine decanter and poured a glass. "You didn't act like a child."

"A woman scorned, then, or something equally dramatic. Try not to contradict me when I'm apologizing."

Despite his best efforts, his lips curved against the rim of his glass. If he didn't watch himself he could find he was crazy about her. "All right. Is there more?"

"Just a little." She picked up one of the few petits fours that were left over, debated with herself, then popped it into her mouth. "I shouldn't let my personal feelings interfere with my running of the inn. The problem is, almost everything I think or feel connects with the inn."

"Neither of us were thinking of the inn last night. Maybe that's the problem."

"Maybe."

"Do you want the couch moved back?"

"Yes." Business as usual, Charity told herself as she walked over to lift her end. The moment it was in place she scooted around to plump the pillows. "I saw you dancing with Miss Millie. It thrilled her."

"I like her."

"I think you do," Charity said slowly, straightening and studying him. "You're not the kind of man who likes easily."

"No."

She wanted to go to him, to lift a hand to his cheek. That was ridiculous, she told herself. Apology notwithstanding, she was still angry with him for last night. "Has life been so hard?" she murmured.

"No."

With a little laugh, she shook her head. "Then again, you wouldn't tell me if it had been. I have to learn not to ask you questions. Why don't we call a truce, Roman? Life's too short for bad feelings."

"I don't have any bad feelings toward you, Charity."

She smiled a little. "It's tempting, but I'm not going to ask what kind of feelings you do have."

"I wouldn't be able to tell you, because I haven't figured it out." He was amazed that the words had come out. After draining the wine, he set the empty glass aside.

"Well." Nonplussed, she pushed her hair back with both hands. "That's the first thing you've told me I can really understand. Looks like we're in the same boat. Do I take it we have a truce?"

"Sure."

She glanced back as another record dropped onto the turntable. "This is one of my favorites. 'Smoke Gets in Your Eyes.'" She was smiling again when she looked back at him. "You never asked me to dance."

"No, I didn't."

"Miss Millie claims you're very smooth." She held out a hand in a gesture that was as much a peace offering as an invitation. Unable to resist, he took it in his. Their eyes stayed locked as he drew her slowly toward him.

Chapter 5

A fire simmered in the grate. Rain pattered against the windows. The record was old and scratchy, the tune hauntingly sad. Whether they wanted it or not, their bodies fitted. Her hand slid gently over his shoulder, his around her waist. With their faces close, they began to dance.

The added height from her heels brought her eyes level with his. He could smell the light fragrance that seemed so much a part of her. Seduced by it, he brought her closer, slowly. Their thighs brushed. Still closer. Her body melted against his.

It was so quiet. There was only the music, the rain, the hissing of the fire. Gloomy light swirled into the room. He could feel her heart beating against his, quick now, and not too steady.

His wasn't any too steady now, either.

Was that all it took? he wondered. Did he only have to touch her to think that she was the beginning and the end of everything? And to wish… His hand slid up her back, fingers spreading until they tangled in her hair. To wish she could belong to him.

He wasn't sure when that thought had sunk its roots in him. Perhaps it had begun the first moment he had seen her. She was—should have been—unattainable for him. But when she was in his arms, warm, just bordering on pliant, dozens of possibilities flashed through his head.

She wanted to smile, to make some light, easy comment. But she couldn't push the words out. Her throat was locked. The way he was looking at her now, as if she were the only woman he had ever seen or ever wanted to see, made her forget that the dance was supposed to be a gesture of friendship.

She might never be his friend, she knew, no matter how hard she tried. But with his eyes on hers she understood how easily she could be his lover.

Maybe it was wrong, but it didn't seem to matter as they glided across the floor. The song spoke of love betrayed, but she heard only poetry. She felt her will ebb away even as the music swelled inside her head. No, it didn't seem to matter. Nothing seemed to matter as long as she went on swaying in his arms.

She didn't even try to think, never attempted to reason. Following her heart, she pressed her lips to his.

Instant. Irresistible. Irrevocable. Emotions funneled from one to the other, then merged in a torrent of need. She didn't expect him to be gentle, though her kiss had offered comfort, as well as passion. He dived into it, into her, with a speed and force that left her reeling, then fretting for more.

So this was what drove people to do mad, desperate acts, she thought as their tongues tangled. This wild, painful pleasure, once tasted, would never be forgotten, would always be craved. She wrapped her arms around his neck as she gave herself to it.

With quick, rough kisses he drove them both to the edge. It was more than desire, he knew. Desire had never hurt, not deeply. It was like a scratch, soon forgotten, easily healed. This was a raw, deep wound.

Lust had never erased every coherent thought from his mind. Still, he could only think of her. Those thoughts were jumbled, and all of them were forbidden. Desperate, he ran his lips over her face, while wild fantasies of touching, of tasting every inch of her whirled in his head. It wouldn't be enough. It would never be enough. No matter how much he took from her, she would draw him back. And she could make him beg. The certainty of it terrified him.

She was trembling again, even as she strained against him. Her soft gasps and sighs pushed him toward the brink of reason. He found her mouth again and feasted on it.

He hardly recognized the change, could find no reason for it. All at once she was like glass in his arms, something precious, something fragile, something he needed to protect and defend. He lifted his hands to her face, his fingers light and cautiously caressing. His mouth, ravenous only a moment before, gentled.

Stunned, she swayed. New, vibrant emotions poured into her. Weak from the onslaught, she let her head fall back. Her arms slipped, boneless, to her sides. There was beauty here, a soft, shimmering beauty she had never known existed. Tenderness did what passion had not yet accomplished. As freely as a bird taking wing, her heart flew out to him.

Love, first experienced, was devastating. She felt tears burn the back of her eyes, heard her own quiet moan of surrender. And she tasted the glory of it as his lips played gently with hers.

She would always remember that one instant when the world changed—the music, the rain, the scent of fresh flowers. Nothing would ever be quite the same again. Nor would she ever want it to be.

Shaken, she drew back to lift a hand to her spinning head. "Roman—"

"Come with me." Unwilling to think, he pulled her against him again. "I want to know what it's like to be with you, to undress you, to touch you."

With a moan, she surrendered to his mouth again.

"Charity, Mae wants to—" Lori stopped on a dime at the top of the stairs. After clearing her throat, she stared at the painting on the opposite wall as if it fascinated her. "Excuse me. I didn't mean to…"

Charity had jerked back like a spring and was searching for composure. "It's all right. What is it, Lori?"

"It's, well…Mae and Dolores… Maybe you could come down to the kitchen when you get a minute." She rushed down the stairs, grinning to herself.

"I should…" Charity paused to draw in a steadying breath but managed only a shaky one. "I should go down." She retreated a step. "Once they get started, they need—" She broke off when Roman took her arm. He waited until she lifted her head and looked at him again.

"Things have changed."

It sounded so simple when he said it. "Yes. Yes, they have."

"Right or wrong, Charity, we'll finish this."

"No." She was far from calm, but she was very determined. "If it's right, we'll finish it. I'm not going to pretend I don't want you, but you're right when you say things have changed, Roman. You see, I know what I'm feeling now, and I have to get used to it."

He tightened his grip when she turned to go. "What are you feeling?"

She couldn't have lied if she'd wanted to. Dishonesty was abhorrent to her. When it came to feelings, she had neither the ability nor the desire to suppress them. "I'm in love with you."

His fingers uncurled from her arm. Very slowly, very carefully, as if he were retreating from some dangerous beast, he released her.

She read the shock on his face. That was understandable. And she read the distrust. That was painful. She gave him a last unsmiling look before she turned away.

"Apparently we both have to get used to it."

She was lying. Roman told himself that over and over as he paced the floor in his room. If not to him, then certainly to herself. People seemed to find love easy to lie about.

He stopped by the window and stared out into the dark. The rain had stopped, and the moon was cruising in and out of the clouds. He jerked the window open and breathed in the damp, cool air. He needed something to clear his head.

She was working on him. Annoyed, he turned away from the view of trees and flowers and started pacing again. The easy smiles, the openhanded welcome, the casual friendliness…then the passion, the uninhibited response, the seduction. He wanted to believe it was a trap, even though his well-trained mind found the idea absurd.

She had no reason to suspect him. His cover was solid. Charity thought of him as a drifter, passing through long enough to take in some sights and pick up a little loose change. It was he who was setting the trap.

He dropped down on the bed and lit a cigarette, more out of habit than because he wanted one. Lies were part of his job, a part he was very good at. She hadn't lied to him, he reflected as he inhaled. But she was mistaken. He had made her want, and she had justified her desire for a relative stranger by telling herself she was in love.

But if it was true…

He couldn't allow himself to think that way. Leaning back against the headboard, he stared at the blank wall. He couldn't allow himself the luxury of wondering what it would be like to be loved, and especially not what it would be like to be loved by a woman to whom love would mean a lifetime. He couldn't afford any daydreams about belonging, about having someone belong to him. Even if she hadn't been part of his assignment he would have to sidestep Charity Ford.

She would think of love, then of white picket fences, Sunday dinners and evenings by the fire. He was no good for her. He would never be any good for her. Roman DeWinter, he thought with a mirthless smile. Always on the wrong side of the tracks. A questionable past, an uncertain future. There was nothing he could offer a woman like Charity.

But God, he wanted her. The need was eating away at his insides. He knew she was upstairs now. He imagined her curled up in the big four-poster, under white blankets, perhaps with a white candle burning low on the table.

He had only to climb the stairs and walk through the door. She wouldn't send him away. If she tried, it would take him only moments to break down her resistance. Believing herself in love, she would yield, then open her arms to him. He ached to be in them, to sink into that bed, into her, and let oblivion take them both.

But she had asked for time. He wasn't going to deny her what he needed himself. In the time he gave her he would use all his skill to do the one thing he knew how to do for her. He would prove her innocence.

Roman watched the tour group check out the following morning. Perched on a stepladder in the center of the lobby, he took his time changing bulbs in the ceiling fixture. The sun was out now, full and bright, bathing the lobby in light as a few members of the tour loitered after breakfast.

At the front desk, Charity was chatting with Block. He was wearing a fresh white shirt and his perpetual smile. Taking a calculator from his briefcase, he checked to see if Charity's tallies matched his own.

Bob poked his head out of the office and handed her a computer printout. Roman didn't miss the quick, uncertain look Bob sent in his direction before he shut himself away again.

Charity and Block compared lists. Still smiling, he took a stack of bills out of his briefcase. He paid in Canadian, cash. Having already adjusted the bill to take the exchange rate into account, Charity locked the cash away in a drawer, then handed Block his receipt.

"Always a pleasure, Roger."

"Your little party saved the day," he told her. "My people consider this the highlight of the tour."

Pleased, she smiled at him. "They haven't seen Mount Rainier yet."

"You're going to get some repeaters out of this." He patted her hand, then checked his watch. "Time to move them out. See you next week."

"Safe trip, Roger." She turned to make change for a departing guest, then sold a few postcards and a few souvenir key chains with miniature whales on them.

Roman replaced the globe on the ceiling fixture, taking his time until the lobby was clear again. "Isn't it strange for a company like that to pay cash?"

Distracted from her reservations list, Charity glanced up at him. "We never turn down cash." She smiled at him as she had promised herself she would. Her feelings, her problem, she reminded herself as he climbed down from the ladder. She only wished the hours she'd spent soul-searching the night before had resulted in a solution.

"It seems like they'd charge, or pay by check."

"It's their company policy. Believe me, with a small, independent hotel, a cash-paying customer like Vision can make all the difference."

"I'll bet. You've been dealing with them for a while?"

"A couple of years. Why?"

"Just curious. Block doesn't look much like a tour guide."

"Roger? No, I guess he looks more like a wrestler." She went back to her papers. It was difficult to make small talk when her feelings were so close to the surface. "He does a good job."

"Yeah. I'll be upstairs."

"Roman." There was so much she wanted to say, but she could feel, though they were standing only a few feet apart, that he had distanced himself from her. "We never discussed a day off," she began. "You're welcome to take Sunday, if you like."

"Maybe I will."

"And if you'd give Bob your hours at the end of the week, he generally takes care of payroll."

"All right. Thanks."

A young couple with a toddler walked out of the dining room. Roman left her to answer their questions on renting a boat.

It wasn't going to be easy to talk to him, Charity decided later. But she had to do it. She'd spent all morning on business, she'd double-checked the housekeeping in the cabins, she'd made every phone call on her list, and if Mae's comments were anything to go on she'd made a nuisance of herself in the kitchen.

She was stalling.

That wasn't like her. All her life she'd made a habit of facing her problems head-on and plowing through them. Not only with business, she thought now. Personal problems had always been given the same kind of direct approach. She had handled being parentless. Even as a child she had never evaded the sometimes painful questions about her background.

But then, she'd had her grandfather. He'd been so solid, so loving. He'd helped her understand that she was her own person. Just as he'd helped her through her first high-school crush, Charity remembered.

He wasn't here now, and she wasn't a fifteen-year-old mooning over the captain of the debating team. But if he had taught her anything, it was that honest feelings were nothing to be ashamed of.

Armed with a thermos full of coffee, she walked into the west wing. She wished it didn't feel so much like bearding the lion in his den.

He'd finished the parlor. The scent of fresh paint was strong, though he'd left a window open to air it out. The doors still had to be hung and the floors varnished, but she could already imagine the room with sheer, billowy curtains and the faded floral-print rug she'd stored in the attic.

From the bedroom beyond, she could hear the buzz of an electric saw. A good, constructive sound, she thought as she pushed the door open to peek inside.

His eyes were narrowed in concentration as he bent over the wood he had laid across a pair of sawhorses. Wood dust flew, dancing gold in the sunlight. His hands, and his arms where he'd rolled his sleeves up past the elbow, were covered with it. He'd used a bandanna to keep the hair out of his eyes. He didn't hum while he worked, as she did. Or talk to himself, she mused, as George had. But, watching him, she thought she detected a simple pleasure in doing a job and doing it well.

He could do things, she thought as she watched him measure the wood for the next cut. Good things, even important things. She was sure of it. Not just because she loved him, she realized. Because it was in him. When a woman spent all her life entertaining strangers in her home, she learned to judge, and to see.

She waited until he put the saw down before she pushed the door open. Before she could speak he whirled around. Her step backward was instinctive, defensive. It was ridiculous, she told herself, but she thought that if he'd had a weapon he'd have drawn it.

"I'm sorry." The nerves she had managed to get under control were shot to hell. "I should have realized I'd startle you."

"It's all right." He settled quickly, though it annoyed him to have been caught off guard. Perhaps if he hadn't been thinking of her he would have sensed her.

"I needed to do some things upstairs, so I thought I'd bring you some coffee on my way." She set the thermos on the stepladder, then wished she'd kept it, as her empty hands made her feel foolish. "And I wanted to check how things were going. The parlor looks great."

"It's coming along. Did you label the paint?"

"Yes. Why?"

"Because it was all done in this tidy printing on the lid of each can in the color of the paint. That seemed like something you'd do."

"Obsessively organized?" She made a face. "I can't seem to help it."

"I liked the way you had the paintbrushes arranged according to size."

She lifted a brow. "Are you making fun of me?"

"Yeah."

"Well, as long as I know." Her nerves were calmer now. "Want some of this coffee?"

"Yeah. I'll get it."

"You've got sawdust all over your hands." Waving him aside, she unscrewed the top. "I take it our truce is back on."

"I didn't realize it had been off."

She glanced back over her shoulder, then looked around and poured the coffee into the plastic cup. "I made you uncomfortable yesterday. I'm sorry."

He accepted the cup and sat down on a sawhorse. "You're putting words in my mouth again, Charity."

"I don't have to this time. You looked as if I'd hit you with a brick." Restless, she moved her shoulders. "I suppose I might have reacted the same way if someone had said they loved me out of the blue like that. It must have been pretty startling, seeing as we haven't known each other for long."

Finding he had no taste for it, he set the coffee aside. "You were reacting to the moment."

"No." She turned back to him, knowing it was important to talk face-to-face. "I thought you might think that. In fact, I even considered playing it safe and letting you. I'm lousy at deception. It seemed more fair to tell you that I'm not in the habit of…what I mean is, I don't throw myself at men as a rule. The truth is, you're the first."

"Charity." He dragged a hand through his hair, pulling out the bandanna and sending more wood dust scattering. "I don't know what to say to you."

"You don't have to say anything. The fact is, I came in here with my little speech all worked out. It was a pretty good one, too…calm, understanding, a couple of dashes of humor to keep it light. I'm screwing it up."

She kicked a scrap of wood into the corner before she paced to the window. Columbine and bluebells grew just below in a bed where poppies were waiting to burst into color. On impulse, she pushed up the window to breathe in their faint, fragile scents.

"The point is," she began, hating herself for keeping her back to him, "we can't pretend I didn't say it. I can't pretend I don't feel it. That doesn't mean I expect you to feel the same way, because I don't."

"What do you expect?"

He was right behind her. She jumped when his hand gripped her shoulder. Gathering her courage, she turned around. "For you to be honest with me." She was speaking quickly now, and she didn't notice his slight, automatic retreat. "I appreciate the fact that you don't pretend to love me. I may be simple, Roman, but I'm not stupid. I know it might be easier to lie, to say what you think I want to hear."

"You're not simple," he murmured, lifting a hand and brushing it against her cheek. "I've never met a more confusing, complicated woman."

Shock came first, then pleasure. "That's the nicest thing you've ever said to me. No one's ever accused me of being complicated."

He'd meant to lower his hand, but she had already lifted hers and clasped it. "I didn't mean it as a compliment."

That made her grin. Relaxed again, she sat back on the windowsill. "Even better. I hope this means we're finished feeling awkward around each other."

"I don't know what I feel around you." He ran his hands up her arms to her shoulders, then down to the elbows again. "But awkward isn't the word for it."

Touched—much too deeply—she rose. "I have to go."

"Why?"

"Because it's the middle of the day, and if you kiss me I might forget that."

Already aroused, he eased her forward. "Always organized."

"Yes." She put a hand to his chest to keep some distance between them. "I have some invoices I have to go over upstairs." Holding her breath, she backed toward the door. "I do want you, Roman. I'm just not sure I can handle that part of it."

Neither was he, he thought after she shut the door. With another woman he would have been certain that physical release would end the tension. With Charity he knew that making love with her would only add another layer to the hold she had on him.

And she did have a hold on him. It was time to admit that, and to deal with it.

Perhaps he'd reacted so strongly to her declaration of love because he was afraid, as he'd never been afraid of anything in his life, that he was falling in love with her.

"Roman!" He heard the delight in Charity's voice when she called to him. He swung open the door and saw her standing on the landing at the top of the stairs. "Come up. Hurry. I want you to see them."

She disappeared, leaving him wishing she'd called him anyplace but that innocently seductive bedroom.

When he walked into her sitting room, she called again, impatience in her tone now. "Hurry. I don't know how long they'll stay."

She was sitting on the windowsill, her upper body out the opening, her long legs hooked just above the ankles. There was music playing, something vibrant, passionate. How was it he had never thought of classical music as passionate?

"Damn it, Roman, you're going to miss them. Don't just stand in the doorway. I didn't call you up to tie you to the bedposts."

Because he felt like a fool, he crossed to her. "There goes my night."

"Very funny. Look." She was holding a brass spy glass, and she pointed with it now, out to sea. "Orcas."

He leaned out the window and followed her guiding hand. He could see a pair of shapes in the distance, rippling the water as they swam. Fascinated, he took the spyglass from Charity's hand.

"There are three of them," he said. Delighted, he joined her on the windowsill. Their legs were aligned now, and he rested his hand absently on her knee. This time, instead of fire, there was simple warmth.

"Yes, there's a calf. I think it might be the same pod I spotted a few days ago." She closed a hand over his as they both stared out to sea. "Great, aren't they?"

"Yeah, they are." He focused on the calf, which was just visible between the two larger whales. "I never really expected to see any."

"Why? The island's named after them." She narrowed her eyes, trying to follow their path. She didn't have the heart to ask Roman for the glass. "My first clear memory of seeing one was when I was about four. Pop had me out on this little excuse for a fishing boat. One shot up out of the water no more than eight or ten yards away. I screamed my lungs out." Laughing, she leaned back against the window frame. "I thought it was going to swallow us whole, like Jonah or maybe Pinocchio."

Roman lowered the glass for a moment. "Pinocchio?"

"Yes, you know the puppet who wanted to be a real boy. Jiminy Cricket, the Blue Fairy. Anyway, Pop finally calmed me down. It followed us for ten or fifteen minutes. After that, I nagged him mercilessly to take me out again."

"Did he?"

"Every Monday afternoon that summer. We didn't always see something, but they were great days, the best days. I guess we were a pod, too, Pop and I." She turned her face into the breeze. "I was lucky to have him as long as I did, but there are times—like this—when I can't help wishing he were here."

"Like this?"

"He loved to watch them," she said quietly. "Even when he was ill, really ill, he would sit for hours at the window. One afternoon I found him sitting there with the spyglass on his lap. I thought he'd fallen asleep, but he was gone." There was a catch in her breath when she slowly let it out. "He would have wanted that, to just slip away while watching for his whales. I haven't been able to take the boat out since he died." She shook her head. "Stupid."

"No." He reached for her hand for the first time and linked his fingers with hers. "It's not."

She turned her face to his again. "You can be a nice man." The phone rang, and she groaned but slipped dutifully from the windowsill to answer it.

"Hello. Yes, Bob. What does he mean he won't deliver them? New management be damned, we've been dealing with that company for ten years. Yes, all right. I'll be right there. Oh, wait." She glanced up from the phone. "Roman, are they still there?"

"Yes. Heading south. I don't know if they're feeding or just taking an afternoon stroll."

She laughed and put the receiver at her ear again. "Bob— What? Yes, that was Roman." Her brow lifted. "That's right. We're in my room. I called Roman up here because I spotted a pod out my bedroom window. You might want to tell any of the guests you see around. No, there's no reason for you to be concerned. Why should there be? I'll be right down."

She hung up, shaking her head. "It's like having a houseful of chaperons," she muttered.

"Problem?"

"No. Bob realized that you were in my bedroom— or rather that we were alone in my bedroom—and got very big-brotherly. Typical." She opened a drawer and pulled out a fabric-covered band. In a few quick movements she had her hair caught back from her face. "Last year Mae threatened to poison a guest who made a pass at me. You'd think I was fifteen."

He turned to study her. She was wearing jeans and a sweatshirt with a silk-screened map of the island. "Yes, you would."

"I don't take that as a compliment." But she didn't have time to argue. "I have to deal with a small crisis downstairs. You're welcome to stay and watch the whales." She started toward the door, but then she stopped. "Oh, I nearly forgot. Can you build shelves?"

"Probably."

"Great. I think the parlor in the family suite could use them. We'll talk about it."

He heard her jog down the stairs. Whatever crisis there might be at the other end of the inn, he was sure she would handle it. In the meantime, she had left him alone in her room. It would be a simple matter to go through her desk again, to see if she'd left anything that would help him move his investigation forward.

It should be simple, anyway. Roman looked out to sea again. It should be something he could do without hesitation. But he couldn't. She trusted him. Sometime during the past twenty-four hours he reached the point where he couldn't violate that trust.

That made him useless. Swearing, Roman leaned back against the window frame. She had, without even being aware of it, totally undermined his ability to do his job. It would be best for him to call Conby and have himself taken off the case. It would simply be a matter of him turning in his resignation now, rather than at the end of the assignment. It was a question of duty.

He wasn't going to do that, either.

He needed to stay. It had nothing to do with being loved, with feeling at home. He needed to believe that. He also needed to finish his job and prove, beyond a shadow of a doubt, Charity's innocence. That was a question of loyalty.

Conby would have said that his loyalty belonged to the Bureau, not to a woman he had known for less than a week. And Conby would have been wrong, Roman thought as he set aside the spyglass. There were times, rare times, when you had a chance to do something good, something right. Something that proved you gave a damn. That had never mattered to him before, but it mattered now.

If the only thing he could give Charity was a clear name, he intended to give it to her. And then get out of her life.

Rising, he looked around the room. He wished he were nothing more than the out-of-work drifter Charity had taken into her home. If he were maybe he would have the right to love her. As it was, all he could do was save her.

Chapter 6

The weather was warming. Spring was busting loose, full of glory and color and scent. The island was a treasure trove of wildflowers, leafy trees and birdsong. At dawn, with thin fingers of fog over the water, it was a mystical, timeless place.

Roman stood at the side of the road and watched the sun come up as he had only days before. He didn't know the names of the flowers that grew in tangles on the roadside. He didn't know the song of a jay from that of a sparrow. But he knew Charity was out running with her dog and that she would pass the place he stood on her return.

He needed to see her, to talk to her, to be with her.

The night before, he had broken into her cash drawer and examined the bills she had neatly stacked and marked for today's deposit. There had been over two thousand dollars in counterfeit Canadian currency. His first impulse had been to tell her, to lay everything he knew and needed to know out in front of her. But he had quashed that. Telling her wouldn't prove her innocence to men like Conby.

He had enough to get Block. And nearly enough, he thought, to hang Bob along with him. But he couldn't get them without casting shadows on Charity. By her own admission, and according to the statements of her loyal staff, a pin couldn't drop in the inn without her knowing it.

If that was so, how could he prove that there had been a counterfeiting and smuggling ring going on under her nose for nearly two years?

He believed it, as firmly as he had ever believed anything. Conby and the others at the Bureau wanted facts. Roman drew on his cigarette and watched the fog melt away with the rising of the sun. He had to give them facts. Until he could, he would give them nothing.

He could wait and make sure Conby dropped the ax on Block on the guide's next trip to the inn. That would give Roman time. Time enough, he promised himself, to make certain Charity wasn't caught in the middle. When it went down, she would be stunned and hurt. She'd get over it. When it was over, and she knew his part in it, she would hate him. He would get over that. He would have to.

He heard a car and glanced over, then returned his gaze to the water. He wondered if he could come back someday and stand in this same spot and wait for Charity to run down the road toward him.

Fantasies, he told himself, pitching his half-finished cigarette into the dirt. He was wasting too much time on fantasies.

The car was coming fast, its engine protesting, its muffler rattling. He looked over again, annoyed at having his morning and his thoughts disturbed.

His annoyance saved his life.

It took him only an instant to realize what was happening, and a heartbeat more to evade it. As the car barreled toward him, he leaped aside, tucking and rolling into the brush. A wave of displaced air flattened the grass before the car's rear tires gripped the roadbed again. Roman's gun was in his hand even as he scrambled to his feet. He caught a glimpse of the car's rear end as it sped around a curve. There wasn't even time to swear before he heard Charity's scream.

He ran, unaware of the fire in his thigh where the car had grazed him and the blood on his arm where he had rolled into a rock. He had faced death. He had killed. But he had never understood terror until this moment, with her scream still echoing in his head. He hadn't understood agony until he'd seen Charity sprawled beside the road.

The dog was curled beside her, whimpering, nuzzling her face with her nose. He turned at Roman's approach and began to growl, then stood, barking.

"Charity." Roman crouched beside her, and felt for a pulse, his hand shaking. "Okay, baby. You're going to be okay," he murmured to her as he checked for broken bones.

Had she been hit? A sickening vision of her being

tossed into the air as the car slammed into her pulsed through his head. Using every ounce of control he possessed, he blocked it out. She was breathing. He held on to that. The dog whined as he turned her head and examined the gash on her temple. It was the only spot of color on her face. He stanched the blood with his bandanna, cursing when he felt its warmth on his fingers.

Grimly he replaced his weapon, then lifted her into his arms. Her body seemed boneless. Roman tightened his grip, half afraid she might melt through his arms. He talked to her throughout the half mile walk back to the inn, though she remained pale and still.

Bob raced out the front door of the inn. "My God! What happened? What the hell did you do to her?"

Roman paused just long enough to aim a dark, furious look at him. "I think you know better. Get me the keys to the van. She needs a hospital."

"What's all this?" Mae came through the door, wiping her hands on her apron. "Lori said she saw—" She went pale, but then she began to move with surprising speed, elbowing Bob aside to reach Charity. "Get her upstairs."

"I'm taking her to the hospital."

"Upstairs," Mae repeated, moving back to open the door for him. "We'll call Dr. Mertens. It'll be faster. Come on, boy. Call the doctor, Bob. Tell him to hurry."

Roman passed through the door, the dog at his heels. "And call the police," he added. "Tell them they've got a hit-and-run."

Wasting no time on words, Mae led the way upstairs. She was puffing a bit by the time she reached the second floor, but she never slowed down. When they moved into Charity's room, her color had returned.

"Set her on the bed, and be careful about it." She yanked the lacy coverlet aside and then just as efficiently, brushed Roman aside. "There, little girl, you'll be just fine. Go in the bathroom," she told Roman. "Get me a fresh towel." Easing a hip onto the bed, she cupped Charity's face with a broad hand and examined her head wound. "Looks worse than it is." She let out a long breath. After taking the towel Roman offered, she pressed it against Charity's temple. "Head wounds bleed heavy, make a mess. But it's not too deep."

He only knew that her blood was still on his hands. "She should be coming around."

"Give her time. I want you to tell me what happened later, but I'm going to undress her now, see if she's hurt anywhere else. You go on and wait downstairs."

"I'm not leaving her."

Mae glanced up. Her lips were pursed, and lines of worry fanned out from her eyes. After a moment, she simply nodded. "All right, then, but you'll be of some use. Get me the scissors out of her desk. I want to cut this shirt off."

So that was the way of it, Mae mused as she untied Charity's shoes. She knew a man who was scared to death and fighting his heart when she saw one. Well, she'd just have to get her girl back on her feet. She didn't doubt for a moment that Charity could deal with the likes of Roman DeWinter.

"You can stay," she told him when he handed her the

scissors. "But whatever's been going on between the two of you, you'll turn your back till I make her decent."

He balled his hands into impotent fists and shoved them into his pockets as he spun around. "I want to know where she's hurt."

"Just hold your horses." Mae peeled the shirt away and put her emotions on hold as she examined the scrapes and bruises. "Look in that top right-hand drawer and get me out a nightshirt. One with buttons. And keep your eyes to yourself," she added, "or I'll throw you out of here."

In answer, he tossed a thin white nightshirt onto the bed. "I don't care what she's wearing. I want to know how badly she's hurt."

"I know, boy." Mae's voice softened as she slipped Charity's limp arm into a sleeve. "She's got some bruises and scrapes, that's all. Nothing broken. The cut on her head's going to need some tending, but cuts heal. Why, she hurt herself worse when she fell out of a tree some time back. There's my girl. She's coming around."

He turned to look then, shirt or no shirt. But Mae had already done up the buttons. He controlled the urge to go to her—barely—and, keeping his distance, watched Charity's lashes flutter. The sinking in his stomach was pure relief. When she moaned, he wiped his clammy hands on his thighs.

"Mae?" As she struggled to focus her eyes, Charity reached out a hand. She could see the solid bulk of her cook, but little else. "What— Oh, God, my head."

"Thumping pretty good, is it?" Mae's voice was

brisk, but she cradled Charity's hand in hers. She would have kissed it if she'd thought no one would notice. "The doc'll fix that up."

"Doctor?" Baffled, Charity tried to sit up, but the pain exploded in her head. "I don't want the doctor."

"Never did, but you're having him just the same."

"I'm not going to…" Arguing took too much effort. Instead, she closed her eyes and concentrated on clearing her mind. It was fairly obvious that she was in bed— but how the devil had she gotten there?

She'd been walking the dog, she remembered, and Ludwig had found a tree beside the road irresistible. Then…

"There was a car," she said, opening her eyes again. "They must have been drunk or crazy. It seemed like they came right at me. If Ludwig hadn't already been pulling me off the road, I—" She wasn't quite ready to consider that. "I stumbled, I think. I don't know."

"It doesn't matter now," Mae assured her. "We'll figure it all out later."

After a brisk knock, the outside door opened. A short, spry little man with a shock of white hair hustled in. He carried a black bag and was wearing grubby overalls and muddy boots. Charity took one look, then closed her eyes again.

"Go away, Dr. Mertens. I'm not feeling well."

"She never changes." Mertens nodded to Roman, then walked over to examine his patient.

Roman slipped quietly out into the sitting room. He needed a moment to pull himself together, to quiet the rage that was building now that he knew she would be all right. He had lost his parents, he had buried his best friend, but he had never, never felt the kind of panic he had experienced when he had seen Charity bleeding and unconscious beside the road.

Taking out a cigarette, he went to the open window. He thought about the driver of the old, rusted Chevy that had run her down. Even as his rage cooled, Roman understood one thing with perfect clarity. It would be his pleasure to kill whoever had hurt her.

"Excuse me." Lori was standing in the hall doorway, wringing her hands. "The sheriff's here. He wants to talk to you, so I brought him up." She tugged at her apron and stared at the closed door on the other side of the room. "Charity?"

"The doctor's with her," Roman said. "She'll be fine."

Lori closed her eyes and took a deep breath. "I'll tell the others. Go on in, sheriff."

Roman studied the paunchy man, who had obviously been called out of bed. His shirttail was only partially tucked into his pants, and he was sipping a cup of coffee as he came into the room.

"You Roman DeWinter?"

"That's right."

"Sheriff Royce." He sat, with a sigh, on the arm of Charity's rose-colored Queen Anne chair. "What's this about a hit-and-run?"

"About twenty minutes ago somebody tried to run down Miss Ford."

Royce turned to stare at the closed door just the way Lori had done. "How is she?"

"Banged up. She's got a gash on her head and some bruises."

"Were you with her?" He pulled out a pad and a stubby pencil.

"No. I was about a quarter mile away. The car swerved at me, then kept going. I heard Charity scream. When I got to her, she was unconscious."

"Don't suppose you got a good look at the car?"

"Dark blue Chevy. Sedan, '67, '68. Muffler was bad. Right front fender was rusted through. Washington plates Alpha Foxtrot Juliet 847."

Royce lifted both brows as he took down the description. "You got a good eye."

"That's right."

"Good enough for you to guess if he ran you down on purpose?"

"I don't have to guess. He was aiming."

Without a flicker of an eye, Royce continued taking notes. He added a reminder to himself to do a routine check on Roman DeWinter. "He? Did you see the driver?"

"No," Roman said shortly. He was still cursing himself for that.

"How long have you been on the island, Mr. DeWinter?"

"Almost a week."

"A short time to make enemies."

"I don't have any—here—that I know of."

"That makes your theory pretty strange." Still scribbling, Royce glanced up. "There's nobody on the island who knows Charity and has a thing against her. If what you're saying's true, we'd be talking attempted murder."

Roman pitched his cigarette out the window. "That's just what we're talking about. I want to know who owns that car."

"I'll check it out."

"You already know."

Royce tapped his pad on his knee. "Yes, sir, you do have a good eye. I'll say this. Maybe I do know somebody who owns a car that fits your description. If I do, I know that that person wouldn't run over a rabbit on purpose, much less a woman. Then again, there's no saying you have to own a car to drive it."

Mae opened the connecting door, and he glanced up. "Well, now, Maeflower."

Mae's lips twitched slightly before she thinned them. "If you can't sit in a chair proper you can stand on your feet, Jack Royce."

Royce rose, grinning. "Mae and I went to school together," he explained. "She liked to bully me then, too. I don't suppose you've got any waffles on the menu today, Maeflower."

"Maybe I do. You find out who hurt my girl and I'll see you get some."

"I'm working on it." His face sobered again as he nodded toward the door. "Is she up to talking to me?"

"Done nothing but talk since she came around." Mae blinked back a flood of relieved tears. "Go ahead in."

Royce turned to Roman. "I'll be in touch."

"Doc said she could have some tea and toast." Mae sniffled, then made a production out of blowing her nose. "Hay fever," she said roughly. "I'm grateful you were close by when she was hurt."

"If I'd been closer she wouldn't have been hurt."

"And if she hadn't been walking that dog she'd have been in bed." She paused and gave Roman a level look. "I guess we could shoot him."

She surprised a little laugh out of him. "Charity might object to that."

"She wouldn't care to know you're out here brooding, either. Your arm's bleeding, boy."

He looked down dispassionately at the torn, blood-stained sleeve of his shirt. "Some."

"Can't have you bleeding all over the floor." She walked to the door, waving a hand. "Well, come on downstairs. I'll clean you up. Then you can bring the girl up some breakfast. I haven't got time to run up and down these steps all morning."

After the doctor had finished his poking and the sheriff had finished his questioning, Charity stared at the ceiling. She hurt everywhere there was to hurt. Her head especially, but the rest of her was throbbing right along in time.

The medication would take the edge off, but she wanted to keep her mind clear until she'd worked everything out. That was why she had tucked the pill Dr. Mertens had given her under her tongue until she'd been alone. As soon as she'd organized her thoughts she would swallow it and check into oblivion for a few hours.

She'd only caught a flash of the car, but it had seemed familiar. While she'd spoken with the sheriff she'd remembered. The car that had nearly run her over belonged to Mrs. Norton, a sweet, flighty lady who crocheted doilies and doll clothes for the local craft shops. Charity didn't think Mrs. Norton had ever driven over twenty-five miles an hour. That was a great deal less than the car had been doing when it had swerved at her that morning.

She hadn't seen the driver, not really, but she had the definite impression it had been a man. Mrs. Norton had been widowed for six years.

Then it was simple, Charity decided. Someone had gotten drunk, stolen Mrs. Norton's car, and taken it for a wild joyride around the island. They probably hadn't even seen her at the side of the road.

Satisfied, she eased herself up in the bed. The rest was for the sheriff to worry about. She had problems of her own.

The breakfast shift was probably in chaos. She thought she could rely on Lori to keep everyone calm. Then there was the butcher. She still had her list to complete for tomorrow's order. And she had yet to choose the photographs she wanted to use for the ad in the travel brochure. The deposit hadn't been paid, and the fireplace in cabin 3 was smoking.

What she needed was a pad, a pencil and a telephone. That was simple enough. She'd find all three at the desk in the sitting room. Carefully she eased her legs over the side of the bed. Not too bad, she decided, but she gave herself a moment to adjust before she tried to stand.

Annoyed with herself, she braced a hand on one of the bedposts. Her legs felt as though they were filled with Mae's whipped cream rather than muscle and bone.

"What the hell are you doing?"

She winced at the sound of Roman's voice, then gingerly turned her head toward the doorway. "Nothing," she said, and tried to smile.

"Get back in bed."

"I just have a few things to do."

She was swaying on her feet, as pale as the nightshirt that buttoned modestly high at the neck and skimmed seductively high on her thighs. Without a word, he set down the tray he was carrying, crossed to her and scooped her up in his arms.

"Roman, don't. I—"

"Shut up."

"I was going to lie back down in a minute," she began. "Right after—"

"Shut up," he repeated. He laid her on the bed, then gave up. Keeping his arms around her, he buried his face against her throat. "Oh, God, baby."

"It's all right." She stroked a hand through his hair. "Don't worry."

"I thought you were dead. When I found you I thought you were dead."

"Oh, I'm sorry." She rubbed at the tension at the back of his neck, trying to imagine how he must have felt. "It must have been awful, Roman. But it's only some bumps and bruises. In a couple of days they'll be gone and we'll forget all about it."

"I won't forget." He pulled himself away from her. "Ever."

The violence she saw in his eyes had her heart fluttering. "Roman, it was an accident. Sheriff Royce will take care of it."

He bit back the words he wanted to say. It was best that she believe it had been an accident. For now. He got up to get her tray. "Mae said you could eat."

She thought of the lists she had to make and decided she had a better chance getting around him if she cooperated. "I'll try. How's Ludwig?"

"Okay. Mae put him out and gave him a ham bone."

"Ah, his favorite." She bit into the toast and pretended she had an appetite.

"How's your head?"

"Not too bad." It wasn't really a lie, she thought. She was sure a blow with a sledgehammer would have been worse. "No stitches." She pulled back her hair to show him a pair of butterfly bandages. A bruise was darkening around them. "You want to hold up some fingers and ask me how many I see?"

"No." He turned away, afraid he would explode. The last thing she needed was another outburst from him, he reminded himself. He wasn't the kind to fall apart—at least he hadn't been until he'd met her.

He began fiddling with bottles and bowls set around the room. She loved useless little things, he thought as he picked up a wand-shaped amethyst crystal. Feeling clumsy, he set it down again.

"The sheriff said the car swerved at you." She drank the soothing chamomile tea, feeling almost human again. "I'm glad you weren't hurt."

"Damn it, Charity." He whirled, then made an effort to get a handle on his temper. "No, I wasn't hurt."

And he was going to see to it that *she* wasn't hurt again. "I'm sorry. This whole business has made me edgy."

"I know what you mean. Want some tea? Mae sent up two cups."

He glanced at the pretty flowered pot. "Not unless you've got some whiskey to go in it."

"Sorry, fresh out." Smiling again, she patted the bed. "Why don't you come sit down?"

"Because I'm trying to keep my hands off you."

"Oh." Her smile curved wider. It pleased her that she was resilient enough to feel a quick curl of desire. "I like your hands on me, Roman."

"Bad timing." Because he couldn't resist, he crossed to the bed to take her hand in his. "I care about you, Charity. I want you to believe that."

"I do."

"No." His fingers tightened insistently on hers. He knew he wasn't clever with words, but he needed her to understand. "It's different with you than it's ever been with anyone." Fighting a fresh wave of frustration, he relaxed his grip. "I can't give you anything else."

She felt her heart rise up in her throat. "If I had known I could get that much out of you I might have bashed my head on a rock before."

"You deserve more." He sat down and ran a gentle finger under the bruise on her temple.

"I agree." She brought his hand to her lips and watched his eyes darken. "I'm patient."

Something was moving inside him, and he was helpless to prevent it. "You don't know enough about me. You don't know anything about me."

"I know I love you. I figured you'd tell me the rest eventually."

"Don't trust me, Charity. Not so much."

There was trouble here. She wanted to smooth it from his face, but she didn't know how. "Have you done something so unforgivable, Roman?"

"I hope not. You should rest." Knowing he'd already said too much, he set her tray aside.

"I was going to, really. Right after I take care of a few things."

"The only thing you have to take care of today is yourself."

"That's very sweet of you, and as soon as I—"

"You're not getting out of bed for at least twenty-four hours."

"That's the most ridiculous thing I've ever heard. What possible difference does it make whether I'm lying down or sitting down?"

"According to the doctor, quite a bit." He picked up a tablet from the nightstand. "Is this the medication he gave you?"

"Yes."

"The same medication that you were supposed to take before he left?"

She struggled to keep from pouting. "I'm going to take it after I make a few phone calls."

"No phone calls today."

"Now listen, Roman, I appreciate your concern, but I don't take orders from you."

"I know. You give them to me."

Before she could respond, he lowered his lips to

hers. Here was gentleness again, whisper-soft, achingly warm. With a little sound of pleasure, she sank into it.

He'd thought it would be easy to take one, only one, fleeting taste. But his hand curled into a fist as he fought the need to demand more. She was so fragile now. He wanted to soothe, not arouse…to comfort, not seduce. But in seconds he was both aroused and seduced.

When he started to pull back, she gave a murmur of protest and pressed him close again. She needed this sweetness from him, needed it more than any medication.

"Easy," he told her, clawing for his self-control. "I'm a little low on willpower, and you need rest."

"I'd rather have you."

She smiled at him, and his stomach twisted into knots. "Do you drive all men crazy?"

"I don't think so." Feeling on top of the world, she brushed his hair back from his brow. "Anyway, you're the first to ask."

"We'll talk about it later." Determined to do his best for her, he held out the pill. "Take this."

"Later."

"Uh-uh. Now."

With a sound of disgust, she popped the pill into her mouth, then picked up her cooling tea and sipped it. "There. Satisfied?"

He had to grin. "I've been a long way from satisfied since I first laid eyes on you, baby. Lift up your tongue."

"I beg your pardon?"

"You heard me. You're pretty good." He put a hand under her chin. "But I'm better. Let's have the pill."

She knew she was beaten. She took the pill out of her mouth, then made a production out of swallowing it. She touched the tip of her tongue to her lips. "It might still be in there. Want to search me for it?"

"What I want—" he kissed her lightly "—is for you to stay in bed." He shifted his lips to her throat. "No calls, no paperwork, no sneaking downstairs." He caught her earlobe between his teeth and felt her shudder, and his own. "Promise."

"Yes." Her lips parted as his brushed over them. "I promise."

"Good." He sat back and picked up the tray. "I'll see you later."

"But—" She set her teeth as he walked to the door. "You play dirty, DeWinter."

"Yeah." He glanced back at her. "And to win."

He left her, knowing she would no more break her word than she would fly out of the window. He had business of his own to attend to.

Chapter 7

An important part of Roman's training had been learning how to pursue an assignment in a thorough and objective manner. He had always found it second nature to do both. Until now. Still, for very personal reasons, he fully intended to be thorough.

When he left Charity, Roman expected to find Bob in the office, and he hoped to find him alone. He wasn't disappointed. Bob had the phone receiver at his ear and the computer monitor blinking above his fingers. After waving a distracted hand in Roman's direction, he went on with his conversation.

"I'll be happy to set that up for you and your wife, Mr. Parkington. That's a double room for the nights of the fifteenth and sixteenth of July."

"Hang up," Roman told him. Bob merely held up a finger, signaling a short wait.

"Yes, that's available with a private bath and includes breakfast. We'd be happy to help you arrange the rentals of kayaks during your stay. Your confirmation number is—"

Roman slammed a hand down on the phone, breaking the connection.

"What the hell are you doing?"

"Wondering if I should bother to talk to you or just kill you."

Bob sprang out of his chair and managed to put the desk between him and Roman. "Look, I know you've had an upsetting morning—"

"Do you?" Roman didn't bother to try to outmaneuver. He simply stood where he was and watched Bob sweat. "Upsetting. That's a nice, polite word for it. But you're a nice, polite man, aren't you, Bob?"

Bob glanced at the door and wondered if he had a chance of getting that far. "We're all a bit edgy because of Charity's accident. You could probably use a drink."

Roman moved over to a stack of computer manuals and unearthed a small silver flask. "Yours?" he said. Bob stared at him. "I imagine you keep this in here for those long nights when you're working late—and alone. Wondering how I knew where to find it?" He set it aside. "I came across it when I broke in here a couple of nights ago and went through the books."

"You broke in?" Bob wiped the back of his hand over suddenly dry lips. "That's a hell of a way to pay Charity back for giving you a job."

"Yeah, you're right about that. Almost as bad as

using her inn to pass counterfeit bills and slip undesirables in and out of the country."

"I don't know what you're talking about." Bob took one cautious sideways step toward the door. "I want you out of here, DeWinter. When I tell Charity what you've done—"

"But you're not going to tell her. You're not going to tell her a damn thing—yet. But you're going to tell me." One look stopped Bob's careful movement cold. "Try for the door and I'll break your leg." Roman tapped a cigarette out of his pack. "Sit down."

"I don't have to take this." But he took a step back, away from the door, and away from Roman. "I'll call the police."

"Go ahead." Roman lit the cigarette and watched him through a veil of smoke. It was a pity Bob was so easily cowed. He'd have liked an excuse to damage him. "I was tempted to tell Royce everything I knew this morning. The problem with that was that it would have spoiled the satisfaction of dealing with you and the people you're with personally. But go ahead and call him." Roman shoved the phone across the desk in Bob's direction. "I can find a way of finishing my business with you once you're inside."

Bob didn't ask him to explain. He had heard the cell door slam the moment Roman had walked into the room. "Listen, I know you're upset...."

"Do I look upset?" Roman murmured.

No, Bob thought, his stomach clenching. He looked cold—cold enough to kill. Or worse. But there had to be a way out. There always was. "You said something about counterfeiting. Why don't you tell me what this is all about, and we'll try to settle this calm—" Before he got the last word out he was choking as Roman hauled him out of the chair by the collar.

"Do you want to die?"

"No." Bob's fingers slid helplessly off Roman's wrists.

"Then cut the crap." Disgusted, Roman tossed him back into the chair. "There are two things Charity doesn't do around here. Only two. She doesn't cook, and she doesn't work the computer. *Can't* would be a better word. She can't cook because Mae didn't teach her. Pretty easy to figure why. Mae wanted to rule in the kitchen, and Charity wanted to let her."

He moved to the window and casually lowered the shades so that the room was dim and private. "It's just as simple to figure why she can't work a basic office computer. You didn't teach her, or you made the lessons so complicated and contradictory she never caught on. You want me to tell you why you did that?"

"She was never really interested." Bob swallowed, his throat raw. "She can do the basics when she has to, but you know Charity—she's more interested in people than machines. I show her all the printouts."

"All? You and I know you haven't shown her all of them. Should I tell you what I think is on those disks you've got hidden in the file drawer?"

Bob pulled out a handkerchief with fumbling fingers and mopped at his brow. "I don't know what you're talking about."

"You keep the books for the inn, and for the little

business you and your friends have on the side. I figure a man like you would keep backups, a little insurance in case the people you work for decided to cut you out." He opened a file drawer and dug out a disk. "We'll take a look at this later," he said, and tossed it onto the desk. "Two to three thousand a week washes through this place. Fifty-two weeks a year makes that a pretty good haul. Add that to the fee you charge to get someone back and forth across the border mixed with the tour group and you've got a nice, tidy sum."

"That's crazy." Barely breathing, Bob tugged at his collar. "You've got to know that's crazy."

"Did you know your references were still on file here?" Roman asked conversationally. "The problem is, they don't check out. You never worked for a hotel back in Ft. Worth, or in San Francisco."

"So I padded my chances a bit. That doesn't prove anything."

"I think we'll turn up something more interesting when we run your prints."

Bob stared down at the disk. Sometimes you could bluff, and sometimes you had to fold. "Can I have a drink?"

Roman picked up the flask, tossed it to him and waited while he twisted off the cap. "You made me for a cop, didn't you? Or you were worried enough to keep your ear to the ground. You heard me asking the wrong questions, were afraid I'd told Charity about the operation and passed it along to your friends."

"It didn't feel right." Bob wiped the vodka from his

lips, then drank again. "I know a scam when I see one, and you made me nervous the minute I saw you."

"Why?"

"When you're in my business you get so you can spot cops. In the supermarket, on the street, buying underwear at a department store. It doesn't matter where, you get so you can make them."

Roman thought of himself and of the years he'd spent on the other side of the street. He'd made his share of cops, and he still could. "Okay. So what did you do?"

"I told Block I thought you were a plant, but he figured I was going loopy. I wanted to back off until you'd gone, but he wouldn't listen. Last night, when you went down for dinner, I looked through your room. I found a box of shells. No gun, just the shells. That meant you were wearing it. I called Block and told him I was sure you were a cop. You'd been spending a lot of time with Charity, so I figured she was working with you on it."

"So you tried to kill her."

"No, not me." Panicked, Bob pressed back in his chair. "I swear. I'm not a violent man, DeWinter. Hell, I like Charity. I wanted to pull out, take a breather. We'd already set up another place, in the Olympic Mountains. I figured we could take a few weeks, run legit, then move on it. Block just said he'd take care of it, and I thought he meant we'd handle next week's tour on the level. That would give me time to fix everything here and get out. If I'd known what he was planning…"

"What? Would you have warned her?"

"I don't know." Bob drained the flask, but the liquor

did little to calm his nerves. "Look, I do scams, I do cons. I don't kill people."

"Who was driving the car?"

"I don't know. I swear it," he said. Roman took a step toward him, and he gripped the arms of his chair. "Listen, I got in touch with Block the minute this happened. He said he'd hired somebody. He couldn't have done it himself, because he was on the mainland. He said the guy wasn't trying to kill her. Block just wanted her out of the way for a few days. We've got a big shipment coming in and—" He broke off, knowing he was digging himself in deeper.

Roman merely nodded. "You're going to find out who was driving the car."

"Okay, sure." He made the promise without knowing if he could keep it. "I'll find out."

"You and I are going to work together for the next few days, Bob."

"But...aren't you going to call Royce?"

"Let me worry about Royce. You're going to go on doing what you do best. Lying. Only now you're going to lie to Block. You do exactly what you're told and you'll stay alive. If you do a good job I'll put in a word for you with my superior. Maybe you can make a deal, turn state's evidence."

After resting a hip on the desk, Roman leaned closer. "If you try to check out, I'll hunt you down. I'll find you wherever you hide, and when I'm finished you'll wish I'd killed you."

Bob looked into Roman's eyes. He believed him. "What do you want me to do?"

"Tell me about the next shipment."

* * *

Charity was sick of it. It was bad enough that she'd given her word to Roman and had to stay in bed all day. She couldn't even use the phone to call the office and see what was going on in the world.

She'd tried to be good-humored about it, poking through the books and magazines that Lori had brought up to her. She'd even admitted—to herself—that there had been times, when things had gotten crazy at the inn, that she'd imagined having the luxury of an idle day in bed.

Now she had it, and she hated it.

The pill Roman had insisted she swallow had made her groggy. She drifted off periodically, only to wake later, annoyed that she didn't have enough control to stay awake and be bored. Because reading made her headache worse, she tried to work up some interest in the small portable television perched on the shelf across the room.

When she'd found *The Maltese Falcon* flickering in black and white she'd felt both pleasure and relief. If she had to be trapped in bed, it might as well be with Bogart. Even as Sam Spade succumbed to the Fat Man's drug, Charity's own medication sent her under. She awoke in a very poor temper to a rerun of a sitcom.

He'd made her promise to stay in bed, she thought, jabbing an elbow at her pillow. And he didn't even have the decency to spend five minutes keeping her company. Apparently he was too busy to fit a sickroom call into his schedule. That was fine for him, she decided, running around doing something useful while she was moldering between the sheets. It wasn't in her nature to do nothing, and if she had to do it for five minutes longer she was going to scream.

Charity smiled a bit as she considered that. Just what would he do if she let out one long bloodcurdling scream? It might be interesting to find out. Certainly more interesting, she decided, than watching a blond airhead jiggle around a set to the beat of a laugh track. Nodding, she sucked in her breath.

"What are you doing?"

She let it out again in a long huff as Roman pushed open the door. Pleasure came first, but she quickly buried it in resentment. "You're always asking me that."

"Am I?" He was carrying another tray. Charity distinctly caught the scent of Mae's prize chicken soup and her biscuits. "Well, what were you doing?"

"Dying of boredom. I think I'd rather be shot." After eyeing the tray, she decided to be marginally friendly. But not because she was glad to see him, she thought. It was dusk, and she hadn't eaten for hours. "Is that for me?"

"Possibly." He set the tray over her lap, then stayed close and took a long, hard look at her. There was no way for him to describe the fury he felt when he saw the bruises and the bandages. Just as there was no way for him to describe the sense of pleasure and relief he experienced when he saw the annoyance in her eyes and the color in her cheeks.

"I think you're wrong, Charity. You're going to live."

"No thanks to you." She dived into the soup. "First you trick a promise out of me, then you leave me to rot for the next twelve hours. You might have come up for a minute to see if I had lapsed into a coma."

He *had* come up, about the time Sam Spade had been unwrapping the mysterious bird, but she'd been sleeping. Nonetheless, he'd stayed for nearly half an hour, just watching her.

"I've been a little busy," he told her, and broke off half of her biscuit for himself.

"I'll bet." Feeling far from generous, she snatched it back. "Well, since you're here, you might tell me how things are going downstairs."

"They're under control," he murmured, thinking of Bob and the phone calls that had already been made.

"It's only Bonnie's second day. She hasn't—"

"She's doing fine," he said, interrupting her. "Mae's watching her like a hawk. Where'd all these come from?" He gestured toward half a dozen vases of fresh flowers.

"Oh, Lori brought up the daisies with the magazines. Then the ladies came up. They really shouldn't have climbed all those stairs. They brought the wood violets." She rattled off more names of people who had brought or sent flowers.

He should have brought her some, Roman thought, rising and thrusting his hands into his pockets. It had never crossed his mind. Things like that didn't, he admitted. Not the small, romantic things a woman like Charity was entitled to.

"Roman?"

"What?"

"Did you come all the way up here to scowl at my peonies?"

"No." He hadn't even known the name for them. He turned away from the fat pink blossoms. "Do you want any more to eat?"

"No." She tapped the spoon against the side of her empty bowl. "I don't want any more to eat, I don't want any more magazines and I don't want anyone else to come in here, pat my hand and tell me to get plenty of rest. So if that's what you've got in mind you can leave."

"You're a charming patient, Charity." Checking his own temper, he removed the tray.

"No, I'm a miserable patient." Furiously, she tossed aside her self-control, and just as furiously tossed a paperback at his head. Fortunately for them both, her aim was off. "And I'm tired of being stuck in here as though I had some communicable disease. I have a bump on the head, damn it, not a brain tumor."

"I don't think a brain tumor's contagious."

"Don't be clever with me." Glaring at him, she folded her arms and dropped them over her chest. "I'm sick of being here, and sicker yet of being told what to do."

"You don't take that well, do you? No matter how good it is for you?"

When she was being unreasonable there was nothing she wanted to hear less than the truth. "I have an inn to run, and I can't do it from bed."

"Not tonight you don't."

"It's my inn, just like it's my body and my head." She tossed the covers aside. Even as she started to scramble out of bed her promise weighed on her like a chain.

Swinging her legs up again, she fell back against the pillows.

Thumbs hooked in his pockets, he measured her. "Why don't you get up?"

"Because I promised. Now get out, damn it. Just get out and leave me alone."

"Fine. I'll tell Mae and the rest that you're feeling more like yourself. They've been worried about you."

She threw another book—harder—but had only the small satisfaction of hearing it slap against the closing door.

The hell with him, she thought as she dropped her chin on her knees. The hell with everything.

The hell with her. He hadn't gone up there to pick a fight, and he didn't have to tolerate a bad-tempered woman throwing things at him, especially when he couldn't throw them back. Roman got halfway down the stairs, turned around and stalked back up again.

Charity was moping when he pushed open the door. She knew it, she hated it, and she wished everyone would leave her in peace to get on with it.

"What now?"

"Get up."

Charity straightened her spine against the headboard. "Why?"

"Get up," Roman repeated. "Get dressed. There must be a floor to mop or a trash can to empty around here."

"I said I wouldn't get up—" she set her chin "—and I won't."

"You can get out of bed on your own, or I can drag you out."

Temper had her eyes darkening and her chin thrusting out even farther. "You wouldn't dare." She regretted the words even as she spoke them. She'd already decided he was a man who would dare anything.

She was right. Roman crossed to the bed and grabbed her arm. Charity gripped one of the posts. Despite her hold, he managed to pull her up on her knees before she dug in. Before the tug-of-war could get much further she began to giggle.

"This is stupid." She felt her grip slipping and hooked her arm around the bedpost. "Really stupid. Roman, stop. I'm going to end up falling on my face and putting another hole in my head."

"You wanted to get up. So get up."

"No, I wanted to feel sorry for myself. And I was doing a pretty good job of it, too. Roman, you're about to dislocate my shoulder."

"You're the most stubborn, hardheaded, unreasonable woman I've ever met," he said. But he released her.

"I have to go along with the first two, but I'm not usually unreasonable." Offering him a smile, she sat cross-legged. The storm was over. At least hers was, she thought. She recognized the anger that was still darkening his eyes. She let out a long sigh. "I guess you could say I was having a really terrific pity party for myself when you came in. I'm sorry I took it out on you."

"I don't need an apology."

"Yes, you do." She would have offered him a hand, but he didn't look ready to sign any peace treaties. "I'm not used to being cut off from what's going on. I'm hardly ever sick, so I haven't had much practice in taking it like a good little soldier." She idly pleated the sheet between her fingers as she slanted a look at him. "I really am sorry, Roman. Are you going to stay mad at me?"

"That might be the best solution." Anger had nothing to do with what he was feeling at the moment. She looked so appealing with that half smile on her face, her hair tousled, the nightshirt buttoned to her chin and skimming her thighs.

"Want to slug me?"

"Maybe." It was hopeless. He smiled and sat down beside her. He balled his hand into a fist and skimmed it lightly over her chin. "When you're back on your feet again I'll take another shot."

"It was nice of you to bring me dinner. I didn't even thank you."

"No, you didn't."

She leaned forward to kiss his cheek. "Thanks."

"You're welcome."

After blowing the hair out of her eyes, she decided to start over. "Did we have a good crowd tonight?"

"I bused thirty tables."

"I'm going to have to give you a raise. I guess Mae made her chocolate mousse torte."

"Yeah." Roman found his lips twitching again.

"I don't suppose there was any left over."

"Not a crumb. It was great."

"You had some?"

"Meals are part of my pay."

Feeling deprived, Charity leaned back against the pillows. "Right."

"Are you going to sulk again?"

"Just for a minute. I wanted to ask you if the sheriff had any news about the car."

"Not much. He found it about ten miles from here, abandoned." He reached over to smooth away a line between her brows. "Don't worry about it."

"I'm not. Not really. I'm just glad the driver didn't hurt anyone else. Lori said you'd cut your arm."

"A little." Their hands were linked. He didn't know whether he had taken hers or she had taken his.

"Were you taking a walk?"

"I was waiting for you."

"Oh." She smiled again.

"You'd better get some rest." He was feeling awkward again, awkward and clumsy. No other woman had ever drawn either reaction from him.

Reluctantly she released his hand. "Are we friends again?"

"I guess you could say that. Good night, Charity."

"Good night."

He crossed to the door and opened it. But he couldn't step across the threshold. He stood there, struggling with himself. Though it was only a matter of seconds, it seemed like hours to both of them.

"I can't." He turned back, shutting the door quietly behind him.

"Can't what?"

"I can't leave."

Her smile bloomed, in her eyes, on her lips. She opened her arms to him, as he had known she would. Walking back to her was nearly as difficult as walking away. He took her hands and held them hard in his.

"I'm no good for you, Charity."

"I think you're very good for me." She brought their joined hands to her cheek. "That means one of us is wrong."

"If I could, I'd walk out the door and keep going."

She felt the sting and accepted it. She'd never expected loving Roman to be painless. "Why?"

"For reasons I can't begin to explain to you." He stared down at their linked hands. "But I can't walk away. Sooner or later you're going to wish I had."

"No." She drew him down onto the bed. "Whatever happens, I'll always be glad you stayed." This time she smoothed the lines from his brow. "I told you before that this wouldn't happen unless it was right. I meant that." Lifting her hands, she linked them behind his neck. "I love you, Roman. Tonight is something I want, something I've chosen."

Kissing her was like sinking into a dream. Soft, drugging and too impossibly beautiful to be real. He wanted to take care, such complete, such tender care, not to hurt her now, knowing that he would have no choice but to hurt her eventually.

But tonight, for a few precious hours, there would be no future. With her he could be what he had never tried to be before. Gentle, loving, kind. With her he could believe it was possible for love to be enough.

He loved her. Though he'd never known he was capable of that strong and fragile emotion, he felt it with her. It streamed through him, painless and sweet, healing wounds he'd forgotten he had, soothing aches he'd lived with forever. How could he have known when he'd walked into her life that she would be his salvation? In the short time he had left he would show her. And in showing her he would give himself something he had never expected to have.

He made her feel beautiful. And delicate, Charity thought as his mouth whispered over hers. It was as though he knew that this first time together was to be savored and remembered. She heard her own sigh, then his, as her hands slid up his back. Whatever she had wished they could have together was nothing compared to this.

He laid her back gently, barely touching her, as the kiss lengthened. Even loving him as she did, she hadn't known he'd possessed such tenderness. Nor could she know that he had just discovered it in himself.

The lamplight glowed amber. He hadn't thought to light the candles. But he could see her in the brilliance of it, her eyes dark and on his, her lips curved as he brought his to meet them. He hadn't thought to set the music. But her nightshirt whispered as she brought her arms around him. It was a sound he would remember always. Air drifted in through the open window, stirring the scent of the flowers others had brought to her. But it was the fragrance of her skin that filled his head. It was the taste of it that he yearned for.

Lightly, almost afraid he might bruise her with a touch, he cupped her breasts in his hands. Her breath caught, then released on a moan against the side of his neck. He knew that nothing had ever excited him more.

Then her hands were on his shirt, her fingers undoing his buttons as her eyes remained on his. They were as dark, as deep, as vibrant, as the water that surrounded her home. He could read everything she felt in them.

"I want to touch you," she said as she drew the shirt from his shoulders. Her heart began to sprint as she looked at him, the taut muscles, the taut skin.

There was a strength in him that excited, perhaps because she understood that he could be ruthless. There was a toughness to his body, a toughness that made her realize he was a man who had fought, a man who would fight. But his hands were gentle on her now, almost hesitant. Her excitement leaped higher, and there was no fear in it.

"It seems I've wanted to touch you like this all my life." She ran her fingertips lightly over the bandage on his arm. "Does it hurt?"

"No." Every muscle in his body tensed when she trailed her hands from his waist to his chest. It was impossible for him to understand how anyone could bring him peace and torment at the same time. "Charity..."

"Just kiss me again, Roman," she murmured.

He was helpless to refuse. He wondered what she would ask him for if she knew that he was powerless to deny her anything at this moment. Fighting back a flood of desperation, he kept his hands easy, sliding and stroking them over her until he felt the tremors begin.

He knew he could give her pleasure. The need to do so pulsed heavily inside him. He could ignite her passions. The drive to fan them roared through him like a brushfire. As he touched her he knew he could make her weak or strong, wild or limp. But it wasn't power that filled him at the knowledge. It was awe.

She would give him whatever he asked, without questions, without restrictions. This strong, beautiful, exciting woman was his. This wasn't a dream that would awaken him to frustration in the middle of the night. This wasn't a wish that he'd have to pretend he'd never made. It was real. She was real, and she was waiting for him.

He could have torn the nightshirt from her with one pull of his hand. Instead, he released button after tiny button, hearing her breath quicken, following the narrow path with soft, lingering kisses. Her fingers dug into his back, then went limp as her system churned. She could only groan as his tongue moistened her flesh, teasing and heating it. The night air whispered over her as he undressed her. Then he was lifting her, cradling her in his arms.

She was twined around him, her heart thudding frantically against his lips. He needed a moment to drag himself back, to find the control he wanted so that he could take her up, take her over. Murmuring to her, he used what skills he had to drive her past the edge of reason.

Her body was rigid against his. He watched her dazed eyes fly open. She gasped his name, and then he covered her mouth with his to capture her long, low moan as her body went limp.

She seemed to slide like water through his hands when he laid her down again. To his delight, her arousal burst free again at his lightest touch.

It was impossible. It was impossible to feel so much and still need more. Blindly she reached for him. Fresh pleasure poured into her until her arms felt too heavy to move. She was a prisoner, a gloriously willing prisoner, of the frantic sensations he sent tearing through her. She wanted to lock herself around him, to keep him there, always there. He was taking her on a long, slow journey to places she had never seen, places she never wanted to leave.

When he slid inside her she heard his low, breathless moan. So he was as much a captive as she.

With his face pressed against her neck, he fought the need to sprint toward release. He was trapped between heaven and hell, and he gloried in it. In her. In them. He heard her sob out his name, felt the strength pour into her. She was with him as no one had ever been.

Charity wrapped her arms around Roman to keep him from shifting away. "Don't move."

"I'm hurting you."

"No." She let out a long, long sigh. "No, you're not."

"I'm too heavy," he insisted, and compromised by gathering her close and rolling so that their positions were reversed.

"Okay." Satisfied, she rested her head on his shoulder. "You are," she said, "the most incredible lover."

He didn't even try to prevent the smile. "Thanks." He stroked a possessive hand down to her hip. "Have you had many?"

It was her turn to smile. The little trace of jealousy in his voice was a tremendous addition to an already-glorious night. "Define *many*."

Ignoring the quick tug of annoyance he felt, he

played the game. "More than three. Three is a few. Anything more than three is many."

"Ah. Well, in that case." She almost wished she could lie and invent a horde. "I guess I've had less than a few. That doesn't mean I don't know an incredible one when I find him."

He lifted her head to stare at her. "I've done nothing in my life to deserve you."

"Don't be stupid." She inched up to kiss him briefly. "And don't change the subject."

"What subject?"

"You're clever, DeWinter, but not that clever." She lifted a brow and studied him in the lamplight. "It's my turn to ask you if you've had many lovers."

He didn't smile this time. "Too many. But only one who's meant anything."

The amusement faded from her eyes before she closed them. "You'll make me cry," she murmured, lowering her head to his chest again.

Not yet, he thought, stroking her hair. Soon enough, but not yet. "Why haven't you ever gotten married?" he wondered aloud. "Had babies?"

"What a strange question. I haven't loved anyone enough before." She winced at her own words, then made herself smile as she lifted her head. "That wasn't a hint."

But it was exactly what he'd wanted to hear. He knew he was crazy to let himself think that way, even for a few hours, but he wanted to imagine her loving him enough to forgive, to accept and to promise.

"How about the traveling you said you wanted to do? Shouldn't that come first?"

She shrugged and settled against him again. "Maybe I haven't traveled because I know deep down I'd hate to go all those places alone. What good is Venice if you don't have someone to ride in a gondola with? Or Paris if there's no one to hold hands with?"

"You could go with me."

Already half-asleep, she laughed. She imagined Roman had little more than the price of a ferry ticket to his name. "Okay. Let me know when to pack."

"Would you?" He lifted her chin to look into her drowsy eyes.

"Of course." She kissed him, snuggled her head against his shoulder and went to sleep.

Roman switched off the lamp beside the bed. For a long time he held her and stared into the dark.

Chapter 8

Charity opened her eyes slowly, wondering why she couldn't move. Groggy, she stared into Roman's face. It was only inches from hers. He had pulled her close in his sleep, effectively pinning her arms and legs with his. Though his grip on her was somewhat guardlike, she found it unbearably sweet.

Ignoring the discomfort, she lay still and took advantage of the moment by looking her fill.

She'd always thought that people looked softer, more vulnerable, in sleep. Not Roman. He had the body of a fighter and the eyes of a man accustomed to facing trouble head-on. His eyes were closed now, and his body was relaxed. Almost.

Still, studying him, she decided that, asleep or awake, he looked tough as nails. Had he always been? she wondered. Had he had to be? It was true that smiling lent a certain charm to his face. It lightened the wariness in his eyes. In Charity's opinion, Roman smiled much too seldom.

She would fix that. Her own lips curved as she watched him. In time she would, gently, teach him to relax, to enjoy, to trust. She would make him happy. It wasn't possible to love as she had loved and not have it returned. And it wasn't possible to share what they had shared during the night without his heart being as lost as hers.

Sooner or later—sooner, if she had her way—he would come to accept how good they were together. And how much better they would become in all the years to follow. Then there would be time for promises and families and futures.

I'm not letting you go, she told him silently. *You don't realize it yet, but I've got a hold on you, and it's going to be mighty hard to break it.*

He had such a capacity for giving, she thought. Not just physically, though she wasn't ashamed to admit that his skill there had dazed and delighted her. He was a man full of emotions, too many of them strapped down. What had happened to him, she wondered, that had made him so wary of love, and so afraid to give it?

She loved him too much to demand an answer. It was a question he had to answer on his own…a question she knew he would answer as soon as he trusted her enough. When he did, all she had to do was show him that none of it mattered. All that counted, from this moment on, was what they felt for each other.

Inching over, she brushed a light kiss on his mouth.

His eyes opened instantly. It took only a heartbeat longer for them to clear. Fascinated, Charity watched their expression change from one of suspicion to one of desire.

"You're a light sleeper," she began. "I just—"

Before she could complete the thought, his mouth, hungry and insistent, was on hers. She managed a quiet moan as she melted into his kiss.

It was the only way he knew to tell her what it meant to him to wake and find her close and warm and willing. Too many mornings he had woken alone in strange beds in empty rooms.

That was what he expected. For years he had deliberately separated himself from anyone who had tried to get close. The job. He'd told himself it was because of the job. But that was a lie, one of many. He'd chosen to remain alone because he hadn't wanted to risk losing again. Grieving again. Now, overnight, everything had changed.

He would remember it all, the pale fingers of light creeping into the room, the high echoing sound of the first birds calling to the rising sun, the scent of her skin as it heated against his. And her mouth…he would remember the taste of her mouth as it opened eagerly under his.

There were such deep, dark needs in him. She felt them, understood them, and met them unquestioningly. As dawn swept the night aside, he stirred her own until their needs mirrored each other's.

Slowly, easily, while his lips cruised over her face, he slipped inside her. With a sigh and a murmur, she welcomed him.

* * *

She felt as strong as an ox and as content as a cat with cream on its whiskers. With her eyes closed, Charity stretched her arms to the ceiling.

"And to think I used to consider jogging the best way to start the day." Laughing, she curled over against him again. "I have to thank you for showing me how very wrong I was."

"My pleasure." He could still feel his own heart thudding like a jackhammer against his ribs. "Give me a minute and I'll show you the best reason for staying in bed in the morning."

Lord, it was tempting. Before her blood could begin to heat she shook her head. She took a quick nip at his chin before she sat up. "Maybe if you've got some time when I get back."

He took her wrist but kept his fingers light. "From where?"

"From taking Ludwig for his run."

"No."

The hand that had lifted to push back her hair paused. Deliberately she continued to lift it to finger-comb the hair away from her face. "No, what?"

He recognized that tone. She was the boss again, despite the fact that her face was still glowing from love-making and she was naked to where the sheets pooled at her waist. This was the woman who didn't take orders. Roman decided he would have to show her again that she was wrong.

"No, you're not taking the dog out for a run."

Because she wanted to be reasonable, she added a

smile. "Of course I am. I kept my promise and stayed in bed all day yesterday. And all night, for that matter. Now I'm going to get back to work."

Around the inn, that was fine. In fact, the sooner everything got back to normal the better it would be. But there was no way he was having her walking down a deserted road by herself. "You're in no shape to go for a mile hike."

"Three miles, and yes, I am."

"Three?" Lifting a brow, he stroked a hand over her thigh. "No wonder you've got such great muscle tone."

"That's not the point." She shifted away before his touch could weaken her.

"You have the most incredible body."

She shoved at his seeking hands. "Roman... I do?"

His lips curved. This was the way she liked them best. "Absolutely. Let me show you."

"No, I..." She caught his hands as they stroked her thighs. "We'll probably kill each other if we try this again."

"I'll risk it."

"Roman, I mean it." Her head fell back and she gasped when he scraped his teeth over her skin. It was impossible, she thought, impossible, for this deep, dark craving to take over again. "Roman—"

"Fabulous legs," he murmured, skimming his tongue behind her knee. "I didn't pay nearly enough attention to them last night."

"Yes, you—" She braced a hand against the mattress as she swayed. "You're trying to distract me."

"Yeah."

"You can't." She closed her eyes. He could, and he was. "Ludwig needs the run," she managed. "He enjoys it."

"Fine." He sat up and circled her waist with his hands. "I'll take him."

"You?" Wanting to catch her breath, she turned her head to avoid his kiss, then shuddered as his lips trailed down her throat. "It's not necessary. I'm perfectly... Roman." She said his name weakly as his thumbs circled her breasts.

"Yes, a truly incredible body," he murmured. "Long and lean and incredibly responsive. I can't seem to touch you and not want you."

She came up on her knees as he dragged another gasp out of her. "You're trying to seduce me."

"Nothing gets by you, does it?"

She was losing, weakening shamelessly. She knew it would infuriate her later, but for now all she could do was cling to him and let him have his way. "Is this your answer for everything?"

"No." He lifted her hips and brought her to him. "But it'll do."

Unable to resist, she wrapped her limbs around him and let passion take them both. When it was spent, she slid bonelessly down in the bed. She didn't argue when he drew the sheets over her shoulders.

"Stay here," he told her, kissing her hair. "I'll be back."

"His leash is on a hook under the steps," Charity murmured. "He gets two scoops of dog food when he gets back. And fresh water."

"I think I can handle a dog, Charity."

She yawned and tugged the blankets higher. "He likes to chase the Fitzsimmonses' cat. But don't worry, he can't catch her."

"That makes me breathe easier." He laced up his shoes. "Anything else I should know?"

"Mmm." She snuggled into the pillow. "I love you."

As always, it knocked him backward to hear her say it, to know she meant it. In silence, he stepped outside.

She wasn't tired, Charity thought as she stretched under the sheets. But Roman was right. Sleep wasn't the best reason for staying in bed in the morning. Despite her bumps and bruises, she knew she'd never felt better in her life.

Still, she indulged herself, lingering in bed, half dreaming, until guilt finally prodded her out.

Moving automatically, she turned on the stereo, then tidied the bed. In the parlor she glanced over the notes she'd left for herself, made a few more. Then she headed for the shower. She was humming along to Tchaikovsky's violin concerto when the curtain swished open.

"Roman!" She pressed both hands to her heart and leaned back against the tile. "You might as well shoot me as scare me to death. Didn't you ever hear of the Bates Motel?"

"I left my butcher knife in my other pants." She had her hair piled on top of her head and a cake of some feminine scented soap in her hand. Her skin was gleaming wet and already soapy. He pulled off his shirt and tossed it aside. "Did you ever consider teaching that dog to heel?"

"No." She grinned as she watched Roman unfasten his jeans. "I guess you could use a shower." Saying nothing, he tossed his jeans on top of his shirt. Charity took a moment to make a long, thorough survey. "Well, apparently that run didn't...tire you out." She was laughing when he stepped in with her.

It was nearly an hour later when Charity made it down to the lobby. "I could eat one of everything." She pressed a hand to her stomach. "Good morning, Bob." She paused at the front desk to smile at him.

"Charity." Bob felt the sweat spring onto his palms when he spotted Roman behind her. "How are you feeling? It's awfully soon for you to be up and around."

"I'm fine." Idly she glanced at the papers on the desk. "Sorry I left you in the lurch yesterday."

"Don't be silly." Fear ground in his stomach as he eyed the wound on her temple. "We were worried about you."

"I appreciate that, but there's no need to worry anymore." She slanted a smile at Roman. "I've never felt better in my life."

Bob caught the look, and his stomach sank. If the cop was in love with her, he thought, things were going to be even stickier. "Glad to hear it. But—"

She stopped his protest by raising a hand. "Is there anything urgent?"

"No." He glanced at Roman again. "No, nothing."

"Good." After setting the papers aside again, Charity studied his face. "What's wrong, Bob?"

"Nothing. What could be wrong?"

"You look a little pale. You're not coming down with anything, are you?"

"No, everything's fine. Just fine. We got some new reservations. July's almost booked solid."

"Great. I'll look things over after breakfast. Get yourself some coffee." She patted his hand and walked into the dining room.

Three tables were already occupied, the patrons enjoying Mae's coffee cake before their meal was served. Bonnie was busy taking orders. The breakfast menu was neatly listed on the board, and music was playing in the background, soft and soothing. The flowers were fresh, and the coffee was hot.

"Something wrong?" Roman asked her.

"No." Charity smoothed down the collar of her shirt. "What could be wrong? It looks like everything's just dandy." Feeling useless, she walked into the kitchen.

There was no bickering to referee. Mae and Dolores were working side by side, and Lori loaded up a tray with her first order.

"We need more butter for the French toast," Mae called out.

"Coming right up." Cheerful as a bird, Dolores began to scoop up neat balls of butter. As she offered the newly filled bowl to Lori, she spotted Charity standing inside the door. "Well, good morning." Her thin face creased with a smile. "Didn't expect to see you up."

"I'm fine."

"Sit down, girl." Hardly glancing around, Mae continued to sprinkle shredded cheese into an omelet. "Dolores will get you some tea."

Charity smiled with clenched teeth. "I don't want any tea."

"Want and need's two different things."

"Glad to see you're feeling better," Lori said as she rushed out with her tray.

Bonnie came in, pad in hand. "Oh, hi, Charity, we thought you'd rest another day. Feeling better?"

"I'm fine," Charity said tightly. "Just fine."

"Great. Two omelets with bacon, Mae. And an order of French toast with sausage. Two herb teas, an English muffin—crisp. And we're running low on coffee." After punching her order sheet on a hook by the stove, she took the fresh pot Dolores handed her and hurried out.

Charity walked over to get an apron, only to have Mae smack her hand away. "I told you to sit."

"And I told you I'm fine. That's *f-i-n-e.* I'm going to help take orders."

"The only orders you're taking today are from me. Now sit." She ran a hand up and down Charity's arm. Nobody recognized or knew how to deal with that stubborn look better than Mae. "Be a good girl, now. I won't worry so much if I know you've had a good breakfast. You don't want me to worry, do you?"

"No, of course not, but—"

"That's right. Now take a seat. I'll fix you some French toast. It's your favorite."

She sat down. Dolores set a cup of tea in front of her and patted her head. "You sure did give us all a fright yesterday. Have a seat, Roman. I'll get your coffee."

"Thanks. You're sulking," he murmured to Charity.

"I am not."

"Doc's coming by this morning to take another look at you."

"Oh, for heaven's sake, Mae—"

"You're not doing nothing till he gives the okay." With a nod, she began preparing Bonnie's order. "Fat lot of good you'll do if you're not a hundred percent. Things were hard enough yesterday."

Charity stopped staring into her tea and looked up. "Were they?"

"Everybody asking questions nobody had the answer to. Whole stacks of linens lost."

"Lost? But—"

"Found them." Mae made room at the stove for Dolores. "But it sure was confusing for a while. Then the dinner shift... Could have used an extra pair of hands for sure." Mae winked at Roman over Charity's head. "We'll all be mighty glad when the doc gives you his okay. Let that bacon crisp, Dolores."

"It is crisp."

"Not enough."

"Want me to burn it?"

Charity smiled and sipped her tea. It was good to be back.

It was midafternoon before she saw Roman again. She had a pencil behind her ear, a pad in one pocket and a dust cloth in another, and she was dashing down the hallway toward her rooms.

"In a hurry?"

"Oh." She stopped long enough to smile at him. "Yes.

I have some papers up in my room that should be in the office."

"What's this?" He tugged at the dust cloth.

"One of the housekeepers came down with a virus. I sent her home." She looked at her watch and frowned. She thought she could spare about two minutes for conversation. "I really hope that's not what's wrong with Bob."

"What's wrong with Bob?"

"I don't know. He just doesn't look well." She tossed her hair back, causing the slender gold spirals in her ears to dance. "Anyway, we're short a housekeeper, and we've got guests checking into units 3 and 5 today. The Garsons checked out of 5 this morning. They won't win any awards for neatness."

"The doctor said you were supposed to rest an hour this afternoon."

"Yes, but— How did you know?"

"I asked him." Roman pulled the dustcloth out of her pocket. "I'll clean 5."

"Don't be ridiculous. It's not your job."

"My job's to fix things. I'll fix 5." He took her chin in his hand before she could protest. "When I'm finished I'm going to go upstairs. If you aren't in bed I'm coming after you."

"Sounds like a threat."

He bent down and kissed her, hard. "It is."

"I'm terrified," she said, and dashed up the stairs.

It wasn't that she meant to ignore the doctor's orders. Not really. It was only that a nap came far down on her list of things to be done. Every phone call she made had to include a five-minute explanation of her injuries.

No, she was really quite well. Yes, it was terrible that someone had stolen poor Mrs. Norton's car and driven it so recklessly. Yes, she was sure the sheriff would get to the bottom of it. No, she had not broken her legs...her arm...her shoulder.... Yes, she intended to take good care of herself, thank you very much.

The goodwill and concern would have warmed her if she hadn't been so far behind in her work. To make it worse, Bob was distracted and disorganized. Worried that he was ill or dealing with a personal problem, Charity took on the brunt of his work.

Twice she'd fully intended to take a break and go up to her rooms, and twice she'd been delayed by guests checking in. Taking it on faith that Roman had spruced up unit 5, she showed a young pair of newlyweds inside.

"You have a lovely view of the garden from here," Charity said as a cover while she made sure there were fresh towels. Roman had hung them on the rack, exactly where they belonged. The bed, with its heart-shaped white wicker headboard, was made up with a military precision she couldn't have faulted. It cost her, but she resisted the temptation to turn up the coverlet and check sheets.

"We serve complimentary wine in the gathering room every evening at five. We recommend that you make a reservation for dinner if you plan to join us, particularly since it's Saturday night. Breakfast is served between seven-thirty and ten. If you'd like to—" She broke off when Roman stepped into the room. "I'll be with you in a minute," she told him, and started to turn back to the newlyweds.

"Excuse me." Roman gave them both a friendly nod before he scooped Charity up in his arms. "Miss Ford is needed elsewhere. Enjoy your stay."

As the first shock wore off she began to struggle. "Are you out of your mind? Put me down."

"I intend to—when I get you to bed."

"You can't just…" The words trailed off into a groan as he carried her through the gathering room.

Two men sitting on the sofa stopped telling fish stories. A family coming in from a hike gawked from the doorway. Miss Millie and Miss Lucy halted their daily game of Scrabble by the window.

"Isn't that the most romantic thing?" Miss Millie said when they disappeared into the west wing.

"You have totally embarrassed me."

Roman shifted her weight in his arms and carried her upstairs. "You're lucky that's all I did."

"You had no right interrupting me when I was welcoming guests. Then, to make matters worse, you decide to play Rhett Butler."

"As I recall, he had something entirely different in mind when he carried another stubborn woman up to bed." He dropped her, none too gently, on the mattress. "You're going to rest."

"I'm tempted to tell you to go to hell."

He leaned down to cage her head between his hands. "Be my guest."

She'd be damned if she'd smile. "My manners are too ingrained to permit it."

"Aren't I the lucky one?" He leaned a little closer. There was amusement in his eyes now, enough of it so she had to bite her lip to keep from laughing. "I don't want you to get out of this bed for sixty minutes."

"Or?"

"Or...I'll sic Mae on you."

"A low blow, DeWinter."

He brushed a kiss just below the fresh bandage on her temple. "Tune out for an hour, baby. It won't kill you."

She reached up to toy with the top button of his shirt. "I'd like it better if you got in with me."

"I said tuned out, not turned on." When the phone in the parlor rang, he held her down with one hand. "Not a chance. Stay here and I'll get it."

She rolled her eyes behind his back as he walked into the adjoining room.

"Yes? She's resting. Tell him she'll get back to him in an hour. Hold her calls until four. That's right." He glanced down idly at a catalog she'd left open on her desk. She had circled a carved gold bracelet with a square-cut purple stone. "You handle whatever needs to be handled for the next hour. That's right."

"What was it?" Charity called from the next room.

"I'll tell you in an hour."

"Damn it, Roman."

He stopped in the doorway. "You want the message, I'll give it to you in an hour."

"But if it's important—"

"It's not."

She sent him a smoldering look. "How do you know?"

"I know it's not more important than you. Nothing is." He closed the door on her astonished expression.

He needed to keep Bob on a tight leash, he thought as he headed downstairs. As long as he was more afraid of him than of Block, things would be fine. He only had to keep the pressure on for a few more days. Block and Vision Tours would be checking in on Tuesday. When they checked out on Thursday morning he would lock the cage.

Roman pushed open the door of the office to find Bob staring at the computer screen and gulping coffee. "For somebody who's made his living from scams you're a mess."

Bob gulped more coffee. "I never worked with a cop looking over my shoulder before."

"Just think of me as your new partner," Roman advised him. He took the mug out of his hand and sniffed at it. "And lay off the booze."

"Give me a break."

"I'm giving you more of one than you deserve. Charity's worried that you're coming down with something—something other than a stretch in federal prison. I don't want her worrying."

"Look, you want me to carry on like it's business as usual. I'm lying to Block, setting him up." His hand shook as he passed it over his hair. "You don't know what he's capable of. *I* don't know what he's capable of." He looked at the mug, which Roman had set out of reach. "I need a little something to help me through the next few days."

"Let this get you through." Roman calmly lit a cigarette. "You pull this off and I'll go to bat for you. Screw up and I'll see to it that you're in a cage for a long time. Now take a break."

"What?"

"I said, take a break, go for a walk, get some real coffee." Roman tapped the ash from his cigarette into a little mosaic bowl.

"Sure." As he rose, Bob rubbed his palms on his thighs. "Look, DeWinter, I'm playing it straight with you. When this goes down, I expect you to keep Block off me."

"I'll take care of Block." That was a promise he intended to keep. When the door closed behind Bob, he picked up the phone. "DeWinter," he said when the connection was made.

"Make it quick," Conby told him. "I'm entertaining friends."

"I'll try not to let your martini get warm. I want to know if you've located the driver."

"DeWinter, an underling is hardly important at this point."

"It's important to me. Have you found him?"

"A man answering the description your informant gave you was detained in Tacoma this morning. He's being held for questioning by the local police." Conby put his hand over the receiver. Roman heard him murmur something that was answered by light laughter.

"We're using our influence to lengthen the procedure," Conby continued. "I'll be flying out there on Monday. By Tuesday afternoon I should be checked into the inn. I'm told I'll have a room overlooking a fish pond. It sounds very quaint."

"I want your word that Charity will be left out of this."

"As I explained before, if she's innocent she has nothing to worry about."

"It's not a matter of *if.*" Struggling to hold his temper, Roman crushed out his cigarette. "She is innocent. We've got it on record."

"On the word of a whimpering little bookkeeper."

"She was damn near killed, and she doesn't even know why."

"Then keep a closer eye on her. We have no desire to see Miss Ford harmed, or to involve her any more deeply than necessary. There's a police officer out there who shares the same passionate opinion of Miss Ford as you do. Sheriff Royce managed to trace you to us."

"How?"

"He's a smart cop with connections. He has a cousin or brother-in-law or some such thing with the Bureau. He wasn't at all pleased at being left in the dark."

"I'll bet."

"I imagine he'll be paying you a visit before long. Handle him carefully, DeWinter, but handle him."

Just as Roman heard the phone click in his ear the office door opened. For once, Roman thought, Conby was right on target. He replaced the receiver before settling back in his chair.

"Sheriff."

"I want to know what the hell's going on around here, Agent DeWinter."

"Close the door." Roman pushed back in the chair and considered half a dozen different ways of handling Royce. "I'd appreciate it if you'd drop the 'Agent' for now."

Royce just laid both palms on the surface of the desk. "I want to know what a federal agent is doing undercover in my territory."

"Following orders. Sit down?" He indicated a chair.

"I want to know what case you're working on."

"What did they tell you?"

Royce snorted disgustedly. "It got to the point where even my cousin started giving me the runaround, DeWinter, but I've got to figure that your being here had something to do with Charity being damn near run down yesterday."

"I'm here because I was assigned here." Roman waited a moment, sending Royce a long, direct look. "But my first priority is keeping Charity safe."

Royce hadn't been in law enforcement for nearly twenty years without being able to take the measure of a man. He took Roman's now, and was satisfied. "I got a load of bull from Washington about her being under investigation."

"She was. Now she's not. But she could be in trouble. Are you willing to help?"

"I've known that girl all her life." Royce took off his hat and ran his fingers through his hair. "Why don't you stop asking fool questions and tell me what's going on?"

Roman briefed him, pausing only once or twice to allow Royce to ask questions. "I don't have time to get into any more specifics. I want to know how many of your men you can spare Thursday morning."

"All of them," Royce said immediately.

"I only want your most experienced. I have information that Block will not only be bringing the counterfeit money, but also a man who'll register as Jack Marshall. His real name is Vincent Dupont. A week ago he robbed two banks in Ontario, killed a guard and wounded a civilian. Block will smuggle him out of Canada in the tour group, keep him here for a couple of days, then send him by short routes to South America. For his travel service to men like Dupont he takes a nice stiff fee. Both Dupont and Block are dangerous men. We'll have agents here at the inn, but we also have civilians. There's no way we can clear the place without tipping them off."

"It's a chancy game you're playing."

"I know." He thought of Charity dozing upstairs. "It's the only way I know how to play it."

Chapter 9

Charity drove back to the inn after dropping a trio of guests at the ferry. She was certain it was the most beautiful morning she'd ever seen. After the most wonderful night of her life, she thought. No, two of the most wonderful nights of her life.

Though she'd never considered herself terribly romantic, she'd always imagined what it would be like to really be in love. Her daydreams hadn't come close to what she was feeling now. This was solid and bewildering. It was simple and staggering. He filled her thoughts just as completely as he filled her heart. She couldn't wait to walk back into the inn, just knowing Roman would be there.

It seemed that every hour they spent together brought them closer. Gradually, step by step, she could feel the barriers he had placed around him lowering. She wanted to be there when they finally dropped completely.

He was in love with her. She was sure he was, whether he knew it or not. She could tell by the way he looked at her, by the way he touched her hair when he thought she was sleeping. By the way he held her so tightly all through the night, as if he were afraid she might somehow slip away from him. In time she would show him that she wasn't going anywhere—and that he wasn't going anywhere, either.

Something was troubling him. That was another thing she was sure of. Her eyes clouded as she drove along the water. There were times when she could feel the tension pulsing in him even when he was across the room. He seemed to be watching, waiting. But for what?

Since the accident he'd barely let her out of his sight. It was sweet, she mused. But it had to stop. She might love him, but she wouldn't be pampered. She was certain that if he had known she planned to drive to the ferry that morning he would have found a way to stop her.

She was right again. It had taken Roman some time to calm down after he had learned Charity wasn't in the office or the kitchen or anywhere else in the inn.

"She's driven up to drop some guests at the ferry," Mae told him, then watched in fascination as he let his temper loose.

"My, my," she said when the air was clear again. "You've got it bad, boy."

"Why did you let her go?"

"Let her go?" Mae let out a rich, appreciative laugh.

"I haven't *let* that girl do anything since she could walk. She just does it." She stopped stirring custard to study him. "Any reason she shouldn't drive to the ferry?"

"No."

"All right, then. Just cool your britches. She'll be back in half an hour."

He sweated and paced, nearly the whole time she was away. Mae and Dolores exchanged glances across the room. There would be plenty of gossip to pass around once they had the kitchen to themselves.

Mae thought of the way Charity had been smiling that morning. Why, the girl had practically danced into the kitchen. She kept her eye on Roman as he brooded over a cup of coffee and watched the clock. Yes, indeed, she thought, the boy had it bad.

"You got today off, don't you?" Mae asked him.

"What?"

"It's Sunday," she said patiently. "You got the day off?"

"Yeah, I guess."

"Nice day, too. Good weather for a picnic." She began slicing roast beef for sandwiches. "Got any plans?"

"No."

"Charity loves picnics. Yes, sir, she's mighty partial to them. You know, I don't think that girl's had a day away from this place in better than a month."

"Got any dynamite?"

Dolores piped up. "What's that?"

"I figure it would take dynamite to blast Charity out of the inn for a day."

It took her a minute, but Dolores finally got the joke. She chuckled. "Hear that, Mae? He wants dynamite."

"Pair of fools," Mae muttered as she cut generous pieces of chocolate cheesecake. "You don't move that girl with dynamite or threats or orders. Might as well bash your head against a brick wall all day." She tried not to sound pleased about it, and failed. "You want her to do something, you make her think she's doing you a favor. Make her think it's important to you. Dolores, you go on in that back room and get me the big wicker hamper. Boy, if you keep walking back and forth you're going to wear out my floor."

"She should have been back by now."

"She'll be back when she's back. You know how to run a boat?"

"Yes, why?"

"Charity always loved to picnic on the water. She hasn't been out in a boat in a long time. Too long."

"I know. She told me."

Mae turned around. Her face was set. "Do you want to make my girl happy?"

He tried to shrug it off, but he couldn't. "Yes. Yes, I do."

"Then you take her out on the boat for the day. Don't let her say no."

"All right."

Satisfied, she turned around again. "Go down in the cellar and get a bottle of wine. French. She likes the French stuff."

"She's lucky to have you."

Her wide face colored a bit, but she kept her voice

brisk. "Around here, we got each other. You're all right," she added. "I wasn't sure of it when you first came around, but you're all right."

He was ready for her when she came back. Even as she stepped out of the van he was walking across the gravel lot, the wicker hamper in his hand.

"Hi."

"Hi." She greeted him with a smile and a quick kiss. Despite the two teenagers shooting hoops on the nearby court, Roman wrapped an arm around her and brought her hard against him for a longer, more satisfying embrace. "Well…" She had to take a deep breath and steady herself against the van. "Hello again." She noted then that he had pulled a loose black sweater over his jeans and was carrying a hamper. "What's this?"

"It's a basket," he told her. "Mae put a few things in it for me. It's my day off."

"Oh." She tossed her braid behind her back. "That's right. Where are you off to?"

"Out on the water, if I can use the boat."

"Sure." She glanced up at the sky, a bit wistfully. "It's a great day for it. Light wind, hardly a cloud."

"Then let's go."

"Let's?" He was already pulling her toward the pier. "Oh, Roman, I can't. I have dozens of things to do this afternoon. And I…" She didn't want to admit she wasn't ready to go out on the water again. "I can't."

"I'll have you back before the dinner shift." He laid a hand on her cheek. "I need you with me, Charity. I need to spend some time with you, alone."

"Maybe we could go for a drive. You haven't seen the mountains."

"Please." He set the hamper down to take both of her arms. "Do this for me."

Had he ever said "Please" before? she wondered. She didn't think so. With a sigh, she looked out at the boat rocking gently against the pier. "All right. Maybe for an hour. I'll go in and change."

The red sweater and jeans would keep her warm enough on the water, he decided. She would know that, too. She was stalling. "You look fine." He kept her hand in his as they walked down the pier. "This could use a little maintenance."

"I know. I keep meaning to." She waited until Roman stepped down into the boat. When he held up a hand, she hesitated, then forced herself to join him. "I have a key on my ring."

"Mae already gave me one."

"Oh." Charity sat down in the stern. "I see. A conspiracy."

It took him only two pulls to start the engine. Mae had told him Charity kept the boat for the staff to use. "From what you said to me the other day, I don't think he'd want you to grieve forever."

"No." As her eyes filled, she looked back toward the inn. "No, he wouldn't. But I loved him so much." She took a deep breath. "I'll cast off."

Before he sent the boat forward, Roman took her hand and drew her down beside him. After a moment she rested her head on his shoulder.

"Have you done much boating?"

"From time to time. When I was a kid we used to rent a boat a couple times each summer and take it on the river."

"Who's we?" She watched the shutters come down over his face. "What river?" she asked instead.

"The Mississippi." He smiled and slipped an arm over her shoulders. "I come from St. Louis, remember?"

"The Mississippi." Her mind was immediately filled with visions of steamboats and boys on wooden rafts. "I'd love to see it. You know what would be great? Taking a cruise all the way down, from St. Louis to New Orleans. I'll have to put that in my file."

"Your file?"

"The file I'm going to make on things I want to do." With a laugh, she waved to a passing sailboat before leaning over to kiss Roman's cheek. "Thanks."

"For what?"

"For talking me into this. I've always loved spending an afternoon out here, watching the other boats, looking at the houses. I've missed it."

"Have you ever considered that you give too much to the inn?"

"No. You can't give too much to something you love." She turned. If she shielded her eyes with her hand she could just see it in the distance. "If I didn't have such strong feelings for it, I would have sold it, taken a job in some modern hotel in Seattle or Miami or...or anywhere. Eight hours a day, sick leave, two weeks paid vacation." Just the idea made her laugh. "I'd wear a nice neat business suit and sensible shoes, have my own office and quietly go out of my mind." She dug into her bag for her sunglasses. "You should understand that. You have good hands and a sharp mind. Why aren't you head carpenter for some big construction firm?"

"Maybe when the time came I made the wrong choices."

With her head tilted, she studied him, her eyes narrowed and thoughtful behind the tinted lenses. "No, I don't think so. Not for you."

"You don't know enough about me, Charity."

"Of course I do. I've lived with you for a week. That probably compares with knowing someone on a casual basis for six months. I know you're very intense and internal. You have a wicked temper that you seldom lose. You're an excellent carpenter who likes to finish the job he starts. You can be gallant with little old ladies." She laughed a little and turned her face into the wind. "You like your coffee black, you're not afraid of hard work…and you're a wonderful lover."

"And that's enough for you?"

She lifted her shoulders. "I don't imagine you know too much more about me. I'm starving," she said abruptly. "Do you want to eat?"

"Pick a spot."

"Head over that way," she told him. "See that little jut of land? We can anchor the boat there."

The land she'd indicated was hardly more than a jumble of big, smooth rocks that fell into the water. As they neared it he could see a narrow stretch of sand crowded by trees. Cutting back the engine, he maneuvered toward the beach, Charity guiding him in with hand signals. As the current lapped at the sides of the boat, she pulled off her shoes and began to roll up her jeans.

"You'll have to give me a hand." As she said it she plunged into the knee-high water. "God, it's cold!" Then she was laughing and securing the line. "Come on."

The water was icy on his bare calves. Together they pulled the boat up onto a narrow spit of sand.

"I don't suppose you brought a blanket."

He reached into the boat and took out the faded red blanket Mae had given him. "This do?"

"Great. Grab the basket." She splashed through the shallows and onto the shore. After spreading the blanket at the base of the sheltering rocks she rolled down the damp legs of her jeans. "Lori and I used to come here when we were kids. To eat peanut butter sandwiches and talk about boys." Kneeling on the blanket, she looked around.

There were pines at her back, deep and green and thick all the way up the slope. A few feet away the water frothed at the rock, which had been worn smooth by wind and time. A single boat cruised in the distance, its sails full and white.

"It hasn't changed much." Smiling, she reached for the basket. "I guess the best things don't." She threw back the top and spotted a bottle of champagne. "Well." With a brow arched, she pulled it out. "Apparently we're going to have some picnic."

"Mae said you liked the French stuff."

"I do. I've never had champagne on a picnic."

"Then it's time you did." He took the bottle and walked back to dunk it in the water, screwing it down in the wet sand. "We'll let it chill a little more." He came back to her, taking her hand before she could explore deeper in the basket. He knelt. When they were thigh to thigh, he gathered her close and closed his mouth over hers.

Her quiet sound of pleasure came first, followed by a gasp as he took the kiss deeper. Her arms came around him, then slid up until her hands gripped his shoulders. Desire was like a flood, rising fast to drag her under.

He needed…needed to hold her close like this, to taste the heat of passion on his lips, to feel her heart thud against him. He dragged his hands through her hair, impatiently tugging it free of the braids. All the while his mouth ravaged hers, gentleness forgotten.

There was a restlessness in him, and an anger that she couldn't understand. Responding to both, she pressed against him, unhesitatingly offering whatever he needed. Perhaps it would be enough. Slowly his mouth gentled. Then he was only holding her.

"That's a very nice way to start a picnic," Charity managed when she found her voice again.

"I can't seem to get enough of you."

"That's okay. I don't mind."

He drew away to frame her face in his hands. The crystal drops at her ears swung and shot out light. But her eyes were calm and deep and full of understanding. It would be better, he thought, and certainly safer, if he simply let her pull out the sandwiches. They could talk about the weather, the water, the people at the inn. There was so much he couldn't tell her. But when he looked into her eyes he knew he had to tell her enough about Roman DeWinter that she would be able to make a choice.

"Sit down."

Something in his tone sent a frisson of alarm down her spine. He was going to tell her he was leaving, she thought. "All right." She clasped her hands together, promising herself she'd find a way to make him stay.

"I haven't been fair with you." He leaned back against a rock. "Fairness hasn't been one of my priorities. There are things about me you should know, that you should have known before things got this far."

"Roman—"

"It won't take long. I did come from St. Louis. I lived in a kind of neighborhood you wouldn't even understand. Drugs, whores, Saturday night specials." He looked out at the water. The spiffy little sailboat had caught the wind. "A long way from here, baby."

So the trust had come, she thought. She wouldn't let him regret it. "It doesn't matter where you came from, Roman. It's where you are now."

"That's not always true. Part of where you come from stays with you." He closed a hand over hers briefly, then released it. It would be better, he thought, to break the contact now. "When he was sober enough, my father drove a cab. When he wasn't sober enough, he sat around the apartment with his head in his hands. One of my first memories is waking up at night hearing my mother screaming at him. Every couple of months she'd threaten to leave. Then he'd straighten up. We'd live in the eye of the hurricane until he'd stop off at the bar to have a drink. So she finally stopped threatening and did it."

"Where did you go?"

"I said she left."

"But...didn't she take you with her?"

"I guess she figured she was going to have it rough enough without dealing with a ten-year-old."

Charity shook her head and struggled with a deep, churning anger. It was hard for her to understand how a mother could desert her child. "She must have been very confused and frightened. Once she—"

"I never saw her again," Roman said. "You have to understand that not everyone loves unconditionally. Not everyone loves at all."

"Oh, Roman." She wanted to gather him close then, but he held her away from him.

"I stayed with my father another three years. One night he hit the gin before he got in the cab. He killed himself and his passenger."

"Oh, God." She reached for him, but he shook his head.

"That made me a ward of the court. I didn't much care for that, so I took off, hit the streets."

She was reeling from what he'd already told her, and she could barely take it all in. "At thirteen?"

"I'd been living there most of my life anyway."

"But how?"

He shook a cigarette out of his pack, lighting it and drawing deep before he spoke again. "I took odd jobs when I could find them. I stole when I couldn't. After a couple of years I got good enough at the stealing that

I didn't bother much with straight jobs. I broke into houses, hot-wired cars, snatched purses. Do you understand what I'm telling you?"

"Yes. You were alone and desperate."

"I was a thief. Damn it, Charity, I wasn't some poor misguided youth. I stopped being a kid when I came home and found my father passed out and my mother gone. I knew what I was doing. I chose to do it."

She kept her eyes level with his, battling the need to take him in her arms. "If you expect me to condemn a child for finding a way to survive, I'll have to disappoint you."

She was romanticizing, he told himself, pitching his cigarette into the water.

"Do you still steal?"

"What if I told you I did?"

"I'd have to say you were stupid. You don't seem stupid to me, Roman."

He paused for a moment before he decided to tell her the rest. "I was in Chicago. I'd just turned sixteen. It was January, so cold your eyes couldn't water. I decided I needed to score enough to take a bus south. Thought I'd winter in Florida and fleece the rich tourists. That's when I met John Brody. I broke into his apartment and ended up with a .45 in my face. He was a cop." The memory of that moment still made him laugh. "I don't know who was more surprised. He gave me three choices. One, he could turn me over to Juvie. Two, he could beat the hell out of me. Three, he could give me something to eat."

"What did you do?"

"It's hard to play it tough when a two-hundred-pound man's pointing a .45 at your belt. I ate a can of soup. He let me sleep on the couch." Looking back, he could still see himself, skinny and full of bitterness, lying wakeful on the lumpy sofa.

"I kept telling myself I was going to rip off whatever I could and take off. But I never did. I used to tell myself he was a stupid bleeding heart, and that once it warmed up I'd split with whatever I could carry. The next thing I knew I was going to school." Roman paused a moment to look up at the sky. "He used to build things down in the basement of the building. He taught me how to use a hammer."

"He must have been quite a man."

"He was only twenty-five when I met him. He'd grown up on the South Side, running with the gangs. At some point he turned it around. Then he decided to turn me around. In some ways he did. When he got married a couple of years later he bought this old run-down house in the suburbs. We fixed it up room by room. He used to tell me there was nothing he liked better than living in a construction zone. We were adding on another room—it was going to be his workshop—when he was killed. Line of duty. He was thirty-two. He left a three-year-old son and a pregnant widow."

"Roman, I'm sorry." She moved to him and took his hands.

"It killed something in me, Charity. I've never been able to get it back."

"I understand." He started to pull away, but she held him fast. "I do. When you lose someone who was that much a part of your life, something's always going to be missing. I still think about Pop all the time. It still makes me sad. Sometimes it just makes me angry, because there was so much more I wanted to say to him."

"You're leaving out pieces. Look at what I was, where I came from. I was a thief."

"You were a child."

He took her shoulders and shook her. "My father was a drunk."

"I don't even know who my father was. Should I be ashamed of that?"

"It doesn't matter to you, does it? Where I've been, what I've done?"

"Not very much. I'm more interested in what you are now."

He couldn't tell her what he was. Not yet. For her own safety, he had to continue the deception for a few more days. But there was something he could tell her. Like the story he had just recounted, it was something he had never told anyone else.

"I love you."

Her hands went slack on his. Her eyes grew huge. "Would you—" She paused long enough to take a deep breath. "Would you say that again?"

"I love you."

With a muffled sob, she launched herself into his arms. She wasn't going to cry, she told herself, squeezing her eyes tight against the threatening tears. She wouldn't be red-eyed and weepy at this, the most beautiful and exciting moment of her life.

"Just hold me a moment, okay?" Overwhelmed, she

pressed her face into his shoulder. "I can't believe this is happening."

"That makes two of us." But he was smiling. He could feel the stunned delight coil through him as he stroked her hair. It hadn't been so hard to say, he realized. In fact, he could easily get used to saying it several times a day.

"A week ago I didn't even know you." She tilted her head back until her lips met his. "Now I can't imagine my life without you."

"Don't. You might change your mind."

"Not a chance."

"Promise." Overwhelmed by a sudden sense of urgency, he gripped her hands. "I want you to make that a promise."

"All right. I promise. I won't change my mind about being in love with you."

"I'm holding you to that, Charity." He swooped her against him, then drained even happy thoughts from her mind. "Will you marry me?"

She jerked back, gaped, then sat down hard. "What? *What?*"

"I want you to marry me—now, today." It was crazy, and he knew it. It was wrong. Yet, as he pulled her up again, he knew he had to find a way to keep her. "You must know somebody, a minister, a justice of the peace, who could do it."

"Well, yes, but…" She held a hand to her spinning head. "There's paperwork, and licenses. God, I can't think."

"Don't think. Just say you will."

"Of course I will, but—"

"No buts." He crushed his mouth to hers. "I want you to belong to me. God, I need to belong to you. Do you believe that?"

"Yes." Breathless, she touched a hand to his cheek. "Roman, we're talking about marriage, a lifetime. I only intend to do this once." She dragged a hand through her hair and sat down again. "I guess everyone says that, but I need to believe it. It has to start off with more than a few words in front of an official. Wait, please," she said before he could speak again. "You've really thrown me off here, and I want to make you understand. I love you, and I can't think of anything I want more than to belong to you. When I marry you it has to be more than rushing to the J.P. and saying 'I do.' I don't have to have a big, splashy wedding, either. It's not a matter of long white trains and engraved invitations."

"Then what is it?"

"I want flowers and music, Roman. And friends." She took his face in her hands, willing him to understand. "I want to stand beside you knowing I look beautiful, so that everyone can see how proud I am to be your wife. If that sounds overly romantic, well, it should be."

"How long do you need?"

"Can I have two weeks?"

He was afraid to give her two days. But it was for the best, he told himself. He would never be able to hold her if there were still lies between them. "I'll give you two weeks, if you'll go away with me afterward."

"Where?"

"Leave it to me."

"I love surprises." Her lips curved against his. "And you...you're the biggest surprise so far."

"Two weeks." He took her hands firmly in his. "No matter what happens."

"You make it sound as though we might have to overcome a natural disaster in the meantime. I'm only going to take a few days to make it right." She brushed a kiss over his cheek and smiled again. "It will be right, Roman, for both of us. That's another promise. I'd like that champagne now."

She took out the glasses while he retrieved the bottle from the water. As they sat together on the blanket, he released the cork with a pop and a hiss.

"To new beginnings," she said, touching her glass to his.

He wanted to believe it could happen. "I'll make you happy, Charity."

"You already have." She shifted so that she was cuddled against him, her head on his shoulder. "This is the best picnic I've ever had."

He kissed the top of her head. "You haven't eaten anything yet."

"Who needs food?" With a sigh, she reached up. He linked his hand with hers, and they both looked out toward the horizon.

Chapter 10

Check-in on Tuesday was as chaotic as it came. Charity barreled her way through it, assigning rooms and cabins, answering questions, finding a spare cookie for a cranky toddler, and waited for the first rush to pass.

She was the first to admit that she usually thrived on the noise, the problems and the healthy press of people that proved the inn's success. At the moment, though, she would have liked nothing better than having everyone, and everything settled.

It was hard to keep her mind on the business at hand when her head was full of plans for her wedding.

Should she have Chopin or Beethoven? She'd barely begun her list of possible selections. Would the weather hold so that they could have the ceremony in the gardens, or would it be best to plan an intimate and cozy wedding in the gathering room?

"Yes, sir, I'll be glad to give you information on renting bikes." She snatched up a pamphlet.

When was she going to find an afternoon free so that she could choose the right dress? It *had* to be the right dress, the perfect dress. Something ankle-length, with some romantic touches of lace. There was a boutique in Eastsound that specialized in antique clothing. If she could just—

"Aren't you going to sign that?"

"Sorry, Roger." Charity pulled herself back and offered him an apologetic smile. "I don't seem to be all here this morning."

"No problem." He patted her hand as she signed his roster. "Spring fever?"

"You could call it that." She tossed back her hair, annoyed that she hadn't remembered to braid it that morning. As long as she was smelling orange blossoms she'd be lucky to remember her own name. "We're a little behind. The computer's acting up again. Poor Bob's been fighting with it since yesterday."

"Looks like you've been in a fight yourself."

She lifted a hand to the healing cut on her temple. "I had a little accident last week."

"Nothing serious?"

"No, just inconvenient, really. Some idiot joyriding nearly ran me down."

"That's terrible." Watching her carefully, he pulled his face into stern lines. "Were you badly hurt?"

"No, only a few stitches and a medley of bruises. Scared me more than anything."

"I can imagine. You don't expect something like that around here. I hope they caught him."

"No, not yet." Because she'd already put the incident behind her, she gave a careless shrug. "To tell you the truth, I doubt they ever will. I imagine he got off the island as soon as he sobered up."

"Drunk drivers." Block made a sound of disgust. "Well, you've got a right to be distracted after something like that."

"Actually, I've got a much more pleasant reason. I'm getting married in a couple of weeks."

"You don't say!" His face split into a wide grin. "Who's the lucky man?"

"Roman DeWinter. I don't know if you met him. He's doing some remodeling upstairs."

"That's handy now, isn't it?" He continued to grin. The romance explained a lot. One look at Charity's face settled any lingering doubts. Block decided he'd have to have a nice long talk with Bob about jumping the gun. "Is he from around here?"

"No, he's from St. Louis, actually."

"Well, I hope he's not going to take you away from us."

"You know I'd never leave the inn, Roger." Her smile faded a bit. That was something she and Roman had never spoken of. "In any case, I promise to keep my mind on my work. You've got six people who want to rent boats." She took a quick look at her watch. "I can have them taken to the marina by noon."

"I'll round them up."

The door to the inn opened, and Charity glanced over. She saw a small, spare man with well-cut auburn hair, wearing a crisp sport shirt. He carried one small leather bag.

"Good morning."

"Good morning." He took a brief study of the lobby as he crossed to the desk. "Conby, Richard Conby. I believe I have a reservation."

"Yes, Mr. Conby. We're expecting you." Charity shuffled through the papers on the desk and sent up a quick prayer that Bob would have the computer humming along by the end of the day. "How was your trip?"

"Uneventful." He signed the register, listing his address as Seattle. Charity found herself both amused and impressed by his careful manicure. "I was told your inn is quiet, restful. I'm looking forward to relaxing for a day or two."

"I'm sure you'll find the inn very relaxing." She opened a drawer to choose a key. "Either Roman or I will drive your group to the marina, Roger. Have them in the parking lot at noon."

"Will do." With a cheerful wave, he sauntered off.

"I'll be happy to show you to your room, Mr. Conby. If you have any questions about the inn, or the island, feel free to ask me or any of the staff." She came around the desk and led the way to the stairs.

"Oh, I will," Conby said, following her. "I certainly will."

At precisely 12:05, Conby heard a knock and opened his door. "Prompt as always, DeWinter." He scanned down to Roman's tool belt. "Keeping busy, I see."

"Dupont's in cabin 3."

Conby decided to drop the sarcasm. This was a big one, much too big for him to let his personal feelings interfere. "You made a positive ID?"

"I helped him carry his bags."

"Very good." Satisfied, Conby finished arranging his ebony-handled clothes brush and shoe horn on the oak dresser. "We'll move in as planned on Thursday morning and take him before we close in on Block."

"What about the driver of the car who tried to kill Charity?"

Always fastidious, Conby walked into the adjoining bath to wash his hands. "You're inordinately interested in a small-time hood."

"Did you get a confession?"

"Yes." Conby unfolded a white hand towel bordered with flowers. "He admitted to meeting with Block last week and taking five thousand to—to put Miss Ford out of the picture. A very minor sum for a hit." His hands dry, Conby tossed the towel over the lip of the sink before walking back into the bedroom. "If Block had been more discerning, he might have had more success."

Taking him by the collar, Roman lifted Conby to his toes. "Watch your step," he said softly.

"It's more to the point for me to tell you to watch yours." Conby pulled himself free and straightened his shirt. In the five years since he had taken over as Roman's superior he had found Roman's methods crude and his attitude arrogant. The pity was, his results were invariably excellent. "You're losing your focus on this one, Agent DeWinter."

"No. It's taken me a while—maybe too long—but I'm focused just fine. You've got enough on Block to pin him with conspiracy to murder. Dupont's practically tied up with a bow. Why wait?"

"I won't bother to remind you who's in charge of this case."

"We both know who's in charge, Conby, but there's a difference between sitting behind a desk and calling the shots in the field. If we take them now, quietly, there's less risk of endangering innocent people."

"I have no intention of endangering any of the guests. Or the staff," he added, thinking he knew where Roman's mind was centered. "I have my orders on this, just as you do." He took a fresh handkerchief out of his drawer. "Since it's apparently so important to you, I'll tell you that we want to nail Block when he passes the money. We're working with the Canadian authorities on this, and that's the way we'll proceed. As for the conspiracy charges, we have the word of a bargain-basement hit man. It may take a bit more to make it stick."

"You'll make it stick. How many have we got?"

"We have two agents checking in tomorrow, and two more as backup. We'll take Dupont in his cabin, and Block in the lobby. Moving on Dupont any earlier would undoubtedly tip off Block. Agreed?"

"Yes."

"Since you've filled me in on the checkout procedures, it should go very smoothly."

"It better. If anything happens to her—anything—I'm holding you responsible."

Charity dashed into the kitchen with a loaded tray. "I don't know how things can get out of hand so fast. When have you ever known us to have a full house on a Wednesday night?" she asked the room at large, whipping out her pad. "Two specials with wild rice, one with baked potato, hold the sour cream, and one child's portion of ribs with fries." She rushed over to get the drinks herself.

"Take it easy, girl," Mae advised her. "They ain't going anywhere till they eat."

"That's the problem." She loaded up the tray. "What a time for Lori to get sick. The way this virus is bouncing around, we're lucky to have a waitress still standing. Whoops!" She backed up to keep from running into Roman. "Sorry."

"Need a hand?"

"I need two." She smiled and took the time to lean over the tray and kiss him. "You seem to have them. Those salads Dolores is fixing go to table 5."

"Girl makes me tired just looking at her," Mae commented as she filleted a trout. She lifted her head just long enough for her eyes to meet Roman's. "Seems to me she rushes into everything."

"Four house salads." Dolores was humming the "Wedding March" as she passed him a tray. "Looks like you didn't need that dynamite after all." Cackling, she went back to fill the next order.

Five minutes later he passed Charity in the doorway again. "Strange bunch tonight," she murmured.

"How so?"

"There's a man at table 2. He's so jumpy you'd think he'd robbed a bank or something. Then there's a couple at table 8, supposed to be on a second honeymoon.

They're spending more time looking at everyone else than each other."

Roman said nothing. She'd made both Dupont and two of Conby's agents in less than thirty minutes.

"And then there's this little man in a three-piece suit sitting at 4. Suit and tie," she added with a glance over her shoulder. "Came here to relax, he says. Who can relax in a three-piece suit?" Shifting, she balanced the tray on her hip. "Claims to be from Seattle and has an Eastern accent that could cut Mae's apple pie. Looks like a weasel."

"You think so?" Roman allowed himself a small smile at her description of Conby.

"A very well-groomed weasel," she added. "Check it out for yourself." With a small shudder, she headed toward the dining room again. "Anyone that smooth gives me the creeps."

Duty was duty though, and the weasel was sitting at her station. "Are you ready to order?" she asked Conby with a bright smile.

He took a last sip of his vodka martini. It was passable, he supposed. "The menu claims the trout is fresh."

"Yes, sir." She was particularly proud of that. The stocked pond had been her idea. "It certainly is."

"Fresh when it was shipped in this morning, no doubt."

"No." Charity lowered her pad but kept her smile in place. "We stock our own right here at the inn."

Lifting a brow, he tapped a finger against his empty glass. "Your fish may be superior to your vodka, but I have my doubts as to whether it is indeed fresh. Nonetheless, it appears to be the most interesting item on your menu, so I shall have to make do."

"The fish," Charity repeated, with what she considered admirable calm, "is fresh."

"I'm sure you consider it so. However, your conception of fresh and mine may differ."

"Yes, sir." She shoved the pad into her pocket. "If you'll excuse me a moment."

She might be innocent, Conby thought, frowning at his empty glass, but she was hardly efficient.

"Where's the fire?" Mae wanted to know when Charity burst into the kitchen.

"In my brain." She stopped a moment, hands on hips. "That—that insulting pipsqueak out there tells me our vodka's below standard, our menu's dull and our fish isn't fresh."

"A dull menu." Mae bristled down to her crepe-soled shoes. "What did he eat?"

"He hasn't eaten anything yet. One drink and a couple of crackers with salmon dip and he's a restaurant critic."

Charity took a turn around the kitchen, struggling with her temper. No urban wonder was going to stroll into her inn and pick it apart. Her bar was as good as any on the island, her restaurant had a triple-A rating, and her fish—

"Guy at table 4 wants another vodka martini," Roman announced as he carried in a loaded tray.

"Does he?" Charity whirled around. "Does he really?"

He couldn't recall ever seeing quite that glint in her eye. "That's right," he said cautiously.

"Well, I have something else to get him first." So saying, she strode into the utility room and then out again.

"Uh-oh," Dolores mumbled.

"Did I miss something?" Roman asked.

"Man's got a nerve saying the food's dull before he's even had a taste of it." Scowling, Mae scooped a helping of wild asparagus onto a plate. "I've a mind to add some curry to his entrée. A nice fat handful of it. We'll see about dull."

They all turned around when Charity strolled back in. She was still carrying the platter. On it flopped a very confused trout.

"My." Dolores covered her mouth with both hands, giggling. "Oh, my."

Grinning, Mae went back to her stove.

"Charity." Roman made a grab for her arm, but she evaded him and glided through the doorway. Shaking his head, he followed her.

A few of the diners looked up and stared as she carried the thrashing fish across the room. Weaving through the tables, she crossed to table 4 and held the tray under Conby's nose.

"Your trout, sir." She dropped the platter unceremoniously in front of him. "Fresh enough?" she asked with a small, polite smile.

In the archway Roman tucked his hands into his pockets and roared. He would have traded a year's salary for a photo of the expression on Conby's face as he and the fish gaped at each other.

When Charity glided back into the kitchen, she

handed the tray and its passenger to Dolores. "You can put this back," she said. "Table 4 decided on the stuffed pork chops. I wish I had a pig handy." She let out a laughing squeal as Roman scooped her off the floor.

"You're the best." He pressed his lips to hers and held them there long after he'd set her down again. "The absolute best." He was still laughing as he gathered her close for a hug. "Isn't she, Mae?"

"She has her moments." She wasn't about to let them know how much good it did her to see them smiling at each other. "Now the two of you stop pawing each other in my kitchen and get back to work."

Charity lifted her face for one last kiss. "I guess I'd better fix that martini now. He looked like he could use one."

Because she wasn't one to hold a grudge, Charity treated Conby to attentive and cheerful service throughout the meal. Noting that he hadn't unbent by dessert, she brought him a serving of Mae's Black Forest cake on the house.

"I hope you enjoyed your meal, Mr. Conby."

It was impossible for him to admit that he'd never had better, not even in Washington's toniest restaurants. "It was quite good, thank you."

She offered an easy smile as she poured his coffee. "Perhaps you'll come back another time and try the trout."

Even for Conby, her smile was hard to resist. "Perhaps. You run an interesting establishment, Miss Ford."

"We try. Have you lived in Seattle long, Mr. Conby?"

He continued to add cream to his coffee, but he was very much on guard. "Why do you ask?"

"Your accent. It's very Eastern."

Conby deliberated only seconds. He knew that Dupont had already left the dining room, but Block was at a nearby table, entertaining part of his tour group with what Conby considered rather boring stories. "You have a good ear. I was transferred to Seattle eighteen months ago. From Maryland. I'm in marketing."

"Maryland." Deciding to forgive and forget, she topped off his coffee. "You're supposed to have the best crabs in the country."

"I assure you, we do." The rich cake and the smooth coffee had mellowed him. He actually smiled at her. "It's a pity I didn't bring one along with me."

Laughing, Charity laid a friendly hand on his arm. "You're a good sport, Mr. Conby. Enjoy your evening."

Lips pursed, Conby watched her go. He couldn't recall anyone having accused him of being a good sport before. He rather liked it.

"We're down to three tables of diehards," Charity announced as she entered the kitchen again. "And I'm starving." She opened the refrigerator and rooted around for something to eat, but Mae snapped it closed again.

"You haven't got time."

"Haven't got time?" Charity pressed a hand to her stomach. "Mae, the way tonight went, I wasn't able to grab more than a stray French fry."

"I'll fix you a sandwich, but you had a call. Something about tomorrow's delivery."

"The salmon. Damn." She tilted her watch forward. "They're closed by now."

"Left an emergency number, I think. Message is upstairs."

"All right, all right. I'll be back in ten minutes." She cast a last longing glance at the refrigerator. "Make that two sandwiches."

To save time, she raced out through the utility room, rounded the side of the building and climbed the outside steps. When she opened the door, she could only stop and stare.

The music was pitched low. There was candlelight, and there were flowers and a white cloth on a table at the foot of the bed. It was set for two. As she watched, Roman took a bottle of wine from a glass bucket and drew the cork.

"I thought you'd never get here."

She leaned back on the closed door. "If I'd known this was waiting, I'd have been here a lot sooner."

"You said you liked surprises."

"Yes." There was both surprise and delight in her eyes as she brushed her tumbled hair back from her forehead. "I like them a lot." Untying her apron, she walked to the table while he poured the wine. It glinted warm and gold in the candlelight. "Thanks," she murmured when he offered her a glass.

"I wanted to give you something." He gripped her hand, holding tight and trying not to remember that this was their last night together before all the questions had to be answered. "I'm not very good with romantic gestures."

"Oh, no, you're very good at them. Champagne picnics, late-night suppers." She closed her eyes for a moment. "Mozart."

"Picked at random," he admitted, feeling foolishly nervous. "I have something for you."

She looked at the table. "Something else?"

"Yes." He reached down to the seat of his chair and picked up a square box. "It just came today." It was the best he could do. He pushed the box into her hand.

"A present?" She'd always liked the anticipation as much as the gift itself, so she took a moment to study and shake the box. But the moment the lid was off she snatched the bracelet out. "Oh, Roman, it's gorgeous." Thoroughly stunned, she turned the etched gold, watching the light glint off the metal and the square-cut amethyst. "It's absolutely gorgeous," she said again. "I'd swear I'd seen this before. Last week," she remembered. "In one of the magazines Lori brought me."

"You had it on your desk."

Overwhelmed, she nodded. "Yes, I'd circled this. I do that with beautiful things I know I'll never buy." She took a deep breath. "Roman, this is a wonderful, sweet and very romantic thing to do, but—"

"Then don't spoil it." He took the bracelet from the box and clasped it on her wrist. "I need the practice."

"No." She slipped her arms around him and rested her cheek against his shoulder. "I think you've got the hang of it."

He held her, letting the music, her scent, the moment, wash over him. Things could be different with her. He could be different with her.

"Do you know when I fell in love with you, Roman?"

"No." He kissed the top of her head. "I've thought more about why than when."

With a soft laugh, she snuggled against him. "I'd thought it was when you danced with me and you kissed me until every bone in my body turned to water."

"Like this?"

He turned his head, meeting her lips with his. Gently he set her on fire.

"Yes." She swayed against him, eyes closed. "Just like that. But that wasn't when. That was when I realized it, but it wasn't when I fell in love with you. Do you remember when you asked me about the spare?"

"The what?"

"The spare." Sighing, she tilted her head to give him easier access to her throat. "You wanted to know where the spare was so you could fix my flat." She leaned back to smile at his stunned expression. "I guess I can't call it love at first sight, since I'd already known you two or three minutes."

He ran his hands over her cheeks, through her hair, down her neck. "Just like that?"

"I'd never thought as much about falling in love and getting married as I suppose most people might. Because of Pop's being sick, and the inn. I always figured if it happened it would happen without me doing a lot of worrying or preparing. And I was right." She linked hands with him. "All I had to do was have a flat tire. The rest was easy."

A flat, Roman remembered, that had been deliberately arranged, just as her sudden need for a handyman had been arranged. As everything had been arranged, he thought, his grip tightening on her fingers. Everything except his falling in love with her.

"Charity..." He would have given anything to be able to tell her the truth, the whole truth. Anything but his knowledge that in ignorance there was safety. "I never meant for any of this to happen," he said carefully. "I never wanted to feel this way about anyone."

"Are you sorry?"

"About a lot of things, but not about being in love with you." He released her. "Your dinner's getting cold."

She tucked her tongue in her cheek. "If we found something else to do for an hour or so we could call it a midnight supper." She ran her hands up his chest to toy with the top button of his shirt. "Want to play Parcheesi?"

"No."

She flicked the button open and worked her way slowly, steadily down. "Scrabble?"

"Uh-uh."

"I know." She trailed a finger down the center of his body to the snap of his jeans. "How about a rip-roaring game of canasta?"

"I don't know how to play."

Grinning, she tugged the snap open. "Oh, I have a feeling you'd catch on." Her laugh was muffled against his mouth.

Her heated thoughts of seducing him spun away as he dragged her head back and plundered her mouth. Her hands, so confident an instant before, faltered, then fisted hard at the back of his shirt. This wasn't the gentle, persuasive passion he had shown her since the night they had become lovers. This was a raw, desperate need, and it held a trace of fury, and a hint of despair. Whirling from the feel of it, she strained against him, letting herself go.

He'd needed her before. Roman had already come to understand that he had needed her long before he'd ever met her. But tonight was different. He'd set the stage carefully—the wine, the candles, the music—wanting to give her the romance she made him capable of. Then he'd felt her cool fingertips on his skin. He'd seen the promising flicker of desire in her eyes. There was only tonight. In a matter of hours she would know everything. No matter how often he told himself he would set things right, he was very much afraid she wouldn't forgive him.

He had tonight.

Breathless, she clung to him as they tumbled onto the bed. Here was the restless, ruthless lover she had known existed alongside the gentle, patient one. And he excited her every bit as much. As frantic as he, she pulled the loosened shirt from his shoulders and gloried in the feel of his flesh under her hands.

He was as taut as wire, as explosive as gunpowder. She felt his muscles tense and tighten as his mouth raced hungrily over her face. With a throaty laugh she tugged at his jeans while they rolled over the bed. If this was a game they were playing, she was determined they would both win.

A broken moan escaped him as her seeking hands drove him toward delirium. With an oath, he snagged her wrists, yanking them over her head. Breath heaving, he watched her face as he hooked a hand in the top of her shirt and ripped it down the center.

She had only time for a gasp before his hot, open mouth lowered to her skin to torment and tantalize. Powerless against the onslaught, she arched against him. When her hands were free, she only pressed him closer, crying out as he sucked greedily at her breast.

There were sensations here, wild and exquisite, that trembled on but never crossed the thin line that separated pleasure from pain. She felt herself dragged under, deep, still deeper, to windmill helplessly down some dark, endless tunnel toward unreasonable pleasures.

She couldn't know what she was doing to him. He was skilled enough to be certain that she was trapped by her own senses. Yet her body wrapped around his, her hands sought, her lips hungered.

In the flickering light her skin was like white satin. Under his hands it flowed like lava, hot and dangerous. Passion heated her light floral scent and turned it into something secret and forbidden.

Impatient, he yanked her slacks down her hips, frantically tasting each new inch of exposed flesh. This new intimacy had her sobbing out his name, shuddering as climax slammed impossibly into climax.

She held on to him, her nails digging in, her palms sliding damply over his slick skin. Her mind was empty, wiped clear of all but sensation. His name formed on her lips again and again. She thought he spoke to her, some mad, frenzied words that barely penetrated her clouded brain. Perhaps they were promises, pleas or prayers. She would have answered all of them if she could.

Then his mouth was on hers, swallowing her cry of release, smothering her groan of surrender, as he drove himself into her.

Fast, hot, reckless, they matched rhythms. Far beyond madness, they clung. Driven by love, locked in desire, they raced. Even when they tumbled back to earth, they held each other close.

Chapter 11

With her eyes half closed, her lips curved, she gave a long, lazy sigh. "That was wonderful."

Roman topped off the wine in Charity's glass. "Are you talking about the meal or the preliminaries?"

She smiled. "Both." Before he could set the bottle down, she touched his hand. It was just a skimming of her fingertip over his skin. His pulse doubled. "I think we should make midnight suppers a regular event."

It was long past midnight. Even cold fish was delicious with wine and love. He hoped that if he held on hard enough it could always be like this. "The first time you looked at me like that I almost swallowed my tongue."

She kept her eyes on his. Even in candlelight they were the color of morning. "Like what?"

"Like you knew exactly what I was thinking, and

was trying not to think. Exactly what I wanted not to think. Exactly what I wanted, and was trying not to want. You scare the hell out of me."

Her lazy smile faltered. "I do?"

"You make too much difference. All the difference." He took both of her hands, wishing that just this once he had smooth words, a little poetry. "Every time you walk into a room…" But he didn't have smooth words, or poetry. "It makes a difference." He would have released her hands, but she turned them in his.

"I'm crazy about you. If I'd gone looking for someone to share my life, and my home, and my dreams, it would have been you."

She saw the shadow of concern in his eyes and willed it away. There was no room for worries in their lives tonight. With a quick, wicked smile, she nibbled on his fingers. "You know what I'd like?"

"More Black Forest cake."

"Besides that." Her eyes laughed at him over their joined hands. "I'd like to spend the night making love with you, talking with you, drinking wine and listening to music. I have a feeling I'd find it much more satisfying than the slumber parties I had as a girl."

She could, with a look and a smile, seduce him more utterly than any vision of black lace or white silk. "What would you like to do first?"

She had to laugh. It delighted her to see him so relaxed and happy. "Actually, there is something I want to talk with you about."

"I've already told you—I'll wear a suit, but no tuxedo."

"It's not about that." She smiled and traced a fingertip over the back of his hand. "Even though I know you'd look wonderful in a tux, I think a suit's more than adequate for an informal garden wedding. I'd like to talk to you about after the wedding."

"After-the-wedding plans aren't negotiable. I intend to make love with you for about twenty-four hours."

"Oh." As if she were thinking it through, she sipped her wine. "I guess I can go along with that. What I'd like to discuss is more long-range. It's something that Block said to me the other day."

"Block?" Alarm sprinted upward, then centered at the base of his neck.

"Just an offhand comment, but it made me think." She moved her shoulders in a quick, restless movement, then settled again. "I mentioned that we were getting married, and he said something about hoping you didn't take me away. It suddenly occurred to me that you might not want to spend your life here, on Orcas."

"That's it?" He felt the tension seep away.

"It's not such a little thing. I mean, I'm sure we can work it out, but you might not be crazy about the idea of living in a…well, a public kind of place, with people coming and going, and interruptions, and…" She let her words trail off, knowing she was rambling, as she did whenever she was nervous. "The point is, I need to know how you feel about staying on the island, living here, at the inn."

"How do you feel about it?"

"It isn't just a matter of what I feel any longer. It's what we feel."

It amazed him that she could so easily touch his heart. He supposed it always would. "It's been a long time since I've felt at home anywhere. I feel it here, with you."

She smiled and linked her fingers with his. "Are you tired?"

"No."

"Good." She rose and corked the wine. "Just let me get my keys."

"Keys to what?"

"The van," she told him as she walked into the next room.

"Are we going somewhere?"

"I know the best place on the island to watch the sun rise." She came back carrying a blanket and jiggling the keys. "Want to watch the sun come up with me, Roman?"

"You're only wearing a robe."

"Of course I am. It's nearly two in the morning. Don't forget the wine." With a laugh, she opened the door and crept down the steps. "Let's try not to wake anyone." She winced a little as she started across the gravel in her bare feet. With a muttered oath, Roman swung her up into his arms. "My hero," she murmured.

"Sure." He dumped her in the driver's seat of the van. "Where are we going, baby?"

"To the beach." She pushed her hair behind her shoulders as she started the van. Symphonic music blared from the radio before she twisted the knob. "I always play it too loud when I'm driving alone." She turned to look guiltily back at the inn. It remained dark and quiet. Slowly she drove out of the lot and onto the road. "It's a beautiful night."

"Morning."

"Whatever." She took a long, greedy gulp of air. "I haven't really had time for big adventures, so I have to take small ones whenever I get the chance."

"Is that what this is? An adventure?"

"Sure. We're going to drink the rest of the wine, make love under the stars and watch the sun come up over the water." She turned her head. "Is that all right with you?"

"I think I can live with it."

It was hours later when she curled up close to him. The bottle of wine was empty, and the stars were blinking out one by one.

"I'm going to be totally useless today." After a sleepy laugh, she nuzzled his neck. "And I don't even care."

He tugged the blanket over her. The mornings were still chilly. Though he hadn't planned it, the long night of loving had given him new hope. If he could convince her to sleep through the morning, he could complete his assignment, close the door on it and then explain everything. That would let him keep her out of harm's way and begin at the beginning.

"It's nearly dawn," she murmured.

They didn't speak as they watched day break. The sky paled. The night birds hushed. For an instant, time hung suspended. Then, slowly, regally, colors seeped into the horizon, bleeding up from the water, reflecting in it. Shadows faded, and the trees were tipped with gold. The first bird of the morning trumpeted the new day.

Roman gathered her to him to love her slowly under the lightening sky.

She dozed as he drove back to the inn. The sky was a pale, milky blue, but it was as quiet now as it had been when they'd left. When he lifted her out of the van, she sighed and nestled her head on his shoulder.

"I love you, Roman."

"I know." For the first time in his life he wanted to think about next week, next month, even next year—anything except the day ahead. He carried her up the stairs and into the inn. "I love you, Charity."

He had little trouble convincing her to snuggle between the sheets of the rumpled bed once he promised to take Ludwig for his habitual run.

Before he did, Roman went downstairs, strapped on his shoulder holster and shoved in his gun.

Taking Dupont was a study in well-oiled police work. By 7:45 his secluded cabin was surrounded by the best Sheriff Royce and the F.B.I. had to offer. Roman had ignored Conby's mutterings about bringing the locals into it and advised his superior to stay out of the way.

When the men were in position, Roman moved to the door himself, his gun in one hand, his shoulder snug against the frame. He rapped twice. When there was no response, he signaled for his men to draw their weapons and close in. Using the key he'd taken from Charity's ring, he unlocked the door.

Once inside, he scanned the room, legs spread, the gun held tight in both hands. The adrenaline was there, familiar, even welcome. With only a jerk of the head he signaled his backup. Guarding each other's flanks, they took a last circle.

Roman cautiously approached the bedroom. For the

first time, a smile—a grim smile—moved across his face. Dupont was in the shower. And he was singing.

The singing ended abruptly when Roman yanked the curtain aside.

"Don't bother to put your hands up," Roman told him as he blinked water out of his eyes. Keeping the gun level, he tossed his first prize a towel. "You're busted, pal. Why don't you dry off and I'll read you your rights?"

"Well done," Conby commented when the prisoner was cuffed. "If you handle the rest of this as smoothly, I'll see that you get a commendation."

"Keep it." Roman holstered his weapon. There was only one more hurdle before he could finally separate past and future. "When this is done, I'm finished."

"You've been in law enforcement for over ten years, DeWinter. You won't walk away."

"Watch me." With that, he headed back to the inn to finish what he had started.

When Charity awoke, it was full morning and she was quite alone. She was grateful for that, because she couldn't stifle a moan. The moment she sat up, her head, unused to the generous doses of wine and stingy amounts of sleep, began to pound.

She had no one but herself to blame, she admitted as she crawled out of bed. Her feet tangled in what was left of the shirt she'd been wearing the night before.

It had been worth it, she thought, gathering up the torn cotton. Well worth it.

But, incredible night or not, it was morning and she

had work to do. She downed some aspirin, allowed herself another groan, then dived into the shower.

Roman found Bob huddled in the office, anxiously gulping laced coffee. Without preamble, he yanked the mug away and emptied the contents into the trash can.

"I just needed a little something to get me through."

He'd had more than a little, Roman determined. His words were slurred, and his eyes were glazed. Even under the best of circumstances Roman found it difficult to drum up any sympathy for a drunk.

He dragged Bob out of his chair by the shirtfront. "You pull yourself together and do it fast. When Block comes in you're going to check him and his little group out. If you tip him off—if you so much as blink and tip him off—I'll hang you out to dry."

"Charity does the checkout," Bob managed through chattering teeth.

"Not today. You're going to go out to the desk and handle it. You're going to do a good job because you're going to know I'm in here and I'm watching you."

He stepped away from Bob just as the office door opened. "Sorry I'm late." Despite her heavy eyes, Charity beamed at Roman. "I overslept."

He felt his heart stop, then sink to his knees. "You didn't sleep enough."

"You're telling me." Her smile faded when she looked at Bob. "What's wrong?"

He grabbed at the thread of opportunity with both hands. "I was just telling Roman that I'm not feeling very well."

"You don't look well." Concerned, she walked over to feel his brow. It was clammy and deepened the worry in her eyes. "You're probably coming down with that virus."

"That's what I'm afraid of."

"You shouldn't have come in at all today. Maybe Roman should drive you home."

"No, I can manage." He walked on shaking legs to the door. "Sorry about this, Charity." He turned to give her a last look. "Really sorry."

"Don't be silly. Just take care of yourself."

"I'll give him a hand," Roman muttered, and followed him out. They walked out into the lobby at the same time Block strolled in.

"Good morning." His face creased with his habitual smile, but his eyes were wary. "Is there a problem?"

"Virus." Bob's face was already turning a sickly green. Fear made a convincing cover. "Hit me pretty hard this morning."

"I called Dr. Mertens," Charity announced as she came in to stand behind the desk. "You go straight home, Bob. He'll meet you there."

"Thanks." But one of Conby's agents followed him out, and he knew he wouldn't be going home for quite a while.

"This virus has been a plague around here." She offered Block an apologetic smile. "I'm short a housekeeper, a waitress and now Bob. I hope none of your group had any complaints about the service."

"Not a one." Relaxed again, Block set his briefcase

on the desk. "It's always a pleasure doing business with you, Charity."

Roman watched helplessly as they chatted and went through the routine of checking lists and figures. She was supposed to be safe upstairs, sleeping deeply and dreaming of the night they'd spent together. Frustrated, he balled his hands at his side. Now, no matter what he did, she'd be in the middle.

He heard her laugh when Block mentioned the fish she'd carried into the dining room. And he imagined how her face would look when the agents moved in and arrested the man she thought of as a tour guide and a friend.

Charity read off a total. Roman steadied himself.

"We seem to be off by...22.50." Block began laboriously running the numbers through his calculator again. Brow furrowed, Charity went over her list, item by item.

"Good morning, dear."

"Hmm." Distracted, Charity glanced up. "Oh, good morning, Miss Millie."

"I'm just on my way up to pack. I wanted you to know what a delightful time we've had."

"We're always sorry to see you go. We were all pleased that you and Miss Lucy extended your stay for a few days."

Miss Millie fluttered her eyelashes myopically at Roman before making her way toward the stairs. At the top, he thought, there would now be an officer posted to see that she and the other guests were kept out of the way.

"I get the same total again, Roger." Puzzled, she

tapped the end of her pencil on the list. "I wish I could say I'd run it through the computer, but…" She let her words trail off, ignoring her headache. "Ah, this might be it. Do you have the Wentworths in cabin 1 down for a bottle of wine? They charged it night before last."

"Wentworth, Wentworth…" With grating slowness, Block ran down his list. "No, nothing here."

"Let me find the tab." After opening a drawer, she flipped her way efficiently through the folders. Roman felt a bead of sweat slide slowly down his back. One of the agents strolled over to browse through some post-cards.

"I've got both copies," she said with a shake of her head. "This virus is really hanging us up." She filed her copy of the receipt and handed Block his.

"No problem." Cheerful as ever, he noted the new charge, then added up his figures again. "That seems to match."

With the ease of long habit, Charity calculated the amount in Canadian currency. "That's 2,330.00." She turned the receipt around for Block's approval.

He clicked open his briefcase. "As always, it's a pleasure." He counted out the money in twenties. The moment Charity marked the bill Paid, Roman moved in.

"Put your hands up. Slow." He pressed the barrel of his gun into the small of Block's back.

"Roman!" Charity gaped at him, the key to the cash drawer in her hand. "What on earth are you doing?"

"Go around the desk," he told her. "Way around, and walk outside."

"Are you crazy? Roman, for God's sake—"

"Do it!"

Block moistened his lips, keeping his hands carefully aloft. "Is this a robbery?"

"Haven't you figured it out by now?" With his free hand, Roman pulled out his ID. After tossing it on the desk, he reached for his cuffs. "You're under arrest."

"What's the charge?"

"Conspiracy to murder, counterfeiting, transporting known felons across international borders. That'll do for a start." He yanked one of Block's arms down and slipped the cuff over his wrist.

"How could you?" Charity's voice was a mere whisper. She held his badge in her hand.

He took his eyes off Block for only a second to look at her. One second changed everything.

"How silly of me," Miss Millie muttered as she waltzed back into the lobby. "I was nearly upstairs when I realized I'd left my—"

For a man of his bulk, Block moved quickly. He dragged Miss Millie against him and had a knife to her throat before anyone could react. The cuffs dangled from one wrist. "It'll only take a heartbeat," he said quietly, staring into Roman's eyes. The gun was trained in the center of Block's forehead, and Roman's finger was twitching on the trigger.

"Think about it." Block's gaze swept the lobby, where other guns had been drawn. "I'll slice this nice little lady's throat. Don't move," he said to Charity. Shifting slightly, he blocked her way.

Wide-eyed, Miss Millie could only cling to Block's arm and whimper.

"Don't hurt her." Charity stepped forward, but she stopped quickly when she saw Block's grip tighten. "Please, don't hurt her." It had to be a dream, she told herself. A nightmare. "Someone tell me what's happening here."

"The place is surrounded." Roman kept his eyes and his weapon on Block. He waited in vain for one of his men to move in from the rear. "Hurting her isn't going to do you any good."

"It isn't going to do you any good, either. Think about it. Want a dead grandmother on your hands?"

"You don't want to add murder to your list, Block," Roman said evenly. And Charity was much too close, he thought. Much too close.

"It makes no difference to me. Now take it outside. All of you!" His voice rose as he scanned the room. "Toss down the guns. Toss them down and get out before I start slicing into her. Do it." He nicked Miss Millie's fragile throat with the blade.

"Please!" Again Charity took a step forward. "Let her go. I'll stay with you."

"Damn it, Charity, get back."

She didn't spare Roman a glance. "Please, Roger," she said again, taking another careful step forward. "She's old and frail. She might get sick. Her heart." Desperate, she stepped between him and Roman's gun. "I won't give you any trouble."

The decision took Block only a moment. He grabbed Charity and dug the point of the blade into her throat. Miss Millie slid bonelessly to the floor.

"Drop the gun." He saw the fear in Roman's eyes

and smiled. Apparently he'd made a much better bargain. "Two seconds and it's over. I don't have anything to lose."

Roman held his hands up, letting his weapon drop. "We'll talk."

"We'll talk when I'm ready." Block shifted the knife so that the length of the blade lay across Charity's neck. She shut her eyes and waited to die. "Get out, now. The first time somebody tries to get back in she dies."

"Out." Roman pointed to the door. "Keep them back, Conby. All of them. There's my weapon," he said to Block. "I'm clean." He lifted his jacket cautiously to show his empty holster. "Why don't I hang around in here? You can have two hostages for the price of one. A federal agent ought to give you some leverage."

"Just the woman. Take off, DeWinter, or I'll kill her before you can think how to get to me. Now."

"For God's sake, Roman. Get her out of here. She needs a doctor." Charity sucked in her breath when the point of the knife pierced her skin.

"Don't." Roman held up his hands again, palms out, as he moved toward the crumpled form near the desk. Keeping his movements slow, he gathered the sobbing woman in his arms. "If you hurt her, you won't live long enough to regret it."

With that last frustrated threat he left Charity alone.

"Stay back." After bundling Miss Millie into waiting arms, he rushed off the porch, fighting to keep his mind clear. "Nobody goes near the doors or any of the windows. Get me a weapon." Before anyone could oblige him, he was yanking a gun away from one of Royce's deputies. With the smallest of gestures Royce signaled to his man to be silent.

"What do you want us to do?"

Roman merely stared down at the gun in his hand. It was loaded. He was trained. And he was helpless.

"DeWinter..." Conby began.

"Back off." When Conby started to speak again, Roman turned on him. "Back off."

He stared at the inn. He could hear Miss Millie crying softly as someone carried her to a car. The guests who had already been evacuated were being herded to safety. Roman imagined that Royce had arranged that. Charity would want to make sure they were well taken care of.

Charity.

Shoving the gun into his holster, he turned around. "Have the road blocked off a mile in each direction. Only official personnel in this area. We'll keep the inn surrounded from a distance of fifty feet. He'll be thinking again," Roman said slowly, "and when he starts thinking he's going to know he's blocked in."

He lifted both hands and rubbed them over his face. He'd been in hostage situations before. He was trained for them. With time and cool heads, the odds of getting a hostage out in a situation of this type were excellent. When the hostage was Charity, excellent wasn't nearly good enough.

"I want to talk to him."

"Agent DeWinter, under the circumstances I have serious reservations about you being in charge of this operation."

Roman rounded on him. "Get in my way, Conby, and I'll hang you up by your silk tie. Why the hell weren't there men positioned in the back, behind him?"

Because his palms were sweating, Conby's voice was only more frigid. "I thought it best to have them outside, prepared if he attempted to run."

Roman battled the red wave of fury that burst behind his eyes. "When I get her out," he said softly, "I'm going to deal with you, you bastard. I need communication," he said to Royce. "Can you handle it?"

"Give me twenty minutes."

With a nod, Roman turned back to study the inn. Systematically he considered and rejected points of entry.

Inside, Charity felt some measure of relief when the knife was removed from her throat. Somehow the gun Block was pointing at her now seemed less personal.

"Roger—"

"Shut up. Shut up and let me think." He swiped a beefy forearm over his brow to dry it. It had all happened so fast, too fast. Everything up to now he had done on instinct. As Roman had calculated, he was beginning to think.

"They've got me trapped in here. I should've used you to get to one of the cars, should've taken off." Then he laughed, looking wildly around the lobby. "We're on a damn island. Can't drive off an island."

"I think if we—"

"Shut up!" He shouted and had her holding her breath as he leveled the gun at her. "I'm the one who needs to think. Feds. That sniveling little wart was right all

along," he muttered, thinking of Bob. "He made DeWinter days ago. Did you?" As he asked, he grabbed her
by the hair and yanked her head back to hold the barrel against her throat.

"No. I didn't know. I didn't. I still don't understand."
She could only give a muffled cry when he slammed
her back against the wall. She'd never seen murder in a
man's eyes before, but she recognized it. "Roger, think.
If you kill me you won't have anything to bargain with."
She tasted fear on her tongue as she forced the words
out. "You need me."

"Yeah." He relaxed his grip. "You've been handy so
far. You'll just have to go on being handy. How many
ways in and out of this place?"

"I—I don't really know." She sucked in her breath
when he gave her hair another cruel twist.

"You know how many two-by-fours are in this
place."

"Five. There are five exits, not counting the windows. The lobby, the gathering room, the outside steps
running to my quarters and a family suite in the east
wing, and the back, through the utility room off the
kitchen."

"That's good." Panting a bit, he considered the possibilities. "The kitchen. We'll take the kitchen. I'll have
water and food there in case this takes a while. Come
on." He kept a hand in her hair and the gun at the base
of her neck.

His eyes on the inn, Roman paced back and forth
behind the barricade of police cars. She was smart,

he told himself. Charity was a smart, sensible woman. She wouldn't panic. She wouldn't do anything stupid.

Oh, God, she must be terrified. He lit a cigarette from the butt of another, but he didn't find himself soothed as the harsh smoke seared into him.

"Where's the goddamn phone?"

"Nearly ready." Royce pushed back his hat and straightened from where he'd been watching a lineman patch in a temporary line. "My nephew," he explained to Roman with a thin smile. "The boy knows his job."

"You got a lot of relatives."

"I'm lousy with them. Listen, I heard you and Charity were getting married. That part of the cover?"

"No." Roman thought of the picnic on the beach, that one clear moment in time. "No."

"In that case, I'm going to give you some advice. You're wrong," he said, before Roman could speak. "You do need it. You're going to have to get yourself calm, real calm, before you pick up that phone. A trapped animal reacts two ways. He either cowers back and gives up or he strikes out at anything in his way." Royce nodded toward the inn. "Block doesn't look like the type to give up easy, and Charity sure as hell's in his way. That line through yet, son?"

"Yes, sir." The young lineman's hands were sweaty with nerves and excitement. "You can dial right through." He passed the damp receiver to Roman.

"I don't know the number," Roman murmured. "I don't know the damn number."

"I know it."

Roman swung around to face Mae. In that one instant he saw everything he felt about himself mirrored in her eyes. There would be time for guilt later, he told himself. There would be a lifetime for it. "Royce, you were supposed to clear the area."

"Moving Maeflower's like moving a tank."

"I don't budge until I see Charity." Mae firmed her quivering lips. "She's going to need me when she comes out. Waste of time to argue," she added. "You want the number?"

"Yes."

She gave it to him. Tossing his cigarette aside, Roman dialed.

Charity jolted in the chair when the phone rang. Across the table, Block simply stared at it. He had had her pile everything she could drag or carry to block the two doors. Extra chairs, twenty-pound canisters of flour and sugar, the rolling butcher block, iron skillets, all sat in a jumble, braced against both entrances.

In the silent kitchen the phone sounded again and again, like a scream.

"Stay right where you are." Block moved across the room to answer it. "Yeah?"

"It's DeWinter. Thought you might be ready to talk about a deal."

"What kind of deal?"

"That's what we have to talk about. First I have to know you've still got Charity."

"Have you seen her come out?" Block spit into the phone. "You know damn well I've got her or you wouldn't be talking to me."

"I have to make sure she's still alive. Let me talk to her."

"You can go to hell."

Threats, abuse, curses, rose like bile in his throat. Still, when he spoke, his voice was dispassionate. "I verify that you still have a hostage, Block, or we don't deal."

"You want to talk to her?" Block gestured with the gun. "Over here," he ordered. "Make it fast. It's your boyfriend," he told Charity when she stood beside him. "He wants to know how you're doing. You tell him you're just fine." He brushed the gun up her cheek to rest it at her temple. "Understand?"

With a nod, she leaned into the phone. "Roman?"

"Charity." Too many emotions slammed into him for him to measure. He wanted to reassure her, to make promises, to beg her to be careful. But he knew he would have only seconds and that Block would be listening to every word spoken. "Has he hurt you?"

"No." She closed her eyes and fought back a sob. "No, I'm fine. He's going to let me fix some food."

"Hear that, DeWinter? She's fine." Deliberately Block dragged her arm behind her back until she cried out. "That can change anytime."

Roman gripped the phone helplessly as he listened to the sound of Charity's sobs. It took every ounce of control he had left to keep the terror out of his voice. "You don't have to hurt her. I said we'd talk about terms."

"We'll talk about terms, all right. My terms." He released Charity's arm and ignored her as she slid to the floor. "You get me a car. I want safe passage to the airport, DeWinter. Charity drives. I want a plane fueled up and waiting. She'll be getting on it with me, so any tricks and we're back to square one. When I get where I'm going, I turn her loose."

"How big a plane?"

"Don't try to stall me."

"Wait. I have to know. It's a small airport, Block. You know that. If you're going any distance—"

"Just get me a plane."

"Okay." Roman wiped the back of his hand over his mouth and forced his voice to level. He couldn't hear her any longer, and the silence was as anguishing as her sobbing. "I'm going to have to go through channels on this. That's how it works."

"The hell with your channels."

"Look, I don't have the authority to get you what you want. I need to get approval. Then I'll have to clear the airport, get a pilot. You'll have to give me some time."

"Don't yank my chain, DeWinter. You got an hour."

"I've got to get through to Washington. You know how bureaucrats are. It'll take me three, maybe four."

"The hell with that. You got two. After two I'm going to start sending her out in pieces."

Charity closed her eyes, lowered her head to her folded arms and wept out her terror.

Chapter 12

"We've got a couple of hours," Roman murmured, continuing to study the inn and the floor plan Royce had given him. "He's not as smart as I thought, or maybe he's too panicked to think it through."

"That could be to our advantage," Royce said when Roman shook his head at his offer of coffee. "Or it could work against us."

Two hours. Roman stared at the quiet clapboard building. He couldn't stand the idea of Charity being held at gunpoint for that long. "He wants a car, safe passage to the airport and a plane." He turned to Conby. "I want you to make sure he thinks he's going to get it."

"I'm aware of how to handle a hostage situation, DeWinter."

"Which one of your men is the best shot?" Roman asked Royce.

"I am." He kept his eyes steady on Roman's. "Where do you want me?"

"They're in the kitchen."

"He tell you that?"

"No, Charity. She told me he was going to let her fix some food. Since I doubt eating's on her mind, she was letting me know their position."

Royce glanced over to where Mae was pacing up and down the pier. "She's a tough girl. She's keeping her head."

"So far." But Roman remembered too well the sound of her muffled sobbing. "We need to shift two of the men around the back. I want them to keep their distance, stay out of sight. Let's see how close we can get." He turned to Conby again. "Give us five minutes, then call him again. Tell him who you are. You know how to make yourself sound important. Stall him, keep him on the phone as long as you can."

"You have two hours, DeWinter. We can call for a SWAT team from Seattle."

"We have two hours," Roman said grimly. "Charity may not."

"I can't take responsibility—"

Roman cut him off. "You'll damn well take it."

"Agent DeWinter, if this wasn't a crisis situation I would cite you for insubordination."

"Great. Just put it on my tab." He looked at the rifle Royce had picked up. It had a long-range telescopic sight. "Let's move."

She'd cried long enough, Charity decided, taking a long, deep breath. It wasn't doing her any good. Like her captor, she needed to think. Her world had whittled down to one room, with fear as her constant companion. This wouldn't do, she told herself, straightening her spine. Her life was being threatened, and she wasn't even sure why.

She rose from where she had been huddled on the floor. Block was still sitting at the table, holding the gun in one hand while the other tapped monotonously on the scrubbed wood. The dangling cuffs jangled. He was terrified, she realized. Perhaps every bit as much as she. There must be some way to use that to her advantage.

"Roger…would you like some coffee?"

"Yeah. That's good, that's a good idea." He took a firmer grip on the gun. "But don't get cute. I'm watching every move."

"Are they going to give you a plane?" She turned the burner on low. The kitchen was full of weapons, she thought. Knives, cleavers, mallets. Closing her eyes, she wondered if she had the courage to use one.

"They're going to give me anything I want as long as I have you."

"Why do they want you?" Stay calm, she told herself. She wanted to stay calm and alert and alive. "I don't understand." She poured the hot coffee into two cups. She didn't think she could swallow, but she hoped that sharing it would put him slightly more at ease. "They said something about counterfeiting."

It didn't matter what she knew. In any case, he had worked hard and was proud of it. "For over two years now I've been running a nice little game back and forth over the border. Twenties and tens in Canadian. I can stamp them out like bottle caps. But I'm careful, you know." He gulped at the coffee. "A couple thousand here, couple thousand there, with Vision as the front. We run a good tour, keep the clients happy."

"You've been paying me with counterfeit money?"

"You, and a couple other places. But you're the longest and most consistent." He smiled at her, as friendly as ever—if you didn't count the gun in his hand. "You have a special place here, Charity, quiet, remote, privately owned. You deal with a small local bank. It ran like a charm."

"Yes." She looked down at her cup, her stomach rolling. "I can see that." And Roman had come not to see the whales but to work on a case. That was all she had been to him.

"We were going to milk this route for a few more months," he continued. "Just lately Bob started getting antsy."

"Bob?" Her hand fisted on her lap. "Bob knew?"

"He was nothing but a nickel-and-dime con man before I took him on. Working scams and petty embezzlements. I set him up here and made him rich. Didn't do badly by you, either," he added with a grin. "You were on some shaky financial ground when I came along."

"All this time," she whispered.

"I'd decided to give it another six months, then move on, but Bob started getting real jumpy about your new handyman. The bastard set me up." He slammed the cup down. "Worked a deal with the feds. I should have caught it, the way he started falling apart after the hit-and-run."

"The accident—you tried to kill me."

"No." He patted her hand, and she cringed. "Truth is, I've always had a liking for you. But I wanted to get you out of the way for a while. Just testing the waters to see how DeWinter played it. He's good," Block mused. "Real good. Had me convinced he was only interested in you. The romance was a good touch. Threw me off."

"Yes." Devastated, she stared at the grain in the wood of the tabletop. "That was clever."

"Sucked me in," Block muttered. "I knew you weren't stringing me along. You haven't got it in you. But DeWinter... They've probably already taken Dupont."

"Who?"

"We don't just run the money. There are people, people who need to leave the country quietly, who pay a lot for our services. Looks like I'm going to have to take myself on as a client." He laughed and drained his cup. "How about some food? One of the things I'll miss most about this place is the food."

She rose silently and went to the refrigerator. It had all been a lie, she thought. Everything Roman had said, everything he'd done...

The pain cut deep and had her fighting back another bout of weeping. He'd made a fool of her, as surely and as completely as Roger Block had. They had used her, both of them, used her and her inn. She would never forgive. She rubbed her hands over her eyes to clear them. And she would never forget.

"How about that lemon meringue pie?" Relaxed, pleased with his own cleverness, Roger tapped the barrel of the gun on the table. "Mae outdid herself on that pie last night."

"Yes." Slowly Charity pulled it out. "There's a little left."

Block had ripped the frilly tiebacks from the sunny yellow curtains, but there was a space two inches wide at the center. Silently Roman eased toward it. He could see Charity reach into a cupboard, take out a plate.

There were tears drying on her cheeks. It tore at him to see them. Her hands were steady. That was something, some small thing to hold on to. He couldn't see Block, though he shifted as much as he dared.

Then, suddenly, as if she had sensed him, their eyes met through the glass. She braced, and in that instant he saw a myriad of emotions run across her face. Then it was set again. She looked at him as she would have looked at a stranger and waited for instructions.

He held up a hand, palm out, doing his best to signal her to hold on, to keep calm. Then the phone rang and he watched her jolt.

"About time," Block said. He was almost swaggering as he walked to the phone. "Yeah? Who the hell's this?" After listening a moment, he gave a pleased laugh. "I like dealing with a title. Where's my plane, Inspector Conby?"

As quickly as she dared, Charity tugged the curtain open another inch.

"Over here," Block ordered.

She dropped her hand, and the plate rattled to the counter. "What?"

He gestured with the gun. "I said over here."

Roman swore as she moved between him and a clear shot.

"I want them to know I'm keeping up my end." Block took Charity by the arm, less roughly this time. "Tell the man I'm treating you fine."

"He hasn't hurt me," she said dully. She forced herself to keep her eyes away from the window. Roman was out there. He would do his best to get her out safely. That was his job.

"The plane'll be ready in a hour," Block told her after he hung up. "Just enough time for that pie and another cup of coffee."

"All right." She crossed to the counter again. Panic sprinted through her when she looked out the window and saw no one. He'd left. Because her fingers were unsteady, she fumbled with the pie. "Roger, are you going to let me go?"

He hesitated only an instant, but that was enough to tell her that his words were just another lie. "Sure. As soon as I'm clear."

So it came down to that. Her heart, her inn and now her life. She set the pie in front of him and studied his face. He was pleased with himself, she thought, and she hated him for it. But he was still sweating.

"I'll get your coffee." She walked to the stove. One foot, then the other. There was a buzzing in her ears. It was more than fear now, she realized as she turned the burner up under the pot. It was rage and despair and a strong, irresistible need to survive. Mechanically she switched the stove off. Then, taking a cloth, she took the pot by the handle.

He was still holding the gun, and he was shoveling pie into his mouth with his left hand. He thought she was a fool, Charity mused. Someone who could be used and duped and manipulated. She took a deep breath.

"Roger?"

He glanced up. Charity looked directly into his eyes.

"You forgot your coffee," she said calmly, then tossed the steaming contents into his face.

He screamed. She didn't think she'd ever heard a man scream like that before. He was half out of his chair, groping blindly for the gun. It happened quickly. No matter how often she played back the scene in her mind, she would never be completely sure what happened first.

She grabbed for the gun herself. Block's flailing hand caught her across the cheekbone. Even as she staggered backward there was the sound of glass breaking.

Roman was through the window. Charity landed on the floor, stunned by the blow, as he burst through. There were men breaking through the barricaded doors and rushing into the room. Someone dragged her from the floor and pulled her out.

Roman held the gun to Block's temple. They were kneeling on the shattered glass—or rather Roman was kneeling and supporting the moaning Block. There were already welts rising up on his wide face. "Please," Roman murmured. "Give me a reason."

"Roman." Royce laid a hand on his shoulder. "It's over."

But the rage clogged his throat. It made his finger slippery on the trigger of the gun. He remembered the way Charity had looked at him when she had seen him outside the window. Slowly he drew back and holstered his gun.

"Yeah. It's over. Get him the hell out of here." He rose and went to find Charity.

He found her in the lobby, wrapped in Mae's arms.

"I'm all right," Charity murmured. "Really." When she saw Roman, her eyes frosted over. "Everything's going to be fine now. I need to speak with Roman for a minute."

"You say your piece." Mae kissed both of her cheeks. "Then you're going to get in a nice hot tub."

"Okay." She squeezed Mae's hand. Strange, but it felt more like a dream now, as if she were pushing her way through layers and layers of gauzy gray curtains. "I think we'll have more privacy upstairs," she said to Roman. Then she turned without looking at him and started up the stairs.

He wanted to hold her. His fingers curled tight into his palms. He needed to lift her against him, touch her hair, her skin, and convince himself that the nightmare was over.

Her knees were shaking. Reaction was struggling to set in, but she fought it off. When she was alone, Charity promised herself. When she was finally alone, she would let it all out.

In her sitting room she turned to face him. She would not, could not, speak to him in the intimacy of her bedroom. "I imagine you have reports to file," she began. Was that her voice? she wondered. It sounded so thin and cold, so foreign. Deliberately she cleared her throat. "I've been told I'll have to make a statement, but I thought we should get this out of the way first."

"Charity." He started toward her, only to be brought up short when her hands whipped out.

"Don't." Her eyes were as cold as her voice. It wasn't a dream, she told herself. It was as harsh and as brutal a reality as she had ever known. "Don't touch me. Not now, not ever again."

His hands fell uselessly to his sides. "I'm sorry."

"Why? You accomplished exactly what you came to do. From what I've been able to gather, Roger and Bob had quite a system going. I'm sure your superiors will be delighted with you."

"It doesn't matter."

She dug his badge out of her pocket, where she had shoved it. "Yes." She threw it at him. "Yes, it does."

Struggling for calm, he pushed it into his pocket. He noted dispassionately that his hands were bleeding. "I couldn't tell you."

"Didn't tell me."

There was a faint bruise on her cheekbone. For a moment all his guilt and impotent fury centered there. "He hit you."

She ran a fingertip lightly across the mark. "I don't break easily."

"I want to explain."

"Do you?" She turned away for a moment. She wanted to keep her anger cold. "I think I get the picture."

"Listen, baby—"

"No, *you* listen, baby." Her composure cracking, she whirled around again. "You lied to me, you used me from the first minute to the last. It was all one huge, incredible lie."

"Not all."

"No? Let's see, how can we separate one from the other? A convenient flat." She saw the anger in his eyes and shoved a chair out of her path. "And George, good old lucky George. I suppose it was worth a few thousand dollars to get him out of the way and leave you an opening. And Bob—you knew all about Bob, didn't you?"

"We couldn't be sure, not at first."

"Not at first," she repeated. As long as she kept her brain cold, she told herself, she could think. She could think and not feel. "I wonder, Roman, were you so sure of me? Or did you think I was part of it?" When he didn't answer, she spun around again. "You did. Oh, I see. I was under investigation all the time. And there you were, so conveniently on the scene. All you had to do was get close to me, and I made it so easy for you." With a laugh, she pressed her hands to her face. "My God, I threw myself at you."

"I wasn't supposed to get involved with you." Fighting desperation, he paced his words carefully. "It just happened. I fell in love with you."

"Don't say that to me." She lowered her hands. Her face was pale and cool behind them. "You don't even know what it means."

"I didn't, until you."

"You can't have love without trust, Roman. I trusted you. I didn't just give you my body. I gave you everything."

"I told you everything I could," he shot back. "Damn it, I couldn't tell you the rest. The things I told you about myself, about the way I grew up, the way I felt, they were all true."

"Do I have your word on that? Agent DeWinter?"

With an oath, he strode across the room and grabbed her arms. "I didn't know you when I took the assignment. I was doing a job. When things changed, the most important part of that job became proving your innocence and keeping you safe."

"If you had told me I would have proven my own innocence." She jerked out of his hold. "This is my inn, and these are my people. The only family I have left. Do you think I would risk it all for money?"

"No. I knew that, I trusted that, after the first twenty-four hours. I had orders, Charity, and my own instincts. If I had told you who I was and what was going on, you would never have been able to keep up a front."

"So I'm that stupid?"

"No. That honest." Digging deep, he found his control again. "You've been through a lot. Let me take you to the hospital."

"I've been through a lot," she repeated, and nearly laughed. "Do you know how it feels to know that for two years, *two years*, people I thought I knew were using me? I always thought I was such a good judge of character." Now she did laugh. She walked to the window. "They made a fool out of me week after week. I'm not sure I'll ever get over it. But that's nothing." She turned, wrapping her fingers around the windowsill. "That's nothing compared to what I feel when I think of how I let myself believe you were in love with me."

"If it was a lie, why am I here now, telling you that I do?"

"I don't know." Suddenly weary, she dragged her hair away from her face. "And it doesn't seem to matter. I'm wrung dry, Roman. For a while today I was sure he was going to kill me."

"Oh, Charity." He gathered her close, and when she didn't resist he buried his face in her hair.

"I thought he would kill me," she repeated, her arms held rigidly at her sides. "And I didn't want to die. In fact, nothing was quite so important to me as staying alive. When my mother fell in love and that love was betrayed, she gave up. I've never been much like her." She stepped stiffly out of his hold. "Maybe I'm gullible, but I've never been weak. I intend to pick up where I left off, before all of this. I'm going to keep the inn running. No matter what it takes, I'm going to erase you and these last weeks from my life."

"No." Furious, he took her face in his hands. "You won't, because you know I love you. And you made me a promise, Charity. No matter what happened, you wouldn't stop loving me."

"I made that promise to a man who doesn't exist." It hurt. She could feel the pain rip through her from one end to the other. "And I don't love the man who does." She took a small but significant step backward. "Leave me alone."

When he didn't move, she walked into the bedroom and flipped the lock.

Mae was busily sweeping up glass in the kitchen. For the first time in over twenty years the inn was closed. She figured it would open again soon enough, but for now she was content that her girl was safe upstairs in bed and the coffee-guzzling police were on their way out.

When Roman came in, she rested her arms on her broom. Mae had rocked Charity for nearly an hour while she'd cried over him. She'd been prepared to be cold and dismissive. It only took one look to change her mind.

"You look worn out."

"I…" Feeling lost, he glanced around the room. "I wanted to ask how she was before I left."

"She's miserable." She nodded, content with the anguish she saw in his eyes. "And stubborn. You got a few cuts."

Automatically he lifted a hand to rub at the nick on his temple. "Will you give her this number?" He dropped a card on the table. "She can reach me there if— She can reach me there."

"Sit down. Let me clean you up."

"No, it's all right."

"I said sit down." She went to a cupboard for a bottle of antiseptic. "She's had a bad shock."

He had a sudden mental image of Block holding the knife to her throat. "I know."

"She bounces back pretty quick from most things. She loves you."

Roman winced a little as she dabbed on the antiseptic, but not from the sting. "Did."

"Does," Mae said flatly. "She just doesn't want to right now. You been an agent for long?"

"Too long."

"Are you going to make sure that slimy worm Roger Block's put away?"

Roman's hands curled into fists. "Yes."

"Are you in love with Charity?"

He relaxed his hands. "Yes."

"I believe you, so I'm going to give you some advice." Puffing a bit, she sat down next to him. "She's hurt, real bad. Charity's the kind who likes to fix things herself. Give her a little time." She picked up the card and slipped it into her apron pocket. "I'll just hold on to this for now."

She was feeling stronger. And not just physically, Charity decided as she jogged along behind Ludwig. In every way. The sweaty dreams that had woken her night after night were fading. It wasn't nearly as difficult to talk, or to smile, or to pretend that she was in control again. She had promised herself she would put her life back together, and she was doing it.

She rarely thought of Roman. On a sigh, she relented. She would never get strong again if she began to lie to herself.

She *always* thought of Roman. It was difficult not to, and it was especially difficult today.

They were to have been married today. Charity veered into the grass as Ludwig explored. The ache came, spread and was accepted. Just after noon, with the music swelling and the sun streaming down on the garden, she would have put her hand in his. And promised.

A fantasy, she told herself, and nudged her dog back

onto the shoulder of the road. It had been fantasy then, and it was a fantasy now.

And yet… With every day that passed she remembered more clearly the times they had spent together. His reluctance, and his anger. Then his tenderness and concern. She glanced down to where the bracelet shimmered on her wrist.

She'd tried to put it back in the box, to push it into some dark, rarely opened drawer. Every day she told herself she would. Tomorrow. And every day she remembered how sweet, how awkward and how wonderful he'd been when he'd given it to her.

If it had only been a job, why had he given her so much more than he had needed to? Not just the piece of jewelry, but everything the circle of gold had symbolized? He could have offered her friendship and respect, as Bob had, and she would have trusted him as much. He could have kept their relationship strictly physical. Her feelings would have remained the same.

But he had said he loved her. And at the end he had all but begged her to believe it.

She shook her head and increased her pace. She was being weak and sentimental. It was just the day…the beautiful spring morning that was to have been her wedding day.

What she needed was to get back to the inn and keep busy. This day would pass, like all the others.

At first she thought she was imagining it when she saw him standing beside the road, looking out at the sunrise over the water. Her feet faltered. Before she could think to prevent it, her knees weakened. Fighting her heart, she walked to him.

He'd heard her coming. As he'd stood in the growing light he'd remembered wondering if he came back, if he would stand just there and wait for Charity to run to him.

She wasn't running now. She was walking very slowly, despite the eager dog. Could she know, he wondered, that she held his life in her hands?

Nerves swarmed through her, making her fingers clench and unclench on the leash. She prayed as she stopped in front of him that her voice would be steadier.

"What do you want?"

He bent down to pat the squirming dog's head. "We'll get to that. How are you feeling?"

"I'm fine."

"You've been having nightmares." There were shadows under her eyes. He wouldn't make it easy on her by ignoring them.

She stiffened. "They're passing. Mae talks too much."

"At least she talks to me."

"We've already said all there is to say."

He closed a hand over her arm as she started by him. "Not this time. You had your say last time, and I had a lot of it coming. Now it's my turn." Reaching down, he unhooked the leash. Free, Ludwig bounded toward home. "Mae's waiting for him," Roman explained before Charity could call the dog back.

"I see." She wrapped the leash around her fisted hand. "You two work all this out?"

"She cares about you. So do I."

"I have things to do."

"Yeah. This is first." He pulled her close and, ignoring her struggling, crushed his mouth to hers. It was like a drink after days in the desert, like a fire after a dozen long cold nights. He plundered, greedy, as though it were the first time. Or the last.

She couldn't fight him, or herself. Almost sobbing, she clung to him, hungry and hurting. No matter how strong she tried to be, she would never be strong enough to stand against her own heart.

Aching, she started to draw back, but he tightened his hold. "Give me a minute," he murmured, pressing his lips to her hair. "Every night I wake up and see him holding a knife at your throat. And there's nothing I can do. I reach for you, and you're not there. For a minute, one horrible minute, I'm terrified. Then I remember that you're safe. You're not with me, but you're safe. It's almost enough."

"Roman." With a helpless sigh, she stroked soothing hands over his shoulders. "It doesn't do any good to think about it."

"Do you think I could forget?" He pulled back, keeping his hands firm on her arms. "For the rest of my life I'll remember every second of it. I was responsible for you."

"No." The anger came quickly enough to surprise both of them. She shoved at his chest. "*I'm* responsible for me. I was and I am and I always will be. And I took care of myself."

"Yeah." He ran his palm over her cheek. The bruise

had faded, even if the memory hadn't. "It was a hell of a way to serve coffee."

"Let's forget it." She shrugged out of his grip and walked toward the water. "I'm not particularly proud of letting myself be duped, so I'd rather not dwell on it."

"They were pros, Charity. You're not the first person they've used."

She pressed her lips together. "And you?"

"When you're undercover you lie, and you use, and you take advantage of anything that's offered." Her eyes were closed when he turned her around to face him. "I came here to do a job. It had been a long time since I'd let myself think beyond anything but the next day. Look at me. Please."

Taking a steadying breath, she opened her eyes. "We've been through this already, Roman."

"No. I'd hurt you. I'd disappointed you. You weren't ready to listen." Gently he brushed a tear from her lashes. "I hope you are now, because I can't make it much longer without you."

"I was too hard on you before." It took almost everything she had, but she managed a smile. "I was hurt, and I was a lot shakier than I knew from being locked up with Roger. After I gave my statement, Inspector Conby explained everything to me, more clearly. About how the operation had been working, what my responsibilities were, what you had to do."

"What responsibilities?"

"About the money. It's put us in somewhat of a hole, but at least we only have to pay back a percentage."

"I see." Roman laughed and shook his head. "He always was a prince."

"The merchant's responsible for the loss." She tilted her head. "You didn't know about the arrangements I've made with him?"

"No."

"But you work for him."

"Not anymore. I turned in my resignation when I got back to D.C."

"Oh, Roman, that's ridiculous. It's like throwing out the baby with the bathwater."

He smiled appreciatively at her innate practicality. "I decided I like carpentry better. Got any openings?"

Running the leash through her hands, she looked over the water. "I haven't given much thought to remodeling lately."

"I work cheap." He tilted her face to his. "All you have to do is marry me."

"Don't."

"Charity." Calling on patience he hadn't been aware he possessed, he held her still. "One of the things I most admire about you is your mind. You're real sharp. Look at me, really look. I figure you've got to know that I'm not beating my head against this same wall for entertainment. I love you. You've got to believe that."

"I'm afraid to," she whispered.

He felt the first true spark of hope. "Believe this. You changed my life. Literally changed it. I can't go back to the way it was before. I can't go forward unless you're with me. How long do you want me to stand here, waiting to start living again?"

With her arms wrapped around her chest, she walked a short distance away. The high grass at the water's edge was still misted with dew. She could smell it, and the fragile fragrances of wildflowers. It occurred to her then that she had blocked such small things out of her life ever since she'd sent him away.

If it was honesty she was demanding from him, how could she give him anything less?

"I've missed you terribly." She shook her head quickly before he could touch her again. "I tried not to wonder if you'd come back. I told myself I didn't want you to. When I saw you standing in the road, all I wanted to do was run to you. No questions, no explanations. But it's not that simple."

"No."

"I do love you, Roman. I can't stop. I have tried," she said, looking back at him. "Not very hard, but I have tried. I think I knew under all the anger and the hurt that you weren't lying about loving me back. I haven't wanted to forgive you for lying about the rest, but— That's just pride, really." Perhaps it was simple after all, she thought. "If I have to make a choice, I'd rather take love." She smiled and opened her arms to him. "I guess you're hired."

She laughed when he caught her up in his arms and swung her around. "We'll make it work," he promised her, raining kisses all over her face. "Starting today."

"We were going to be married today."

"Are going to be." He hooked his arm under her legs to carry her.

"But we—"

"I have a license." Closing his mouth over hers, he swung her around again.

"A marriage license?"

"It's in my pocket, with two tickets to Venice."

"To—" Her hand slid limply from his shoulder. "To *Venice?* But how—?"

"And Mae bought you a dress yesterday. She wouldn't let me see it."

"Well." The thrill was too overwhelming to allow her to pretend annoyance. "You were awfully sure of yourself."

"No." He kissed her again, felt the curve of her lips, and the welcoming. "I was sure of you."

* * * * *

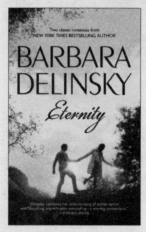

REQUEST YOUR FREE BOOKS!

2 FREE NOVELS
FROM THE ROMANCE COLLECTION
PLUS 2 FREE GIFTS!

NORA ROBERTS

(limited quantities available)

TOTAL AMOUNT	$ _____
POSTAGE & HANDLING	$ _____
($1.00 FOR 1 BOOK, 50¢ for each additional)	
APPLICABLE TAXES*	$ _____
TOTAL PAYABLE	$ _____

(check or money order—please do not send cash)

To order, complete this form and send it, along with a check or money order for the total above, payable to Harlequin Books, to: **In the U.S.:** 3010 Walden Avenue, P.O. Box 9077, Buffalo, NY 14269-9077; **In Canada:** P.O. Box 636, Fort Erie, Ontario, L2A 5X3.

Name: _____
Address: _____ City: _____
State/Prov.: _____ Zip/Postal Code: _____
Account Number (if applicable): _____
075 CSAS

*New York residents remit applicable sales taxes.
*Canadian residents remit applicable GST and provincial taxes.

Silhouette®
Where love comes alive™

Visit Silhouette Books at www.Harlequin.com   PSNR1212BL